HAMLET

Translated

SJ Hills

and

William Shakespeare

Faithfully Translated
into Performable Modern English
Side by Side with Original Text

Includes Stage Directions

THE TRAGEDY OF HAMLET

Book 24 in a series of 42

This Work First Published In 2019
by DTC Publishing, London.
www.InteractiveShakespeare.com

This revised paperback edition published in 2022

Typeset by DTC Publishing.

Translated from *The Tragedy of Hamlet, Prince of Denmark*,
by Shakespeare, circa 1602.

Revised Edition, 2022 XIIWS

ISBN 978-1-0776-1743-8

Interactive Shakespeare
Making the past accessible

SJ Hills Writing Credits: Dramatic Works.

Shakespeare Translated Series. Modern English With Original Text.
  Faithfully translated line by line for students, actors and fans of Shakespeare.
Macbeth Translated
Romeo & Juliet Translated
Hamlet Translated
A Midsummer Night's Dream Translated
Othello Translated

Shakespeare Translated For All Ages Series.
  Highly accurate Modern English with illustrations and simplified text on each
facing page for young readers to enjoy.
    Macbeth For All Ages

Dramatised Classic Works.
    Twenty-two dramatised works written and produced by SJ Hills for
Encyclopaedia Britannica, based on classic stories including Shakespeare, for
audiences of all ages around the world.
Greatest Tales of the World. Vol 1.
Greatest Tales of the World. Vol 2.

New Works Inspired By Classic Restoration Comedy Plays.
    Scarborough Fair - inspired by *The Relapse*
    To Take A Wife - inspired by *The Country Wife*
    Wishing Well - inspired by *Epsom Wells*
    Love In A Nunnery - inspired by *The Assignation*.

Modernised English Classic Works.
    The Faerie Queene
    Beowulf
    The Virtuous Wife
    Love's Last Shift
    Wild Oats
    The Way of the World

Dedicated to my four little terrors;
Melody
Eve
James
Hamilton

"From an ardent love of literature, a profound admiration of the men who have left us legacies of thought and beauty, and, I suppose, from that feature in man that induces us to strive to follow those we most admire, and looking upon the pursuit of literature as one of the noblest in which no labour should be deemed too great, I have sought to add a few thoughts to the store already bequeathed to the world. If they are approved, I shall have gained my desire; if not, I shall hope to receive any hints in the spirit of one who loves his work and desires to progress."

R. Hilton. 1869

PREFACE

When we studied Shakespeare at school we had to flick back and forth to the notes at the back of the book to understand a confusing line, words we were not familiar with, expressions lost in time, or even current or political references of Shakespeare's time.

What if the text was rewritten to make each line clear without looking up anything?

There are plenty of modern translations just for this. But they are cumbersome to read, no flow, matter of fact translations (and most this author has found are of varying inaccuracy, despite being approved by exam boards).

As a writer and producer of drama, I wanted not only to translate the play faithfully line by line, but also to include the innuendos, the political satire, the puns and the bawdy humour in a way which would flow and bring the work to life for students, actors prepping for a performance or lovers of the work to enjoy today, faithful to the feel and meaning of the original script and language without going into lengthy explanations for a modern day audience.

A faithful line-by-line translation into modern phrasing that flows, along with additional staging directions making the play interesting to read, easy to understand, and very importantly, an invaluable study aid.

For me it all started at about eight or nine years of age. I was reading a comic which contained the story of Macbeth serialized in simple comic strip form. I could not wait to see what happened next so I rushed out to the public library to get a copy of the book. Of course, when I got it home I didn't even recognise it as being the same story. It made no sense to me, being written in 'Olde English' and often using 'flowery' language. I remember thinking at the time that one day I should write my version of the story for others to understand.

Years went by and I had pretty much forgotten my idea. Then quite by chance I was approached by Encyclopaedia Britannica to produce a series of dramatised classic dramas as educational aids for children learning English as a second language. Included in the selection was Romeo And Juliet which I was to condense down to fifty minutes using modern English.

This brought flooding back the memories of being eight years old again, reading my comic and planning my modern version of Shakespeare. In turn it also led me to the realisation that even if a reader could understand English well, this did not mean they could fully understand and enjoy Shakespeare. I could understand English, yet I did not fully understand some of Shakespeare's text without serious research. So what hope did a person whose first language was not English have?

After some investigation, I discovered there was a great desire around the world to understand the text fully without the inconvenience of referring to footnotes or sidelines, or worse still, the internet. How can one enjoy the wonderful drama with constant interruption? I was also surprised to discover the desire was equally as great in English speaking countries as ones whose first language was not English.

The final kick to get me started was meeting fans of Shakespeare's works who knew scripts off by heart but secretly admitted to me that they did have trouble fully understanding the meaning of some lines. Although they knew the storyline well they could miss some of the subtlety and innuendo Shakespeare was renowned for. It is hardly surprising in this day and age as many of the influences, trends, rumours, beliefs and current affairs of Shakespeare's time are not valid today.

I do not pretend my work is any match for the great master, but I do believe in the greater enjoyment for all. These great works deserve to be understood by all, Shakespeare himself wrote for all levels of audience, he would even aim his work to suit a particular audience at times – for example changing historical facts if he knew a member of royalty would be seeing his play and it would cause them any embarrassment, or of course to curry favour with a monarch by the use of flattery.

I have been as faithful as possible with my version, but the original, iambic pentameter, (the tempo and pace the lines were written for), and other Elizabethan tricks of the trade that Shakespeare was so brilliant at are not included unless vital to the text and meaning. For example, rhyming couplets to signify the end of a scene, for in Shakespeare's day there were no curtains, no lights and mostly static scenery, so scene changes were not so obvious, these couplets, though not strictly necessary, are included to maintain the feel of the original.

This makes for a play that sounds fresh to today's listening audience. It is also a valuable educational tool; English Literature courses often include a section on translating Shakespeare. I am often asked the meaning of a particular line, sometimes scholars argue over the meaning of particular lines. I have taken the most widely agreed version and the one which flows best with the story line where there is dispute, and if you read this translation before reading the original work or going to see a stage version, you will find the play takes on a whole new meaning, making it infinitely more enjoyable.

SJ Hills. London. 2018

Author's Note: This version contains stage directions. These are included purely as a guide to help understand the script better. Any director staging the play would have their own interpretation of the play and decide their own directions. These directions are my own personal interpretation and not those of Shakespeare. You may change these directions to your own choosing or ignore them completely. For exam purposes these should be only regarded as guidance to the dialogue and for accuracy should not be quoted in any studies or examinations.

Hamlet (or to give the play its full title, *The Tragedy of Hamlet, Prince of Denmark*) is a tragedy. A tragedy is typically a serious drama based around a central character, usually flawed, culminating in an unhappy or disastrous ending. The origin of tragedies can be traced back to ancient Greece, particularly Aristotle in his work, *Poetics*. The tragic hero would usually be a great man who made a grave mistake, and have weaknesses we as an audience can relate to or sympathise with. The four major tragedies Shakespeare wrote are *Hamlet, Macbeth, Othello,* and *King Lear*.

To aid in understanding speeches and for learning lines, where possible, speeches by any character are not broken over two pages unless they have a natural break. As a result of this, gaps will be noticeable at the bottom of pages where the next speech will not fully fit onto the page. This was intentional. A speech can not be fully appreciated if one has to turn the page back and forth when studying or learning lines.

Coming soon, *Hamlet for All Ages* by SJ Hills, by SJ Hills, which includes the script in modern English with study note stickies, illustrations and simplified text running alongside the main text for younger readers to share with students, actors and fans of the great work.

And available soon, a wonderful, innovative app, a huge undertaking and the very first of its kind, which will include full, new interactive filmed versions of Shakespeare's plays in both original and modern English.

For further info

www.InteractiveShakespeare.com

www.facebook.com/InteractiveShakespeare

@iShakes1 on Twitter

Historical Notes

The sources for Hamlet can be found as far back as the 12th century in Icelandic tales. A Scandinavian version of *Hamlet*, *Amleth* or *Amlóði* - a Norse word meaning, "not sane" - was written down in the 12th century by Danish historian, *Saxo Grammaticus* entitled *Gesta Danorum* (Deeds of the Danes). Similar storylines can be found in the Icelandic Saga, *Hrolf Kraki*, and the Roman legend *Lucius Junius Brutus*, both include heroes who pretend to be insane in order to gain revenge. A version of *Saxo's* story was translated into French in 1570 by *François de Belleforest* in his *Histoires Tragiques* from which Shakespeare would obtain many sources for his plays. *Belleforest* added to *Saxo's* text substantially, doubling its length, and introducing the hero's gloomy sadness.

Another source Shakespeare used was an earlier play of which no known copy survives, referred to today as the *Ur-Hamlet*, possibly written by *Thomas Kyd* around 1589. This was the first known version to include a ghost in the story. Some scholars suggest that the *Ur-Hamlet* is an early draft by Shakespeare rather than the work of *Kyd*. Whoever the author was, Shakespeare, as he always did, added elements of his own to the original versions, including additional characters and a change of location to Elsinore Castle.

Shakespeare's use of pre-existing material was not considered a lack of originality. In Elizabethan times copyright law did not exist, copying whole passages of text was frequently practiced and not considered theft as it is today. Nowadays, stage and movie productions are frequently 'adaptations' from other sources, the only difference being the need to obtain permission or rights to do so, unless the work is out of copyright.

The real skill Shakespeare displays is in how he adapts his sources in new ways, displaying a remarkable understanding of human psyche and emotion, and including a talent at building characters, adding characters for effect - in the case of Hamlet, completely reinventing the hero's personality - dramatic pacing, tension building, interspersed by short bouts of relief before building the tension even further, and above all of course, his extraordinary ability to use and miss-use language to his and dramatic, bawdy or playful advantage.

It has been said Shakespeare almost wrote screenplays, predating modern cinema by over 400 years, however you view it, he wrote a powerful story and understood how to play on human emotions and weaknesses.

A piece of Hamlet trivia: there is a tradition going back centuries of productions using a real skull for the character Yorick in the graveyard scene (Act 5, Scene 1), with many people donating their skulls to be used after their death.

Kronborg Castle from a 1580 geography book.

Elsinore Castle is based on Kronborg Castle in Helsingør, Denmark. It is strategically placed, overlooking a narrow stretch of sea between Denmark and present day Sweden allowing passage through to the Baltic Sea. The platform would have been a gun placement, with cannons aimed at any threat from the sea and also as a threat to ships which were required to pay a 'Sound Fee' to pass this point.

Circa 1750 relief drawing of Kronborg castle

DRAMATIS PERSONAE

PRINCE HAMLET	Son of the late King Hamlet of Denmark
KING CLAUDIUS	New crowned King of Denmark, uncle of Prince Hamlet
QUEEN GERTRUDE	Prince Hamlet's mother, widow of King Hamlet, recently married to King Claudius, brother of her late husband
GHOST	The ghost of the late King Hamlet
POLONIUS	An elderly councillor in the royal court
LAERTES	Son of Polonius, a student studying abroad
OPHELIA	Daughter of Polonius, love interest of Hamlet
HORATIO	Friend of Prince Hamlet, scholar
ROSENCRANTZ	Courtier. Formerly a fellow student of Prince Hamlet
GUILDENSTERN	Courtier. Formerly a fellow student of Prince Hamlet
PRINCE FORTINBRAS	Prince of Norway, enemy of Denmark
VOLTEMAND	Danish councillor
CORNELIUS	Danish councillor
MARCELLUS	Member of the king's guard
FRANCISCO	Member of the king's guard
OSRIC	A fashionable courtier
REYNALDO	Servant to Polonius
GRAVEDIGGER	
GRAVEDIGGER'S ASSISTANT	
CAPTAIN	Captain in Fortinbras's army
PLAYERS	Actors
GENTLEMAN	In the Danish court
PRIEST	
SAILORS	
LORDS	
LADIES	
SOLDIERS	
MESSENGERS	
ATTENDANTS	

CONTENTS

ACT I

DENMARK
ELSINORE, WHERE OUR TALE IS SET.

SIXTEENTH CENTURY A.D.

ACT I

ACT I SCENE I

ELSINORE. A PLATFORM BEFORE THE CASTLE. MIDNIGHT.

> *Note: Elsinore Castle is based on Kronborg Castle in Helsingør, Denmark. The platform would have been a gun placement for cannons.*
>
> *To show characters are comedic or to vary the overall structure of the play, Shakespeare sometimes writes lines in prose rather than the usual blank verse (a form of poetry which doesn't rhyme except for dramatic effect). He moves between prose and verse to give his characters more depth and variety by breaking the rhythm.*
>
> *Deliberate bawdy use of words is underlined, rhymed lines are in italics.*

THE PLAY STARTS WITH FRANCISCO, A SOLDIER, STANDING WATCH ON A GUARD PLATFORM OF THE ROYAL CASTLE AT ELSINORE IN DENMARK. IT IS BITTERLY COLD AND FRANCISCO IS DEPRESSED, HE IS SUFFERING FROM THE COLD MORE SO THIS NIGHT AS HE IS NOT FEELING WELL.

AS THE CLOCK TOWER BELL STRIKES TWELVE, BARNARDO, THE GUARD WHO IS TO RELIEVE FRANCISCO, ARRIVES. IT IS TOO DARK TO FULLY RECOGNISE ANYONE BY SIGHT UNLESS THEY STAND BY A BURNING TORCH. FRANCISCO RAISES HIS PYKE IN CHALLENGE.

BARNARDO	BARNARDO
(*arriving*) Who goes there?	Who's there?
FRANCISCO	FRANCISCO
No, you answer me. Halt and reveal yourself.	Nay, answer me. Stand and unfold* yourself.

> *Note: 'Unfold' means to pull back his hood, it also suggests to us it is cold.*

FRANCISCO PULLS BACK THE HOOD SHIELDING HIM FROM THE COLD TO REVEAL HIS IDENTITY AND GIVES THE PASSWORD.

BARNARDO	BARNARDO
Long live the king!	Long live the king!
FRANCISCO	FRANCISCO
Bernardo?	Barnardo?

BARNARDO Himself.	BARNARD He.
FRANCISCO You arrive most punctually on the hour.	FRANCISCO You come most carefully upon your hour.
BARNARDO The clock has already struck twelve, get to bed, Francisco.	BARNARDO 'Tis now struck twelve; get thee to bed, Francisco.
FRANCISCO I'm most grateful you are relieving me, it's bitterly cold and I'm not feeling so good.	FRANCISCO For this relief much thanks; 'tis bitter cold, And I am sick at heart.
BARNARDO Has your guard been a quiet one?	BARNARDO Have you had quiet guard?
FRANCISCO Not even a mouse is stirring.	FRANCISCO Not a mouse stirring.
BARNARDO Well, goodnight then. If you see my fellow watchers, Horatio and Marcellus, tell them to hurry up.	BARNARDO Well, good night. If you do meet Horatio and Marcellus, The rivals* of my watch, bid them make haste.

Note: 'Rivals' - used here in its original meaning of people who share something. But people who share often fall out or become competitive, hence the current meaning of rival. From Latin, Rivalis, a group of people who lived on a bank of the same river.

BARNARDO WALKS AWAY, STARTING HIS GUARD DUTY.
FRANCISCO COLLECTS HIS THINGS PREPARING TO LEAVE.

FRANCISCO (*aside*) I think I hear them. (*calls*) Halt! Who goes there?	FRANCISCO I think I hear them. Stand ho! Who is there?

ENTER MARCELLUS, A SOLDIER, AND HORATIO, A CIVILIAN.

HORATIO Friends of this land.	HORATIO Friends to this ground.
MARCELLUS And loyal subjects of the Danish king.	MARCELLUS And liegemen to the Dane.
FRANCISCO I wish you a good night then.	FRANCISCO Give you good night.

Note: It seems strange that he doesn't ask them to reveal themselves as he did Barnardo, especially as they gave a different answer when challenged.

FRANCISCO MAKES TO LEAVE.

MARCELLUS

Oh, goodnight, good soldier. Who has relieved you?

FRANCISCO

Barnardo has taken my place. Good night to you.

MARCELLUS

O, farewell, honest soldier. Who hath relieved you?

FRANCISCO

Barnardo hath my place. Give you good night.

FRANCISCO LEAVES.

MARCELLUS

(*calling out*) Hello? Barnardo?

BARNARDO

(*calling back*) Who calls? Is that Horatio?

MARCELLUS

Holla, Barnardo!

BARNARDO

Say, what, is Horatio there?

BARNARDO APPEARS OUT OF THE DARKNESS.

HORATIO OFFERS HIS HAND TO SHAKE.

HORATIO

A piece of him.

BARNARDO

Welcome, Horatio. Welcome, good Marcellus.

HORATIO

Well, has the thing appeared again tonight?

BARNARDO

I've seen nothing.

MARCELLUS

Horatio says it's just our imagination, and refuses to believe in the frightening sight we've seen twice now. That's why I've brought him along to spend the long minutes of this night watching with us. If the apparition appears again he may confirm what we've seen and speak to it himself.

HORATIO

Tush, tush. It will not appear.

HORATIO

A piece of him.

BARNARDO

Welcome Horatio. Welcome good Marcellus.

HORATIO

What, has this thing appeared again tonight?

BARNARDO

I have seen nothing.

MARCELLUS

Horatio says 'tis but our fantasy,
And will not let belief take hold of him,
Touching this dreaded sight twice seen of us.
Therefore I have entreated him along
With us to watch the minutes of this night,
That if again this apparition come,
He may approve our eyes and speak to it.

HORATIO

Tush, tush, 'twill not appear.

BARNARDO

Sit here awhile, and let us once again assault your ears with the story of what we have seen these past two nights that you are so set against believing.

HORATIO

Very well, let us sit down and hear what Barnardo has to say.

BARNARDO

Sit down a while,
And let us once again assail your ears,
That are so fortified against our story,
What we have two nights seen.

HORATIO

Well, sit we down,
And let us hear Barnardo speak of this.

THEY SIT.

BARNARDO

Just last night, when that same star up there, west of the Northern Star, had made its way to illuminate that part of the heavens where it now shines, and just as the clock was chiming one, Marcellus and myself...

BARNARDO

Last night of all,
When yond same star that's westward from the
  pole*
Had made his course t' illume that part of heaven
Where now it burns, Marcellus and myself,
The bell then beating one -

A CLOCK STRIKES ONE.

A GHOST ENTERS IN THE LIKENESS OF THE RECENTLY DECEASED KING OF DENMARK, OLD HAMLET, WEARING BATTLE ARMOUR.

*Note: The Pole Star, or the North Star is a constant position bright star in the northern hemisphere, always due north in the sky. It was used by sailors or travellers as a reference to the direction they were travelling.

MARCELLUS

(hushed) Wait, be quiet. Look, here it comes again!

MARCELLUS

Peace, break thee off. Look where it comes again!

BARNARDO

In the same likeness of the dead king.

BARNARDO

In the same figure like the king that's dead.

MARCELLUS

You're the educated one, Horatio, speak to it.

MARCELLUS

Thou art a scholar, speak to it, Horatio.

BARNARDO

Doesn't it look like the king? See, Horatio?

BARNARDO

Looks a' not like the king? Mark it, Horatio.

HORATIO

Very like him. It chills me with fear and astonishment.

HORATIO

Most like. It harrows me with fear and wonder.

BARNARDO

It wishes to be spoken to.

BARNARDO

It would be spoke to.

MARCELLUS

Ask it a question, Horatio.

MARCELLUS

Question it*, Horatio.

> *Note: It was believed that a ghost could only speak if it was spoken to first. In Shakespeare's day everyone believed ghosts existed.*

HORATIO

(*to Ghost*) Who are you that disturbs our peace this time of night? And clad in armour like the late King of Denmark sometimes wore? By the heavens above, I order you to speak!

HORATIO

What art thou that usurp'st this time of night,
Together with that fair and warlike form
In which the majesty of buried Denmark
Did sometimes march? By heaven, I charge thee
speak!

THE GHOST TURNS, THEN SLOWLY AND REGALLY WALKS AWAY.

MARCELLUS

You've offended it.

MARCELLUS

It is offended.

BARNARDO

Look, it strides away.

BARNARDO

See, it stalks away.

HORATIO

(*to Ghost*) Wait, speak, speak! I order you to speak!

HORATIO

Stay, speak, speak! I charge thee speak!

THE GHOST DISAPPEARS.

MARCELLUS

It's gone, and would not answer.

MARCELLUS

'Tis gone, and will not answer.

BARNARDO

Well, Horatio? You're shaking, and look pale. Is this not something more than wild imagination? What do you think now?

BARNARDO

How now, Horatio? You tremble and look pale.
Is not this something more than fantasy?
What think you on't?

HORATIO

As God is my witness, I would not have believed this if not for the sober confirmation of my own eyes.

HORATIO

Before my God, I might not this believe
Without the sensible and true avouch
Of mine own eyes.

MARCELLUS

Does it not look like the king?

MARCELLUS

Is it not like the king?

HORATIO

As alike as you are to yourself. Wearing the very same armour he wore in his fight against the arrogant king of Norway. Scowling the way he did in an angry exchange before he defeated the Polish army on the snow fields. It's very strange.

MARCELLUS

Twice before, in the dead of night at exactly this hour, he has marched past us.

HORATIO

I don't know what to think about this, but from the limits of my experience I suspect this is a forewarning of new disruption for our country.

MARCELLUS

In that case, sit here and tell me, who would know why there is such a strict nightly watch over this land, and why so many bronze cannons and implements of war are manufactured and imported daily? Why ship builders are ordered to work seven days a week, even on Sunday? What might be the reason for such arduous haste to labour night and day? Who can tell me that?

HORATIO

I can tell you. At least, as far as rumour goes;

HORATIO

As thou art to thyself.
Such was the very armour he had on
When he the ambitious Norway combated;
So frowned he once when in an angry parle
He smote the sledded Polacks on the ice.
'Tis strange.

MARCELLUS

Thus twice before, and jump at this dead hour,
With martial stalk hath he gone by our watch.

HORATIO

In what particular thought to work I know not,
But, in the gross and scope of my opinion,
This bodes some strange eruption to our state.

MARCELLUS

Good now, sit down, and tell me, he that knows,
Why this same strict and most observant watch
So nightly toils the subject of the land,
And why such daily cast of brazen cannon,
And foreign mart for implements of war,
Why such impress of shipwrights, whose sore task
Does not divide the Sunday from the week;
What might be toward that this sweaty haste
Doth make the night joint-labourer with the day:
Who is't that can inform me?

HORATIO

That can I;
At least, the whisper goes so:

THEY HUDDLE CLOSER TO LISTEN.

HORATIO (CONTD)

Our late king, whose image you have just seen before you, was, as you know, goaded - due to the arrogant pride of King Fortinbras of Norway - to a duel, in which our valiant King Hamlet, revered around the world, killed this Fortinbras, who, by order of a sealed contract, approved by law and the ancient rules of combat, forfeited, along with his life, all his lands to the conqueror. Our king had put forward lands of equal size which would have been inherited by Fortinbras had he won by the same terms. Hence Fortinbras' lands fell to King Hamlet.

HORATIO

our last king,
Whose image even but now appeared to us,
Was, as you know, by Fortinbras of Norway,
Thereto pricked on by a most emulate pride,
Dared to the combat; in which our valiant Hamlet -
For so this side of our known world esteemed him -
Did slay this Fortinbras, who, by a sealed compact
Well ratified by law and heraldry,
Did forfeit with his life all those his lands
Which he stood seized of, to the conqueror;
Against the which a moiety competent
Was gaged by our king, which had returned
To the inheritance of Fortinbras,
Had he been vanquisher; as, by the same cov'nant
And carriage of the article designed,
His fell to Hamlet.

> Note: Later on in Act 5, Scene 1 we will learn this happened 30 years ago.

HORATIO (CONT'D)

Now, sir, his son, young Fortinbras, unproven in battle but itching for a fight, has, from the outlying regions of Norway, gathered up a group of unpaid lawless reprobates, willing in return for food and shelter to fight and stand as cannon fodder, in - as it appears to our generals - some daring attempt to retake by force the lands his father lost. This, I take is the main reason behind our preparations for war, the reason for our guard duty, and the cause of this rush of activity and the stockpiling throughout our land.

HORATIO

Now, sir, young Fortinbras,
Of unimproved metal hot and full,
Hath, in the skirts of Norway here and there,
Sharked up a list of lawless resolutes,
For food and diet, to some enterprise
That hath a stomach in't, which is no other -
As it doth well appear unto our state -
But to recover of us, by strong hand
And terms compulsatory, those foresaid lands
So by his father lost; and this, I take it,
Is the main motive of our preparations,
The source of this our watch, and the chief head
Of this posthaste and rummage* in the land.

> *Note: 'Rummage' meant to stow in a ship's hold. Spelled 'romage' in some texts.

BARNARDO

I think there can be no other reason. It may well explain why this ominous armoured figure appears during our watch, and why it looks so like the king who was, and still is, the reason behind these disputes.

BARNARDO

I think it be no other but e'en so.
Well may it sort that this portentous figure
Comes armed through our watch, so like the king
That was and is the question of these wars.

Act I Scene I - Elsinore. A Platform Before The Castle. Midnight.

HORATIO

A speck of dust to trouble the mind's eye. When almighty Rome was at its height, just before the fall of the mighty Caesar, graves stood empty and their shrouded dead contents squawked and gibbered in the Roman streets, and comets with tails of fire and dripping blood were expelled from the sun as ominous signs, and the moon, which influences Neptune's ocean tides was eclipsed like a doomsday precursor of terrible things to come. And many similar signs, messengers preceding our fate, omens of the destruction to follow have been demonstrated by Heaven and earth to our country and countrymen.

HORATIO

A mote it is to trouble the mind's eye.*
In the most high and palmy state* of Rome,
A little ere the mightiest Julius fell,
The graves stood tenantless and the sheeted dead
Did squeak and gibber in the Roman streets;
*As stars with trains of fire and dews of blood,
Disasters in the sun; and the moist star,*
Upon whose influence Neptune's empire stands,
Was sick almost to doomsday with eclipse;
And even the like precurse of feared events,
As harbingers preceding still the fates
And prologue to the omen coming on,
Have heaven and earth together demonstrated
Unto our climatures* and countrymen.

Note: The 'Mind's Eye' is the imagination, forming or recalling a mental image.

'Palmy state' – the palm leaf was an ancient symbol of victory in war.

'As stars with trains...' most scholars agree that there are one or two lines omitted here, probably unintentionally.

'Moist star' – the moon (with its watery beams), and 'climatures' were regions with different climates. For example, Denmark's cold northern climate.

This speech is based on Jesus foretelling the end of the world in the Holy Bible, Mathew, 24:29; "Immediately after the tribulation of those days shall the sun be darkened, and the moon shall not give her light, and the stars shall fall from heaven, and the powers of the heavens shall be shaken."

RE-ENTER GHOST.

HORATIO (CONT'D)

Wait, look! Here it comes again! I'll confront it, though it may destroy me. (*to Ghost*) Wait, spirit. If you are able to make a sound or have a voice, speak to me...

HORATIO

But soft, behold! Lo where it comes again!
I'll cross it* though it blast me. Stay, illusion.
If thou hast any sound or use of voice,
Speak to me.

Note: 'I'll cross it' – it was believed that if you walked across the path of a ghost you became under its power and influence, and if you upset it by doing so it could destroy you, 'blast me' – meaning to obliterate me completely.

THE GHOST DOES NOT SPEAK BUT SPREADS ITS ARMS WIDE AS IF IN REPLY.

HORATIO (CONT'D)

If there is any good thing I can do that may ease your passage and not harm my standing in heaven, speak to me...

(*the ghost does not speak*)

HORATIO

If there be any good thing to be done
That may to thee do ease, and grace to me,
Speak to me.

> Note: It was believed that ghosts returned because of some unfinished business during their life on earth. If someone could complete the task on their behalf they could rest in peace. Another reason for them to appear was to warn loved ones of some impending future event, or because someone had caused their death and they wanted the truth to be known. Horatio broaches all reasons.

HORATIO (CONT'D)

If you have any knowledge of your country's fate – which with forewarning could be avoided – speak out...

(*the ghost does not speak*)

Or if, in your life you hoarded ill-gotten treasures buried in the bowels of the earth, the reason for which your spirit is doomed to walk the earth, tell me. Stay and tell me!

HORATIO

If thou art privy to thy country's fate -
Which happily* foreknowing may avoid -
O, speak.
Or if thou hast uphoarded in thy life
Extorted treasure in the womb of earth,
For which, they say, your spirits oft walk in death,
Speak of it, stay and speak!

> *Note: 'Happily' – perhaps. Derived from the word 'haply'.

A COCK CROWS, INTERRUPTING HIM AND SIGNIFYING THE BREAK OF DAY.

AT THE SOUND, THE GHOST QUICKLY TURNS TO LEAVE.

HORATIO (CONT'D)

Stop it, Marcellus!

MARCELLUS

Shall I strike it with my spear?

HORATIO

Do it, if it will not stay.

HORATIO

Stop it, Marcellus.

MARCELLUS

Shall I strike it with my partisan?

HORATIO

Do, if it will not stand.

AS HE LUNGES AT THE GHOST IT VANISHES AND APPEARS INSTANTLY IN A NEW PLACE REPEATEDLY AS THEY TRY TO STRIKE IT.

BARNARDO

It's here!

HORATIO

Now it's here!

BARNARDO

'Tis here!

HORATIO

'Tis here!

THE GHOST FINALLY DISAPPEARS COMPLETELY.

THEY LOOK AROUND FRANTICALLY FOR WHERE IT MAY REAPPEAR. IT DOESN'T.

MARCELLUS

It's gone!
We did wrong to show violence to a royal entity. It's like the air, untouchable, and our vain blows are malicious and disrespectful.

BARNARDO

It was about to speak just as the cock crowed.

HORATIO

And then it fled like a guilty person upon hearing a fateful summons. I've heard that the cock is the trumpet of the morning, awakening the God of day with his shrill penetrating throat, and at his warning the wandering spirit, whether in sea, fire, earth or air, rushes back to its confines; as we saw proof of just now.

MARCELLUS

It disappeared as the cock crowed. Some say that whenever the season comes when we celebrate our Saviour's birth, the bird of the dawn crows all night long, and then, they say, no spirit dares walk abroad. The nights are free of evil, no planets exert influence, no fairies bewitch anyone, no witch has the power to cast spells, so hallowed and blessed is the time.

MARCELLUS

'Tis gone!
We do it wrong, being so majestical,
To offer it the show of violence;
For it is as the air, invulnerable,
And our vain blows malicious mockery.

BARNARDO

It was about to speak when the cock crew.

HORATIO

And then it started like a guilty thing
Upon a fearful summons. I have heard
The cock, that is the trumpet to the morn,
Doth with his lofty and shrill-sounding throat
Awake the god of day, and at his warning,
Whether in sea or fire, in earth or air,
Th' extravagant and erring spirit hies
To his confine; and of the truth herein
This present object made probation.

MARCELLUS

It faded on the crowing of the cock.
Some say that ever 'gainst that season comes
Wherein our Saviour's* birth is celebrated,
The bird of dawning singeth all night long,
And then, they say, no spirit dare stir abroad,
The nights are wholesome, then no planets strike,
No fairy takes, nor witch hath power to charm,
So hallowed and so gracious is that time.

*Note: 'Our Saviour' refers to Jesus Christ, whose birth is celebrated every year at Christmas time (December 25th)

HORATIO

So I have heard, and I do in part believe it. But look, the morning, clad in its russet gown, walks over the dew of the high eastern hill. Our watch is ended, and my advice is that we share what we have seen tonight with young Hamlet, for, upon my life, I'll wager this spirit that refuses to talk to us will talk to him. Do you agree we should tell him about it, out of loyalty befitting of our duty?

HORATIO

So have I heard, and do in part believe it.
But look, the morn in russet* mantle clad
Walks o'er the dew of yon high eastward* hill.
Break we our watch up; and, by my advice,
Let us impart what we have seen tonight
Unto young Hamlet, for, upon my life,
This spirit, dumb to us, will speak to him.
Do you consent we shall acquaint him with it,
As needful in our loves, fitting our duty?

Note: 'Russet' is a reddy brown colour, often associated with Autumn.

Some editions prefer 'eastern' to 'eastward'.

MARCELLUS

Let's do it, I say, and this morning I know where he can be most conveniently found.

MARCELLUS

Let's do't, I pray; and I this morning know
Where we shall find him most conveniently.

ACT I SCENE II

A STATE ROOM IN THE ROYAL CASTLE.

THE ROYAL COURT OF DENMARK, AFTER A ROYAL WEDDING.
TRUMPETS FLOURISH, HERALDING THE ARRIVAL OF CLAUDIUS, THE NEW
KING OF DENMARK, AFTER HIS BROTHER, THE LATE KING HAMLET, HAD
DIED TWO MONTHS PREVIOUSLY. HE IS ACCOMPANIED BY HIS NEW WIFE,
QUEEN GERTRUDE, RECENT WIDOW OF KING HAMLET.

THEY ARE FOLLOWED BY THE COUNCILLORS, VOLTEMAND AND CORNELIUS,
WITH POLONIUS, THE KING'S CHIEF ADVISOR AND HIS SON, LAERTES, AND
OTHER OFFICIALS (CUM ALLIS – WITH OTHERS - THE WHOLE CAST ON STAGE).

LASTLY HAMLET, THE THIRTY YEAR OLD SON OF THE LATE KING HAMLET
AND QUEEN GERTRUDE, SULKILY ENTERS THE ROOM. STILL MOURNING HIS
FATHER'S DEATH, HE IS DRESSED IN BLACK, DESPITE EVERYONE ELSE BEING
DRESSED IN THEIR FINERY FOR THIS WEDDING BEING CELEBRATED.

Note: The King uses the plural terms 'we' and 'our', when he means 'I' or 'mine'. It is known as 'the royal we'. The English monarch still uses the plural in speech to denote they speak on behalf of the country. It is not used in the translation.

Gertrude was previously his sister-in-law, not an actual blood relative of Claudius

---

KING CLAUDIUS

Though the memory of my dear brother, King Hamlet's death is still fresh in our minds, and while it is natural to grieve openly, as a kingdom mourning together in sorrow, it is time now to restrain our grief and think not only of his memory but of our own affairs. Therefore my one time sister, and now my and your queen, the joint imperial ruler of this warring country, has, as it were, with saddened joy, having one eye open in celebration of a funeral, and one closed in sadness at matrimony, bringing joy to sadness and sadness to joy in equal measure, taken to become my wife. We have listened to public opinion, which we have allowed to be freely given on this matter, and for all your support and approval we give our thanks.

KING CLAUDIUS

Though yet of Hamlet our* dear brother's death
The memory be green, and that it us befitted
To bear our hearts in grief, and our whole
   kingdom
To be contracted in one brow of woe;
Yet so far hath discretion fought with nature
That we with wisest sorrow think on him
Together with remembrance of ourselves.
Therefore our sometime sister, now our queen,
Th' imperial jointress to this warlike state,
Have we, as 'twere with a defeated joy,
With one auspicious and one dropping eye,
With mirth in funeral and with dirge in marriage,
In equal scale weighing delight and dole,
Taken to wife; nor have we herein barred
Your better wisdoms, which have freely gone
With this affair along. For all, our thanks.

THE KING PICKS UP A LETTER SEALED WITH A WAX ROYAL SEAL.

KING CLAUDIUS (CONT'D)

In further news, you all know Fortinbras junior, who, holding a poor opinion of our resolve, or thinking that with my late, dear brother's death our country would be disjointed and in disorder, combined with his ambitious dreams, has not failed to pester us with messages demanding the surrender of the lands lost, quite lawfully, by his late father to my most valiant brother. Well, he can think again.

KING CLAUDIUS

Now follows that you know young Fortinbras,
Holding a weak supposal of our worth,
Or thinking by our late dear brother's death
Our state to be disjoint and out of frame,
Colleagued with the dream of his advantage,
He hath not failed to pester us with message
Importing the surrender of those lands
Lost by his father, with all bands of law,
To our most valiant brother. So much for him.

MURMURS OF APPROVAL FROM THOSE GATHERED.

KING CLAUDIUS (CONT'D)

Now, as for myself, and the purpose of this meeting, in response to his actions I have here a letter I've written to the King of Norway, uncle of young Fortinbras - now so sick and bedridden he barely knows what his nephew is up to - demanding that he suppress his nephew's stance, reminding him that Norway's military personnel and supplies are all subject to his control. I hereby dispatch you, good Cornelius, and you, Voltemand, as bearers of this letter to the aged King, with no power of negotiation outside the range of the detailed articles within this letter.

KING CLAUDIUS

Now for ourself, and for this time of meeting,
Thus much the business is: we have here writ
To Norway, uncle of young Fortinbras,
Who, impotent and bed-rid, scarcely hears
Of this his nephew's purpose, to suppress
His further gait herein, in that the levies,
The lists, and full proportions, are all made
Out of his subject; and we here dispatch
You, good Cornelius, and you, Voltemand,
For bearers of this greeting to old Norway,
Giving to you no further personal power
To business with the king more than the scope
Of these dilated articles allow.

THE KING HANDS VOLTEMAND AND CORNELIUS THE LETTER.

KING CLAUDIUS (CONT'D)

Farewell, you may commence your duty with your immediate departure.

KING

Farewell, and let your haste commend your duty.

VOLTEMAND & CORNELIUS

In this and all things we will do our duty.

VOLTEMAND & CORNELIUS

In that and all things will we show our duty.

KING CLAUDIUS

I do not doubt it. A fond farewell.

KING

We doubt it nothing; heartily farewell.

VOLTEMAND AND CORNELIUS EXIT BOWING.

THE KING TURNS TO POLONIUS'S SON, LAERTES.

KING CLAUDIUS (CONT'D)

And now you, Laertes, what news do you have for me? You mentioned a request you had.

KING

And now, Laertes, what's the news with you? You told us of some suit.

LAERTES DOESN'T IMMEDIATELY REPLY.

KING CLAUDIUS (CONT'D)

What is it, Laertes? Your voice is not lost with any reasonable request to the ruler of Denmark.

KING

What is't, Laertes?
You cannot speak of reason* to the Dane
And lose your voice.

> *Note: 'Speak of reason...' has the double meaning of asking a reasonable question and the King being a reasonable man. 'Lose your voice' meaning both, 'your voice would not be wasted' and also not being able to speak up when requested because he had lost his voice or was timid. A public demonstration that he is a benevolent ruler who listens and you need not be afraid to ask his favour.

KING CLAUDIUS (CONT'D)

What could you possibly ask for, Laertes, that I would not freely give but for the asking? A head is not joined closer to the heart, nor a hand to the mouth, than I, the King of Denmark am to your father. What is it you wish to ask, Laertes?

KING

What wouldst thou beg, Laertes,
That shall not be my offer, not thy asking?
The head is not more native to the heart,
The hand more instrumental to the mouth,
Than is the throne of Denmark to thy father.
What wouldst thou have, Laertes?

LAERTES

My revered lord, your gracious permission to return to France, from where I willingly came to Denmark to show my respects at your coronation. But now that my duty is done, I must confess, my thoughts and wishes once again direct themselves towards France, subject to your gracious permission and pardon.

LAERTES

My dread lord,
Your leave and favour to return to France,
From whence though willingly I came to
  Denmark
To show my duty in your coronation,
Yet now, I must confess, that duty done,
My thoughts and wishes bend again toward
  France,
And bow them to your gracious leave and
  pardon.

KING CLAUDIUS

Do you have your father's permission? What does Polonius say?

KING

Have you your father's leave? What says Polonius?

THE KING TURNS TOWARDS POLONIUS.

POLONIUS

My lord, he so wore me down with his persistent pleading, that in the end I succumbed and gave my reluctant consent. I do beg you, give him permission to go.

POLONIUS

He hath, my lord, wrung from me my slow leave
By laboursome petition, and at last
Upon his will I sealed my hard consent.
I do beseech you, give him leave to go.

THE KING TURNS BACK TO LAERTES.

KING CLAUDIUS

Leave when best suits you, Laertes, the time is yours, put your talents to best use as you wish!
But now, my nephew Hamlet, also my son...

KING

Take thy fair hour, Laertes; time be thine,
And thy best graces spend it at thy will!
But now, my cousin* Hamlet, and my son -

FINALLY THE KING TURNS TO PRINCE HAMLET.

Note: The King chooses to address Hamlet last, which displeases an already unhappy Hamlet. Hamlet's first line below tells this, it has a double meaning, 'kind' meaning either 'by nature' or 'considerate', and he is not the kind of man Claudius is, and Claudius is not nice.

'Cousin' then meant relative of any kind.

HAMLET

(*aside*) Related by nature, but not in nature.

HAMLET

[*Aside.*] A little more than kin, and less than kind*.

KING CLAUDIUS

Why is it that dark clouds still hang over you?

KING

How is it that the clouds still hang on you?

HAMLET

Not so, my lord. I've had too much of the sun.

HAMLET

Not so, my lord. I am too much i'th' sun.*

Note: He uses 'sun' as a deliberate pun; son and sun.

QUEEN GERTRUDE

Dearest Hamlet, take that dark look off your face, and let your eye look on the King of Denmark as a friend. Do not seek your noble father in the dust forever with those downcast eyes. You know this is commonplace, everything that lives must die, passing through nature to the eternal ever after.

QUEEN

Good Hamlet, cast thy nighted colour off,
And let thine eye look like a friend on Denmark.
Do not for ever with thy vailed lids
Seek for thy noble father in the dust.
Thou know'st 'tis common: all that lives must die,
Passing through nature to eternity.

HAMLET

(*sarcasm*) Yes, madam, it is 'common'.

HAMLET

Ay, madam, it is common*.

Note: He is being sarcastic. What his mother has done is far from normal, and 'common' is a pun on usual occurrence and lowly thing to do.

QUEEN GERTRUDE

If it is, then why does it seem to affect you so much?

QUEEN

If it be,
Why seems it so particular with thee?

HAMLET

Seem, madam? No, it *does*. I don't know why you think '*seem*'. It's not just my dark mood, good mother, or my black mourning suits, or my windy expulsion of deep sighs. No, nor is it the constant stream in my eye, or the dejected look of my face, along with all other expressions, moods and displays of grief that can truly show my feelings. These may '*seem*' to, as they are the actions a man can put on,
I feel inside exactly as I show.
There's no pretence in my feelings of woe.

HAMLET

Seems, madam? Nay, it is, I know not ` seems'.
'Tis not alone my inky cloak, good mother,
Nor customary suits of solemn black,
Nor windy suspiration of forced breath,
No, nor the fruitful river in the eye,
Nor the dejected haviour of the visage,
Together with all forms, moods, shows of grief,
That can denote me truly. These indeed seem,
For they are actions that a man might play;
But I have that within which passeth show,
These but the trappings and the suits of woe.

Note: Hamlet is suggesting that his grief is real, unlike his mother who rushed to remarry.

31

KING CLAUDIUS

It is commendable to your sweet nature, Hamlet, to show such duty to mourning your father. But you know, your father lost a father, and that father lost his, and each surviving son felt duty bound for a period to mourn his loss. But to persist in this obstinate sorrow is irreligious stubborness. Such grief is not manly, and most disrespectful to the heavens. It suggests a weak heart, a slow witted mind, an ignorant and uneducated understanding. We know it is inevitable, it is normal, unlike some unexpected terrible occurrence.

KING

'Tis sweet and commendable in your nature, Hamlet,
To give these mourning duties to your father;
But you must know, your father lost a father,
That father lost, lost his, and the survivor bound
In filial obligation for some term
To do obsequious sorrow. But to persever
In obstinate condolement is a course
Of impious stubbornness, 'tis unmanly grief,
It shows a will most incorrect to heaven,
A heart unfortified, a mind impatient,
An understanding simple and unschooled;
For what we know must be and is as common
As any the most vulgar thing to sense -

HAMLET SAYS NOTHING, CONTINUING TO STARE AT THE GROUND.

KING CLAUDIUS (CONT'D)

Why take it so obstinately to heart? Goodness me, it offends heaven, disrespects the dead, and goes against nature, which despite your absurd reasoning, in its natural course takes the life of all fathers, from the first to die to the one who died today, with its cry of 'that is the way it is'. I pray you bury this unproductive grief, and think of me as a father now. Let it be known to all, you are the immediate heir to the throne, and that I look on you with the same fondness of any father to a dearest son. For this reason your desire to return back to Wittenberg University is contrary to my wish, and I beseech you, reconsider and remain here in the warm comfort of our court, as my chief courtier, kinsman and my son.

KING

Why should we in our peevish opposition
Take it to heart? Fie, 'tis a fault to heaven,
A fault against the dead, a fault to nature,
To reason most absurd, whose common theme
Is death of fathers, and who still hath cried
From the first corpse till he that died today,
`This must be so.' We pray you, throw to earth
This unprevailing woe, and think of us
As of a father; for let the world take note
You are the most immediate to our throne,
And with no less nobility of love
Than that which dearest father bears his son
Do I impart toward you. For your intent
In going back to school in Wittenberg,
It is most retrograde to our desire,
And we beseech you, bend you to remain
Here in the cheer and comfort of our eye,
Our chiefest courtier, cousin, and our son.

QUEEN GERTRUDE

Do not let your mother's wishes be in vain, Hamlet. I beg you, stay with us, don't go to Wittenberg.

QUEEN

Let not thy mother lose her prayers, Hamlet.
I pray thee, stay with us; go not to Wittenberg.

HAMLET

I shall do my best to obey you, madam.

HAMLET

I shall in all my best obey you, madam.

KING CLAUDIUS

Why, that is a good, respectful answer. Stay here in Denmark in stately honour. (*to wife*) Come madam, Hamlet's offer of kind accord warms my heart. In celebration of this, a great cannon shall inform the clouds of every toast I drink today, rousing the heavens into re-echoing the king's message with a roar of thunder. Come, let us go.

KING

Why, 'tis a loving and a fair reply:
Be as ourself in Denmark. - Madam, come;
This gentle and unforced accord of Hamlet
Sits smiling to my heart, in grace whereof,
No jocund health that Denmark drinks today
But the great cannon to the clouds shall tell,
And the king's rouse the heavens shall bruit
  again,
Re-speaking earthly thunder. Come away.

TRUMPETS HERALD (FLOURISH).

EXIT ALL EXCEPT HAMLET WHO NOW RECITES HIS 1ST SOLILOQUY.

Note: Soliloquy means talking thoughts out loud.

HAMLET

Oh, how I wish my sullied, hardened flesh would melt away, like water, and form itself as dew on the ground, or that the Almighty had not made taking one's own life a sin. Oh God, Oh God! (*he sighs*) How weary, dull, drab and useless this world seems to me! A curse on it, damn it! It's an untended garden that's gone to seed, overrun with rank and ugly weeds. That it should come to this! Only dead two months - no, less even that that – such an excellent king, compared to this one…

HAMLET

O that this too too solid flesh would melt,
Thaw, and resolve itself into a dew,
Or that the Everlasting had not fixed
His canon 'gainst self-slaughter! O God, O God!
How weary, stale, flat, and unprofitable
Seem to me all the uses of this world!
Fie on't, ah fie! 'Tis an unweeded garden
That grows to seed; things rank and gross in
  nature
Possess it merely. That it should come to this!
But two months dead -nay, not so much, not two-
So excellent a king, that was to this…

HE INDICATES THE DIRECTION KING CLAUDIUS LEFT THE ROOM.

HAMLET (CONT'D)

Like a Titan to a beast. So loving of my mother he'd not even allow the winds from heaven to blow too roughly on her face. Heavens above! I can't get it out of my mind. She would cling to him as if the more she had of him the more her appetite grew. And yet within a month…

HAMLET

Hyperion to a satyr, so loving to my mother
That he might not beteem the winds of heaven
Visit her face too roughly. Heaven and earth!
Must I remember? Why, she should hang on him
As if increase of appetite had grown
By what it fed on, and yet within a month -

Hamlet compares his late father to a Greek god and his new step-father to a beast.

HAMLET PAUSES, THEN PULLS HIMSELF TOGETHER.

HAMLET (CONT'D)	HAMLET
Let me think of it no more. Women, so weak in character! A little more than a month since she wore those same shoes following my poor father's body, weeping like Niobe. Why? Her of all people...	Let me not think on't. Frailty, thy name is woman! A little month, or ere those shoes were old With which she followed my poor father's body, Like Niobe*, all tears; why she, even she -

*Note: Niobe was a mother in Greek mythology, married to the king of Thebes. She boasted to Leto, a mother of only two children, namely Apollo and Artemis, of her fourteen children to show she was superior. Apollo and Artemis in rage at the insult killed all fourteen of her children. Niobe's husband committed suicide in grief at his loss. Niobe ran to Mount Sipylus to plead with the gods to end her misery. Zeus took pity on her and turned her to stone so she would have no feeling. The rock exists today, still weeping tears, and is regarded as a moving reminder of a mother's eternal mourning.

HAMLET (CONT'D)	HAMLET
Oh, God. A senseless beast would have mourned longer! Married to my uncle, my father's brother, but no more like my father than I am like Hercules. Within a month, even before the salt of deceitful tears had ceased flushing her swollen eyes, she remarried. Oh, such wicked haste, to jump with such ease between incestuous sheets! It is not good, nor can any good come of it. It breaks my heart, but I have to suffer in silence.	O God, a beast that wants discourse of reason Would have mourned longer! - married with my uncle, My father's brother, but no more like my father Than I to Hercules. Within a month, Ere yet the salt of most unrighteous tears Had left the flushing in her galled eyes, She married. O most wicked speed, to post With such dexterity to incestuous* sheets! It is not, nor it cannot come to good. But break, my heart, for I must hold my tongue.

*Note: Incest in Shakespeare's time included distant relatives and in-laws. The church forbade a man marrying his brother's widow, yet this is exactly what Henry VIII had done some years before Hamlet was written. Later, Henry, desperate for a son and heir, proclaimed the marriage incestuous and had it annulled. This lead to England breaking away from the Roman Catholic Pope and forming The Church of England with the ruling monarch as its head. In another coincidence, within a month of having Anne Boleyn beheaded, Henry married Anne's lady in waiting.

ENTER HORATIO, MARCELLUS, AND BARNARDO.

HORATIO
Greetings to your lordship!

HAMLET
I'm glad to see you are well, Horatio, it is Horatio isn't it?

HORATIO
It is, my lord, your humble servant as ever.

HAMLET
My good sir, and good friend, I too am yours. And what brings you from Wittenberg, Horatio?

HORATIO
Hail to your lordship!

HAMLET
I am glad to see you well.
Horatio, or I do forget myself.

HORATIO
The same, my lord, and your poor servant ever.

HAMLET
Sir, my good friend; I'll change that name with you.
And what make you from Wittenberg,* Horatio?

*Note: Hamlet means the famous Wittenberg university in Germany, further emphasising that Horatio is a learned gentleman. It was founded in 1502 with Martin Luther attending who in 1517 would pin his ninety-five thesis to the All Saints Castle Church door protesting against the selling of indulgences in Wittenberg. This marked the beginning of the protestant reformation, a movement against the Catholic Church. This was relevant in Shakespeare's England with the recently formed Church of England banning Catholicism.

HAMLET NOTICES THE COMPANIONS WITH HORATIO.

HAMLET (CONT'D)
Marcellus?

MARCELLUS
(bowing) Indeed, my good lord.

HAMLET
I'm very glad to see you.
(to Barnardo) And good evening, sir.

HAMLET
Marcellus?

MARCELLUS
My good lord.

HAMLET
I am very glad to see you. [To Barnado.] Good even, sir.

BARNARDO BOWS IN ACKNOWLEDGEMENT.

HAMLET TURNS HIS ATTENTIONS BACK TO HORATIO.

HAMLET (CONT'D)
(to Horatio) But please, Horatio, tell me what brings you from Wittenberg?

HORATIO
I am playing truant, my good lord.

HAMLET
But what, in faith, make you from Wittenberg!

HORATIO
A truant disposition, good my lord.

35

HAMLET

I would not believe that from your enemies, nor shall I allow you to offend my ears by talking yourself down. I know you are no truant. So, what is your business in Elsinore? We'll teach you to take a good drink before you depart.

HORATIO

My lord, I came for your father's funeral.

HAMLET

I beg you, do not mock me, fellow student. I believe is was for my mother's wedding.

HORATIO

Indeed, my lord, it followed close behind.

HAMLET

Saving money, Horatio. The funeral feast was served cold on the marriage tables. I'd rather have died and met my worst enemy in Heaven than seen that day, Horatio. My father... I still see my father.

HAMLET

I would not hear your enemy say so,
Nor shall you do mine ear that violence
To make it truster of your own report
Against yourself. I know you are no truant.
But what is your affair in Elsinore?
We'll teach you to drink deep ere you depart.

HORATIO

My lord, I came to see your father's funeral.

HAMLET

I prithee do not mock me, fellow-student;
I think it was to see my mother's wedding.

HORATIO

Indeed, my lord, it followed hard upon.

HAMLET

Thrift, thrift, Horatio. The funeral baked meats
Did coldly furnish* forth the marriage tables.
Would I had met my dearest foe* in heaven
Ere I had seen* that day, Horatio.
My father, methinks I see my father.

Note: 'Coldly furnish' – served cold, unfeeling, a play on words.

'Dearest foe'- Dearest was used for strong feelings of both love and hate.

'Ere I had seen' – some editions say 'Or ever I had seen'. 'Ere' is a better syllable count to match the next line.

HORATIO

Where my lord?

HORATIO

Where, my lord?

HORATIO LOOKS AROUND SHOCKED. HAMLET POINTS TO HIS HEAD.

HAMLET

In my memories, Horatio.

HAMLET

In my mind's eye, Horatio.

HORATIO

I met him once, he was a good king.

HORATIO

I saw him once. He was a goodly king.

HAMLET

He was a good man. The best of anyone in everything. I shall not see the like of him again.

HAMLET

He was a man. Take him for all in all,
I shall not look upon his like again.

HORATIO

My lord... I think I saw him last night.

HORATIO

My lord, I think I saw him yesternight.

HAMLET
Saw? Who?

HAMLET
Saw? Who?*

HAMLET
Saw? Who?*

Note: Some editions change this line to "Saw who?', but it was probably meant as two separate questions.

HORATIO
The king, your father, my lord.

HORATIO
My lord, the king your father.

HAMLET
(*shocked*) The king my father!

HAMLET
The king my father!

HORATIO
Calm your shock for a moment, and listen carefully to what I have to say, with these two gentlemen as witnesses to the astonishing event.

HORATIO
Season your admiration for a while
With an attent ear, till I may deliver,
Upon the witness of these gentlemen,
This marvel to you.

HAMLET
For the love of God, tell me.

HAMLET
For God's love, let me hear.

HORATIO
Two nights in a row, these gentlemen, Marcellus and Barnardo, on their guard duty in the dead quiet of the midnight hour had an encounter. A figure looking like your father appeared before them wearing exactly the armour he wore and marched slowly and regally past them. Three times he walked past their disbelieving, fearful eyes, as close as the length of his staff, whilst they, quivering like jelly out of fear, stood dumbstruck, unable to speak a word to him. In dire secrecy they revealed this to me. On the third night I kept watch with them, where, every word they had told me both in time and description was proven good and true. The apparition came. I knew your father, it was as alike as these two hands. (*holds up his hands*)

HORATIO
Two nights together had these gentlemen,
Marcellus and Barnardo, on their watch,
In the dead waste and middle of the night
Been thus encountered. A figure like your father,
Armed at point* exactly, cap-a-pe,*
Appears before them, and with solemn march
Goes slow and stately by them. Thrice he walked
By their oppressed and fear-surprised eyes,
Within his truncheon's length;* whilst they,
  distilled
Almost to jelly with the act of fear,
Stand dumb and speak not to him. This to me
In dreadful secrecy impart they did,
And I with them the third night kept the watch;
Where, as they had delivered, both in time,
Form of the thing, each word made true and
  good,
The apparition comes. I knew your father;
These hands are not more like.

Note: 'Armed at point' - dressed ready for battle.

'Cap-a-pe' - head to toe, 'pe' probably stemming from the French 'pied' for foot.

'Truncheon' – a staff up to 6 feet (2m) long, used by someone in high position, not the later police baton.

HAMLET
But where was this?

MARCELLUS
On the platform of the watch tower, my lord.

HAMLET
Did you speak to it?

HORATIO
I did, my lord, but it made no reply. Yet on one occasion I thought it lifted its head as if to speak, but just then the cock crowed loudly, and at the sound it turned and hastened away, vanishing from our sight.

HAMLET
That's very strange.

HORATIO
Upon my life I swear it's true, my noble Lord, and we believed it our duty to tell you.

HAMLET
Indeed, indeed, sirs, but this troubles me. Are you on watch duty tonight?

BARNADO & MARCELLUS
We are, my lord.

HAMLET
It was armoured you say?

BARNADO & MARCELLUS
Armoured, my lord.

HAMLET
From top to toe?

BARNADO & MARCELLUS
From head to foot, my lord.

HAMLET
Then you saw his face?

HORATIO
Oh yes, my lord, his visor was up.

HAMLET
But where was this?

MARCELLUS
My lord, upon the platform where we watched.

HAMLET
Did you not speak to it?

HORATIO
My lord, I did,
But answer made it none; yet once methought
It lifted up it head and did address
Itself to motion, like as it would speak;
But even then the morning cock crew loud,
And at the sound it shrunk in haste away
And vanished from our sight.

HAMLET
'Tis very strange.

HORATIO
As I do live, my honoured lord, 'tis true,
And we did think it writ down in our duty
To let you know of it.

HAMLET
Indeed, indeed, sirs; but this troubles me.
Hold you the watch tonight?

BARNARDO & MARCELLUS
We do, my lord.

HAMLET
Armed, say you?

BARNARDO & MARCELLUS
Armed, my lord.

HAMLET
From top to toe?

BARNARDO & MARCELLUS
My lord, from head to foot.

HAMLET
Then saw you not his face?

HORATIO
O yes, my lord; he wore his beaver up.

HAMLET How did he look? Fierce?	HAMLET What looked he? Frowningly?
HORATIO He looked more in sorrow than in anger.	HORATIO A countenance more in sorrow than in anger.
HAMLET Pale or red in the face?	HAMLET Pale or red?
HORATIO Pale, very pale.	HORATIO Nay, very pale.
HAMLET And his eyes were fixed upon you?	HAMLET And fixed his eyes upon you?
HORATIO All the time.	HORATIO Most constantly.
HAMLET I wish I had been there.	HAMLET I would I had been there.
HORATIO It would have been a shock to you.	HORATIO It would have much amazed you.
HAMLET Very likely, very likely. Did it stay long?	HAMLET Very like, very like. Stayed it long?
HORATIO As long as one can count slowly to a hundred.	HORATIO While one with moderate haste might tell a hundred.
BARNARDO & MARCELLUS Longer, it was longer.	BARNARDO & MARCELLUS Longer, longer.
HORATIO Not when I saw it.	HORATIO Not when I saw't.
HAMLET His beard was gray, yes?	HAMLET His beard was grizzled, no?
HORATIO As I remember it in real life, dark with silver streaks.	HORATIO It was as I have seen it in his life, A sable* silvered.

*Note: In heraldry sable is black. Shakespeare also uses sable for black later - "he whose sable arms black as his purpose".

HAMLET I will watch with you tonight. Perhaps it will walk again.	HAMLET I will watch tonight; Perchance 'twill walk again.

HORATIO
I'm sure it will.

HAMLET
If it has assumed my noble father's likeness, I'll speak to it even if hell itself howls a warning from its gaping mouth for me to hold my peace. I ask you all, if you have not spoken of this sight, to remain silent about it, and whatever happens tonight observe but say nothing. I will repay your loyalty. So, go about your duties. I'll visit you between eleven and twelve on the guard platform.

ALL
Our duty is to your honour.

HAMLET
May your affections be as great as mine are for you. Farewell.

HORATIO
I warrant you it will.

HAMLET
If it assume my noble father's person,
I'll speak to it though hell itself should gape
And bid me hold my peace. I pray you all,
If you have hitherto concealed this sight,
Let it be tenable in your silence still,
And whatsoever else shall hap tonight,
Give it an understanding but no tongue.
I will requite your loves. So, fare you well.
Upon the platform 'twixt eleven and twelve
I'll visit you.

ALL
Our duty to your honour.

HAMLET
Your loves, as mine to you. Farewell.

EXEUNT ALL EXCEPT HAMLET.

HAMLET (CONT'D)
(*aside*) My father's armoured spirit! All is not well. I suspect foul play. I wish it were night already.
Till then, stay calm, my soul. Foul deeds will rise,
Though all the world would keep them from men's eyes.

HAMLET
My father's spirit in arms! All is not well.
I doubt some foul play. Would the night were come.
Till then sit still, my soul. Foul deeds will rise,
Though all the earth o'erwhelm them, to men's eyes. *

EXEUNT

Note: The rhyming couplet at the end of Hamlet's speech signified to the audience the end of the scene at a time when there was little if any scenery on stage, no curtains and no lights to dim. Rhymes are in italics to identify them.

ACT I SCENE III

A ROOM IN THE HOUSE OF POLONIUS.

ENTER LAERTES AND HIS SISTER OPHELIA.
LAERTES IS PREPARING TO DEPART FOR PARIS.

LAERTES

My Luggage is on board. Farewell sister. And whenever the winds blow in a favourable direction to convey your words to me, do not forget to let me hear from you.

OPHELIA

Did you doubt me?

LAERTES

As for Hamlet trifling for your favours, consider it a youthful fad, a hot-blooded impulse, like a flower in the youth of Spring, its bloom not permanent, its sweetness not lasting, the perfume and beauty of the minute, no more.

OPHELIA

No more than that?

LAERTES

Think of it as nothing more. In nature it's not only the body that grows, but as life's experiences service the mind and soul it too grows and widens its scope.

LAERTES

My necessaries are embarked. Farewell.
And, sister, as the winds give benefit
And convoy is assistant, do not sleep,
But let me hear from you.

OPHELIA

Do you doubt that?

LAERTES

For Hamlet, and the trifling of his favour,
Hold it a fashion and a toy in blood,
A violet in the youth of primy nature,
Forward not permanent. sweet not lasting,
The perfume and suppliance of a minute,
No more.

OPHELIA

No more but so?

LAERTES

Think it no more.
For nature crescent* does not grow alone
In thews* and bulks, but as this temple* waxes*
The inward service of the mind and soul
Grows wide withal.

---

*Note: 'Crescent' – growing, developing.

'Thews' – muscles, sinews, strength..

'Temple' – body.

'Waxes' – to grow larger. Note how 'Crescent' and 'Wax' are two terms most notably used to refer to the moon, how it's body appears to 'grow wide' throughout its cycle. The moon is the symbol of female chastity, which is also relevant.

LAERTES (CONT'D)

Perhaps he loves you now, and his intentions may be honourable, but you must be wary of his high position. He cannot make his own choices, his birth dictates his life. He cannot live like lesser people, his decisions affect the well-being of the entire country. He can make no choice without approval of the nation he will head.

LAERTES

Perhaps he loves you now,
And now no soil nor cautel doth besmirch*
The virtue of his will;* but you must fear,
His greatness weighed, his will is not his own,
For he himself is subject to his birth;
He may not, as unvalued persons do,
Carve for himself, for on his choice depends
The sanity and health of the whole state;
And therefore must his choice be circumscribed*
Unto the voice and yielding of that body
Whereof he is the head.

*Note: 'No soil nor cautel doth besmirch' – 'soil' is a stain or slur on his character, 'cautel' is a Latin legal term, from it we get the word 'caution', and 'besmirch' is damage or blemish, particularly a person's reputation. So a literal translation would read; No stain nor cautionary thing does blemish the integrity of his intention.

'Will': Punning three meanings of will; intention, mind and choice.

'Circumscribed' – restricted.

LAERTES (CONT'D)

So if he says he loves you, you'll know it can only go as far as he may have any say in any particular act or deed, which is no further than the King of Denmark allows. So weigh the loss your honour would receive by too readily listening to his songs of love, or by giving your heart, or by surrendering your treasured chastity to his passionate pleading. Be wary, Ophelia, be wary, my dear sister, step back and keep your affections in check, out of the range and danger of desire. Even the most careful maiden is reckless if she reveals her full beauty to the moon.

LAERTES

Then if he says he loves you,
It fits your wisdom so far to believe it
As he in his particular act and place
May give his saying deed; which is no further
Than the main voice of Denmark goes withal.
Then weigh what loss your honour may sustain,
If with too credent ear you list his songs,
Or lose your heart, or your chaste treasure open
To his unmastered importunity.
Fear it, Ophelia, fear it, my dear sister;
And keep you in the rear of your affection,
Out of the shot and danger of desire.
The chariest maid is prodigal enough
If she unmask her beauty to the moon.*

*Note: The moon was associated with Diana, the virgin goddess of the moon and the protector of women. Laertes lectures Ophelia about holding onto her most valuable asset, her virginity. There was a myth that if a virgin exposed her naked body to the moon she would succumb to temptation, the moon being the symbol of virginity.

LAERTES (CONT'D)
Virtue itself is no defence against malicious rumour. The worm penetrates the buds of spring too often before they have fully bloomed, and in the morning dew of youth, contagious immorality is most prevalent. So be wary, the safest course lies in fear, youth by nature rebels against common sense.

LAERTES
Virtue itself 'scapes not calumnious strokes;
The canker* galls the infants of the spring*
Too oft before their buttons be disclosed,
And in the morn and liquid dew of youth
Contagious blastments are most imminent.
Be wary then; best safety lies in fear;
Youth to itself rebels, though none else near.

> *Note: More sexual innuendo. The canker worm penetrating the buds of spring before they had properly matured. Laertes is warning his sister that Hamlet cannot marry her, and she would be damaged goods if she allowed Hamlet to deflower her as her virginity is her most valuable asset when seeking a husband. Along with a warning that youth tends to rebel against common sense.*

OPHELIA
I shall take heed of this good advice and keep it as protector of my heart. But, my dear brother, don't be like some ungodly preacher who shows me the steep thorny path to heaven while he, like a bloated, reckless libertine, walks the primrose path of indulgence, and heeds not his own advice.

OPHELIA
I shall th' effect of this good lesson keep
As watchman to my heart. But, good my brother,
Do not, as some ungracious pastors do,
Show me the steep and thorny way to heaven
Whiles, like a puffed and reckless libertine,
Himself the primrose path of dalliance treads
And recks not his own rede.

LAERTES
Oh, don't worry about me.
– I should be leaving.
(*sarcastic*) And here comes my father, he can send me off with his blessings a second time, fortune smiles on me twice.

LAERTES
O, fear me not.
I stay too long.
But here my father comes.
A double blessing is a double grace;
Occasion smiles upon a second leave.

ENTER POLONIUS.

POLONIUS
Still here, Laertes? Get aboard, get aboard, shame on you! The wind is in your favour, they wait for you.

POLONIUS
Yet here, Laertes? Aboard, aboard, for shame!
The wind sits in the shoulder of your sail,
And you are stayed for.

> *Note: Laertes has given his sister a lecture on her behaviour in his absence, now it is his own turn to receive a long lecture from his father, despite him being late and his father telling him to hurry. The following lecture by Polonius is one of the famous speeches in Hamlet. Many lines from it are referenced today.*

POLONIUS EMBRACES LAERTES IN A FATHERLY HUG.

POLONIUS (CONT'D)

There, my blessings go with you, and with them these few principles to imprint in your memory. Keep your thoughts to yourself, and don't act in haste on any of them. Be friendly but not over friendly, the friends you have, once they've proved themselves to you, clasp to your soul with bands of steel, but do not offer your hand in friendship to every new unproven, fawning acquaintance. Beware of getting into quarrels, but if you do, ensure your opponent is made wary of you in future. Give every man your ear, but few your voice. Take every man's criticism, but keep your own judgements to yourself. Dress as well as your purse allows, but don't be over extravagant, look rich not gaudy, for often people judge a man by his apparel, and those in France of the highest rank are the most select and particular in this respect. Be neither a borrower nor a lender, for a loan often causes the loss of both the sum and the friendship, and borrowing leads to carelessness in one's finances. And above all, be true to yourself, then it follows, as night follows day, that you cannot be false to any other man. Farewell, may my blessing instil this in you.

POLONIUS

There, my blessing with thee,
And these few precepts in thy memory
Look thou character. Give thy thoughts no tongue,
Nor any unproportioned thought his act.
Be thou familiar but by no means vulgar.
The friends thou hast, and their adoption tried,
Grapple them to thy soul with hoops of steel,
But do not dull thy palm with entertainment
Of each new-hatched unfledged courage. Beware
Of entrance to a quarrel, but, being in,
Bear't that th' opposed may beware of thee.
Give every man thine ear but few thy voice.
Take each man's censure, but reserve thy judgement.
Costly thy habit as thy purse can buy,
But not expressed in fancy; rich, not gaudy,
For the apparel oft proclaims the man,
And they in France of the best rank and station
Are of all most select and generous chief in that.
Neither a borrower nor a lender be,
For loan oft loses both itself and friend,
And borrowing dulls the edge of husbandry.
This above all - to thine own self be true,
And it must follow, as the night the day,
Thou canst not then be false to any man.
Farewell; my blessing season* this in thee!

*Note: The sense of 'season' here, is as in the practice of seasoning wood to made it long lasting and durable.

LAERTES

I most humbly take my leave of you, my lord.

LAERTES

Most humbly do I take my leave, my lord.

LAERTES BOWS TO HIS FATHER.

POLONIUS

The hour is calling you. Go, your servants await.

POLONIUS

The time invites you. Go, your servants tend.

LAERTES Farewell, Ophelia, and remember well all I have said to you.	**LAERTES** Farewell, Ophelia, and remember well What I have said to you.
OPHELIA It's locked away in my memory, and you alone shall keep the key to it.	**OPHELIA** 'Tis in my memory locked, And you yourself shall keep the key of it.
LAERTES Farewell.	**LAERTES** Farewell.

LAERTES LEAVES.

POLONIUS What is it he said to you, Ophelia?	POLONIUS What is't, Ophelia, he hath said to you?
OPHELIA As it pleases you, something about Prince Hamlet.	OPHELIA So please you, something touching the Lord Hamlet.
POLONIUS Indeed, a timely word. I've heard he has often of late been seen alone with you, and you yourself have been free and generous of your time with him. If what I have been told is true, by those concerned with your actions, I have to say you clearly do not understand the behaviour befitting a daughter of mine, and her honour. What is going on between the two of you? Tell me the truth.	POLONIUS Marry, well bethought. 'Tis told me he hath very oft of late Given private time to you, and you yourself Have of your audience been most free and bounteous. If it be so - as so 'tis put on me, And that in way of caution - I must tell you You do not understand yourself so clearly As it behoves my daughter, and your honour. What is between you? Give me up the truth.
OPHELIA My lord, he has of late made many offers of his affections to me.	OPHELIA He hath, my lord, of late made many tenders Of his affection to me.
POLONIUS Affections! Pah! – you speak like an immature girl, naïve in such perilous matters. Do you believe his 'offers' as you call them?	POLONIUS Affection! Pooh! - you speak like a green girl Unsifted in such perilous circumstance. Do you believe his `tenders' as you call them?
OPHELIA I do not know what to believe, my lord.	OPHELIA I do not know, my lord, what I should think.

45

POLONIUS

Then I'll tell you: you are a foolish baby to have accepted these 'offers' at face value when they have no worth. Set yourself a higher price, or, not to labour an over-used saying and to put it bluntly, you'll offer me up as a fool if you get with child.

POLONIUS

Marry, I'll teach you: think yourself a baby
That you have ta'en these tenders for true pay,
Which are not sterling.* Tender yourself more dearly,
Or - not to crack the wind of the poor phrase,
Running it thus - you'll tender me a fool.*

OPHELIA IS TAKEN ABACK AT THIS STATEMENT.

*Note: 'Sterling' has the double meaning of the currency of England (not Denmark) and also something that is excellent or first rate.

'You'll tender me a fool' had a double meaning of 'you'll make me look a fool' and 'you'll present me with an illegitimate grandchild', as Fool was an affectionate term for a child, with wordplay on the word 'tender'.

OPHELIA

(shocked) My lord, his advances of love have been in an honourable fashion.

OPHELIA

My lord, he hath importuned* me with love
In honourable fashion.

*Note: 'Importune' has the triple meaning, all relevant to this statement, of; 1, to press or beset with enticement, 2, to make improper advances, 3, to beg persistently to the point of annoyance.

POLONIUS

Aye, as fleeting as fashion. Foolish nonsense.

POLONIUS

Ay, fashion you may call it. Go to, go to.*

*Note: 'Go to' was a common sarcastic expression of contempt or disbelief.

OPHELIA

And he has vowed by all that is holy in heaven that his words are genuine, my lord.

OPHELIA

And hath given countenance to his speech, my lord,
With almost all the holy vows of heaven.

POLONIUS

Aye, traps to catch gullible fools. I know how free and easy the tongue is with meaningless vows when the blood is hot. These fiery outbursts give more light than heat, disappearing the moment the promise is made. Don't confuse these with real fire. From now on be more sparing of your innocent company, set your price higher than a request to talk. As for Prince Hamlet, believe only so much from him, remember he is young and with more free reign than you may ever have. In short, Ophelia, do not believe his promises, they are brokers, falsely representing their investments, mere exponents of sinful deals, behaving like sanctimonious and pious whores in order to lead you astray.

POLONIUS

Ay, springes to catch woodcocks.* I do know,
When the blood burns, how prodigal the soul
Lends the tongue vows. These blazes, daughter,
Giving more light than heat, extinct in both
Even in their promise, as it is a-making,
You must not take for fire. From this time
Be something scanter of your maiden presence,
Set your entreatments at a higher rate
Than a command to parley. For Lord Hamlet,
Believe so much in him, that he is young,
And with a larger tether may he walk
Than may be given you. In few, Ophelia,
Do not believe his vows, for they are brokers,
Not of that dye which their investments show,
But mere implorators of unholy suits,
Breathing like sanctified and pious bawds
The better to beguile.

*Note: Woodcocks are proverbially known as gullible as they were so easily caught.

POLONIUS (CONT'D)

These are my final words: I will not, in plain terms, allow you to misuse any leisure time you may have by sending word or talking with Prince Hamlet. See that you obey my orders. Come, let us leave.

POLONIUS

This is for all:
I would not, in plain terms, from this time forth
Have you so slander any moment leisure
As to give words or talk with the Lord Hamlet.
Look to't, I charge you. Come your ways.

OPHELIA

I will obey, my lord.

OPHELIA

I shall obey, my lord.

ACT I SCENE IV

THE PLATFORM OF THE WATCHTOWER IN FRONT OF THE CASTLE.

ENTER HAMLET, HORATIO, AND MARCELLUS. IT IS NIGHT-TIME.

HAMLET The air is biting, it's very cold.	**HAMLET** The air bites shrewdly, it is very cold.
HORATIO It is nippy and a bitter wind	**HORATIO** It is a nipping and an eager air.
HAMLET What time is it now?	**HAMLET** What hour now?
HORATIO Almost twelve I think.	**HORATIO** I think it lacks of twelve.
MARCELLUS No, the clock has struck twelve.	**MARCELLUS** No, it is struck.
HORATIO It did? I didn't hear it. Then it draws near the time when the spirit normally walks.	**HORATIO** Indeed? I heard it not. It then draws near the season Wherein the spirit held his wont to walk.

 A FLOURISH OF TRUMPETS AND DRUMMING IS HEARD INSIDE THE CASTLE. TWO CANNONS ARE FIRED.

HORATIO (CONT'D) What does that signify, my lord?	**HORATIO** What does this mean, my lord?
HAMLET The king stays awake tonight, partying, singing, and dancing wild reels as he drains his mugs of Rhine wine. (*sarcastic*) The kettle-drums and trumpets blare out the triumph of his toasting.	**HAMLET** The king doth wake tonight and takes his rouse, Keeps wassail, and the swagg'ring up-spring reels, And, as he drains his draughts of Rhenish down, The kettle-drum and trumpet thus bray out The triumph of his pledge.*

> *Note: 'Pledge' - toast. Taking a drink to celebrate. Hamlet sarcastically explains the sound celebrates the king finishing yet another drink. The kettle drums are sounded when the king drinks as a signal to the cannons outside.*

HORATIO
Is it a custom to do this?

HAMLET
Aye, indeed it is, but to my mind, even though I was born here and am accustomed to it, it would be a custom more honourable in the breaking of than in its practise. This drunken revelry across the country damages our reputation in the eyes of other nations. They call us drunkards, and with sarcastic voice mock us. And indeed it takes away from our achievements, great as they are, and damages our reputation. Often it happens in individuals too that because of some inherited defect of nature at birth over which they have no control – since they cannot choose their ancestors – they may suffer an excess of some trait or other, often breaking the barriers of reasonable behaviour, or they are afflicted by some habit that oversteps the boundaries of acceptable manners, so that these men - carrying as I said, the stamp of one defect or another as a result of nature or misfortune, despite the man's virtues - he may otherwise be the most god fearing man, and as fine a man as any could be – he shall by general concensus be viewed from the point of view of that particular fault. The drop of evil outweighs all the noble goodness in a man, to his detriment.

HORATIO
Is it a custom?

HAMLET
Ay, marry, is't,
But to my mind, though I am native here
And to the manner born, it is a custom
More honoured in the breach than the
  observance.
This heavy-headed revel east and west
Makes us traduced, and taxed of other nations.
They clepe us drunkards, and with swinish phrase
Soil our addition; and indeed it takes
From our achievements, though performed at
  height,
The pith and marrow of our attribute.
So, oft it chances in particular men
That for some vicious mole of nature in them,
As in their birth, wherein they are not guilty,
Since nature cannot choose his origin,
By their o'ergrowth of some complexion,
Oft breaking down the pales and forts of reason,
Or by some habit that too much o'erleavens
The form of plausive manners, that these men,
Carrying, I say, the stamp of one defect,
Being nature's livery or fortune's star,
His virtues else, be they as pure as grace,
As infinite as man may undergo,
Shall in the general censure take corruption
From that particular fault. The dram* of evil
Doth all the noble substance of a doubt
To his own scandal.

*Note: This is more likely a social comment on the drunken revelry rife in England at the time, rather than in Denmark.

Dram – small measure of liquid, often associated with whisky.

ENTER THE GHOST.

HORATIO NOTICES IT AND POINTS WITH NERVOUS EXCITEMENT.

HORATIO
Look my lord, here it comes.

HORATIO
Look, my lord, it comes.

HAMLET

Angels and ministers of God defend us! Whether you are a good spirit or an evil demon, bringing a sweet chorus from heaven or the fiery blasts from hell, and whether your intentions are wicked or good, you come in such a recognisable shape that I will speak with you. I'll call you Hamlet, King, father, Danish monarch. Oh, answer me! Do not let me burst in ignorance, tell me why your saintly bones, carried away in death, have burst from their place of rest? And why the tomb, where I saw you peacefully interred has opened its mighty marble jaws to cast you out again? What does it mean, that you, a dead corpse, once again clad in your armour, should revisit here under the watchful eye of the moon, terrifying the night, and making us foolish mortals, shake so horribly with thoughts beyond our comprehension? Tell me why this is? Why? What should we do?

HAMLET

Angels and ministers of grace defend us!
Be thou a spirit of health or goblin damned,
Bring with thee airs from heaven or blasts from hell,
Be thy intents wicked or charitable,
Thou com'st in such a questionable shape
That I will speak to thee. I'll call thee Hamlet,
King, father, royal Dane. O, answer me!
Let me not burst in ignorance, but tell
Why thy canonized bones, hearsed in death,
Have burst their cerements? Why the sepulchre,
Wherein we saw thee quietly enurned,
Hath oped his ponderous and marble jaws
To cast thee up again? What may this mean,
That thou, dead corpse, again in complete steel,
Revisits thus the glimpses of the moon,
Making night hideous, and we fools of nature
So horridly to shake our disposition
With thoughts beyond the reaches of our souls?
Say, why is this? Wherefore? What should we do?

THE GHOST BECKONS TO HAMLET.

HORATIO

It beckons to you to go with it, as if it wishes to share something with you alone.

HORATIO

It beckons you to go away with it,
As if it some impartment did desire
To you alone.

MARCELLUS

Look how courteously it directs you to a more private location, but don't go with it.

MARCELLUS

Look with what courteous action
It waves you to a more removed ground.
But do not go with it.

HORATIO

No, not by any means.

HORATIO

No, by no means.

HAMLET

It will not speak here, so I'll follow it.

HAMLET

It will not speak; then I will follow it.

HORATIO RESTRAINS HAMLET.

HORATIO

Do not go, my lord!

HORATIO

Do not, my lord.

HAMLET

Why not? What have I to fear? I value my life no more than the price of a pin, and as for my soul, what can it do to that, considering it is as immortal as the thing itself?

HAMLET

Why, what should be the fear?
I do not set my life at a pin's fee,
And for my soul, what can it do to that,
Being a thing immortal as itself?

THE GHOST BECKONS TO HAMLET.

HAMLET (CONT'D)

It waves me over again. I'll follow it.

HAMLET

It waves me forth again, I'll follow it.

AGAIN, HORATIO RESTRAINS HAMLET.

HORATIO

What if it tempts you towards the sea, my lord, or to the perilous summit of the cliff that overhangs the waves below, and then assumes some horrible form which might deprive you of your royal reasoning and drag you into madness? Think about it. Such lofty heights drives a mind to desperate thoughts just by looking into the depths of the sea or hearing the roar far below, without need of further incentive.

HORATIO

What if it tempt you toward the flood, my lord,
Or to the dreadful summit of the cliff
That beetles o'er his base into the sea,
And there assume some other horrible form
Which might deprive your sovereignty of reason,
And draw you into madness? Think of it.
The very place puts toys of desperation,
Without more motive, into every brain
That looks so many fathoms to the sea
And hears it roar beneath.

THE GHOST AGAIN BECKONS TO HAMLET.

HAMLET

Still it beckons me.
(to Ghost) Lead on, I'll follow you.

HAMLET

It waves me still. [To Ghost.] Go on, I'll follow thee.

MARCELLUS

You shan't go, my lord.

MARCELLUS

You shall not go, my lord.

MARCELLUS AND HORATIO RESTRAIN HAMLET.

HAMLET

Take your hands from me!

HAMLET

Hold off your hands!

HAMLET STRUGGLES AGAINST THEM, BUT THEY HOLD HIM BACK.

HORATIO

Have some sense, don't go.

HORATIO

Be ruled, you shall not go.

HAMLET
My fate calls me, it gives every sinew in my body the strength and nerve of the Nemean lion which fought Hercules.

HAMLET
My fate cries out,
And makes each petty arture in this body
As hardy as the Nemean lion's nerve.*

Note: The 'Nemean lion' is a monstrous creature Hercules kills as one of his twelve labours. Its golden fur protected it from weapons and its claws could cut through any armour. Hercules finally killed it by trapping it in a cave and strangling it.

THE GHOST CONTINUES BECKONING TO HAMLET.

HAMLET (CONT'D)
Still it calls me. Unhand me, gentlemen! By heavens, I'll make a ghost of the man who tries to stop me!

HAMLET
Still am I called. Unhand me, gentlemen.
By heaven, I'll make a ghost of him that lets me!

HAMLET HALF DRAWS HIS SWORD TO SHOW HE MEANS WHAT HE SAYS.

HAMLET (CONT'D)
(*firmly*) Away, I say!

HAMLET
I say, away.

THEY RELUCTANTLY RELEASE HAMLET.

HAMLET (CONT'D)
(*to Ghost*) Lead on, I'll follow you.

HAMLET
[*To Ghost.*] Go on, I'll follow thee.

HAMLET FOLLOWS THE GHOST LEAVING THE OTHERS LOOKING ON.

HORATIO
He's lost his mind.

HORATIO
He waxes desperate with imagination.

MARCELLUS
Let's follow them, it's not right to do as he orders.

MARCELLUS
Let's follow; 'tis not fit thus to obey him.

HORATIO
Go on then, but what is the meaning of all this?

HORATIO
Have after. To what issue will this come?

MARCELLUS
Something is rotten in the state of Denmark.

MARCELLUS
Something is rotten in the state* of Denmark.

Note: A double meaning of the word 'state' - the condition of the country, and the country itself. This line is still often quoted today if things are going wrong.

HORATIO
Heaven will guide it.

HORATIO
Heaven will direct it.*

Note: He means heaven (God) will direct (look after) Denmark.

MARCELLUS
Let's not leave it to chance, let's follow him.

MARCELLUS
Nay, let's follow him.

THEY DEPART IN THE DIRECTION THE GHOST AND HAMLET TOOK.

ACT I SCENE V

ANOTHER PART OF THE PLATFORM.

THE GHOST AND HAMLET WALK TO A REMOTE
PART OF THE PLATFORM OUT OF SIGHT OF ANYONE.

HAMLET
Where are you leading me? Speak to me. I'll go no further.

GHOST
Listen carefully.

HAMLET
I will.

GHOST
The time has almost come when I must return to the acrid torment of the flames of purgatory.

*Note: To the Roman Catholic faith (the practice of which was banned in Shakespeare's time) Purgatory is the suspended state of a soul after death in which those destined for heaven must first undergo 'purification'. For those not qualifying for admittance to heaven, and not destined for hell, there was also a permanent state known as Limbo. Both were introduced in the middle ages by the Roman Catholic church, which has the Pope as its head, rather than taken from the Bible proper.

HAMLET
Alas, you poor ghost!

GHOST
Do not pity me, listen carefully to what I have to reveal.

HAMLET
Speak, I am duty bound to hear.

GHOST
And so will you be for revenge, once you've heard what I have to say.

HAMLET
What?

HAMLET
Whither wilt thou lead me? Speak; I'll go no further.

GHOST
Mark me.

HAMLET
I will.

GHOST
My hour is almost come
When I to sulph'rous and tormenting flames
Must render up myself.*

HAMLET
Alas, poor ghost!

GHOST
Pity me not, but lend thy serious hearing
To what I shall unfold.

HAMLET
Speak, I am bound to hear.

GHOST
So art thou to revenge, when thou shalt hear.

HAMLET
What?

GHOST

I am the ghost of your father, destined for a period of time to walk at night and to a fiery confinement by day until the foul crimes I committed in life are purged by burning. I am forbidden, but if I could reveal the secrets of my imprisonment you would hear a tale where even the slightest detail would distress your soul, sending ice through your young veins, making your eyes pop out of their sockets, and unravelling your hair till every strand stood on end like a frightened porcupine. But a revelation of the afterlife is not for ears of flesh and blood. So listen, listen, I beg you, hear me well!

If you ever loved your dear father...

GHOST

I am thy father's spirit,

Doomed for a certain term to walk the night,

And for the day confined to fast in fires,

Till the foul crimes done in my days of nature

Are burnt and purged away. But that I am forbid

To tell the secrets of my prison-house

I could a tale unfold whose lightest word

Would harrow up thy soul, freeze thy young
  blood,

Make thy two eyes like stars start from their
  spheres,*

Thy knotted and combined locks to part,

And each particular hair to stand an end

Like quills upon the fretful porcupine.

But this eternal blazon must not be

To ears of flesh and blood. List, list, O, list!

If thou didst ever thy dear father love –

---

*Note: 'Start from their spheres' – Back then, thanks to Ptolemy, astronomers believed the seven visible planets (including the Moon and the Sun) were carried around the Earth in invisible spheres, with an outer eighth sphere containing them and all the stars (the firmament). The whole system was contained in a ninth sphere, the Primum Mobile, itself contained within the Empyrean, the fastest moving sphere, revolving around the earth (the centre of the system) in twenty-four hours carrying the inner spheres with it. However, Copernicus had proved by 1543 that the earth revolved around the Sun, but the Church considered this heresy.

HAMLET

Oh God!

HAMLET

O God!

GHOST

...you must revenge his foul and most unnatural murder.

GHOST

Revenge his foul and most unnatural* murder.

---

*Note: He says 'unnatural' to emphasise that it was not death by natural causes and nor was it from an enemy, but from a close blood relative, his brother.

HAMLET

Murder!

HAMLET

Murder!

GHOST

Murder most foul, as murder always is, but this murder was especially foul, despicable and unnatural.

GHOST

Murder most foul,* as in the best it is; But this most foul, strange, and unnatural.

> *Note: 'Murder most foul' is a phrase still in use today and was also the title of a British movie based on the Agatha Christie novel, 'Mrs McGinty's Dead', which had nothing to do with Shakespeare.

HAMLET

Quickly tell me, so with wings as swift as my thoughts of love for you I may swoop to gain revenge.

HAMLET

Haste me to know't, that I with wings as swift As meditation or the thoughts of love May sweep to my revenge.*

> *Note: Another hawking reference, a bird of prey swooping down on its victim.

GHOST

Your words please me. You'd have as much spirit in you as the fat weeds that laze on the banks of the forgetful river of Lethe if this did not rouse you.

GHOST

I find thee apt; And duller shouldst thou be than the fat weed That rots* itself in ease on Lethe* wharf Wouldst thou not stir in this.

> *Note: The Lethe river is the legendary river of forgetfulness in Hades. Anyone drinking the water from it would forget the past.
>
> Early editions say 'roots', later editions say 'rots' which agrees with a similar line in Antony & Cleopatra and makes better overall sense.

GHOST (CONT'D)

Now, Hamlet, listen to me. It's been widely reported that a serpent stung me while I slept in my orchard. All of Denmark has been terribly misled by this false account of my death. But know this, my noble son, the snake whose sting took your father's life now wears his crown.

GHOST

Now, Hamlet, hear: 'Tis given out that, sleeping in mine orchard* A serpent stung* me; so the whole ear of Denmark Is by a forged process of my death Rankly abused. But know, thou noble youth, The serpent that did sting* thy father's life Now wears his crown.

> *Note: A serpent, or a snake, does not technically have a sting, like a scorpion does for example, it injects its venom by biting its victim. The word 'sting' is used here in the wordplay of robbing his father's life, a carefully planned operation of deception, and injecting poison.
>
> Orchard then meant garden (or yard).

HAMLET

Oh, by my soul, as I suspected! My uncle?

HAMLET

O my prophetic soul! Mine uncle?

GHOST

Yes, that incestuous, adulterous beast, with cunning trickery and treacherous skill - oh, such wicked cunning and skill to deceive so well! - and with his shameful lust, seduced the will of my most seemingly virtuous queen. Oh, Hamlet, what a failing that was to me, me whose love was dignified and went hand in hand always with the unswerving vow I made to her in marriage, and to lower herself to that wretch whose merits were so inferior to mine.

GHOST

Ay, that incestuous, that adulterate beast,
With witchcraft of his wit, with traitorous gifts -
O wicked wit and gifts that have the power
So to seduce! - won to his shameful lust
The will of my most seeming-virtuous queen.
O Hamlet, what a falling off was there
From me, whose love was of that dignity
That it went hand in hand even with the vow
I made to her in marriage, and to decline
Upon a wretch whose natural gifts were poor
To those of mine.

THE GHOST SHAKES ITS HEAD IN DISBELIEF AND DESPAIR.

GHOST (CONT'D)

True virtue can never be overcome, even from lewd temptation in heavenly disguise, but lust, even when married to one so heavenly pure, will satisfy its pleasure in the holy matrimonial bed, and prey on garbage outside of it.

GHOST

But virtue, as it never will be moved,
Though lewdness court it in a shape of heaven,
So lust, though to a radiant angel linked,
Will sate itself in a celestial bed
And prey on garbage.

THE GHOST PAUSES AS IF NOTICING SOMETHING.

GHOST (CONT'D)

But wait! - I think I smell the morning air. I must be brief. I was sleeping in my garden, as was my custom in the afternoon, and at my most vulnerable time your uncle stole up on me with the cursed juice of hebenon in a vial, which he poured into the opening of my ear.

GHOST

But soft! - methinks I scent the morning air.
Brief let me be. Sleeping within my orchard,
My custom always in the afternoon,
Upon my secure hour thy uncle stole
With juice of cursed hebenon* in a vial,
And in the porches of mine ears did pour

*Note: Hebenon is an unknown plant or substance. Shakespeare either got the name wrong, or made the name up, or it was a printing error. No one is sure what the substance actually was, it has been the source of speculation for centuries. The three most likely suspects are, Hemlock, Yew, or Henbane. Yew has similar symptoms to those described and a yew bow was known as a Heben Bow. Henbane could be a combined misspelling and printing error, as could Hemlock, though hemlock was a well known poison which Shakespeare refers to by its correct name in other works. We will never know for sure.

GHOST (CONT'D)

The poisonous essence causes such a hostile reaction in a man's blood, that as swift as quicksilver it courses though the veins of the body rapidly setting and curdling the blood, the thin healthy blood, like acid dropping into milk. As it did to mine. And in an instant my smooth skin erupted into scabs as rough as bark on a tree, like Lazarus had, covering my body in a thick, loathsome crust

GHOST

The leperous* distilment, whose effect
Holds such an enmity with blood of man
That swift as quicksilver* it courses* through
The natural gates and alleys of the body,
And with a sudden vigour it doth posset*
And curd, like eager droppings into milk,
The thin and wholesome blood. So did it mine,
And a most instant tetter barked about,
Most lazar-like,* with vile and loathsome crust,
All my smooth body.

*Note: 'Leperous' - skin blotches similar to leprosy.

'Quicksilver' – mercury. So named because it looks like silver but is liquid and flows rapidly as water does.

'Courses' – Liquid flowing rapidly without hindrance.

'Posset' - a drink made of hot milk curdled with ale, wine, or other alcohol and typically flavoured with spices. A popular drink of the time.

'Lazer-like' – Like the skin affliction Lazarus has in the biblical 'Rich man and Lazarus' story in Luke 16. Not to be confused with the Lazarus who Jesus raises from the dead. There is relevance in this story. Briefly, the rich man has all he wants in life, whereas Lazarus is a beggar covered in sores who survives on scraps fallen from the rich man's table. Both men die, the rich man, finding he is in hell, looks up and sees Lazarus standing next to Abraham (forefather of all Jews) in heaven and pleads with him to send Lazarus to give him water to cool his tongue from the fires of hell. Abraham reminds the rich man that in life he had only good things whereas Lazarus had bad things, but now that is reversed for eternity, and neither can ever cross to the other side.

GHOST (CONT'D)

There, as I slept, I was robbed of my life, my crown, my queen, all by a brother's hand. In an instant cut down while my sinful life still blossomed. No last rites, no spiritual preparation, no blessing, no making my peace before God, but sent to my maker with all my sins still upon my head. Oh, so horrible! So horrible! Most horrible! If you have any feeling in you, do not stand for it, don't let the royal bed of Denmark be a cradle of lust and damned incest.

GHOST

Thus was I, sleeping, by a brother's hand
Of life, of crown, of queen, at once dispatched,
Cut off even in the blossoms of my sin,
Unhouseled, disappointed, unaneled,
No reck'ning made*, but sent to my account
With all my imperfections on my head.
O, horrible! O, horrible! Most horrible!
If thou hast nature in thee, bear it not.
Let not the royal bed of Denmark be
A couch for luxury and damned incest.

*Note: 'No reckoning made...' - Not making his peace before God before he died will have great significance later in the play.

GHOST (CONT'D)

But, however you take vengeance on this act, do not poison your mind, or let your soul plot against your mother. Leave her to heaven and to the thorns within her bosom that prick and sting her conscience. A quick farewell, the glow-worm's artificial fire begins to pale indicating the morning is close. Adieu, adieu, adieu! Remember my words.

GHOST

But, howsoever thou pursuest this act,
Taint not thy mind, nor let thy soul contrive
Against thy mother aught. Leave her to heaven,
And to those thorns that in her bosom lodge
To prick and sting her. Fare thee well at once.
The glowworm shows the matin to be near,
And 'gins to pale his uneffectual fire.*
Adieu, adieu, adieu! Remember me.

*Note: Only the female glow-worm glows. It should say 'her uneffectual fire'.

THE GHOST DISAPPEARS. HAMLET RECITES HIS 2ND SOLILOQUY.

HAMLET

Oh, I will, by all you host up in heaven! And on earth!

HAMLET

O all you host of heaven! O earth!*

*Note: Hamlet promised to remember by the 'heavens', which is where he imagined his father to be. Then he remembers that he met him down on earth. Then wonders where he might be now as his father had mentioned purgatory,

HAMLET (CONT'D)

Where else? Should I include hell?

HAMLET

What else?
And shall I couple hell?

HE BECOMES DISTRESSED AT THE THOUGHT, CLUTCHING HIS CHEST.

HAMLET (CONT'D)

Oh, no! Be strong my heart, and you, my sinews, do not weaken like an old man, bear me firmly upright.
(*now about his father*) Remember your words? Aye, you poor ghost, while my memory keeps residence in this distracted skull of mine I'll remember your words. I'll erase all trivial memories, all I've learnt, every image, all the past worries of youth stored there, and your order alone shall be stored there within the database of my mind, separate from all trivial matter. Yes, by heavens!

HAMLET

O, fie! Hold, hold, my heart,
And you, my sinews, grow not instant old,
But bear me stiffly up. Remember thee?
Ay, thou poor ghost, while memory holds a seat
In this distracted globe. Remember thee?
Yea, from the table of my memory
I'll wipe away all trivial fond records,
All saws of books, all forms, all pressures past,
That youth and observation copied there,
And thy commandment all alone shall live
Within the book and volume of my brain,
Unmixed with baser matter. Yes, by heaven!

HE RECALLS UGLY MEMORIES, DESPITE HIS FATHER TELLING HIM NOT TO
HATE OR BLAME HIS MOTHER, HE CURSES HIS MOTHER AND STEP-FATHER.

HAMLET (CONT'D)
Oh, most wicked woman! And that villain,
that smiling, damned villain!

HAMLET
O most pernicious woman!
O villain, villain, smiling, damned villain!

HE FETCHES A NOTEBOOK HE USES FOR HIS STUDIES FROM HIS POCKET.

HAMLET (CONT'D)
My notebook, I'll write it down - that a
man may smile, and smile, and still be a
villain. At least I'm sure that's the way it is
with the new king.

HAMLET
My tables - meet it is I set it down
That one may smile, and smile, and be a villain.
At least I'm sure it may be so in Denmark.

HE WRITES IN HIS BOOK.

HAMLET (CONT'D)
So, uncle... there you are. Now to my
promise, it was; *Adieu, adieu, remember
my words.* There, I have sworn to
remember.

HAMLET
So, uncle, there you are. Now to my word;
It is `Adieu, adieu, remember me.'
I have sworn't.

HORATIO
(*off, calling*) My lord? My lord.

HORATIO
[*Calling within.*]   My lord, my lord.

MARCELLUS
(*off, calling*) Prince Hamlet!

MARCELLUS
[*Calling within.*]   Lord Hamlet.

HORATIO
Heaven keep him safe.

HORATIO
Heaven secure him.

HAMLET
(*aside*) So be it!

HAMLET
So be it!*

*Note: Some early editions give the above line to Marcellus in reply to Horatio's
prayer. 'So be it' is 'amen' in English, the common reply to a prayer.*

HAMLET PUTS THE NOTEBOOK BACK IN HIS POCKET.

ENTER HORATIO AND MARCELLUS, THEY SEE HAMLET AT A DISTANCE AND
APPROACH, CALLING TO HIM AS A FALCONER CALLS TO HIS FALCON.

MARCELLUS
(*calling*) Halloo! Ho, ho, my lord.

MARCELLUS
[*Calling.*] Illo, ho, ho, my lord.

HAMLET
Halloo, ho, ho, boy.
(*he whistles*) Come bird, come.

MARCELLUS
How did it go, my noble lord?

HORATIO
What news, my lord?

HAMLET
Wonderful news!

HORATIO
Good, my lord, tell us.

HAMLET
No, you will reveal it.

HORATIO
Not I, my lord, I swear by the heavens.

MARCELLUS
Nor I, my lord.

HAMLET
What would you say if...
Would any man ever believe it?...
You'll keep it secret?

HORATIO & MARCELLUS
Yes, I swear, my lord.

HAMLET
Hillo, ho, ho, boy. Come, bird, come.

MARCELLUS
How is't, my noble lord?

HORATIO
What news, my lord?

HAMLET
O, wonderful!

HORATIO
Good my lord, tell it.

HAMLET
No, you will reveal it.

HORATIO
Not I, my lord, by heaven.

MARCELLUS
Nor I, my lord.

HAMLET
How say you, then; would heart of man once
  think it?
But you'll be secret?

HORATIO & MARCELLUS
Ay, by heaven, my lord.

HAMLET DRAWS THEM CLOSE AS IF TO TELL THEM THE SECRET.

HAMLET
There's not a villain living in all Denmark
that's not an out and out rogue.

HAMLET
There's never a villain dwelling in all Denmark
But he's an arrant knave.

THE MEN PULL AWAY FROM HAMLET FEELING THEY HAD BEEN FOOLED.

HORATIO
It needs no ghost from the grave to tell us
this, my lord.

HORATIO
There needs no ghost, my lord, come from the
  grave
To tell us this.

HAMLET

How right you are in that, and so without further ado I think it fitting that we shake hands and part. You to where your business and pleasures take you, for every man has business and pleasures whatever they may be - and for my own poor part, I tell you, I must go pray.

HORATIO

These are just wild, meaningless words, my lord.

HAMLET

I'm heartily sorry they offend you, yes indeed, heartily.

HORATIO

There was no offence, my lord.

HAMLET

Yes, by St. Patrick there was, Horatio, and a great offence too. Regarding what we saw here, it was a real ghost, I can tell you that. As to your desire to know what was said between us, overcome it as best you can. And now, good friends, as you are my friends, scholars and supporters, grant me one small request.

HAMLET

Why, right, you are i'th' right;
And so, without more circumstance at all,
I hold it fit that we shake hands and part,
You as your business and desire shall point you -
For every man hath business and desire,
Such as it is - and for mine own poor part,
Look you, I'll go pray.

HORATIO

These are but wild and whirling words, my lord.

HAMLET

I'm sorry they offend you, heartily;
Yes, faith, heartily.

HORATIO

There's no offence, my lord.

HAMLET

Yes, by Saint Patrick,* but there is, Horatio,
And much offence too. Touching this vision here,
It is an honest ghost, that let me tell you.
For your desire to know what is between us,
O'ermaster 't as you may. And now, good friends,
As you are friends, scholars, and soldiers,
Give me one poor request.

*Note: According to ancient scriptures, St. Patrick was shown a pit in Ireland by Christ and told this was the entrance to purgatory – where the ghost had said he came from. St. Patrick was known as the keeper of the entrance to Purgatory. The location was well known in Shakespeare's time and even appeared on maps.

HORATIO

We will. What is it, my lord?

HAMLET

Never reveal what you have seen tonight.

HORATIO & MARCELLUS

We will not, my lord.

HAMLET

No, you must swear it.

HORATIO

I swear, my lord, I will not.

HORATIO

What is't, my lord? We will.

HAMLET

Never make known what you have seen tonight.

HORATIO & MARCELLUS

My lord, we will not.

HAMLET

Nay, but swear't.

HORATIO

In faith, my lord, not I.

MARCELLUS	MARCELLUS
Nor I, my lord, I swear.	Nor I, my lord, in faith.
HAMLET	HAMLET
Swear upon my sword.	Upon my sword.

HE HOLDS HIS SWORD VERTICAL, POINT DOWN, THE HILT FORMING A CROSS.

MARCELLUS	MARCELLUS
We have already sworn, my lord.	We have sworn, my lord, already.
HAMLET	HAMLET
Indeed, but not upon my sword, indeed.	Indeed, upon my sword, indeed.*

*Note: word play on 'in deed' – indeed and the deed of swearing on the cross.

THE GHOST'S VOICE COMES FROM SOMEWHERE BELOW THE STAGE.

GHOST	GHOST
(*calls off, from below*) Swear.	[*Cries under the stage.*] Swear.
HAMLET	HAMLET
(*to Ghost*) Ah, ha, boy, you say so too? Are you there old faithful?	Ah, ha, boy, sayst thou so? Art thou there, truepenny?*
(*to men*) Come on, you can hear the fellow in the cellar. Agree to swear.	Come on, you hear this fellow in the cellarage; Consent to swear.

*Note: 'Truepenny' meant a trusty, honest fellow, from days when many coins were counterfeit. From the two words 'true' and 'penny'.

HORATIO	HORATIO
Propose the oath, my lord.	Propose the oath, my lord.
HAMLET	HAMLET
You are never to speak a word of what you have seen. Swear by my sword.	Never to speak of this that you have seen. Swear by my sword.

THE GHOST'S VOICE REPLIES FROM A DIFFERENT AREA BELOW.

GHOST	GHOST
(*off*) Swear.	Swear.

THEY PLACE THEIR HANDS ON HIS SWORD AND SWEAR THE OATH AGAIN.

HAMLET REALISES THE GHOST VOICE HAS MOVED AND MOVES TO WHERE
THE VOICE HAD COME FROM

HAMLET

Here, there and everywhere, eh? Then we'll move.

HAMLET

Hic et ubique?* Then we'll shift our ground

> *Note: 'Hic et Ubique' is Latin, a language taught in private schools and universities and used to mock those of a lesser education (such as Shakespeare) who were not as fluent in it, in a time where it was deemed inappropriate for lesser educated people to write plays. It means, 'here, there and everywhere'.*

HAMLET (CONT'D)

Come here, gentlemen, and lay your hands again on my sword. Swear by my sword never to speak again of what you have heard.

HAMLET

Come hither, gentlemen,
And lay your hands again upon my sword.
Swear by my sword,
Never to speak of this that you have heard.

THE GHOST'S VOICE COMES FROM A NEW LOCATION BELOW AGAIN.

GHOST

(*off*) Swear by his sword.

GHOST

Swear by his sword.

THEY SWEAR AGAIN.

HAMLET

Well said, old mole! Can you tunnel your way through the earth so fast? A skilful miner! Let's move once more, good friends.

HAMLET

Well said, old mole! Canst work i'th' earth so fast? A worthy pioneer! Once more remove, good friends.

HORATIO

Oh, as night and day is my witness, this is incredibly strange!

HORATIO

O day and night, but this is wondrous strange!

HAMLET

So therefore as it is a stranger give it a warm welcome. There are more things in heaven and earth than you or your teachings ever dreamt of, Horatio. But come, over here.

HAMLET

And therefore as a stranger give it welcome.
There are more things in heaven and earth, Horatio,
Than are dreamt of in your philosophy. But come,

HAMLET MOVES TO A NEW LOCATION AND HOLDS OUT HIS SWORD.

HAMLET (CONT'D)	HAMLET
Swear as before, that never, so help you god, no matter how strange or odd my behaviour – because in future I may think it helpful to put on an act of insanity – swear that if you see me at such a time, you will never, with arms folded like so...	Here, as before, never, so help you mercy, How strange or odd soe'er I bear myself - As I perchance hereafter shall think meet To put an antic disposition on - That you, at such times seeing me, never shall, With arms encumbered thus,

HAMLET CROSSES HIS ARMS.

HAMLET (CONT'D)	HAMLET
Or by shaking your head like this...	or this headshake,

HAMLET SHAKES HIS HEAD IN DEMONSTRATION.

HAMLET (CONT'D)	HAMLET
Or by muttering cryptic phrases such as 'Well, we know' or 'We could, if we so wished...', or 'If we cared to speak', or 'There are those, who if they did...', or some other such ambiguous phrase to hint you know anything of my actions. This you will not do, so swear, by the grace and mercy of god in your hour of need.	Or by pronouncing of some doubtful phrase As `Well, well, we know' or `We could, an if we would', Or `If we list to speak' or `There be, an if they might', Or such ambiguous giving out, to note That you know aught of me. This not to do, So grace and mercy at your most need help you, swear.
GHOST	GHOST
(*off below*) Swear.	Swear.

THEY SWEAR.

HAMLET	HAMLET
Rest, rest, troubled spirit! So, gentlemen, I offer you my love and affection, and everything else a man as poor as Hamlet may offer to express his love and friendship to you, God willing. Let us go back inside together, and remember, keep your fingers to your lips.	Rest, rest, perturbed spirit! So, gentlemen, With all my love I do commend me to you, And what so poor a man as Hamlet is May do t' express his love and friending to you,* God willing, shall not lack. Let us go in together, And still your fingers on your lips, I pray.

Note: Hamlet speaks of himself in the third person. Shakespeare uses this to suggest not only a philosophical man, but also an arrogant man.

HAMLET LOOKS UP TO THE HEAVENS.

HAMLET (CONT'D)

Now, the time is wrong. Oh, curse you spite,

That ever I was born to set it right!

HAMLET

The time is out of joint. O cursed spite,

That ever I was born to set it right!

HAMLET HAS FINISHED TALKING, HE MAKES TO LEAVE, THEY STAND ASIDE TO
LET HIM PASS.

HAMLET (CONT'D)

No, come, we'll walk together.

HAMLET

Nay, come, let's go together.

> *Note: The rhyming couplet near the end of Hamlet's speech signified to the audience that the scene was ending at a time when there was little if any scenery on stage, no curtains and no lights to dim. It was not always in the last two lines, and sometimes it could be four lines, but the audience would recognise the significance and know a scene was ending.*

ACT II

INTO THE MADNESS WHEREIN NOW HE RAVES

ACT II

ACT II SCENE I

A ROOM IN POLONIUS'S HOUSE

ENTER POLONIUS AND HIS SERVANT REYNALDO.

THEY TALK ABOUT LAERTES, WHO HAS SINCE DEPARTED FOR PARIS.

*Note: This scene is often omitted from performances as it is not required for the story and it shortens the run time.

Laertes is not referred to by name, leaving the audience to assume the identity. His name has been inserted into the first line of the translation to make it clear to those studying the scene.

POLONIUS
Give Laertes* this money and these letters, Reynaldo.

REYNALDO
I will, my lord.

POLONIUS
You would be very wise, my good Reynaldo, to make inquiries into his behaviour before you visited him.

REYNALDO
I had intended to, my lord.

POLONIUS
Give him this money and these notes, Reynaldo.*

REYNALDO
I will, my lord.

POLONIUS
You shall do marvellous wisely, good Reynaldo,
Before you visit him, to make inquire
Of his behaviour.

REYNALDO
My lord, I did intend it.

*Note: the name 'Reynaldo' means 'fox-like', which suits the character well, as he is sent off on a mission of cunning and trickery by Polonius.

Polonius's pompous and overbearing manner in this scene could have been a satirical jibe at Lord Burghley, Queen Elizabeth's chief minister. It was said he set strict rules for his son and had him spied upon in Paris.

POLONIUS

Well, that's good, that's very good. And listen, sir, first, find out for me what Danes are in Paris, and why, and who they are, and their financial means, and where they stay, what company they keep, and how much it costs them. And find out if they know my son by roundabout means and vague questions, it will bring you closer to the truth than direct questioning. Pretend you have some distant connection with him, such as 'I know his father and some friends of his, and know him a little'. Are you taking this in, Reynaldo?

REYNALDO

Yes, very well, my lord.

POLONIUS

'I know him a little, but...' then you may add, 'not very well, but if he's the one I'm thinking of, he's a very wild, addicted so-and-so', and there you can add whatever vices you please, but none that may damage his reputation, be careful of that. But, sir, the kind of wanton, wild misbehaviour usually associated with youth and new found freedom.

POLONIUS

Marry, well said, very well said. Look you, sir,
Inquire me first what Danskers are in Paris,
And how, and who, what means, and where they
  keep,
What company, at what expense; and finding
By this encompassment and drift of question
That they do know my son, come you more
  nearer
Than your particular demands will touch it.
Take you, as 'twere, some distant knowledge of
  him,
As thus: ' I know his father and his friends,
And in part him'. Do you mark this, Reynaldo?

REYNALDO

Ay, very well, my lord.

POLONIUS

'And in part him, but', you may say, 'not well;
But if't be he I mean, he's very wild,
Addicted so and so';* and there put on him
What forgeries you please; marry, none so rank
As may dishonour him, take heed of that;
But, sir, such wanton, wild, and usual slips
As are companions noted and most known
To youth and liberty.

*Note: 'So and so' - a person who is disliked or is considered to have a particular unfavourable characteristic.

REYNALDO

Such as gambling, my lord.

POLONIUS

Yes, or drinking, fencing, swearing, arguing, whoring – you can go that far.

REYNALDO

My lord, that would dishonour him.

REYNALDO

As gaming, my lord.

POLONIUS

Ay, or drinking, fencing, swearing,
Quarrelling, drabbing - you may go so far.

REYNALDO

My lord, that would dishonour him.

POLONIUS

Goodness, no, as you can lighten it in the telling. You must not damage his reputation by saying he practises immoral behaviour, that's not what I meant, just mention his faults lightly as if they are mere frivolities of youthful liberty. The impulsive behaviour of a heated mind, the hot blooded wildness young men are inclined to.

POLONIUS

Faith, no, as you may season it in the charge.
You must not put another scandal on him,
That he is open to incontinency;
That's not my meaning, but breathe his faults so
  quaintly
That they may seem the taints of liberty,
The flash and outbreak of a fiery mind,
A savageness in unreclaimed* blood,
Of general assault.

Note: 'Unreclaimed' – another reference to hawking (falconry). A bird was 'reclaimed' by loud whooping to recall it if had become disobedient.

REYNALDO

But my good lord...

REYNALDO

But, my good lord -

POLONIUS

(finishing Reynaldo's sentence) Why am I asking you to do this?

POLONIUS

Wherefore should you do this?

REYNALDO

Yes, my lord. I'd like to know.

REYNALDO

Ay, my lord,
I would know that.

POLONIUS

Well, sir, here's my reasoning, and I believe it to be a cunning plan; you accuse my son of these slight misdemeanours, as if they were minor blemishes of character. Now take note, the person you are conversing with, the one you wish to question, if he's ever seen the youth you mention practicing any of the crimes you mention, be assured, he'll open up to you saying something like; 'Dear sir', or such like, or 'friend', or 'gentleman' according to the customary term of address of the man and his country.

POLONIUS

Marry, sir, here's my drift,
And I believe it is a fetch of warrant:
You laying these slight sullies on my son,
As 'twere a thing a little soiled i'th' working,
Mark you, your party in converse, him you would
  sound,
Having ever seen in the prenominate crimes
The youth you breathe of guilty, be assured
He closes with you in this consequence:
`Good sir', or so, or 'friend', or 'gentleman',
According to the phrase or the addition
Of man and country.

REYNALDO

I understand, my lord.

REYNALDO

Very good, my lord.

POLONIUS

And then, sir, he does, erm... he does... what was I about to say? By heavens, I was about to say something. Where was I up to?

POLONIUS

And then, sir, does a' this - a' does - what was I about to say? By the mass, I was about to say something. Where did I leave?

REYNALDO
At 'he opens up to you with', then 'friend or such like' and 'gentleman'.

POLONIUS
At 'opens up to you with' – oh yes, indeed, he opens up to you with this; 'I know the gentleman, I saw him yesterday, or the other day, or some other time, with such and such, or such and such, and, as you say, there was gambling, there was excessive drinking, quarrelling over a tennis match', or perhaps, 'I saw him enter a house of ill-repute', in other words, a brothel, and so on. So you can see, your bait of small lies catches the bigger fish of truth. And this is how we men of wisdom and understanding, by slowly drawing people in and with subtle deviation and misdirection get a direct answer. So shall you about my son if you follow my directions and advice. You understand me, I hope?

REYNALDO
At 'closes in the consequence', at 'friend or so', and 'gentleman'.

POLONIUS
At ʻcloses in the consequence' - ay, marry;
He closes with you thus: 'I know the gentleman,
I saw him yesterday, or t'other day,
Or then, or then, with such, or such; and, as you
   say,
There was a' gaming, there o'ertook in's rouse,
There falling out at tennis', or perchance
'I saw him enter such a house of sale',
Videlicet,* a brothel, or so forth. See you now,
Your bait of falsehood takes this carp* of truth;
And thus do we of wisdom and of reach,
With windlasses* and with assays of bias,*
By indirections find directions out.
So, by my former lecture and advice,
Shall you my son. You have me, have you not?

Note: Carp is a fresh water fish which can grow to a large size.

Videlicet – Latin, meaning 'namely'.

Windlass is a winch which slowly winds in a rope, typically on a ship.

Assays of bias: A term derived from lawn bowling where a bowler makes his ball curve around an opponent's ball to hit a target behind it. In modern terms 'throw him a curveball'.

REYNALDO
I do, my lord.

POLONIUS
God go with you then, farewell.

REYNALDO
Thank you, my lord.

REYNALDO
My lord, I have.

POLONIUS
God-buy-ye; fare ye well.

REYNALDO
Good my lord!

REYNALDO TURNS TO LEAVE. AS HE DOES, POLONIUS CALLS AFTER HIM.

POLONIUS
Observe his behaviour for yourself as well.

POLONIUS
Observe his inclination in yourself.

REYNALDO
I will, my lord.

REYNALDO
I shall, my lord.

POLONIUS
And do not try to restrict his behaviour.

POLONIUS
And let him ply his music.

REYNALDO
I understand, my lord.

REYNALDO
Well, my lord.

POLONIUS
Farewell!

POLONIUS
Farewell!

EXIT REYNALDO.

ENTER OPHELIA IN A DISTRESSED STATE.

POLONIUS (CONT'D)
What's wrong, Ophelia? Whatever is the matter?

POLONIUS
How now, Ophelia! What's the matter?

OPHELIA
Alas, my lord, I have been so frightened.

OPHELIA
Alas, my lord, I have been so affrighted.

POLONIUS
By what, in the name of God?

POLONIUS
With what, i'th' name of God?

OPHELIA
My lord, as I was sewing in my room, Lord Hamlet came in with his jacket unbuttoned, no hat on his head, his socks muddy and hanging like shackles around his ankles, his palour as pale as his shirt, his knees knocking together, and with a look so pitiful, as if he had been let loose from hell to tell of the horrors.

OPHELIA
My lord, as I was sewing in my closet,
Lord Hamlet, with his doublet all unbraced,
No hat upon his head, his stockings fouled,
Ungartered and down-gyved* to his ankle,
Pale as his shirt, his knees knocking each other,
And with a look so piteous in purport
As if he had been loosed out of hell
To speak of horrors, he comes before me.

*Note: Down-gyved. Gyves were ankle shackles used on prisoners.

POLONIUS
Mad for your love?

POLONIUS
Mad for thy love?

OPHELIA
Father, I do not know, but in truth I fear it may be.

OPHELIA
My lord, I do not know,
But truly I do fear it.

POLONIUS
What did he say?

POLONIUS
What said he?

OPHELIA

He took me by the wrist and held me so I couldn't move. Then he stretched out his arm, and with his other hand over his brow like this...

OPHELIA

He took me by the wrist and held me hard;
Then goes he to the length of all his arm,
And with his other hand thus o'er his brow

SHE HOLDS HER HAND TO HER FOREHEAD LIKE A SHIP'S LOOKOUT.

OPHELIA (CONT'D)

He studied my face with the intensity of someone who planned on drawing it. He stayed that way a long time, until at last he shook my arm a little, nodded his head up and down three times like so...

OPHELIA

He falls to such perusal of my face
As a' would draw it. Long stayed he so.
At last, a little shaking of mine arm,
And thrice his head thus waving up and down,

SHE NODS HER HEAD SLOWLY AND SADLY TO DEMONSTRATE.

OPHELIA (CONT'D)

...then let out such a pitiful and deep sigh that it seemed to resonate through his whole body as if it would shake it apart and end his life. Having done that, he let me go and with his head turned back over his shoulder seemed to find his way out without using his sight, because he left without the aid of his eyes, which to the last moment remained fixed on me.

OPHELIA

He raised a sigh so piteous and profound
As it did seem to shatter all his bulk
And end his being. That done, he lets me go,
And with his head over his shoulder turned,
He seemed to find his way without his eyes,
For out o' doors he went without their help,
And to the last bended their light on me.

POLONIUS

Come with me, we'll go to the king. This is the madness of love, which by its violent nature undoes itself and bends the will to self-destructive actions as sure as any passion under heaven that afflicts our emotions. I'm sorry...

POLONIUS

Come, go with me; I will go seek the king.
This is the very ecstasy of love,
Whose violent property fordoes itself
And leads the will to desperate undertakings
As oft as any passion under heaven
That does afflict our natures. I am sorry.

HE STOPS MID-SENTENCE.

POLONIUS (CONT'D)

Wait, have you been speaking harshly to him lately?

POLONIUS

What, have you given him any hard words of late?

OPHELIA

No, father, just as you ordered, I rejected his letters and denied him access to me.

POLONIUS

That has made him mad. I am sorry, with better hindsight and judgement I should have realised. I feared he was trifling with you and meant to damage your reputation. Damn my jealousy! By heavens, it is as improper for my generation to be so over confident in our opinions as it is for younger ones to be so naïve. Come, we must go to the king.
This must be told, to keep shtum might create
More grief hidden than openness caused hate.
Come.

OPHELIA

No, my good lord, but, as you did command,
I did repel his letters and denied
His access to me.

POLONIUS

That hath made him mad.
I am sorry that with better heed and judgement
I had not quoted him. I feared he did but trifle
And meant to wreck thee; but beshrew my
  jealousy!
By heaven, it is as proper to our age
To cast beyond ourselves in our opinions
As it is common for the younger sort
To lack discretion. Come, go we to the king.
This must be known, which, being kept close, might
  move
More grief to hide than hate to utter love. *
Come.

---

*Note: If you noticed the end of scene rhyming couplet and recognised the significance, you're well on the way to becoming a Shakespearean expert.

The meaning of the rhyming couplet is rather convoluted, being shoe-horned into two lines. It means – Hiding what has happened could have more dire consequences to us if the concealment were discovered, than any consequences (hate) from revealing his behaviour would bring upon us, no matter how good our motive (love) was to protect him by hiding it. So we must tell the king what happened. A lot of meaning from just two lines.

EXEUNT

ACT II SCENE II

THE COURT OF THE KING AT CASTLE ELSINORE.

A FLOURISH OF TRUMPETS ANNOUNCES THE ENTRANCE OF KING CLAUDIUS AND QUEEN GERTRUDE TO A GREAT HALL, FOLLOWED BY ROYAL ATTENDANTS, AND ROSENCRANTZ AND GUILDENSTERN, WHO ARE CHILDHOOD FRIENDS OF HAMLET.

> *Note: This is a very long scene.*
>
> *Historic: Two noblemen from Denmark visited England in 1592 (the decade Hamlet was probably written) by the names of Frederik Rosenkrantz and Knud Gyldenstierne. both common surnames among Scandinavian noblility.*

KING CLAUDIUS

Welcome, dear Rosencrantz and Guildenstern. Although we have missed seeing you, the reason for so hastily summoning you is of a certain need we have of you. You may have heard something of the metamorphosis in Hamlet recently, as I call it, since outwardly and inwardly he no longer resembles the man he once was. Apart from his father's death, whatever it is that has caused him to become so confused in himself I cannot imagine. I ask you both, as you grew up from childhood with him and so are familiar with his character and behaviour, that you stay here a while in court in his company, and by indulging and entertaining him, see if you can ascertain any clue as to what afflicts him so, which, when discovered, may lead us to a remedy.

KING

Welcome, dear Rosencrantz and Guildenstern.
Moreover that we much did long to see you,
The need we have to use you did provoke
Our hasty sending. Something have you heard
Of Hamlet's transformation; so I call it,
Since nor th' exterior nor the inward man
Resembles that it was. What it should be,
More than his father's death, that thus hath put
  him
So much from th' understanding of himself,
I cannot dream of. I entreat you both
That, being of so young days brought up with
  him
And since so neighboured to his youth and
  haviour,
That you vouchsafe your rest here in our court
Some little time, so by your companies
To draw him on to pleasures, and to gather,
So much as from occasion you may glean,
Whether* aught to us unknown afflicts him thus
That, opened, lies within our remedy.

> **Note: 'Whether' is pronounced here as a single syllable, sounding like 'where'.*
>
> *The King does not want Hamlet to know the purpose of his friend's visit. It is likely he wants to know if Hamlet suspects anything about his father's death, rather than showing concern out of love or kindness.*

QUEEN GERTRUDE

Dear gentlemen, Hamlet has often talked about you, and I'm sure there are not two men living he is fonder of. It would be a wonderful show of kindness and generosity if you spent your time with us seeking the answer to our plight. In return you would receive thanks befitting of a king's gratitude.

ROSENCRANTZ

Your majesties have, by royal command, the power to order us to fulfil your desires, you have no need to plead with us.

GUILDENSTERN

But we both agree to put ourselves at your full disposal, and freely offer up our services to your command.

QUEEN

Good gentlemen, he hath much talked of you,
And sure I am two men there is not living
To whom he more adheres. If it will please you
To show us so much gentry and good will
As to expend your time with us a while
For the supply and profit of our hope,
Your visitation shall receive such thanks
As fits a king's remembrance.

ROSENCRANTZ

Both your majesties
Might, by the sovereign power you have of us,
Put your dread pleasures more into command
Than to entreaty.

GUILDENSTERN

But we both obey,
And here give up ourselves, in the full bent,
To lay our service freely at your feet
To be commanded.

> Note: One is saying you do not need to beg us, the other is saying you do not need to pay us; they do it willingly to further themselves in the king's favour.

KING CLAUDIUS

Thank you, Rosencrantz and kind Guildenstern.

QUEEN GERTRUDE

Thank you, Guildenstern and kind Rosencrantz. I plead with you to visit my much altered son immediately.
(*to attendants*) Go, a few of you, find Hamlet and take these gentleman to him.

GUILDENSTERN

I pray that our presence and our pleasantries prove helpful to him!.

QUEEN GERTRUDE

Yes, amen to that!

KING

Thanks, Rosencrantz and gentle Guildenstern.

QUEEN

Thanks, Guildenstern and gentle Rosencrantz.
And I beseech you instantly to visit
My too much changed son. Go, some of you,
And bring these gentlemen where Hamlet is.

GUILDENSTERN

Heavens make our presence and our practices
Pleasant and helpful to him!

QUEEN

Ay, amen!

> Note: Amen is Latin, used in prayer, meaning, "So be it". Derived from Greek and Hebrew meaning, "Truth" or "Certainty".

POLONIUS ENTERS AS ROSENCRANTZ AND GUILDENSTERN LEAVE.

POLONIUS
My lord, (*he bows*) the ambassadors to Norway have joyously returned.

KING CLAUDIUS
You've always been the champion of good news!

POLONIUS
Have I, my lord? I assure you, your majesty, I dedicate my duty, as I do my soul, to God and my gracious king, and unless this brain of mine is no longer the keen deductive sleuth it once was, I think I have discovered the very cause of Hamlet's madness.

KING CLAUDIUS
Oh, tell me more, this I've been longing to hear.

POLONIUS
But first grant admittance to the ambassadors, my news shall be the dessert to follow their great feast.

KING CLAUDIUS
I give you the honour of inviting them in.

POLONIUS LEAVES TO FETCH THE AMBASSADORS.

KING CLAUDIUS (CONT'D)
My dear Gertrude, he tells me he has discovered the cause of your son's disorder.

QUEEN GERTRUDE
I doubt it is anything other than the obvious, his father's death and our over-hasty marriage.

KING CLAUDIUS
Well, we will ask him.

RE-ENTER POLONIUS, ACCOMPANIED BY VOLTEMAND AND CORNELIUS
BEARING A DOCUMENT.

POLONIUS
Th' ambassadors from Norway, my good lord,
Are joyfully returned.

KING
Thou still hast been the father of good news.

POLONIUS
Have I, my lord? Assure you, my good liege,
I hold my duty as I hold my soul,
Both to my God and to my gracious king;
And I do think, or else this brain of mine
Hunts not the trail of policy so sure
As it hath used to do, that I have found
The very cause of Hamlet's lunacy.

KING
O speak of that; that do I long to hear.

POLONIUS
Give first admittance to th' ambassadors;
My news shall be the fruit to that great feast.

KING
Thyself do grace to them, and bring them in.

KING
He tells me, my dear Gertrude, he hath found
The head and source of all your son's distemper.

QUEEN
I doubt it is no other but the main,
His father's death and our o'erhasty marriage.

KING
Well, we shall sift him.

KING CLAUDIUS (CONT'D)
Welcome, my good friends. Tell me, Voltemand, what message from my fellow king of Norway?

VOLTEMAND
A most favourable return of your greetings and your demands. As soon as he'd read your message he sent orders to disband his nephew's armies, which he had thought were raised in preparation for war against Poland. The more he looked into it, the more apparent it became it was in fact against your highness instead. Aggrieved that in his sickness and advanced years his leadership was being disrespected, resulting in him being misled, he sent orders for Fortinbras to cease his actions, which, in brief, he obeyed, acknowledged the King of Norway's disapproval and most significantly, made a vow to his uncle never again to raise arms against your majesty. Overcome with joy at this news, the old king of Norway gave Fortinbras three thousand crowns a year payment and commissioned him to reassign the army he had previously raised, but this time against the Poles, with a request, the details of which are contained in here...

KING
Welcome, my good friends.
Say, Voltemand, what from our brother Norway?

VOLTEMAND
Most fair return of greetings and desires.
Upon our first he sent out to suppress
His nephew's levies, which to him appeared
To be a preparation 'gainst the Polack;
But better looked into, he truly found
It was against your highness; whereat grieved
That so his sickness, age, and impotence
Was falsely borne in hand, sends out arrests
On Fortinbras, which he, in brief, obeys,
Receives rebuke from Norway, and, in fine,
Makes vow before his uncle never more
To give th' assay of arms against your majesty.
Whereon old Norway, overcome with joy,
Gives him three thousand crowns in annual fee
And his commission to employ those soldiers
So levied as before, against the Polack,
With an entreaty, herein further shown,

HE PASSES THE DOCUMENT TO THE KING.

VOLTEMAND (CONT'D)
...That it might please your majesty to give free passage through your lands for this purpose, the details of securities and permissions being stated within.

VOLTEMAND
That it might please you to give quiet pass
Through your dominions for this enterprise,
On such regards of safety and allowance
As therein are set down.

KING CLAUDIUS

It suits me well. And at a more convenient time I'll read and answer it, and consider the implications. Meanwhile, I thank you for your most successful mission. Go get some rest, tonight we'll feast together. You are most welcome home.

KING

It likes us well,
And at our more considered time we'll read,
Answer, and think upon this business.
Meantime, we thank you for your well-took
  labour.
Go to your rest, at night we'll feast together.
Most welcome home.

EXEUNT VOLTEMAND AND CORNELIUS (NEVER TO REAPPEAR).

POLONIUS

This business ended well. Your majesty, and madam, to argue about what kingship is, or what duty is, or why day is day, night is night or time is time, is nothing but a waste of night, day and time. So, as brevity is the heart and soul of wit, and tediousness is its off-shoots and meandering adornments, I will be brief. Your noble son is mad. I say mad, though to define true madness, wouldn't one have to be completely mad oneself? But we'll not get into that now.

POLONIUS

This business is well ended.
My liege, and madam, to expostulate
What majesty should be, what duty is,
Why day is day, night night, and time is time,
Were nothing but to waste night, day, and time.
Therefore, since brevity is the soul of wit,
And tediousness the limbs and outward
  flourishes,
I will be brief.* Your noble son is mad.
Mad call I it, for, to define true madness,
What is't but to be nothing else but mad?
But let that go.

*Note: Rather than being brief he has meandered on at length.

QUEEN GERTRUDE

More substance, less embellishment.

QUEEN

More matter with less art.

POLONIUS

Madam, I swear, I'm not embellishing at all. The fact he is mad is true. That it's true is a pity, and it's a pity that it's true. A foolish figure of speech, and that's the end of it, as I won't use embellishment. Mad we'll call him then, and it now remains that we must find the cause of this effect, or rather the cause of this defect, for this effect is defective by cause. So it remains, and the remainder is such...

POLONIUS

Madam, I swear I use no art at all.
That he is mad 'tis true; 'tis true 'tis pity,
And pity 'tis 'tis true. A foolish figure;
But farewell it, for I will use no art.
Mad let us grant him then; and now remains
That we find out the cause of this effect,
Or rather say the cause of this defect,
For this effect defective comes by cause.
Thus it remains, and the remainder thus:

HE TAKES A LETTER FROM HIS POCKET AS HE SPEAKS.

POLONIUS (CONT'D)

Now listen to this - I have a daughter, or I have until she marries, who in her duty and obedience, take note, has given me this. (*he waves the letter*) Now gather round and draw your conclusions.

POLONIUS

Perpend,
I have a daughter, have while she is mine,*
Who in her duty and obedience, mark,
Hath given me this. Now gather and surmise.

> *Note: Once a woman marries she becomes the property of her husband and he has to keep her. A woman could not live with a man back then unless they were married. Hence Polonius saying he has her while she is still his, because after that she is her husband's property and responsibility, and Polonius wants to better himself by finding his daughter a good husband. This is where we get the expression 'the father of the bride giving her away'.*

HE READS THE LETTER ALOUD, FULL OF HIS IMPORTANCE.

POLONIUS (CONT'D)

(*reads*)
"To the heavenly idol of my soul, the most beautified Ophelia" –
That's a poor phrase, a vile phrase, "beautified" is a vile phrase. But I'll read more –
"in her excellent white bosom, these...", etc, etc.

POLONIUS

[*Reads.*]
"To the celestial and my soul's idol, the most beautified Ophelia" -
That's an ill phrase, a vile phrase, ` beautified' is a vile phrase. But you shall hear thus -
"in her excellent white bosom, * these", etc.

> *Note: 'White bosom' - Women would keep love letters tucked in their clothes next to their heart, but it is also suggestive and Polonius feels uncomfortable reading it to the Queen.*

HE FEELS IT INAPPROPRIATE TO CONTINUE THAT LINE AND SCANS THE LETTER TO LOOK FOR A GOOD PART TO READ OUT.

QUEEN GERTRUDE

This was from Hamlet to your daughter?

QUEEN

Came this from Hamlet to her?

POLONIUS

Dear madam, bear with me, I'll read it faithfully.

POLONIUS

Good madam, stay awhile, I will be faithful.

HE READS IT ALOUD TO THE END WITHOUT COMMENT THIS TIME.

POLONIUS (CONT'D)

(reads) "Doubt that the stars are afire,
Doubt that the sun does move,
Doubt truth to be a liar,
But never doubt my love."
"Oh, dearest Ophelia, I am not good at poetry. I have no ability to express my heartaches, except that I love you more than anyone, oh, much more, believe me. Adieu. Yours ever more, most dearest lady, while I still have life in me,
   Hamlet."

POLONIUS

[Reads.] "Doubt thou the stars are fire,
Doubt that the sun doth move,*
Doubt truth to be a liar,
But never doubt I love."*
"O dear Ophelia, I am ill at these numbers. I have not art to reckon my groans; but that I love thee best, O most best, believe it. Adieu.
Thine evermore, most dear lady, whilst this machine is to him,
   Hamlet."

POLONIUS LOOKS UP FROM THE LETTER.

Note: Shakespeare often rhymes 'love' with 'move' or 'prove' – words which don't rhyme when spoken in modern English, but look like they do when written. The vowel sounds have changed over the centuries, and regional variations are very marked, add to that the poetic pronunciation of some words and it all gets lost today. Shakespeare played on poetic and regional pronunciation of words in his sonnets to make puns not obvious today.

Shakespeare also often rhymes 'eye' with a word we would pronounce ending in an 'ee' sound, for example in Midsummer Night's Dream, "My ear should catch your voice, my eye your eye, / My tongue should catch your tongue's sweet melody." Eye is rhymed with melody. In Shakespeare's day, this would have been a perfect rhyme. The technical reason for this is 'secondary stress'. This was commonplace in Middle English, especially in poetry. The word 'melody' would have a secondary stress on the final syllable '-dy', pronouncing it 'die', which of course rhymes with 'eye'.

Today we know the Earth revolves around the sun, back then it was believed the Sun and stars revolved around the Earth (the sun doth move). Copernicus had already proved this was false, but the church had declared this was heresy.

POLONIUS (CONT'D)

As an obedient daughter, Ophelia showed this to me, and further to this, she has told me details of his courting, as it happened; times, means, places.

POLONIUS

This in obedience hath my daughter shown me,
And, more above, hath his solicitings,
As they fell out by time, by means, and place,
All given to mine ear.

KING CLAUDIUS

And how receptive was she to his love?

KING

But how hath she
Received his love?

POLONIUS

What kind of man do you think I am?

POLONIUS

What do you think of me?

KING CLAUDIUS

A loyal and honourable man.

KING

As of a man faithful and honourable.

POLONIUS

As I strive to be, but what would you have thought, when I saw this passionate love take off, - as I perceived it to be before my daughter confided in me, I have to tell you, what would you or your good majesty the queen here, have thought, if I had reacted like an inanimate desk or a notebook, and suppressed my conscience, acting deaf and dumb, turning a blind eye, what would you think? No, I got to work on my young mistress and said this to her: *'Lord Hamlet is a prince, out of your class, this must end'*. I then ordered her to lock herself away from his advances, allow no messengers, receive no love tokens. This she did, she understood the wisdom of my advice, and he, rejected, – to make my tale short – fell into depression, then wouldn't eat, then couldn't sleep, then went into a decline, became delirious, and as a result fell into this madness which he suffers from now, for which we all grieve.

POLONIUS

I would fain prove so; but what might you think,
When I had seen this hot love on the wing,
As I perceived it, I must tell you that,
Before my daughter told me, what might you,
Or my dear majesty your queen here, think,
If I had played the desk or table-book,
Or given my heart a winking, mute and dumb,
Or looked upon this love with idle sight,
What might you think? No, I went round to work,
And my young mistress thus I did bespeak:
` Lord Hamlet is a prince out of thy star;
This must not be'. And then I precepts gave her,
That she should lock herself from his resort,
Admit no messengers, receive no tokens;
Which done, she took the fruits of my advice,
And he, repelled - a short tale to make -
Fell into a sadness, then into a fast,
Thence to a watch, thence into a weakness,
Thence to a lightness; and by this declension
Into the madness wherein now he raves,
And all we mourn for.

THE KING TURNS TO HIS QUEEN AND SPEAKS TO HER.

KING CLAUDIUS

Do you think this is it?

KING

Do you think 'tis this?

QUEEN GERTRUDE

It may be, it's possible.

QUEEN

It may be; very like.

POLONIUS

Has there ever been a time – I'd like to know – that I have definitely said, "*This is what it is*" and I have been proved wrong?

POLONIUS

Hath there been such a time - I'd fain know that -
That I have positively said "'Tis so"
When it proved otherwise?

KING CLAUDIUS

Not that I know of.

KING

Not that I know.

POLONIUS

Take this head...

POLONIUS

Take this...

POLONIUS POINTS TO HIS HEAD.

POLONIUS (CONT'D)

From these shoulders...

POLONIUS

from this...

POLONIUS (CONT'D)	POLONIUS
...if I'm proved wrong. If I get wind of anything, I will find where the truth is concealed, even if it is buried deep in the centre of the earth.	... if this be otherwise. If circumstances lead me, I will find Where truth is hid, though it were hid indeed Within the centre.

KING CLAUDIUS
How can we test your theory?

KING
How may we try it further?

POLONIUS
You know sometimes he paces for hours on end here in the hall.

POLONIUS
You know sometimes he walks four hours*
  together
Here in the lobby.

Note: In Elizabethan times 'four hours' was often written in place of 'for hours'. They meant the same thing – an unspecified long period of time.

QUEEN GERTRUDE
He does indeed.

QUEEN
So he does indeed.

POLONIUS
When he next does, I'll release my daughter to him.
(*to King*) You and I will hide behind the hanging tapestry there and observe the encounter. If he doesn't love her, and that's not the reason he's lost all reasoning, then let me be minister of state no longer, and run a lowly farm instead.

POLONIUS
At such a time I'll loose my daughter to him.
Be you and I behind an arras* then;
Mark the encounter. If he love her not,
And be not from his reason fall'n thereon,
Let me be no assistant for a state,
But keep a farm and carters.*

Note: An arras is a hanging wall tapestry, typically used to conceal an alcove where a man may easily hide undetected. Named after the town 'Arras' in France, famous for its tapestries.

A "carter", named after carts and cart horses, was a farm labourer.

KING CLAUDIUS
We will try it.

KING
We will try it.

QUEEN GERTRUDE
But look, how sadly the poor wretch approaches, reading his book.

QUEEN
But look, where sadly the poor wretch comes reading.

POLONIUS
Leave, I beg you both, leave. I'll engage him now... oh, if you'll pardon my forwardness.

POLONIUS
Away, I do beseech you both, away. I'll board him* presently. O, give me leave.*

> *Note: 'Board him' is taken from the nautical term to go onto another ship, often when raiding it, in this case for information.*
>
> *'Give me leave' puns apologising for ordering the King to leave.*

THE KING, QUEEN AND ATTENDANTS QUICKLY AND QUIETLY LEAVE.

POLONIUS (CONT'D)
How is my dear Prince Hamlet?

POLONIUS
How does my good Lord Hamlet?

HAMLET
Well, God permitting.

HAMLET
Well, God-a-mercy.

POLONIUS
Do you recognise me, my lord?

POLONIUS
Do you know me, my lord?

HAMLET
Very well, you are a fishmonger.

HAMLET
Excellent well, you are a fishmonger.*

POLONIUS
No, not I, my lord.

POLONIUS
Not I, my lord.

> *Note: There are suggestions that fishmonger was slang for a pimp, a man who offers the services of prostitutes. There is no evidence of this being the case, however it does make sense with the text, with Hamlet accusing him of 'pimping' out his daughter to further himself, although this may also be the reason it was later applied. It could also suggest that Polonius is 'fishing' for the truth.*
>
> *As this is a comic interlude, both men speak in prose rather than blank verse.*

HAMLET
Then I would hope you are as honest a man as one.

HAMLET
Then I would you were so honest a man.

POLONIUS
(*indignant*) Honest, my lord?

POLONIUS
Honest, my lord?

HAMLET
Yes sir, the way the world is nowadays, an honest man is one in ten thousand.

HAMLET
Ay, sir; to be honest, as this world goes, is to be one man picked out of ten thousand.

POLONIUS
That's very true, my lord.

POLONIUS
That's very true, my lord.

HAMLET RECITES A PASSAGE FROM HIS BOOK.

HAMLET
"If the sun breeds maggots in a dead dog, being a good kissing carrion... "

HAMLET
For if the sun breed maggots in a dead dog, being a good kissing carrion* -

HE PAUSES, LOOKING UP FROM HIS BOOK.

Note: 'Carrion' is 'road kill' – decaying bodies lying on the ground. 'Kissing' - refer to 'sun kissed'. He is suggesting that Polonius is feeding off him, using Hamlet to his own advantage through his daughter. Carrion is punned with the words 'carry-on' which means questionable behaviour of a sexual nature.

HAMLET (CONT'D)
...Do you have a daughter?

HAMLET
- Have you a daughter?

POLONIUS
I do, my lord.

POLONIUS
I have, my lord.

HAMLET
Don't let her walk in the sun. Conception is a blessing, but as your daughter may conceive – look out, my friend.

HAMLET
Let her not walk i'th' sun. Conception* is a blessing, but as your daughter may conceive* - friend, look to't.

Note: Hamlet is playing with double meanings of words here. 'Conception' can mean both 'understanding' as well as 'becoming pregnant' – which he knows Polonius fears in his daughter. He plays the pun twice, using 'conceive' the second time. This follows on from the 'sun kissed' line above.

POLONIUS
(*aside*) Why does he say that? Still harping on about my daughter! Yet he didn't recognise me at first, and said I was a fishmonger. He is far gone, far gone, however, when I was in my youth I suffered extremely for love, very similar to this in fact. I'll speak to him again.

POLONIUS
[*Aside.*] How say you by that? Still harping on* my daughter. Yet he knew me not at first, a' said I was a fishmonger. A' is far gone, far gone; and truly, in my youth I suffered much extremity for love; very near this. I'll speak to him again.

Note: 'Harping on' means to persistently talk about something to the point of tedium, where it becomes annoying.

POLONIUS TURNS TO HAMLET AGAIN TO RESUME QUESTIONING.

POLONIUS (CONT'D)
What are you reading, my lord?

POLONIUS
What do you read, my lord?

HAMLET
Words, words, words.

HAMLET
Words, words, words.

POLONIUS
What is the matter, my lord?

HAMLET
Between who?

POLONIUS
What is the matter, my lord?*

HAMLET
Between who?*

> *Note: Hamlet deliberately twists the meaning, Polonius means, 'what is the subject matter', Hamlet takes the alternative meaning, 'what is the problem'.

POLONIUS
I mean the subject matter you are reading, my lord.

HAMLET
Lies, sir. The satirical rogue says here that old men have grey beards, their faces are wrinkled, their eyes oozing thick amber and gum tree resin, and that they have a lack of intelligence, together with very weak hips. All of which, sir, though I most fervently believe to be true, I also consider poor taste to be written down. As for yourself, sir, you could be as old as I am, if, like a crab, you could go backwards.

POLONIUS
I mean, the matter that you read, my lord.

HAMLET
Slanders, sir; for the satirical rogue says here that old men have grey beards, that their faces are wrinkled, their eyes purging thick amber and plum-tree gum, and that they have a plentiful lack of wit, together with most weak hams.* All which, sir, though I most powerfully and potently believe, yet I hold it not honesty to have it thus set down; for yourself, sir, shall be old as I am, if, like a crab, you could go backward.

> *Note: 'Hams' was slang for buttocks. This also suggests he was stooped, bent at the waist, like the proverbial old man with a walking stick.

POLONIUS
(aside) Though this is madness, there is some logic to it.
(to Hamlet) Will you come in out of the draft, my lord?

POLONIUS
[Aside.] Though this be madness, yet there is method in't.
[To Hamlet.] Will you walk out of the air,* my lord?

> *Note: It was believed that standing in a draft, or cold air, made an illness worse. All illnesses were treated in the same way prior to medical advances.

HAMLET
Into my grave.

HAMLET
Into my grave.

POLONIUS
Indeed, that's out of the draft.

(*aside*) How witty and original his replies are! A habit madness often indulges in, and which sanity could not so readily deliver. I will leave him, and immediately contrive a meeting somehow between him and my daughter.

(*to Hamlet*) My lord, I will take my leave of you.

HAMLET
You can take nothing from me, sir, that I would not willingly part with – except my life, except my life, my life.

POLONIUS
Farewell, my lord.

POLONIUS
Indeed, that's out of the air.

[*Aside.*] How pregnant sometimes his replies are! A happiness that often madness hits on, which reason and sanity could not so prosperously be delivered of. I will leave him, and suddenly contrive the means of meeting between him and my daughter.

[*To Hamlet.*] My lord, I will take my leave of you.

HAMLET
You cannot, sir, take from me anything that I will not more willingly part withal - except my life, except my life, my life.

POLONIUS
Fare you well, my lord.

AS POLONIUS IS LEAVING, HAMLET MUTTERS ABOUT OLD POLONIUS.

HAMLET
(*aside*) These tedious old fools!

HAMLET
These tedious old fools!

RE-ENTER ROSENCRANTZ AND GUILDENSTERN.

POLONIUS
(*leaving*) If you seek Prince Hamlet, there he is.

ROSENCRANTZ
(*to Polonius*) God bless you, sir.

POLONIUS
You go to seek the Lord Hamlet; there he is.

ROSENCRANTZ
[*To Polonius.*] God save you, sir.

EXIT POLONIUS.

GUILDENSTERN AND ROSENCRANTZ GREET HAMLET.

GUILDENSTERN
My honoured prince!

ROSENCRANTZ
My most dear prince!

HAMLET
My very good friends. How are you, Guildenstern? Ah, and Rosencrantz – good lads. How are you both?

GUILDENSTERN
Mine honoured lord!

ROSENCRANTZ
My most dear lord!

HAMLET
My excellent good friends. How dost thou, Guildenstern? Ah, Rosencrantz - Good lads, how do you both?

ROSENCRANTZ
Just two uneventful people of this world.

GUILDENSTERN
Happy that we're not overly happy. We're not the shiny button on lady luck's cap.

HAMLET
Or the sole of her shoe?

ROSENCRANTZ
Not that either, my lord.

HAMLET
Then you are somewhere around her waist, (*bawdy*) or in the middle of her favours.

Note: A lady offered her 'favours', meaning herself sexually.

GUILDENSTERN
(*bawdy*) Then we are in her *privates*!

Note: 'Privates' is short for 'private parts' – polite term for sexual organs.

HAMLET
In the secret parts of lady luck? Oh, then truly, she is a whore. – So, what news?

Note: A strumpet is a promiscuous woman of loose morals, she offers herself to men freely, often as a prostitute.

ROSENCRANTZ
No news, my lord, except the world has grown more honest.

Note: R and G have been summoned to find out what Hamlet's problem is, so they struggle to answer Hamlet's prying questions.

HAMLET
Then the end of the world is near. But your news is not genuine. Let me question you more specifically. Dear friends, what have you done to deserve lady luck sending you to this prison here?

GUILDENSTERN
Prison, my lord?

ROSENCRANTZ
As the indifferent children of the earth.

GUILDENSTERN
Happy, in that we are not overhappy;
On Fortune's cap we are not the very button.

HAMLET
Nor the soles of her shoe?

ROSENCRANTZ
Neither, my lord.

HAMLET
Then you live about her waist, or in the middle of her favours.*

GUILDENSTERN
Faith, her privates* we.

HAMLET
In the secret parts of Fortune? O, most true, she is a strumpet.* What news?

ROSENCRANTZ
None, my lord, but the world's grown honest.

HAMLET
Then is doomsday near. But your news is not true. Let me question more in particular. What have you, my good friends, deserved at the hands of Fortune, that she sends you to prison hither?

GUILDENSTERN
Prison, my lord?

HAMLET
Denmark is a prison.

ROSENCRANTZ
Then the world is one too.

HAMLET
A substantial one, in which there are many cells, asylums and dungeons. Denmark being one of the worst.

ROSENCRANTZ
We don't think so, my lord.

HAMLET
Well, then it isn't to you, for there is nothing good or bad in anything unless one thinks it is so. To me it is a prison.

ROSENCRANTZ
Well, then your ambitions make it seem so, its prospects are too narrow for your liking.

HAMLET
Denmark's a prison.

ROSENCRANTZ
Then is the world one.

HAMLET
A goodly one, in which there are many confines, wards, and dungeons; Denmark being one o'th' worst.

ROSENCRANTZ
We think not so, my lord.

HAMLET
Why, then 'tis none to you, for there is nothing either good or bad but thinking makes it so. To me it is a prison.

ROSENCRANTZ
Why, then your ambition* makes it one; 'tis too narrow for your mind.

Note: They suspect Hamlet's ambitions are the cause of his madness, that he is frustrated as he wants to be king. They are testing him on this.

HAMLET
Oh God, I could be bound in a nutshell and still consider myself king of the boundless universe, were it not for these bad dreams I have.

HAMLET
O God, I could be bounded in a nutshell and count myself a king of infinite* space, were it not that I have bad dreams.

Note: 'Infinite' meant boundless, without liimits, before it became the mathematical term we recognise today.

In the following confusing exchange, R & G tell Hamlet that ambition is a lowly characteristic, leading Hamlet to say this makes beggars (with no ambitions) at the top with kings and the ambitious people mere shadows of them.

GUILDENSTERN
These dreams are in fact ambition, for the goals of ambitious people are merely reflections of their dreams.

HAMLET
A dream itself is a reflection's shadow.

GUILDENSTERN
Which dreams indeed are ambition;* for the very substance of the ambitious is merely the shadow of a dream.

HAMLET
A dream itself is but a shadow.

ROSENCRANTZ
Indeed, and I see ambition as being so unsubstantial a quality that it is merely a shadow of a shadow.

HAMLET
Then our beggars are the bodies and our kings and ambitious heroes are mere shadows of the beggars. Shall we debate this in court? For, by my word, I cannot figure it out.

ROSENCRANTZ
Truly, and I hold ambition of so airy and light a quality that it is but a shadow's shadow.

HAMLET
Then are our beggars bodies, and our monarchs and outstretched heroes the beggars' shadows. Shall we to th' court? For, by my fay,* I cannot reason.

*Note: 'Fay' is short for faith, used in oaths (by my fay!).

ROSENCRANTZ
We offer our services to you.

HAMLET
Not at all. I don't class you as one of my servants, for, to be honest with you, their service is dreadful. But, my long suffering friends, what brings you to Elsinore?

ROSENCRANTZ & GUILDENSTERN
We'll wait upon you.

HAMLET
No such matter. I will not sort you with the rest of my servants, for, to speak to you like an honest man, I am most dreadfully attended. But, in the beaten way of friendship, what make you at Elsinore?*

*Note: Hamlet suspects the true motive of their visit. R & G have still given no reasonable explanation for their visit.

ROSENCRANTZ
To visit you, my lord. No other reason.

HAMLET
I am a beggar, I'm even poor in giving thanks, but I thank you, even though, dear friends, my thanks are not worth so much as a halfpenny. Were you not sent for? Have you come on your own inclination? Is this visit freely come by? Come, come, be open with me. Come on, tell me.

ROSENCRANTZ
To visit you, my lord; no other occasion.

HAMLET
Beggar that I am, I am even poor in thanks, but I thank you; and sure, dear friends, my thanks are too dear a halfpenny.* Were you not sent for? Is it your own inclining? Is it a free visitation? Come, come, deal justly with me. Come, come. Nay, speak.

*Note: Halfpenny was pronounced 'hape- knee' - two syllables.

GUILDENSTERN
What would you like us to say, my lord?

GUILDENSTERN
What should we say, my lord?

HAMLET
Well, anything – but to the point. You were sent for. There's a kind of guilt in your innocent looks you are unable to conceal. I know the good king and queen sent for you.

HAMLET
Why, anything - but to th' purpose.* You were sent for, and there is a kind of confession in your looks which your modesties have not craft enough to colour. I know the good king and queen have sent for you.

*Note: 'Well , anything – but to the purpose.' He is saying tell me the truth, or sarcastically, tell me anything, but in either case stop evading the question.

ROSENCRANTZ
For what reason, my lord?

ROSENCRANTZ
To what end, my lord?

HAMLET
That you must tell me. But let me beg you by the honour of our friendship, by the bonds of our youth, by the obligation of our time honoured love, and by whatever more precious reason there may be, that you are honest and direct with me. Were you sent for. Yes or no?

HAMLET
That you must teach me. But let me conjure you by the rights of our fellowship, by the consonancy of our youth, by the obligation of our ever-preserved love, and by what more dear a better proposer could charge you withal, be even and direct with me, whether you were sent for or no.

ROSENCRANTZ
(aside to Guildenstern) What do you say?

ROSENCRANTZ
[Aside to Guildenstern.] What say you?

HAMLET
Now then, I can see what you're up to. If you love me, don't hold back.

HAMLET
Nay then, I have an eye of you. If you love me, hold not off.

GUILDENSTERN
My lord, we were sent for.

GUILDENSTERN
My lord, we were sent for.

HAMLET
I'll tell you why; in that way you are without blame, and your sworn secrecy to the king and queen will not have been broken. I don't know why, but of late I've lost my sense of humour, given up my daily exercise, and my depression weighs so heavily upon me that this wonderful planet about us feels to me like a sterile lump of rock, this most excellent canopy above, the air, (he points up) look – this noble overhanging sky, this majestical roof, patterned with golden fire, why, it appears nothing more to me than a foul, diseased, concoction of vapours.

HAMLET
I will tell you why; so shall my anticipation prevent your discovery, and your secrecy to the king and queen moult no feather.* I have of late -but wherefore I know not - lost all my mirth, forgone all custom of exercises; and indeed it goes so heavily with my disposition that this goodly frame, the earth, seems to me a sterile promontory, this most excellent canopy, the air, look you, this brave o'erhanging firmament, this majestical roof fretted with golden fire, why, it appears no other thing to me but a foul and pestilent congregation of vapour.*

Note: Moult no feather – lose no esteem. A bird moults its colourful plumage and for a while is not so glorious as it once was.

Hamlet is describing the painted ceiling over the stage of the Globe Theatre. 'Fretted' means decorative strips of repeating ornamental designs, which we know from written descriptions bordered the Globe Theatre ceiling.

HAMLET (CONT'D)

What a work of art a man is! How noble in reasoning, how infinite in mind, in body and movement, how precise and graceful, and how angelic in action, and in restraint how like a god – the splendour of this world, the king of the animals! And yet, to me, what is this embodiment of dust?

HAMLET

What piece of work is a man! How noble in reason, how infinite in faculty, in form and moving how express and admirable, in action how like an angel, in apprehension how like a god - the beauty of the world, the paragon of animals! And yet, to me, what is this quintessence* of dust?

Note: 'Quintessence', or the fifth essence, was the purest essence. In ancient philosophy it is superior to the other four essences it was believed the world consisted of (air, fire, earth, water). Hamlet's phrase, "quintessence of dust" is ironic. Dust to dust, from the funeral service, where we all come from dust and return to dust after death, will be mentioned a few more times in the play.

HAMLET (CONT'D)

Man holds no delight for me...

HAMLET

Man delights not me,

THE TWO MEN SMIRK AT THIS STATEMENT, THEY ARE ATTACHING A RUDE MEANING TO HAMLET'S WORDS.

HAMLET (CONT'D)

...no, nor woman either, though by your smiling faces you think they do.

HAMLET

no, nor woman neither, though by your smiling you seem to say so.

ROSENCRANTZ

My lord, there was nothing of the kind in my thoughts.

ROSENCRANTZ

My lord, there was no such stuff in my thoughts.

HAMLET

Why did you laugh then, when I said 'man holds no delight for me'?

HAMLET

Why did ye laugh then, when I said ` man delights not me'?

AN EMBARRASSED ROSENCRANTZ STRUGGLES TO DIG HIS WAY OUT OF HIS PREDICAMENT.

ROSENCRANTZ

My lord, I was thinking that if you take no delight from men, what dull entertainment the actors will be for you. We passed them on the way here, and they are coming to offer you their services

ROSENCRANTZ

To think, my lord, if you delight not in man what Lenten* entertainment the players shall receive from you. We coted* them on the way; and hither are they coming to offer you service.

> *Note: 'Lenten' – sparce, named from the fasting period of Lent, a period of forty days when no public theatres were allowed to perform plays, so they were performed in private during this period.
>
> 'Coted' meant overtook, pass-by or surpass. Derived from dog hunting.

HAMLET

The man who plays the king shall be welcome, his stateliness shall be paid my full respect.

HAMLET

He that plays the king shall be welcome; his majesty shall have tribute of me;*

> *Note: As opposed to the real King for whom Hamlet has no respect.

HAMLET (CONT'D)

The adventurous knight shall use his sword and shield, the lover shall have reason to sigh, the villain shall end his act without interruption, the comic shall make those whose lungs are tickled at nothing laugh, and the lady shall speak her mind freely, unless the blank verse is hesitant. Which actors are they?

HAMLET

...the adventurous knight shall use his foil and target; the lover shall not sigh gratis; the humorous man shall end his part in peace;* the clown shall make those laugh whose lungs are tickle o' th' sere;* and the lady shall say her mind freely, or the blank verse* shall halt for't. What players are they?

> *Note: 'End his part in peace' means the villain will not be heckled or booed off the stage as often happened.

> 'O' th' sere' – it loosely means 'hair trigger' – the slightest touch will set it off. The 'sere' was a mechanism to hold the firing pin back.

> Blank verse was how Shakespeare usually wrote (although the speech above is in prose), when written correctly it flows easily with a poetic rhythm when spoken.

ROSENCRANTZ

The same ones you used to take delight in. The actors of tragedies from the city.

ROSENCRANTZ

Even those you were wont to take such delight in, the tragedians of the city.*

> *Note: 'The city' meant City of London, though Hamlet is set in Denmark. This is Shakespeare's commentary on the state of the theatre in London at the time.

HAMLET

Why are they touring? Their resident theatre is better for both their reputation and profit.

ROSENCRANTZ

I think their theatre closed because of recent changes in trends.

HAMLET

Are they held in the same esteem as they were when I was in the city? Do they still have a good following?

ROSENCRANTZ

No, I'm afraid they do not.

HAMLET

How come? Did they grow stale?

ROSENCRANTZ

No, their endeavours are kept up at the same pace, but there is, sir, a nest of children, little chicks, that cry out at the top of their voices and are fanatically applauded for it. They are now all the rage, and belittle the common playhouses – as they call them – so much so, that many sword bearing gentlemen are now so afraid of writer's quills, they daren't go.

HAMLET

How chances it they travel? Their residence, both in reputation and profit, was better both ways.

ROSENCRANTZ

I think their inhibition comes by the means of the late innovation.

HAMLET

Do they hold the same estimation they did when I was in the city? Are they so followed?

ROSENCRANTZ

No, indeed, are they not.

HAMLET

How comes it? Do they grow rusty?

ROSENCRANTZ

Nay, their endeavour keeps in the wonted pace; but there is, sir, an eyrie* of children, little eyases,* that cry out on the top of question and are most tyrannically clapped for't. These are now the fashion, and so berattle the common stages* - so they call them - that many wearing rapiers are afraid of goose-quills, and dare scarce come thither.

> Note: 'Eyrie'- the nest of a bird of prey. 'Eyases' – young hawks taken from the nest for training. Yet another reference to falconry. It seems it was never far from Shakespeare's mind.

> 'Common stages' – 'common' was used as an insult, meaning lowly or lower class.

HAMLET

What? They are children? Who manages them? How are they funded? Will they be popular only until their voices break? If they grow up themselves to become 'common actors' - as is most likely as they'll have nothing left to offer – will they not say afterwards that the writers wronged them by making them sing out against their own future profession?

HAMLET

What, are they children? Who maintains 'em? How are they escoted? Will they pursue the quality no longer than they can sing? Will they not say afterwards, if they should grow themselves to common players - as it is most like, if their means are no better - their writers do them wrong to make them exclaim against their own succession?*

94

Note: This passage (not present in the earlier Quarto editions) is a jibe at the new popular singing children. They contributed to the older London playhouses having to close and go on tour to earn a living. The writers did indeed have the young boys (no girls or women allowed on stage) mock the 'common players' - lowering them to the class of street buskers – and it was Ben Johnson no less who wrote these slurs.

Queen Elizabeth signed a decree permitting children to be 'stolen' by theatre companies and forced to perform. They were often kidnapped on their way home from school and whipped if they didn't perform. Distraught parents could do nothing, and in one famous case a father tried to steal back his 13 year old son, Thomas Clifton, but was physically restrained. Troops of performing children were popular among predominantly male audiences, with dubious morals. Even Christopher Marlowe, a contemporary playwright, included one very dubious scene involving a boy in his play, Dido.

ROSENCRANTZ

Indeed, there's been much abuse on both sides, and the public sees fit to encourage productions to be controversial. There was a period when no theatre would buy a play unless it caused a fight between the writers and the playhouse actors.

ROSENCRANTZ

Faith, there has been much to-do on both sides, and the nation holds it no sin to tarre them to controversy. There was for a while no money bid for argument unless the poet and the player went to cuffs in the question.

HAMLET

How is this possible?

HAMLET

Is't possible?

GUILDENSTERN

Oh, there has been a great deal of heated debate on the subject.

GUILDENSTERN

O, there has been much throwing about of brains.

HAMLET

Do the boys come out the winners?

HAMLET

Do the boys carry it away?

ROSENCRANTZ

Yes, they do, my lord, even above the Globe theatre.

ROSENCRANTZ

Ay, that they do, my lord; Hercules and his load too.

Note: The Globe theatre was the home of Shakespeare's theatre company, and famously had the emblem of Hercules carrying a globe.

HAMLET

It doesn't surprise me, my uncle is King of Denmark, and those who made faces at him while my father was alive give twenty, forty, fifty, even a hundred ducats each for his miniature portrait. Streuth, there's something unnatural about all this, if only we could figure it out what it is.

HAMLET

It is not very strange; for my uncle is King of Denmark, and those that would make mouths at him while my father lived give twenty, forty, fifty, a hundred ducats* apiece for his picture in little. 'Sblood, there is something in this more than natural, if philosophy could find it out.

*Note: Ducats were gold coins common across Europe used as universal currency. Each country had their own design(s) but the value was the same. Each bore the inscription 'Sit tibi, Christe, datus Quem tu regis iste Ducatus', 'Lord, let this duchy which you rule be dedicated to you'.

A FLOURISH OF TRUMPETS HERALD THE ARRIVAL OF THE ACTORS TO THE CASTLE.

GUILDENSTERN

That will be the actors.

GUILDENSTERN

There are the players.

HAMLET

(to his two friends) Gentlemen, you are welcome here in Elsinore. Shake hands, come on. A welcome is not complete without the customary ceremony. Let me honour you in this fashion, in case my welcome to the actors, which I can tell you will be full and open, appears more enthusiastic than yours. You are welcome here. But my uncle-father and aunt-mother have been deceived.

HAMLET

Gentlemen, you are welcome to Elsinore. Your hands, come then. The appurtenance of welcome is fashion and ceremony. Let me comply with you in this garb, lest my extent to the players, which, I tell you, must show fairly outward, should more appear like entertainment than yours. You are welcome. But my uncle-father and aunt-mother are deceived.

GUILDENSTERN

In what way, my dear lord?

GUILDENSTERN

In what, my dear lord?

HAMLET

I'm only mad when the wind is nor-nor-westerly, when the wind is southerly, I know a hawk from a handsaw.

HAMLET

I am but mad north-north-west; when the wind is southerly I know a hawk* from a handsaw.*

Note: A hawk is the flat board a plasterer uses to carry plaster. The handsaw could have been a bird pun of hernshaw (heron) mistyped. Hamlet is saying he is only mad some of the time, in case he wants to persuade his friends to participate in a particular endeavour later, then he can switch to being sane.

RE-ENTER POLONIUS.

POLONIUS
Good health to you, gentlemen.

HAMLET
(*aside to his friends*) Listen, Guildenstern, and you too Rosencrantz, each lend me an ear – that great big baby you see there (*he nods towards Polonius*) is not yet out of diapers.

POLONIUS
Well be with you, gentlemen.

HAMLET
Hark you, Guildenstern, and you too - at each ear a hearer - that great baby you see there is not yet out of his swaddling clouts.*

Note: 'Swaddling clouts (clothes)' are those which babies were tightly wrapped in, preventing movement and keeping them warm and quiet so they could be left unattended while the parents worked. A practise not common these days.

ROSENCRANTZ
(*quietly*) Perhaps it's his second time around for them. They say an old man is a child twice.

HAMLET
(*quietly*) I'll wager he comes to tell me about the actors, you mark my words – (*aloud to his friends*) You are correct, sir, on Monday morning it was, yes indeed.

ROSENCRANTZ
Haply he's the second time come to them, for they say an old man is twice a child.

HAMLET
I will prophesy he comes to tell me of the players; mark it. - You say right, sir, a' Monday morning; 'twas then indeed.

POLONIUS
(*to Hamlet*) My lord, I have news for you.

HAMLET
My lord, I have news for *you*. When Roscius was an actor in Rome...

POLONIUS
My lord, I have news to tell you.

HAMLET
My lord, I have news to tell you. When Roscius* was an actor in Rome -

---

Note: Roscius was a famous actor in Roman times.

POLONIUS
(*interrupting Hamlet*) The actors are here now, my lord.

HAMLET
(*pretending it is a fly*) Buzz, buzz.

POLONIUS
The actors are come hither, my lord.

HAMLET
Buzz, buzz.*

Note: Buzz means latest trend/news etc, as in 'buzz word' but here Hamlet also makes the jibe that Polonius is like a fly annoyingly buzzing around him.

HAMLET SMILES AT HIS FRIENDS THAT HE WAS RIGHT.

POLONIUS
I swear it's true.

POLONIUS
Upon my honour.

HAMLET
(*dramatically quoting from a popular rhyme*) "Then came each actor on his ass."

HAMLET
Then came each actor on his ass.*

Note: Ass means donkey. In British English ass has never meant buttocks. It can be pronounced so it sounds like 'arse' which is buttocks in British English.

POLONIUS
(*referring to the actors*) They are the best actors in the world, whether in tragedy, comedy, history, religion, religious-comedy, historical-religion, trag-ical-history, tragical–comical–historical-religion, single act plays or unrestrained poetry. Seneca's plays not too weighty for them nor Plautus' too light. For traditional or contemporary works, these men are the best.

POLONIUS
The best actors in the world, either for tragedy, comedy, history, pastoral, pastoral-comical, historical-pastoral, tragical-historical, tragical-comical-historical-pastoral, scene individable, or poem unlimited. Seneca* cannot be too heavy, nor Plautus* too light. For the law of writ and the liberty, these are the only men.

Note: Lucius Annaeus SENECA, (4 bc – 65 ad), Roman statesman, philosopher, and dramatist. His 'Epistulae Morales' is a notable heavy-going, stoic work.

Titus Maccius PLAUTUS, (250–184 bc), Roman comic dramatist whose plays were based on Greek 'New Comedy'. The three forms of Ancient Greek theatre were Tragedy, Satyr and Comedy, the latter divided into three periods, Old, Middle and New Comedy.

Although Shakespeare had not studied classical literature at university, as was the norm for playwrights of his era, (he left school at 14), he had studied literature to a high level by today's standards at grammar school, and almost certainly carried on reading them after leaving school. It seems he wanted to demonstrate his knowledge of the classics in his works, both to silence his critics and because he must have been heavily influenced by them at a young age. He certainly 'borrowed' plots and themes from them.

HAMLET
(*reciting a line from a ballad*)
"Oh, Jephthah, judge of Israel, what a treasure you had!"

HAMLET
O Jephthah, judge of Israel, what a treasure hadst thou!

POLONIUS
What treasure did he have, my lord?

POLONIUS
What a treasure had he, my lord?

HAMLET

(reciting another line from the ballad)
Why, 'One fair daughter, and no more,
That he loved very well'.

HAMLET

Why, ` One fair daughter, and no more,
The which he loved passing well'. *

Note: The rhyme was a dig at Polonius. It is the line from a ballad of the time about the biblical story of Jephthah leading the Israelites in a battle against the Ammonites. On the eve of the battle, Jephthah vowed to God that if victory was his, he would offer as sacrifice the first person to enter his door to meet him after the battle. The first person to meet him was his daughter, his only child. He tells her of his vow. She tells him he has to keep his word with God, but asks that she can have two months to roam the mountains and lose her virginity. When she returns her father kept his word and killed her.

This story was Hamlet's way of saying that in a similar vein Polonius is using his only daughter selfishly to further his ambitions.

POLONIUS

(aside) Still on about my daughter.

POLONIUS

[*Aside.*] Still on my daughter.

HAMLET

Am I not right, old Jephthah?

HAMLET

Am I not i'th' right, old Jephthah?

POLONIUS

Since you call me Jephthah, my lord, I do have a daughter that I love very well.

POLONIUS

If you call me Jephthah, my lord, I have a
    daughter that I love passing well.

HAMLET

No, that doesn't follow.

HAMLET

Nay, that follows not.*

Note: A double meaning. Hamlet means that what Polonius says about his daughter is not correct, and that his words are not the next line in the verse.

POLONIUS

What does follow then, my lord?

POLONIUS

What follows then, my lord?

HAMLET

(reciting more from the ballad) Why,
'As by chance, God knows,' - and you know,
'It came to pass as it had to'.
The next verse of the pious ballad will tell you more, for look, my break has just arrived.

HAMLET

Why,
` As by lot, God wot,' and then you know,
` It came to pass as most like it was' -
The first row of the pious hanson will show you
    more, for look where my abridgement comes.

Note: The next verse (2 of 8) of the ballad is;
When Jepha was appointed now, / Chiefe captain of the company,
To God the Lord he made a vow, /If he might have the victory,
At his return to burn / For his offerings the first quick thing,
Should meet him then, / From his house when he came agen, agen

THE ACTORS MAKE AN ENTRANCE.

HAMLET (CONT'D)

Welcome, gentlemen, welcome to you all. (*shakes hands with one*) I am glad to see you well. (*to all*) Welcome, good friends! (*to a young man*) Oh, my old friend! You've grown a beard since I last saw you. Have you come to face me in Denmark as a man?

HAMLET

You are welcome, masters, welcome all. I am glad to see thee well. Welcome, good friends. O, my old friend! Thy face is valanced since I saw thee last; com'st thou to beard me in Denmark?*

Note: In Shakespeare's times, young men played the female parts in a play. It was illegal for women to act. As the actor now had a beard he was obviously no longer playing female parts.

HAMLET (CONT'D)

(*to a young, effeminate man*) What, my young lady and mistress! By my word, your ladyship is nearer to heaven than when I last saw you by the height of a woman's heel. I pray that your voice, like a counterfeit coin, is not broken and worthless.

HAMLET

What, my young lady and mistress! By'rlady, your ladyship is nearer heaven than when I saw you last by the altitude of a chopine.* Pray God your voice, like a piece of uncurrent gold, be not cracked within the ring.*

Note: 'Chopine' – blocks worn under ladies' shoes to raise their height. 'Nearer to heaven' – taller, and also older.

'Cracked within the ring' – Coins had an outer ring around an insert of the king's head. The outer edges would be shaved off to sell the precious metal and would often crack around the outer edge making them worthless. Counterfeit coins would also crack because they used cheap, inferior metal.

HAMLET (CONT'D)

(*to all*) Gentlemen, you are all welcome. Like French falconers we'll not be choosy and have a go at anything we please. Let's have a speech right away. Come, give us a taste of your skills. Come on, a passionate speech.

HAMLET

Masters, you are all welcome. We'll e'en to't like French falconers, fly at anything we see. We'll have a speech straight. Come, give us a taste of your quality. Come, a passionate speech.

Note: French falconers were reputedly less choosy over the prey they set their birds upon.

1ST ACTOR

Which speech, my good lord?

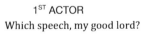

1ST PLAYER

What speech, my good lord?

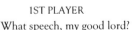

HAMLET

I heard you recite a speech once, but the play was never performed, or if it was, not more than once. As I recall it was not a play for the masses, like caviar it was only for the connoisseur. But it was - in my opinion, and of those whose judgement in such things is better than mine - an excellent play, with well constructed scenes, and written with equal measures of cunning and restraint. I remember one critic said there was no seasoning in the lines to add spice to the substance, and no substance in the wording to suggest any pretention by the author, he called it an honest style, sweetly wholesome, plain rather than extravagant. One speech in it I particularly liked – it was Aeneas' tale to Dido, and within that especially when he speaks of Priam's slaughter. If it lives in your memory, begin at this line: - let me see now, let me see: (*trying to recall it*)

HAMLET

I heard thee speak me a speech once, but it was never acted, or, if it was, not above once; for the play, I remember, leased not the million; 'twas caviare to the general. But it was - as I received it, and others whose judgements in such matters cried in the top of mine - an excellent play, well digested in the scenes, set down with as much modesty as cunning. I remember one said there were no sallets in the lines to make the matter savoury, nor no matter in the phrase that might indict the author of affectation, but called it an honest method, as wholesome as sweet, and by very much more handsome than fine. One speech in it I chiefly loved - 'twas Aeneas'* tale to Dido, and thereabout of it especially when he speaks of Priam's* slaughter. If it live in your memory, begin at this line: - let me see, let me see:

*Note: Hamlet refers to a story of the sacking of Troy as told by Aeneas to Queen Dido in the epic poem The Aeneid by Virgil

Priam was the legendary king of Troy during the Trojan war. He was father of Hector and Paris. Hecuba was his wife. Paris had abducted Helen, wife of the King of Sparta. The war was in order to rescue her.

HAMLET (CONT'D)

"*The rugged Pyrrhus, like the Hycranian tiger*" –

No that's wrong, it begins with Pyrrhus –

HAMLET

"*The rugged Pyrrhus,* * like th' Hyrcanian beast*"* - 'tis not so; it begins with Pyrrhus -

HE PAUSES, ATTEMPTING TO REMEMBER THE LINES.

*Note: Pyrrhus, son of Achilles, was one of the Greeks hidden in the legendary wooden Trojan Horse. He killed and butchered Priam, King of Troy.

'Hycranian Beast' was a tiger from Arcania also referred to in The Aeneid.

HAMLET (CONT'D)

"The rugged Pyrrhus, with black armour, black as his intentions, resembling the night, lies in wait in the ominous Trojan horse. And more dreadful than this fearful black appearance, his body smeared head to foot completely red, horribly painted with the blood of fathers, mothers, daughters and sons, baked into a paste on the burning streets that now shine a cruel damning light towards their ruler's murder. In this manner, ablaze in wrath and fire, smeared with coagulated gore, and eyes like fiery red gems, the hellish Pyrrhus seeks old grandfather Priam."
- So, you carry on from there.

HAMLET

"The rugged Pyrrhus, he whose sable arms,
Black as his purpose, did the night resemble
When he lay couched in the ominous horse,
Hath now this dread and black complexion smeared
With heraldry more dismal; head to foot
Now is he total gules,* horridly tricked
With blood of fathers, mothers, daughters, sons,
Baked and impasted with the parching streets,
That lend a tyrannous and a damned light
To their lord's murder.* Roasted in wrath and fire,
And thus o'ersized with coagulate gore,
With eyes like carbuncles, the hellish Pyrrhus
Old grandsire Priam seeks."
So, proceed you.

*Note: 'Gules' is the colour red in heraldry.

"To their lord's murder" – early versions used 'vile murder' which makes sense of the blood belonging to the murdered victims. The use of 'Lord's' suggests a different meaning, the light from burning streets (the Grecian army set the streets on fire) lights the way towards the ruler's murder (King Priam), which is mentioned shortly. Most editions now use 'lord's murder'.

POLONIUS

Before God, my lord, that was well spoken, with good diction and good delivery.

POLONIUS

Fore God, my lord, well spoken, with good accent and good discretion.

1ST ACTOR

(continuing) "Before long he finds him, striking harmlessly at Greeks; his aged sword, rebelling against his frail arm, falls and lies on the ground, refusing to obey. Unfairly matched, young Pyrrhus charges at old Priam. In a rage his strike misses; but at the flailing wind of his fierce-some sword, the weakened father falls. Then the unfeeling tower of Ilium, seeming to sense this blow, all aflame crashes to its foundations with such a hideous crash it deafens and stuns Pyrrhus. Suddenly, his sword, which was descending on the grey haired head of righteous Priam, seemed to stick in the air."

1ST PLAYER

"Anon he finds him
Striking too short at Greeks; his antique sword,
Rebellious to his arm, lies where it falls,
Repugnant to command. Unequal matched,
Pyrrhus at Priam drives, in rage strikes wide;
But with the whiff and wind of his fell sword
Th' unnerved father falls. Then senseless Ilium,*
Seeming to feel this blow, with flaming top
Stoops to his base, and with a hideous crash
Takes prisoner Pyrrhus' ear; for lo, his sword,
Which was declining on the milky head
Of reverend Priam, seemed i'th' air to stick;"

Note: Illium is the Latin name for Troy.

The famous Trojan Horse was constructed to conceal a small number of warriors. Sinon delivered the horse inside the gates of Troy. At nightfall the warriors escaped the horse through a trapdoor, unlocked the city gates and let the Grecian army into Troy to sack the city and rescue Helen (of Troy).

1ST ACTOR (CONT'D)

"So, like a painting of a tyrant, Pyrrhus stood, and, powerless in will and body, did nothing. But like the often seen silence in the heavens before the storm, with the sky stood still, the bold winds silent, and the earth below as quiet as a grave, before the dreadful thunder comes to tear apart the air, likewise, after Pyrrhus' pause, a newly roused vengeance set upon him; and never did the Cyclops' hammers fall on Mars's armour, forged for everlasting strength, with less mercy than the blood stained sword of Pyrrhus then fell on Priam.

Out, out, you whore, Fortune! All you gods combine and remove her power. Break all the spokes and rims of her wheel, and bowl the round hub down the hill from heaven, all the way down to hell!"

1ST PLAYER

"So, as a painted tyrant, Pyrrhus stood, And, like a neutral to his will and matter, Did nothing.

But as we often see against some storm A silence in the heavens, the rack stand still, The bold winds speechless, and the orb below As hush as death, anon the dreadful thunder Doth rend the region; so, after Pyrrhus' pause, A roused vengeance sets him new a-work; And never did the Cyclops'* hammers fall On Mars's* armour, forged for proof eterne, With less remorse than Pyrrhus' bleeding sword Now falls on Priam.

Out, out, thou strumpet, Fortune!* All you gods In general synod take away her power, Break all the spokes and fellies from her wheel, * And bowl the round nave down the hill of heaven As low as to the fiends!"

Note: Cyclops giants were the legendary makers of armour and arms for the gods in Vulcan's smithy. (Smithy is a blacksmith's workshop). Mars was the god of war.

Fortune – The Goddess of luck and chance had a wheel she turned, people on one side were on the way up, the other side were on the way down. Up or down on their luck. Breaking her wheel would take away any luck from a person.

POLONIUS

This is too long.

POLONIUS

This is too long.

HAMLET

It shall visit the hairdresser, along with your beard.

(to Actor 1) Please go on. He likes a jig, or a bawdy tale, or he falls asleep. Go on, get to Hecuba.

HAMLET

It shall to th' barber's, with your beard. Prithee say on. He's for a jig or a tale of bawdry, or he sleeps. Say on, come to Hecuba.*

---

*Note: Hecuba was the wife of Priam, mother of Hector, Troilus and Cassandra in Homer's Iliad. Hamlet has a reason he wants to get to the widowed wife part.

1ST ACTOR

"But whoever, oh, whoever saw the muffled queen...

1ST PLAYER

"But who, O who had seen the mobled* queen -"

---

*Note: 'Mobled' likely means 'muffled' - wrapped up and silenced.

HAMLET

(interrupting) "The muffled queen"?

HAMLET

`The mobled queen.'

POLONIUS

That's all right. 'muffled queen' is good.

POLONIUS

That's good, `mobled queen' is good.

1ST ACTOR

"...Running barefoot up and down, threatening to extinguish the flames with her blinding tears, a cloth upon that head where of late the crown had sat, and for a robe, a blanket around her thin, and overworked childbearing loins, hastily grabbed in the panic of fear: - Whosoever saw this, would have cried 'treason' with a venomous tongue against the state Fortune had left her in. But if the gods themselves did see her then, as she saw the malicious attack Pyrrhus made with his sword, mutilating her husband's limbs, and they had heard the instant mournful wailing she made, unless mortal matters do not move them, it would have doused even the burning stars in the heavens with tears, and raised sorrow even in the gods."

1ST PLAYER

"Run barefoot up and down, threat'ning the flames
With bisson rheum, a clout upon that head
Where late the diadem stood, and for a robe,
About her lank and all o'erteemed loins, *
A blanket, in th' alarm of fear caught up: -
Who this had seen, with tongue in venom steeped
Gainst Fortune's* state would treason have
    pronounced;
But if the gods themselves did see her then,
When she saw Pyrrhus make malicious sport
In mincing with his sword her husband's limbs, *
The instant burst of clamour that she made,
Unless things mortal move them not at all,
Would have made milch the burning eyes of heaven,
And passion in the gods."

HE SPEAKS WITH SUCH PASSION TEARS STREAM DOWN HIS FACE.

> **Note: According to legend, Hecuba bore most of her husband, Priam's, fifty sons. Hence o'oerteemed (overworked) loins.*
>
> *'Fortune' - The Goddess of luck's wheel. See earlier note.*
>
> *Christopher Marlowe (a playwright and suspected spy, who some think wrote Shakespeare's plays even though he was murdered in a pub brawl before most were written) wrote in his play, 'Dido, Queen of Carthage', that Pyrrhus cut off Priam's hands before killing him. Shakespeare made a number of references to Marlowe's work and was greatly influenced by him.*

POLONIUS
Look, can't you see he has turned pale, and has tears in his eyes? Please, no more.

HAMLET
(*to actor*) That's fine. I'll have you speak the rest of this soon.
(*to Polonius*) My good lord, will you see the players are settled in? Do you hear? – Let them be well cared for, for they are the observers and chroniclers of our time. It is better to have a bad epitaph after your death than their bad account while you live.

POLONIUS
My lord, I will treat them as they deserve.

HAMLET
For God's sake, man! Treat them better. Treat every man as he deserves and who'd escape a flogging? Treat them as you would someone of your own honour and dignity; if they deserve less, then the more the balance goes in your favour. See to them.

POLONIUS
Look, whe'er he has not turned his colour, and has tears in's eyes. Prithee no more.

HAMLET
'Tis well; I'll have thee speak out the rest of this soon. [*To Polonius.*] Good my lord, will you see the players well estowed? Do you hear? – let them be well used, for they are the abstract and brief chronicles of the time. After your death you were better have a bad epitaph than their ill report while you live.

POLONIUS
My lord, I will use them according to their desert.

HAMLET
God's bodykins,* man, much better. Use every man after his desert, and who should 'scape whipping? Use them after your own honour and dignity; the less they deserve, the more merit is in your bounty. Take them in.

> **Note: 'God's bodykins' was a mild term of exclamation of the time, meaning the body of Christ, kin being his son, Jesus Christ.*

POLONIUS
(*to actors*) Come, sirs.

POLONIUS
Come, sirs.

EXIT POLONIUS, THE OTHER ACTORS START TO FOLLOW.

HAMLET

Follow him, friends. We'll hear a play tomorrow.

(*to 1st Actor*) Did you hear me, my friend, can you play the *Murder of Gonzago*?

1ST ACTOR

Yes, my lord.

HAMLET

We'll have it tomorrow night. You could, for a reason I have, learn a speech of some dozen or so lines which I will write down and insert them in it, could you not?

1ST ACTOR

Yes, my lord.

HAMLET

Very good. Follow that gentleman, and try not to mock him.

HAMLET

Follow him, friends. We'll hear a play tomorrow.

[*To 1st Player.*] Dost thou hear me, old friend; can you play the Murder of Gonzago?

1ST PLAYER

Ay, my lord.

HAMLET

We'll ha't tomorrow night. You could, for a need, study a speech of some dozen or sixteen lines which I would set down and insert in't, could you not?

1ST PLAYER

Ay, my lord.

HAMLET

Very well. Follow that lord, and look you mock him not.

EXEUNT ACTORS FOLLOWING POLONIUS.

HAMLET TURNS TO ROSENCRANTZ AND GUILDENSTERN.

HAMLET (CONT'D)

(*to R & G*) My good friends, I'll leave you now until this evening. You are most welcome in Elsinore.

ROSENCRANTZ

Very good, my lord!

HAMLET

Yes, so, goodbye to you.

HAMLET

My good friends, I'll leave you till night. You are welcome to Elsinore.

ROSENCRANTZ

Good my lord!

HAMLET

Ay, so, God-buy* to you.

Note: 'God-buy', means 'Goodbye' which is short for 'God be with you'.

EXEUNT ROSENCRANTZ AND GUILDENSTERN.

HAMLET NOW RECITES HIS 3RD SOLILOQUY.

HE REVERTS TO BLANK VERSE.

HAMLET (CONT'D)

Now I am alone. Oh, what a rogue and worthless being I am! Is it not monstrous that this actor here, in a work of fiction, in pretend passion, could force his emotions from his own imagination to the point he was so overwhelmed his face paled, with real tears in his eyes, distress in his face, a breaking voice, his whole performance matching the depths of his imagination? And all for nothing! ... No, for Hecuba!

What is Hecuba to him, or him to Hecuba, that he should weep for her? What would he do if he had the motive and the reason for grief that I have? He would drown the stage with tears and destroy people's ears with heart-breaking speeches, drive the guilty insane, appal the innocent, bewilder the ignorant, and make ears and eyes doubt their reasoning. Yet I, a spiritless, miserable rascal, mope around in a sleepy daze, lacking in cause, saying nothing, not a thing, not even for the king whose property and dear life was most foully taken. Am I a coward? Who is calling me a villain, breaking my head in two, plucking off my beard and blowing it in my face, tweaking me by the nose and calling me a liar to my face, a liar of the worst kind? Has anyone? Ha! Streuth, I'd have to take it though, for it can only be that I am lily-livered and lack the guts to stand up to bitter criticism, because before this I would have fattened all this country's vultures with that villain's entrails. Bloody, lewd bastard! Remorseless, treacherous, lecherous, unfeeling bastard! Oh, vengeance!

HAMLET

Now I am alone.

O, what a rogue and peasant slave am I!
Is it not monstrous that this player here,
But in a fiction, in a dream of passion,
Could force his soul so to his own conceit
That from her working all this visage wanned,
Tears in his eyes, distraction in's aspect,
A broken voice, and his whole function suiting
With forms to his conceit? And all for nothing!
For Hecuba!
What's Hecuba to him, or he to Hecuba,
That he should weep for her? What would he do
Had he the motive and the cue for passion
That I have? He would drown the stage with tears
And cleave the general ear with horrid speech,
Make mad the guilty, and appal the free,
Confound the ignorant, and amaze indeed
The very faculties of eyes and ears. Yet I,
A dull and muddy-mettled rascal, peak
Like John-a-dreams, unpregnant of my cause,
And can say nothing - no, not for a king
Upon whose property* and most dear life
A damned defeat was made. Am I a coward?
Who calls me villain, breaks my pate across,
Plucks off my beard and blows it in my face,
Tweaks me by th' nose, gives me the lie i'th'
  throat
As deep as to the lungs?* Who does me this?
Ha! 'Swounds, I should take it; for it cannot be
But I am pigeon-livered,* and lack gall
To make oppression bitter, or ere this
I should-a fatted all the region kites*
With this slave's offal. Bloody, bawdy villain!
Remorseless, treacherous, lecherous, kindless
  villain!
Oh, vengeance!

*Note: 'Property' cruelly taken refers to the old King of Denmark's crown and his wife. In Shakespeare's age a wife was considered a husband's property.

HAMLET PAUSES, TAKING STOCK OF HIS SITUATION.

Note: 'Lie i'th throat as deep as the lungs' – the lowest level of lie, from 'you lie', to 'you lie in the throat' to the deepest lie which is in the lungs.

'Pigeon-livered' – The pigeon in this saying is the dove, symbol of peace, and considered weak because it secreted no gall. lily-livered is a similar term in use today also meaning weak and cowardly.

A 'Kite' is a bird of prey which feeds on dead meat. A barbaric punishment of the time was to remove the victim's entrails while he was still alive and throw it to the birds to eat. Though there were no vultures in Denmark it is a bird everyone associates with eating dead bodies so has been used here.

HAMLET (CONT'D)

Why, what an ass I am! How brave of me, that I, the son of a dear murdered father, urged to seek revenge by heaven and hell, instead, like a whore expose my feelings only in words, and lower myself to cursing like a common slut, a skivvy! A curse upon it! Pah! (*he pauses again, gathering himself*)

I must gather my thoughts. Hmm... I have heard that guilty people attending a play have been struck by the power of the performance so deeply to the core they have immediately confessed their crimes. Because murder, though it has no tongue, will speak via the most miraculous means. I'll have these actors act out something like the murder of my father in front of my uncle. I'll watch how he reacts, scrutinise him minutely. If he flinches, I'll know my course of action. The ghost I've seen may be a devil in disguise, the devil has the power to assume any pleasing shape. Yes, and perhaps taking advantage of my weakness and sadness, he uses a ghost with powerful cunning to trick me and damn my soul.

I will need better proof, so with a play,
The conscience of a king I'll trap this way.

HAMLET

Why, what an ass am I! This is most brave,
That I, the son of a dear father murdered,
Prompted to my revenge by heaven and hell,
Must like a whore unpack my heart with words,
And fall a-cursing like a very drab,
A scullion! Fie upon't! Foh!
About, my brains. Hum, I have heard
That guilty creatures sitting at a play
Have, by the very cunning of the scene,
Been struck so to the soul that presently
They have proclaimed their malefactions;
For murder, though it have no tongue, will speak
With most miraculous organ. I'll have these
  players
Play something like the murder of my father
Before mine uncle. I'll observe his looks,
I'll tent him to the quick. If he do blench,
I know my course. The spirit that I have seen
May be a devil, and the devil hath power
T' assume a pleasing shape; yea, and perhaps
Out of my weakness and my melancholy,
As he is very potent with such spirits,
Abuses me to damn me. I'll have grounds
*More relative than this. The play's the thing**
Wherein I'll catch the conscience of the king.

Note: Hamlet worries the devil is tricking him into killing an innocent man and so damning his soul to hell. Or he is finding excuses not to do the deed.

ACT III

THE PLAY'S THE THING

ACT III

ACT III SCENE I

A ROOM IN THE CASTLE.

THE KING, QUEEN, POLONIUS, AND OPHELIA ARE PRESENT.

THE KING IS QUESTIONING ROSENCRANTZ AND GUILDENSTERN.

KING CLAUDIUS And you can not by hints of conversation get from him why he seems so distracted, why his peace is disturbed so harshly each day with wild and unsettling lunacy?	**KING** And can you by no drift of circumstance Get from him why he puts on this confusion, Grating so harshly all his days of quiet With turbulent and dangerous lunacy?
ROSENCRANTZ He does confess to feeling distracted in himself, but we cannot get the cause from him by any means.	**ROSENCRANTZ** He does confess he feels himself distracted, But from what cause a' will by no means speak.
GUILDENSTERN Nor do we find him open to being questioned, instead, with the cunning of a madman he avoids the subject when we enquire as to the true cause of his condition.	**GUILDENSTERN** Nor do we find him forward to be sounded, But, with a crafty madness, keeps aloof When we would bring him on to some confession Of his true state.
QUEEN GERTRUDE Was he pleased to see you?	**QUEEN** Did he receive you well?
ROSENCRANTZ He greeted us like a gentleman.	**ROSENCRANTZ** Most like a gentleman.
GUILDENSTERN But with great effort to restrain his condition.	**GUILDENSTERN** But with much forcing of his disposition.
ROSENCRANTZ Short in conversation, but he freely replied to our questions.	**ROSENCRANTZ** Niggard of question, but of our demands Most free in his reply.

Note: This is the very opposite of what occurred.

QUEEN GERTRUDE
Did you convince him to join you in any activities?

QUEEN
Did you assay him
To any pastime?

ROSENCRANTZ
Madam, it so happened that we overtook some actors on the way here, which we told him about, and he did seem to show some excitement to hear of them. They are here in court, and, so I believe, have already been ordered to perform for him tonight.

ROSENCRANTZ
Madam, it so fell out that certain players
We o'erraught on the way; of these we told him,
And there did seem in him a kind of joy
To hear of it. They are here about the court,
And, as I think, they have already order
This night to play before him.

POLONIUS
I can confirm it's true. And he begged me to invite your majesties to hear and see their performance.

POLONIUS
'Tis most true,
And he beseeched me to entreat your majesties
To hear and see the matter.

KING CLAUDIUS
With all my heart I'd go, and it does greatly comfort me to hear him find an interest in something. Good gentlemen, give him a helping hand and encourage him in this pursuit.

KING
With all my heart; and it doth much content me
To hear him so inclined.
Good gentlemen, give him a further edge,
And drive his purpose into these delights.

ROSENCRANTZ
We shall, my lord.

ROSENCRANTZ
We shall, my lord.

THE KING BECKONS THEM TO LEAVE.

EXIT ROSENCRANTZ AND GUILDENSTERN.

KING CLAUDIUS
Sweet Gertrude, leave us too, I have secretly sent for Hamlet to be here so that he may meet Ophelia as if by accident.
Her father and I, as justifiable spies, shall hide, so that unseen we may judge for ourselves their encounter and ascertain by his behaviour if the affliction he suffers is caused by his love or not.

KING
Sweet Gertrude, leave us too,
For we have closely sent for Hamlet hither,
That he, as 'twere by accident, may here
Affront Ophelia.
Her father and myself, lawful espials,
Will so bestow ourselves that, seeing unseen,
We may of their encounter frankly judge,
And gather by him, as he is behaved,
If't be th' affliction of his love or no
That thus he suffers for.

QUEEN GERTRUDE
I will do as you ask.
(*to Ophelia*) And for your part, Ophelia, I do hope your beauty is the happy cause of Hamlet's madness, and I also hope your goodness will bring him round to his old ways again, to the benefit of you both.

OPHELIA
Madam, I hope so too.

QUEEN
I shall obey you.
And for your part, Ophelia, I do wish
That your good beauties be the happy cause
Of Hamlet's wildness; so shall I hope your virtues
Will bring him to his wonted way again,
To both your honours.

OPHELIA
Madam, I wish it may.

QUEEN GERTRUDE LEAVES THE ROOM.

POLONIUS GUIDES OPHELIA TO A GOOD VANTAGE POINT FOR HIM TO OVERHEAR HER CONVERSATION WITH HAMLET.

POLONIUS
Ophelia, come stand here.
(*to the King*) Your majesty, if you please, we will secrete ourselves.
(*to Ophelia*) Here, read this prayer book, a show of such activity may excuse your being alone.

POLONIUS
Ophelia, walk you here. - Gracious, so please you,
We will bestow ourselves. - Read on this book,
That show of such an exercise may colour
Your loneliness.

POLONIUS HANDS OPHELIA A PRAYER BOOK.

POLONIUS (CONT'D)
(*to the King*) We are often to blame in such matters, as has been much proven, behind our façade of devotion and sincere behaviour we could sugar over the acts of the devil himself.

POLONIUS
We are oft to blame in this:
'Tis too much proved that with devotion's visage
And pious action we do sugar o'er
The devil himself.

KING CLAUDIUS
(*aside*) Oh, it's so true! How stinging a lash that speech gives my conscience. The harlot's cheek, beautified with make-up, is no more ugly behind the powder that hides it, than my deed which hides behind my falsely painted words. Oh, what a heavy burden!

KING
[*Aside.*] O, 'tis too true!
How smart a lash that speech doth give my conscience.
The harlot's cheek, beautied with plast'ring art,
Is not more ugly to the thing that helps it
Than is my deed to my most painted word.
O heavy burden!

POLONIUS
I hear him coming! Let's hide, my lord.

POLONIUS
I hear him coming. Let's withdraw, my lord.

THE KING AND POLONIUS CONCEAL THEMSELVES.

HAMLET

To live, or not to live, that is the question. Is it nobler for the conscience to endure the stones and arrows thrown by dreadful fate, or to take up arms against a sea of troubles and by fighting them stop them? To die is to sleep, nothing more, and if by sleep we mean ending the heartache and the thousand worries that man is a slave to, it's an end whole-heartedly to be wished for. To die, to sleep; to sleep, perhaps to dream. Yes, there's the catch, for in that sleep of death whatever dreams may come to us when we have left the turmoil of life gives us pause to think. That's the fear that makes us suffer so long a life, for who would suffer the pains and abuse that come with time; the tyrant's wrongdoing, the arrogant man's insults, the pains of unrequited love, the delay of legal recourse, the insolence of bureaucracy, and the insults the innocent man has to patiently endure when he could just end his problems with a simple dagger? Who would bear these burdens, to groan and sweat through a weary life, if not for the dread of something after death, that undiscovered territory from whose clutches no traveller returns, it confounds the resolve, and makes us suffer those pains we have rather than flee to others we know nothing of? So, our conscience makes cowards of us all, and the normal radiance of strength is sullied with the pale hue of overthinking, and with this mindset, enterprises of great urgency and importance divert their streams off course and all direction is lost.

HAMLET

To be, or not to be, that is the question:
Whether 'tis nobler in the mind to suffer
The slings and arrows of outrageous fortune,
Or to take arms against a sea of troubles
And by opposing end them. To die - to sleep,
No more; and by a sleep to say we end
The heartache and the thousand natural shocks
That flesh is heir to. 'Tis a consummation
Devoutly to be wished. To die, to sleep;
To sleep, perchance to dream. Ay, there's the
  rub;*
For in that sleep of death what dreams may come
When we have shuffled off this mortal coil
Must give us pause. There's the respect
That makes calamity of so long life,
For who would bear the whips and scorns of
  time,
Th' oppressor's wrong, the proud man's
  contumely,
The pangs of disprized love, the law's delay,
The insolence of office, and the spurns
That patient merit of th' unworthy takes,
When he himself might his quietus make
With a bare bodkin? Who would these fardels
  bear,
To grunt and sweat under a weary life,
But that the dread of something after death,
The undiscovered country from whose bourn
No traveller returns*, puzzles the will,
And makes us rather bear those ills we have
Than fly to others that we know not of?
Thus conscience does make cowards of us all,
And thus the native hue of resolution
Is sicklied o'er with the pale cast of thought,
And enterprises of great pith and moment
With this regard their currents turn awry
And lose the name of action.

Note: Shakespeare would often include extracts from classics he studied at school. The phrase 'The undiscovered country... no traveller returns' is lifted from Virgil's 'Aenead'.

'The rub' is from lawn bowling, being the lay of the grass and how it deflects the ball from traveling in a direct line, known as the rub of the green. Here he means 'obstacle' or 'catch' in the path of the decision.

HAMLET (CONT'D)

(*aside, seeing Ophelia reading*) Thoughts be quiet, it's the beautiful Ophelia!

(*to Ophelia*) Young lady, in your prayers remember to include my sins.

HAMLET

Soft you now,
The fair Ophelia! Nymph, in thy orisons
Be all my sins remembered.

OPHELIA

Very good, my lord, and how is your honourable self these days?

OPHELIA

Good my lord,
How does your honour for this many a day?

HAMLET

I humbly thank you, I'm well, well, well.

HAMLET

I humbly thank you, well, well, well.

OPHELIA

My lord, I have keepsakes of yours I have been wanting to return for some time, I trust you will now take them back.

OPHELIA

My lord, I have remembrances of yours
That I have longed long to re-deliver;
I pray you now receive them.

HAMLET

No, not I, I never gave you anything.

HAMLET

No, not I;
I never gave you aught.

OPHELIA

My honourable lord, you know very well you did, and with them were words composed with such sweet breath they made the items more precious. Their perfume has now faded. Take them back, for to the honourable mind, rich gifts are made poor when givers prove to be untrue. There, my lord.

OPHELIA

My honoured lord, you know right well you did,
And with them words of so sweet breath
  composed
As made these things more rich. Their perfume
  lost,
Take these again; for to the noble mind
Rich gifts wax poor when givers prove unkind.
There, my lord.

OPHELIA OFFERS LETTERS.
HAMLET WAVES THEM AWAY.

HAMLET

Ha, ha! Are you pure?

HAMLET

Ha, ha! Are you honest?*

Note: 'Honest' also meant 'chaste' or a 'virgin'. Hence Ophelia's shock.

OPHELIA
(*shocked*) My lord?

HAMLET
Are you beautifully good?

OPHELIA
My lord?

HAMLET
Are you fair?*

> *Note: 'Fair' means both beautiful and honourable. Again this is deliberate double meaning which could be referring to her virginity or her beauty.*

OPHELIA
What does your lordship mean?

HAMLET
If you are pure and beautiful, your purity should prevent access to your beauty.

OPHELIA
What means your lordship?

HAMLET
That if you be honest and fair, your honesty should admit no discourse to your beauty.

OPHELIA
Wouldn't beauty, my lord, have better value if coupled with purity?

HAMLET
Yes, truly, because the power of beauty would sooner convert purity into sinfulness, than the power of purity would convert beauty into innocence. This was once contrary to belief, but present circumstances proves it is true. I did love you once.

OPHELIA
Could beauty, my lord, have better commerce than with honesty?

HAMLET
Ay, truly, for the power of beauty will sooner transform honesty from what it is to a bawd than the force of honesty can translate beauty into his likeness. This was sometime a paradox, but now the time gives it proof.* I did love you once.

> *Note: The 'paradox' now proved true is a reference to his mother. She was beautiful and honest once but her beauty attracted Claudius, so her beauty corrupted her and now Hamlet has lost all love for her.*

OPHELIA
Indeed, my lord, so you led me to believe.

HAMLET
You should not have believed me, purity does not quell our sinful desires, it makes us want to relish in them. It was not love I had for you.

OPHELIA
I was certainly deceived.

OPHELIA
Indeed, my lord, you made me believe so.

HAMLET
You should not have believed me, for virtue cannot so inoculate our old stock but we shall relish of it. I loved you not.

OPHELIA
I was the more deceived.

115

HAMLET

Go live in a nunnery. Why would you want to bear sinners? I am reasonably moral, but I could accuse myself of faults that would make it better if my mother hadn't had me. I am very proud, vindictive, ambitious, with more crimes I have in mind than I have the mind to store them, or the imagination to plan them, or the time to put them into action. What right should a man such as I have to crawl upon this earth? We men are utter scoundrels. Believe none of us. Take yourself to a nunnery. Where's your father?

HAMLET

Get thee to a nunnery.* Why wouldst thou be a breeder of sinners? I am myself indifferent honest, but yet I could accuse me of such things that it were better my mother had not borne me: I am very proud, revengeful, ambitious, with more offences at my beck than I have thoughts to put them in, imagination to give them shape, or time to act them in. What should such fellows as I do crawling between heaven and earth? We are arrant knaves, all. Believe none of us. Go thy ways to a nunnery. Where's your father?

> *Note: 'Nunnery' was also slang for a whorehouse (being a house full of women) so Hamlet is playing on that pun.
>
> It is possible that Hamlet suspects her father or the King are eavesdropping. Remember the King had said earlier he had secretly summoned Hamlet so he would meet Ophelia as if by accident. Reading the meeting with Ophelia with this in mind makes a different sense of Hamlet's words.

OPHELIA

At home, my lord.

OPHELIA

At home, my lord.

HAMLET

Let the doors be locked so he can play the fool only in his own house. Farewell.

HAMLET

Let the doors be shut upon him, that he may play the fool nowhere but in's own house. Farewell.*

> *Note: Hamlet says farewell three times, each time turning to say more as he walks away.

OPHELIA

(upset at the madness) Oh, sweet heavens, help him!

OPHELIA

O, help him, you sweet heavens!

HAMLET

If you do marry, I'll give you this thought to plague you as a wedding gift; be as cold as ice, as pure as snow, and you will still not avoid malicious gossip. Get yourself to a nunnery, go, farewell. Or if you have to marry, marry a fool. For wise men know very well what fools you make of them by cheating. To the nunnery, go, and quickly. Farewell.

HAMLET

If thou dost marry, I'll give thee this plague for thy dowry: be thou as chaste as ice, as pure as snow, thou shalt not escape calumny. Get thee to a nunnery, go, farewell. Or, if thou wilt needs marry, marry a fool; for wise men know well enough what monsters* you make of them. To a nunnery, go, and quickly too. Farewell.

Note: Hamlet is suggesting that a beautiful woman is more likely to cheat on her husband, her beauty tempting other men. And even if she didn't, others jealous of her beauty would make up stories to damage her reputation.

Making monsters of men alludes to the myth that horns grew out of the head of men whose wives were unfaithful to them.

OPHELIA
Oh, may the heavens cure him!

HAMLET
I've heard about your make-up too, you women. God has given you one face and you make yourselves another. You wiggle, you waddle, you put on fancy accents, you call people cute names, and pretend ignorance of your wanton display. Go, I'll have no more of it, it makes me mad. I say we should stop all marriages. Those that are already married – all except one – shall live on, the rest shall stay as they are. To a nunnery, go!

OPHELIA
O heavenly powers, restore him!

HAMLET
I have heard of your paintings, too, well enough. God hath given you one face and you make yourselves another. You jig, you amble, and you lisp, and nickname God's creatures, and make your wantonness your ignorance. Go to, I'll no more on't; it hath made me mad. I say we will have no more marriage. Those that are married already - all but one* - shall live, the rest shall keep as they are. To a nunnery, go.

Note: 'All but one', meaning all but his mother's marriage, he says 'live' instead of 'stay the same' or 'carry on', another dig about his late father and about wanting revenge by killing the king.

HAMLET FINALLY DOES LEAVE.

OPHELIA
(*aside*) Oh, what a noble mind has been destroyed! The regal looks, educated tongue, top swordsmanship, the hope and glory of being head of state, the leader of fashion, perfection in body, the one to be looked up to - utterly, utterly fallen! And I, the most dejected and wretched of women, who fed on the sweet music of his vows of love, now see his noble and regal reasoning is tuneless, like sweet sounding bells ringing out of time. That unrivalled figure and quality of youth in full bloom destroyed by madness.
Oh, such a great loss, how sad it makes me,
To see what I've seen, and now see what I see!

OPHELIA
O what a noble mind is here o'erthrown!
The courtier's, soldier's, scholar's, eye, tongue, sword,
Th' expectancy and rose of the fair state,
The glass of fashion and the mould of form,
Th' observed of all observers, quite, quite down!
And I, of ladies most deject and wretched,
That sucked the honey of his music vows,
Now see that noble and most sovereign reason
Like sweet bells jangled out of time, and harsh,
That unmatched form and feature of blown youth
Blasted with ecstasy. O, woe is me,
T' have seen what I have seen, see what I see!

THE KING AND POLONIUS EMERGE FROM THEIR CONCEALMENT.

KING CLAUDIUS

Love! His affections do not lie in that direction, and though it lacked sense a little, what he said did not sound like madness. There's something deep inside which his sadness broods on, and I don't doubt the outcome will be harmful. To prevent this, I have this instant decided to send him with all speed to England to demand the overdue payment owed to Denmark. Hopefully, the sea crossing and the different country and its sights will purge this unsettled matter from his heart, which, still beating on his mind puts him out of sorts with himself. What do you think?

KING

Love! His affections do not that way tend,
Nor what he spake, though it lacked form a little,
Was not like madness. There's something in his soul
O'er which his melancholy sits on brood,*
And I do doubt the hatch and the disclose
Will be some danger; which for to prevent
I have in quick determination
Thus set it down: - he shall with speed to England
For the demand of our neglected tribute.
Haply the seas and countries different,
With variable objects, shall expel
This something-settled matter in his heart,
Whereon his brains still beating puts him thus
From fashion of himself. What think you on't?

*Note: 'Brood'. A bird sits on her eggs and 'broods' - waits for them to hatch.

POLONIUS

It would do him good. But still I do believe the origin of his grief springs from unrequited love.
(*he notices Ophelia's grief*) What's this, Ophelia? You need not tell us what Lord Hamlet said, we heard it all.
(*to the King*) My lord, do as you please, but after the play, if you see fit, allow his queen mother to meet him in private to enquire the reason for his grief. Let her be blunt with him, and I'll be placed - with your permission - within earshot of the conversation. If she does not find the answer, send him to England, or confine him wherever your wisdom thinks best.

POLONIUS

It shall do well. But yet do I believe
The origin and commencement of his grief
Sprung from neglected love. How now, Ophelia?
You need not tell us what Lord Hamlet said,
We heard it all. My lord, do as you please;
But if you hold it fit, after the play
Let his queen mother all alone entreat him
To show his grief. Let her be round with him,
And I'll be placed, so please you, in the ear
Of all their conference. If she find him not,
To England send him, or confine him where
Your wisdom best shall think.

KING CLAUDIUS

Let it be done.
For madness within the great and the good,
Must not be allowed to go on ignored.

KING

                    It shall be so:
Madness in great ones must not unwatched go.

ACT III SCENE II

A HALL IN THE CASTLE.

> Note: This is another very long scene.

HAMLET

Recite the speech, I beg you, in the manner I said it to you, tripping easily off the tongue. If you are overly dramatic, as many of you actors are, I might as well ask the town crier to speak the lines. And do not saw the air with your hand like this, but use gentle natural movement, for in the torrent, the storm, and if I may call it, the whirlwind of passionate highs, you must find a restraint that gives it smoothness. Oh, it offends me to the core to hear an over-excited fellow in a powdered wig reduce the passion to tatters, tearing it apart, splitting the ears of the lower audience, who are for the most part only capable of understanding inexplicable mime shows and noise. I would have such a fellow whipped for overplaying Termagent. It out-herods Herod, make sure you avoid it.

HAMLET

Speak the speech, I pray you, as I pronounced it to you, trippingly on the tongue; but if you mouth it, as many of your players do, I had as lief the town-crier spoke my lines. Nor do not saw the air too much with your hand thus, but use all gently, for in the very torrent, tempest, and, as I may say, whirlwind of your passion, you must acquire and beget a temperance that may give it smoothness. O, it offends me to the soul to hear a robustious periwig-pated fellow tear a passion to tatters, to very rags, to split the ears of the groundlings,* who for the most part are capable of nothing but inexplicable dumb-shows and noise. I would have such a fellow whipped for o'erdoing Termagant.* It out-herods Herod:* pray you, avoid it.

> *Note: Groundlings were the 'cheap seats' in the audience. They were less educated and stood around the stage whereas the sophisticated audience sat around the outside in covered areas. Groundlings paid a penny, this was collected in a box with a slot in the top. During a performance the box was kept in the back office of the theatre, which is where the term 'box office' originated, still in use today.

> *Note: Termagent and Herod were well known as noisy, over-dramatic characters in medieval drama.

1ST ACTOR

I will, your highness.

1ST PLAYER

I warrant your honour.

HAMLET

Don't be too weak either, let your intuition be your guide. Match your actions to the words, and the words to the actions, but with one special proviso, don't overstep natural behaviour, for anything overdone defeats the purpose of acting, whose purpose, from the earliest days till now, was to hold, as it were, a mirror up to nature, to reflect the good features, and to scorn the bad, and to record faithfully the life and struggles of our times. If overdone or underdone, it may make the ignorant laugh, but can only make those more discerning grieve, their disapproval outweighing all other theatre goers' opinions. Oh, there are actors that I have seen act, and heard others praise them, and highly too, who have neither the speech of good god-fearing people nor the pretence of any decent, indecent or even basic human behaviour, who have strutted and bellowed so loudly I thought nature had made these men - and not made them well - by using unskilled labourers, they imitated mankind so badly.

HAMLET

Be not too tame neither, but let your own discretion be your tutor. Suit the action to the word, the word to the action, with this special observance, that you o'erstep not the modesty of nature; for anything so o'erdone is from the purpose of playing, whose end, both at the first and now, was and is to hold as 'twere the mirror up to nature, to show virtue her own feature, scorn her own image, and the very age and body of the time his form and pressure. Now, this overdone or come tardy off, though it make the unskilful laugh, cannot but make the judicious grieve, the censure of which one must in your allowance o'erweigh a whole theatre of others. O, there be players that I have seen play, and heard others praise, and that highly, not to speak it profanely, that neither having th' accent of Christians, nor the gait of Christian, pagan, nor man, have so strutted and bellowed that I have thought some of nature's journeymen had made men, and not made them well, they imitated humanity so abominably.*

Note: In some texts, abominably is spelt 'abhominably' which could have been a pun on the word 'humanity' as 'ab homine' in Latin means 'inhuman'.

1ST ACTOR

I hope we have overcome that pretty well in our performance, sir.

1ST PLAYER

I hope we have reformed that indifferently with us, sir.

HAMLET

Oh, overcome it completely! And let those who play your comics say no more than is written for them to say. There are some who will laugh at themselves to get a bunch of mindless spectators to laugh along too, and at a point where some important part of the play should be concentrated on. That's unforgivable, and shows a pitiful ambition in the fool who tries it. Go, get yourself ready.

HAMLET

O, reform it altogether! And let those that play your clowns speak no more than is set down for them; for there be of them that will themselves laugh to set on some quantity of barren spectators to laugh too, though in the meantime some necessary question of the play be then to be considered. That's villainous, and shows a most pitiful ambition in the fool that uses it. Go, make you ready.

HAMLET (CONT'D)

(*see note above*) And there's quite a few more who keep just one suit of jokes, in the same way a man is known by one suit of clothing, and gentlemen write his jokes down in their notebooks before they come to the play; such as, 'Can you not stay till I've eaten my porridge', and 'You owe me three month's wages', and 'My coat needs a patch', and 'Your beer is sour', and blabbering with his lips, he joins in with the jokes, when, God knows, the mediocre comedian cannot make an original joke unless by accident, much as a blind man would catch a hare, so experts tell him.

HAMLET

(*see note above*) And then you have quite some again that keeps one suit of jests, as a man is known by one suit of apparel; and gentlemen quote his jests down in their tables before they come to the play; as thus, 'Cannot you stay till I eat my porridge?', and 'You owe me a quarter's wages', and 'My coat wants a cullusion', and 'Your beer is sour', and blabbering with his lips, and thus keeping in his cinquepace of jests, when, God knows, the warm clown cannot make a jest unless by chance, as the blind man catcheth a hare. Masters, tell him of it.

THE ACTORS FILE OUT THE ROOM.

ENTER POLONIUS, ROSENCRANTZ, AND GUILDENSTERN.

HAMLET (CONT'D)

(*to Polonius*) Greetings, my lord. Will the king be attending this masterpiece?

HAMLET

How now, my lord. Will the king hear this piece of work?*

*Note: 'Piece of work' also means masterpiece, or a great work of art, Hamlet is being sarcastic, he knows what is coming.

POLONIUS

And the queen too, she's on her way.

POLONIUS

And the queen too, and that presently.

HAMLET

Tell the actors to hurry then.

HAMLET

Bid the players make haste.

POLONIUS HURRIES OUT.

HAMLET (CONT'D)

Will you two help to hurry them up?

HAMLET

Will you two help to hasten them?

ROSENCRANTZ

Yes, my lord.

ROSENCRANTZ

Ay, my lord.

ROSENCRANTZ AND GUILDENSTERN LEAVE.

ROSENCRANTZ AND GUILDENSTERN LEAVE.

HAMLET
(*Calling*) Horatio!

HAMLET
What ho, Horatio!

ENTER HORATIO WHO HAD PRESUMABLY BEEN WAITING JUST OUTSIDE.

HORATIO
Here, sweet lord, I'm at your service.

HORATIO
Here, sweet lord, at your service.

HAMLET
Horatio, you are as well-grounded a man as any I've conversed with.

HAMLET
Horatio, thou art e'en as just a man
As e'er my conversation coped withal.

HORATIO
(*blushing*) Oh, my dear lord.

HORATIO
O, my dear lord.

HAMLET
No, don't think I'm flattering you, what good may I hope to achieve with you who has no worth apart from your good intentions to feed and clothe yourself? Why should I flatter the poor? No, let the sweet tongue outrageously flatter the great and the grand, and bend the hinges of the knee pointedly only where reward may follow such slavish devotion. Do you hear?

HAMLET
Nay, do not think I flatter,
For what advancement may I hope from thee
That no revenue hast but thy good spirits
To feed and clothe thee? Why should the poor
 be flattered?
No, let the candied tongue lick absurd pomp,
And crook the pregnant* hinges of the knee
Where thrift may follow fawning. Dost thou
 hear?

> *Note: 'Pregnant' here means, meaningful, suggestive, telling, pointedly, etc. A deliberate act with obvious intention. Such as a pregnant pause.

HAMLET (CONT'D)
Since my dear soul was first master of its own choices, and could distinguish the qualities in men, it has singled you out for closeness, because you have seen such suffering you are used to it, a man who has taken fortune's losses and gains with equal tolerance. And blessed are those whose passion and judgement are so well balanced that they're not a flute for fortune's finger to play whatever tune she pleases.

HAMLET
Since my dear soul was mistress of her choice,
And could of men distinguish her election,
Sh'ath sealed thee for herself, for thou hast been
As one, in suff'ring all, that suffers nothing,
A man that fortune's buffets and rewards
Hast ta'en with equal thanks; and blest are those
Whose blood and judgement are so well
 commeddled*
That they are not a pipe for fortune's finger
To sound what stop she please.

> *Note: 'Commeddled' or 'commingled' in some editions means mingled.

HAMLET (CONT'D)

Give me a man who is not a slave to his emotions, and I will take him to my heart's core, yes, in my heart of hearts, as I do you. Anyway, enough of this. A play will be performed before the king tonight, one scene of it is close to the circumstances which I have told you about my father's death. When it gets to that part, using the fine judgement of your intuition, I ask that you observe my uncle. If no sign of his hidden guilt is revealed in one particular speech, then it was an evil ghost we saw, and my imagination is as foul as Hell's sweatshop. Pay close attention to him, my eyes will be riveted to his face, and afterwards we'll compare our observations of his behaviour.

HAMLET

Give me that man
That is not passion's slave, and I will wear him
In my heart's core, ay, in my heart of heart,
As I do thee. Something too much of this.
There is a play tonight before the king;
One scene of it comes near the circumstance
Which I have told thee of my father's death.
I prithee, when thou seest that act afoot,
Even with the very comment of thy soul
Observe my uncle. If his occulted guilt
Do not itself unkennel* in one speech,
It is a damned ghost that we have seen,
And my imaginations are as foul
As Vulcan's stithy.* Give him heedful note;
For I mine eyes will rivet to his face,
And after we will both our judgements join
In censure of his seeming.

*Note: 'Unkennel' – discover. Literally, 'to release from the kennel'.

'Vulcan's stithy' is what we now call a 'smithy', short for blacksmith. Vulcan is the god of fire and arms, volcanoes are named after him. The stithy was the workshop where the Cyclops giants forged weapons and armour using the volcano's heat as mentioned earlier by the actors.

HORATIO

Well, my lord, if he steals anything past me while the play is performed and escapes detection, I'll pay the price for the theft.

HORATIO

Well, my lord.
If a' steal aught the whilst this play is playing,
And 'scape detecting, I will pay the theft.

TRUMPETS ANNOUNCE THE KING'S ARRIVAL.

HAMLET

They are coming for the play. I must look natural. Get yourself a seat.

HAMLET

They are coming to the play. I must be idle.*
Get you a place.

*Note: Some scholars interpret the word 'idle' to mean pretending to be mad, it does seem to make more sense if it means looking disinterested, unconcerned, trying not to give the game away.

KING CLAUDIUS
(*to Hamlet*) How fares our kinsman Hamlet?

HAMLET
Excellent, indeed, dining on the chameleon's diet of '*air*' and empty promises. You cannot feed capons that way.

KING
How fares* our cousin Hamlet?

HAMLET
Excellent, i'faith, of the chameleon's* dish. I eat the air,* promise-crammed. You cannot feed capons* so.

Note: Hamlet puns the word 'fare' with its other meaning of food. Hence his reply about his eating habits. In these habits he again puns but this time on the word 'air' with 'heir'. The chameleon fed on insects almost too small to see, so was believed to live on air alone.

A capon is a male chicken, caged and castrated when young to fatten it. Hamlet is saying that he refuses to be penned in, powerless, like a capon.

KING CLAUDIUS
I don't follow this answer, Hamlet, these words are not related to mine.

HAMLET
No, nor mine now.
(*to Polonius*) My lord, you acted once at university, didn't you say?

KING
I have nothing with this answer, Hamlet; these words are not mine.*

HAMLET
No, nor mine now.* [*To Polonius.*] My lord, you played once i'th' university, you say?

Note: 'Words not mine' – Hamlet's reply is based on the proverb, "A man's words are his own only as long as he keeps them unspoken".

POLONIUS
That I did, my lord, and was considered a good actor.

HAMLET
What part did you play?

POLONIUS
I played Julius Caesar. I was killed in the Capitol. Brutus killed me.

POLONIUS
That did I, my lord, and was accounted a good actor.

HAMLET
What did you enact?

POLONIUS
I did enact Julius Caesar. I was killed i'th' Capitol; Brutus killed me.

Note: The Capitol is the temple of Jupiter on Capitoline Hill in ancient Rome. On March 15, 44 B.C., Julius Caesar was assassinated by a group of rival consuls in the Curia Pompeii, (not the Capitol). The Curia, where the murder took place, was part of Pompey's Theatre. Perhaps Shakespeare meant the capital city of Rome in order to use the pun in the next line.

HAMLET

He was a brute to kill so capital a calf there. Are the actors ready?

HAMLET

It was a brute part of him to kill so capital a calf* there. Be the players ready?

Note: Another pun, this time based around a sacrificial calf.

ROSENCRANTZ

Yes, my lord, they are ready when you are.

ROSENCRANTZ

Ay, my lord, they stay upon your patience.

QUEEN GERTRUDE

Come here, my dear Hamlet, sit by me.

QUEEN

Come hither, my good Hamlet, sit by me.

HAMLET

No, dear mother, I'm drawn to something more attractive.

HAMLET

No, good mother, here's metal more attractive.*

Note: He is describing Ophelia as a magnet.

HAMLET GOES TO OPHELIA AND SITS AT HER FEET.

POLONIUS

(*aside to King*) Oh, ho, ho, did you hear that?

POLONIUS

[*Aside to the KING.*] O ho, do you mark that?

HAMLET

(*to Ophelia*) Lady, shall I <u>lie</u> in your lap?

HAMLET

Lady, shall I lie* in your lap?

Note: 'Lie with' meant the same as 'sleep with' does today, it is a double meaning for having sex with someone, a deliberate pun. Hamlet makes this clearer a little later.

OPHELIA

(*embarrassed*) No, my lord.

OPHELIA

No, my lord.

HAMLET

I mean my *head* on your lap.

HAMLET

I mean my head upon your lap?

OPHELIA

I see, my lord.

OPHELIA

Ay, my lord.

HAMLET

Did you think I meant '<u>country</u>' matters?

HAMLET

Do you think I meant country matters?*

Note: Again Shakespeare is being bawdy, using wordplay of the word 'country' and a familiar swear word for female genitalia. The term 'country matters' also refers to what they do in the country, where people were considered less refined and had more liberal behaviour than the city.

OPHELIA
I thought *nothing*, my lord.

OPHELIA
I think nothing,* my lord.

Note: Some stage productions have her make a letter 'O' with her hand. 'Nothing', had a sexual meaning, slang for a vagina. A common term for a woman's genitalia of the time was her 'nothing' - a man has something between his legs, a woman has nothing.

Plays were strictly regulated in Shakespeare's time and he frequently used innuendos to get around this.

HAMLET
That's a good thought to <u>lie</u> between a young lady's legs.

HAMLET
That's a fair thought to lie between maids' legs.

OPHELIA
What is, my lord?

OPHELIA
What is, my lord?

HAMLET
Nothing.

HAMLET
Nothing.*

Note: Another innuendo. Her 'nothing' lies between her legs.

OPHELIA
You are merry, my lord.

OPHELIA
You are merry,* my lord.

Note: Merry can mean happy or drunk, and often both and it can also mean you are jesting.

HAMLET
Who, me?

HAMLET
Who, I?

OPHELIA
Yes, my lord.

OPHELIA
Ay, my lord.

HAMLET
(*ironic*) Oh God yes, your best song and dance man! What else should a man be but merry? See how cheerful my mother looks, and my father dead less than two hours.

HAMLET
O God, your only jig-maker!* What should a man do but be merry? For look you how cheerfully my mother looks, and my father died within's two hours.

Note: Jig-maker, someone who composes happy songs to dance to, especially when drinking, or 'making merry'.

OPHELIA

No, it's two, but two months, my lord.

OPHELIA

Nay, 'tis twice two months,* my lord.

Note: There is confusion how long it has been since Hamlet's father's death. Hamlet says it is two hours, Ophelia says it is twice two months, which could be four months. Perhaps rather than say four, Shakespeare plays on the number two. The translation has followed the wordplay on the number two, which would be lost if it said, four months, and Hamlet says two months in the following speech.

HAMLET

(*overdoing being merry*) That long? Then let the devil wear black, and I'll have a suit of dark sable fur to match. Oh heavens! Died two months ago, and not yet forgotten? Then there is hope a great man's memory outlives him by half a year. But by heavens, he'll have to build churches or else suffer being forgotten, like the hobby horse only remembered in song,

(*sings*) "For oh, for oh, the hobby horse is forgot".*

HAMLET

So long? Nay then, let the devil wear black, for I'll have a suit of sables. O heavens! - die two months ago, and not forgotten yet? Then there's hope a great man's memory may outlive his life half a year. But, by'rlady, a' must build churches then, or else shall a' suffer not thinking on, with the hobby-horse, whose epitaph is `For O, for O, the hobby-horse is forgot.'

Note: Hamlet recites a line from a popular ballad mocking the banning of popular May Day games by puritans (a highly moral religious group who believed in self-restraint). A man sings it wearing a horse costume around his waist with a model of a horse's head attached – known as a hobby horse.

TRUMPETS SOUND TO INTRODUCE THE MIME SHOW.

Note: The following mime show enacts the plot of the play called 'The Murder of Gonzago', which will follow straight after the mime.

A mime is performed entirely without words, the story being played out in silence by actions alone.

TWO ACTORS DRESSED AS A KING AND A QUEEN ENTER.

THE QUEEN LOVINGLY EMBRACES THE KING.
SHE KNEELS BEFORE HIM, AS IF PLEADING.

THE KING MAKES HER STAND AND RESTS HIS HEAD UPON HER NECK.
HE LIES DOWN UPON A BED OF FLOWERS. SHE SEES HE IS ASLEEP AND EXITS.

A MAN COMES IN, REMOVES THE SLEEPING KING'S CROWN, HOLDS IT ALOFT
AND KISSES IT. HE POURS POISON IN THE KING'S EAR AND EXITS.

THE QUEEN RETURNS, UPON FINDING THE KING IS DEAD SHE WEEPS AND
MOURNS PASSIONATELY.

THE MURDERER RETURNS WITH FOUR OTHER MEN, HE COMFORTS THE
QUEEN WHILE THE MEN CARRY AWAY THE BODY. HE THEN WOOS THE
QUEEN WITH GIFTS. AT FIRST SHE REBUKES HIS ATTENTIONS, BEFORE
FINALLY ACCEPTING HIS LOVE.

THEY ALL EXIT.

Note: The mime suggests Gertrude had nothing to do with her husband's murder
and that she did not have an affair with Claudius before her husband's death.

OPHELIA	OPHELIA
What does this all mean, my lord?	What means this, my lord?
HAMLET	HAMLET
Well, this is satire, mischievous satire.	Marry, this is miching mallecho;* it means mischief.*

*Note: "Mallecho" is a Spanish word in common use at the time meaning a bad
deed or wickedness, "miching" means hidden or skulking. Hidden (disguised)
wickedness. Satire can be described as such, so it has been used here.

"It means mischief" can be saying that the words 'miching mallecho' mean
mischief (which in a simple way they do), or that the reason for the play is to cause
mischief.

OPHELIA	OPHELIA
I assume this mime show outlines the plot of the play to come.	Belike this show imports the argument of the play.

ONE ACTOR ENTERS TO READ THE PROLOGUE.

HAMLET	HAMLET
We'll find out from this fellow. The actors can't keep it secret, they have to reveal everything.	We shall know by this fellow. The players cannot keep counsel; they'll tell all.

128

OPHELIA
Will he explain what this show is?

HAMLET
(*bawdy*) Yes, or anything else you'd care to show him. If you're not ashamed to show him, he'll not be ashamed to explain what it's for.

OPHELIA
You are naughty, very naughty. I'll watch the play.

PROLOGUE ACTOR
For us and for our tragedy,
Here hoping for your sympathy,
We beg you listen patiently.

OPHELIA
Will a' tell us what this show meant?

HAMLET
Ay, or any show that you will show him. Be not you ashamed to show, he'll not shame to tell you what it means.

OPHELIA
You are naught, you are naught. I'll mark the play.

PROLOGUE
For us and for our tragedy,
Here stooping to your clemency,
We beg your hearing patiently.

THE PROLOGUE ACTOR EXITS.

Note: The prologue is the introduction to the play to be performed, it gives a brief overview of what is to come. This prologue was unusually brief and gives no plot details, to which Hamlet comments in the next line.

HAMLET
Is this a prologue, or the inscription on a love token?

OPHELIA
It was brief, my lord.

HAMLET
Like a woman's love.

HAMLET
Is this a prologue, or the posy of a ring?

OPHELIA
'Tis brief, my lord.

HAMLET
As woman's love.

ENTER THE ACTORS PLAYING KING AND QUEEN.

Note: The King and Queen's lines are written in old fashioned couplets. In most performances these lines are drastically cut, but it's worth knowing the outline of the performance and its philosophical elements. If this section is cut from a performance you are watching, a brief summary is;

The King and Queen have been married thirty years, and now the King is dying. He tells the Queen he hopes she'll find another husband as good to her as he has been. She swears she'll never marry again. The King answers with a long rambling speech of how we all make plans and promises which we fail to keep, and how we should not dwell on them but move on with our lives, because people and circumstances change with time. This is related to Hamlet's belief he is a coward for not fulfilling his promise to kill King Claudius.

ACTOR KING

For thirty years the Sun God's cart's gone round
Neptune's salt waves and mother earth's
ground,
And thirty dozen moon's reflected beams
Around the world have twelve times thirty been
Since love joined hearts and marriage joined
our hands
In mutual bond with sacred golden bands.

ACTOR QUEEN

As many journeys may the sun and moon
Make us count again ere love is done
But, sad to say, you've been so ill of late,
So far from healthy cheer of your old state,
I fear for you. Yet, though I fear a lot,
To worry you, my lord, it so must not.
For women's fear and love, are held equal,
The more they love the more they are fearful.
Now, what my love is, has been proved to you,
And as my love is great, my fear is too.
Where love is great, the smallest doubts are
fear;
Where little fears grow great, great love grows
there.

ACTOR KING

True, I must leave you, love, and very soon.
My failing health, its functions all but gone,
In this fair world you will be left behind,
Honoured, loved, and hopefully one as kind
A husband you shall...

ACTOR QUEEN

(interrupting) ...Oh, don't say the rest!
For love like that's a traitor to my breast.
With second husband let my life be cursed
For they who wed the second killed the first.

HAMLET

(aside) Harsh, harsh.

PLAYER KING

Full thirty times hath Phoebus' cart gone round
Neptune's salt wash and Tellus' orbed ground,
And thirty dozen moons with borrowed sheen
About the world have times twelve thirties been
Since love our hearts and Hymen did our hands
Unite commutual in most sacred bands.

PLAYER QUEEN

So many journeys may the sun and moon
Make us again count o'er ere love be done.
But, woe is me, you are so sick of late,
So far from cheer and from your former state,
That I distrust you. Yet, though I distrust,
Discomfort you, my lord, it nothing must.
And women's fear and love hold quantity,
In neither aught, or in extremity.
Now, what my love is, proof hath made you know,
And as my love is sized, my fear is so.
Where love is great, the littlest doubts are fear;
Where little fears grow great, great love grows there.

PLAYER KING

Faith, I must leave thee, love, and shortly too.
My operant powers their functions leave to do;
And thou shalt live in this fair world behind,
Honoured, beloved; and haply one as kind
For husband shalt thou -

PLAYER QUEEN

                    - O confound the rest!
Such love must needs be treason in my breast.
In second husband let me be accurst;
None wed the second but who killed the first.

HAMLET

*[Aside.] Wormwood, wormwood.**

Note: Wormwood has a very bitter taste, it was used for babies by rubbing on the nipple to ween the child from breastfeeding. It is a synonym for bitter.

130

ACTOR QUEEN

The motives that a second marriage has
Is based on wealth, and not on love, alas.
A second time I kill first husband dead,
When second husband kisses me in bed.

ACTOR KING

I do believe you mean what you now speak,
But promises we make we often break.
Their strength a victim of our memory,
Though strong at first, no continuity;
The unripe fruit which now clings to the tree,
Falls with the wind of distant memory.
Most sad it is that we will soon forget
To pay ourselves our long forgotten debt.
What to ourselves in passion we propose,
When passion ends we do the promise lose.
Excessiveness of either grief or joy
Then by their own excess themselves' destroy.
With joy most great, then grief does show its
*   face,*
Grief to joy, joy to grief, by slender chance.
The world is not forever, nor 'tis strange
That even our love should with our fortunes
*   change.*

It is a question left as yet to prove,
Is love lead by fortune, or fortune by love?
When great men fall you watch his favourites
*   flee,*
While rising poor makes friends of enemy.
And fortune up till now does guide love's ends,
For those who have it all will lack no friends,
But those in need turn to a friend with plea,
Finds suddenly he is his enemy.
But, orderly to end where I'd begun,
Our fate and wishes oppositely run
So all our plans are still all overthrown;
Our thoughts are ours, their outcome not our
*   own.*
A second husband you think you'll not wed,
But your thoughts die when your first one is
*   dead.*

PLAYER QUEEN

The instances that second marriage move
Are base respects of thrift, but none of love.
A second time I kill my husband dead,
When second husband kisses me in bed.

PLAYER KING

I do believe you think what now you speak,
But what we do determine, oft we break.
Purpose is but the slave to memory,
Of violent birth, but poor validity;
Which now, the fruit unripe, sticks on the tree,
But fall unshaken when they mellow be.
Most necessary 'tis that we forget
To pay ourselves what to ourselves is debt.
What to ourselves in passion we propose,
The passion ending, doth the purpose lose.
The violence of either grief or joy
Their own enactures with themselves destroy.
Where joy most revels, grief doth most lament;
Grief joys, joy grieves, on slender accident.
This world is not for aye, nor 'tis not strange
That even our loves should with our fortunes change:

For 'tis a question left us yet to prove,
Whether love lead fortune, or else fortune love.
The great man down, you mark his favourite flies;
The poor advanced makes friends of enemies.
And hitherto doth love on fortune tend;
For who not needs shall never lack a friend,
And who in want a hollow friend doth try
Directly seasons him his enemy.
But, orderly to end where I begun,
Our wills and fates do so contrary run
That our devices still are overthrown;
Our thoughts are ours, their ends none of our own.
So think thou wilt no second husband wed;
But die thy thoughts when thy first lord is dead.

ACTOR QUEEN

Let earth not give me food, nor heaven light,
No joy in day, and no repose at night,
To desperation turn my hopes and wishes,
A tramp's meagre diet be my dishes,
And ev'rything that steals the look of joy
And ev'rything I now hold dear, destroy,
Both here and after give me lasting strife,
If, once a widow, I become a wife!

HAMLET

If she broke her promise after saying that!

ACTOR KING

Now it's deeply sworn, leave me a while;
My breath grows weak, and I would gladly wile
The day away with sleep. (yawns)

THE ACTOR KING LAYS DOWN TO SLEEP.

ACTOR QUEEN

Sleep come to you.
Let no mishap e'er tear us both in two.

> *Note: 'Rock thy brain' was not Shakespeare predicting modern expressions about music, he meant rock as in rock the cradle. Rock someone to sleep.*

THE ACTOR QUEEN EXITS LEAVING THE ACTOR KING FEIGNING SLEEP.

HAMLET

(*to Queen*) Madam, how do you like the play?

QUEEN GERTRUDE

The lady promises too much, I think.

> *Note: This line is one of Shakespeare's famous lines and is still quoted in regular conversation today, with the 'methinks' often said as the first word rather than the last. The meaning has also changed a little. Today, "protest" means "to object", i.e. someone objecting or denying something too much to be trusted and inadvertently showing their guilt. Shakespeare meant 'confirms' or 'states' her vows too much thereby losing her credibility.*

HAMLET

(*sarcastic*) Oh, but she'll keep her promise.

PLAYER QUEEN

Nor earth to me give food, nor heaven light,
Sport and repose lock from me day and night,
To desperation turn my trust and hope,
An anchor's cheer in prison be my scope,
Each opposite that blanks the face of joy
Meet what I would have well, and it destroy,
Both here and hence pursue me lasting strife,
If, once a widow, ever I be a wife!

HAMLET

If she should break it now!

PLAYER KING

'Tis deeply sworn, leave me here a while;
My spirits grow dull, and fain I would beguile
The tedious day with sleep.

PLAYER QUEEN

Sleep rock thy brain, *
And never come mischance between us twain.

HAMLET

[*To Queen.*] Madam, how like you this play?

QUEEN

The lady doth protest too much*, methinks.

HAMLET

O, but she'll keep her word.

132

KING CLAUDIUS

Do you know the plot? It's not offensive is it?

KING

Have you heard the argument? Is there no offence in't?

HAMLET

No, no, it's make believe, the poison isn't real, no offence is committed.

HAMLET

No, no, they do but jest, poison in jest; no offence* i'th' world.

*Note: Hamlet has deliberately twisted the king's meaning of the word 'offence', and managed to get a sarcastic jibe into the words aimed at the king.

KING CLAUDIUS

What is the play called?

KING

What do you call the play?

HAMLET

The Mousetrap. My, what an appropriate title! The play is a re-enactment of a murder committed in Vienna. Gonzago is a duke, Baptista is his wife. You'll see soon. It's a provocative piece of work, but what of it? It will not affect your majesty, or any of us who are free of guilt. Let the guilty wince, our consciences are clear.

HAMLET

The Mousetrap. Marry, how tropically!* This play is the image of a murder done in Vienna. Gonzago is the duke's name, his wife, Baptista. You shall see anon. 'Tis a knavish piece of work, but what o' that? Your majesty, and we that have free souls, it touches us not. Let the galled jade wince, our withers are unwrung.

*Note: "Marry, how tropically" in some editions is written as "Marry, how? Tropically". Tropically here is from the word "trope" – which means 'figure of speech, or a metaphor. He is meaning that the word 'trap' is appropriate.

ENTER THE ACTOR PLAYING LUCIANUS.

HAMLET

This is Lucianus, nephew of the king.

HAMLET

This is one Lucianus, nephew to the king.

OPHELIA

You are as good as a narrator, my lord.

OPHELIA

You are as good as a chorus, my lord.

HAMLET

(bawdy) I could narrate the action between you and your lover too if I could <u>see the performance</u>.

HAMLET

I could interpret between you and your love if I could see the puppets dallying.*

*Note: In a puppet show, the puppet master narrated the performance and was called the "interpreter". "Dally" meant act playfully, particularly with amorous intent and wanton flirting. Hamlet accuses Ophelia of having a lover with whom she 'dallies'. He also calls her a puppet, controlled by others.

OPHELIA

You are sharp, my lord, very sharp.

OPHELIA

You are keen, my lord, you are keen.

HAMLET
(*bawdy*) I'd have you <u>moaning and groaning</u> before you could take the edge off me.

OPHELIA
Even better, and yet worse.

HAMLET
For better, for worse, how husbands are 'mis-taken'.
(*to Lucianus*) Begin, murderer. Pah, stop making those ridiculous faces and begin. Come on, (*dramatically*) "*the croaking raven doth bellow for revenge*".

HAMLET
It would cost you a groaning to take off my edge.

OPHELIA
Still better, and worse.

HAMLET
So you mistake* your husbands. [*To Lucianus.*] Begin, murderer. Pox,* leave thy damnable faces, and begin. Come, the croaking raven* doth bellow for revenge.

---

*Note: Hamlet twists the words to the marriage vow of a husband "do you take this man for better or for worse."

He also uses the word "mistake" as the two word pun on 'miss-take'. i.e. She takes her marriage vows and breaks them, misuses them.

'Pox' was a commonly used exclamation, pox was syphilis, a sexually transmitted disease, for which there was no cure until the twentieth century with the advent of antibiotics.

'Croaking raven' - a melodramatic imitation of old revenge tragedies.

ACTOR LUCIANUS
Black thoughts, hands set, drug mixed, and
*   time agreeing,*
Right opportunity, no one else seeing;
A mixture of foul deadly plants collected,
With triple curses infused and infected,
Its natural magic and dire property
Will take away a life, immediately.

LUCIANUS
Thoughts black, hands apt, drugs fit, and time
*   agreeing;*
Confederate season, else no creature seeing;
Thou mixture rank, of midnight weeds collected,
With Hecate's ban thrice blasted, thrice infected,*
Thy natural magic and dire property
On wholesome life usurps immediately.

---

*Note: Hecate is the goddess of dark places, and appears in Macbeth as the lead witch (though probably added to Macbeth by a later author. See Macbeth Translated by SJ Hills for more detailed information).

HE TAKES OUT A VIAL AND UNCORKS IT DRMATICALLY HOLDING IT ALOFT.

HE THEN POURS ITS POISONOUS CONTENTS
INTO THE SLEEPING ACTOR KING'S EAR.

HAMLET

He poisons him in the garden for his possessions. His name's Gonzago. The story is still performed in pretentious Italian. You'll see soon how the murderer gets the love of Gonzago's wife.

HAMLET

A' poisons him i'th' garden for's estate.* His name's Gonzago. The story is extant, and writ in very choice Italian. You shall see anon how the murderer gets the love of Gonzago's wife.

*Note: 'Estate' - the property of a man. In those days a wife was not allowed to own property, A husband owned everything, including his wife. Here Hamlet insinuates the king murdered to become king himself and to take the murdered king's wife.

KING CLAUDIUS RISES TO HIS FEET.

OPHELIA

The king has risen from his seat.

OPHELIA

The king rises.

HAMLET

What, frightened by blank shots?

HAMLET

What, frighted with false fire?

QUEEN GERTRUDE

(to Claudius) What is it, my lord?

QUEEN

How fares my lord?

POLONIUS

Stop the play.

POLONIUS

Give o'er the play.

KING CLAUDIUS

Bring me some light. We're leaving!

KING

Give me some light.* Away!

*Note: At night, in the days before gas or electric lighting, one would need to carry a torch or a lantern (a light). A king would have others carry lights for him.

POLONIUS

Bring lights, lights, lights!

POLONIUS

Lights, lights, lights!

EXEUNT ALL EXCEPT HAMLET AND HORATIO.

HAMLET

(theatrically)

So, let the wounded deer go weep,

The stag, uninjured play;

For some must live, while some must sleep,

The world it runs this way.

HAMLET

(reciting)

Why, let the strucken deer go weep,

The hart ungalled play;

For some must watch, while some must sleep;

So runs the world away.

HAMLET TURNS TO HORATIO.

HAMLET (CONT'D)

(to Horatio) If my fortunes turn turtle on me, with a plume of feathers in my cap and rosettes on my dancing shoes, would this performance have got me a place in a company of actors?

HORATIO

A half share in the company.

HAMLET

Would not this, sir, and a forest of feathers - if the rest of my fortunes turn Turk with me - with two Provincial roses on my razed shoes, get me a fellowship in a cry of players?

HORATIO

Half a share.*

*Note: A 'share' would be a percentage of the company's earnings.

HAMLET

I'd want a whole share.

(theatrically)

For you don't know, oh, Damon dear,

This kingdom was deposed alas,

Of king himself, and now reigns here

A one and only... (pauses) peacock.

HORATIO

You might have made it rhyme.

HAMLET

A whole one, I.

(reciting)

For thou dost know, O Damon* dear,

This realm dismantled was

Of Jove himself; and now reigns here

A very, very - pacock.

HORATIO

You might have rhymed.*

*Note: Presumably the missing rhyme would have been 'ass' or 'arse', Hamlet pauses to let us think this. In Shakespeare's time the peacock represented pride and envy, as well as cruelty and lust. How Hamlet saw the new king.

'Damon' - a perfect friend. In classical legend, Damon and Pythias were devoted friends. When Pythias was condemned to death he wanted time to arrange his affairs, Damon pledged his life on his friend returning. Pythias returned and both were pardoned.

HAMLET

Oh, good Horatio, I'll back the ghost's words with a thousand pounds. Did you see?

HORATIO

Very clearly, my lord.

HAMLET

When the talk was about poisoning?

HORATIO

Very much I noticed him.

HAMLET

O good Horatio, I'll take the ghost's word for a thousand pound. Didst perceive?

HORATIO

Very well, my lord.

HAMLET

Upon the talk of the poisoning?

HORATIO

I did very well note him.

HAMLET
Ah, ha! Call for music! Call for pipes!
(theatrically)
For if the king likes not the comedy,
It's likely he dislikes it, assuredly.
Come, let's have some music!

HAMLET
Ah, ha! Come, some music! Come, the
  recorders!
For if the king like not the comedy,
Why then, belike he likes it not, perdy.
Come, some music!

RE-ENTER ROSENCRANTZ AND GUILDENSTERN.

GUILDENSTERN
My good lord, grant me a word with you.

GUILDENSTERN
Good my lord, vouchsafe me a word with you.

HAMLET
Sir, you may have a whole essay.

HAMLET
Sir, a whole history.

GUILDENSTERN
The king, sir...

GUILDENSTERN
The king, sir -

HAMLET
Yes, sir, what of him?

HAMLET
Ay, sir, what of him?

GUILDENSTERN
He has retired to his quarters extremely unsettled.

GUILDENSTERN
Is in his retirement marvellous distempered.

HAMLET
With drink, sir?

HAMLET
With drink, sir?

GUILDENSTERN
No, my lord, he is sick with rage.

GUILDENSTERN
No, my lord, rather with choler.*

Note: 'Choler' – anger. It can also mean billiousness, hence Hamlet taking the alternative meaning and suggest a doctor.

HAMLET
It would make better sense if you were to notify a doctor. If I were to give him a taste of his own medicine it would plunge him into even greater depths.

HAMLET
Your wisdom should show itself more richer to signify this to the doctor; for, for me to put him to his purgation would perhaps plunge him into far more choler.

GUILDENSTERN
My good lord, try to control yourself and not stray so wildly off subject.

GUILDENSTERN
Good my lord, put your discourse into some frame, and start not so wildly from my affair.

HAMLET
I am calm now, sir. Proceed.

HAMLET
I am tame, sir. Pronounce.

GUILDENSTERN
Your mother, the queen, in the greatest distress, has sent me to you.

GUILDENSTERN
The queen your mother, in most great affliction of spirit, hath sent me to you.

HAMLET
You are most welcome here.

GUILDENSTERN
No, my good lord, this kind of courtesy is not appropriate. If it pleases you to give me a sensible answer, I will do as your mother commanded. If not, your permission for me to leave and return to her will end this business.

HAMLET
Sir, I cannot.

GUILDENSTERN
Cannot what, my lord?

HAMLET
Give you a sensible answer. My mind is diseased. But, sir, whatever answer I can give, shall be yours to command, or rather as you say, my mother's. Enough of that, back to the matter in hand. My mother, you say?

ROSENCRANTZ
Then this is what she says; your behaviour has astonished and confused her.

HAMLET
Oh, a wonderful son that can so astonish a mother! But is there no follow up on the back of this mother's confusion? Tell me.

ROSENCRANTZ
She desires to speak with you in her chamber before you go to bed.

HAMLET
You are welcome.

GUILDENSTERN
Nay, good my lord, this courtesy is not of the right breed. If it shall please you to make me a wholesome answer, I will do your mother's commandment; if not, your pardon and my return shall be the end of business.

HAMLET
Sir, I cannot.

GUILDENSTERN
What, my lord?

HAMLET
Make you a wholesome answer. My wit's diseased. But, sir, such answer as I can make, you shall command, or rather, as you say, my mother. Therefore no more, but to the matter. My mother, you say?

ROSENCRANTZ
Then thus she says: your behaviour hath struck her into amazement and admiration.

HAMLET
O wonderful son that can so 'stonish a mother! But is there no
sequel at the heels of this mother's admiration? Impart.

ROSENCRANTZ
She desires to speak with you in her closet ere you go to bed.

HAMLET ADOPTS A REGAL POSE.

HAMLET
(adopting a regal manner) We shall obey as if she were our mother ten times over. Have you any further business with us?

HAMLET
We* shall obey, were she ten times our mother. Have you any further trade with us?*

Note: Hamlet uses the 'royal' we, instead of saying I, and uses 'us' for me.

ROSENCRANTZ
My lord, you were once fond of me.

HAMLET
I still am, by these picking and stealing hands.

ROSENCRANTZ
My lord, you once did love me.

HAMLET
So I do still, by these pickers and stealers.*

Note: From a religious instruction saying we should prevent hands from being pickers and stealers – pick-pocketing and stealing.

ROSENCRANTZ
Good my lord, what is the cause of your disorder? You surely close the door on your recovery by denying your ailments to your friend.

HAMLET
Sir, my ambitions are lacking.

ROSENCRANTZ
Good my lord, what is your cause of distemper? You do surely bar the door upon your own liberty if you deny your griefs to your friend.

HAMLET
Sir, I lack advancement.*

Note: Hamlet means he is not taking revenge for his father, but disguises the fact with an ambiguous statement. Rosencrantz assumes the other meaning.

ROSENCRANTZ
How can that be when the king of Denmark himself announced you as heir to the throne?

HAMLET
Yes, sir, but *"While the grass grows..."* (*he pauses forgetting the rest*) ...the proverb is somewhat stale in my memory.

ROSENCRANTZ
How can that be when you have the voice of the king himself for your succession in Denmark?

HAMLET
Ay, sir, but ` While the grass grows,' - the proverb is something musty.*

RE-ENTER SOME ACTORS WITH RECORDERS.

Note: The proverb Hamlet cannot remember is, 'While the grass grows, often the silly horse starves'. Meaning if he does nothing he may never get the throne.

HAMLET
Oh, the recorders! Let me see one.

HAMLET
O, the recorders! Let me see one.

AN ACTOR HANDS HAMLET A RECORDER.

HAMLET (CONT'D)
(*drawing R and G aside*) To confide in you – why do you strive to get me to talk, as if you were driving me into a trap.

HAMLET
To withdraw with you - why do you go about to recover the wind of me, as if you would drive me into a toil?

GUILDENSTERN
Oh, my lord, if I am being too bold, it is my affection for you causing my rudeness.

HAMLET
I'm not sure I understand that.
(*indicating his recorder*) Will you play upon this pipe.

GUILDENSTERN
O my lord, if my duty be too bold, my love is too unmannerly.

HAMLET
I do not well understand that. Will you play upon this pipe?*

> *Note: 'Play upon this pipe' can be played with bawdy innuendo. The whole passage is both suggestive and also a tale of Hamlet being lied to and made a fool of.*

GUILDENSTERN
My lord, I cannot.

HAMLET
I'd like you to.

GUILDENSTERN
Believe me, I cannot.

HAMLET
I beg of you.

GUILDENSTERN
I know not how to touch it, my lord.

HAMLET
It's as easy as *lying*. Control these openings with your fingers and thumb, give it breath with your mouth, and it will emit the sweetest music. Look, these are the openings.

GUILDENSTERN
My lord, I cannot.

HAMLET
I pray you.

GUILDENSTERN
Believe me, I cannot.

HAMLET
I do beseech you.

GUILDENSTERN
I know no touch of it, my lord.

HAMLET
'Tis as easy as lying.* Govern these ventages with your fingers and thumb, give it breath with your mouth, and it will discourse most eloquent music. Look you, these are the stops.*

> *Note: Lying with someone meant the same as sleep with someone means today – have sex with someone, but he also accuses Guildenstern of not being honest.*
>
> *'Stops' are the finger holes in a Recorder.*

GUILDENSTERN
But I cannot control these with any semblance of harmony, I don't have the skill.

GUILDENSTERN
But these cannot I command to any utterance of harmony; I have not the skill.

HAMLET Why, look how small you make me look! You would play me, you seem to know my openings, you would pluck out the heart of my secret, you would sound me out from my lowest note to the top of my range, and there is a lot of music with excellent voice in this little organ, yet you cannot make it sing. Streuth, do you think I am easier to play than a pipe? Call me whatever instrument you like, though you can fret me, you cannot play me.	**HAMLET** Why, look you now how unworthy a thing you make of me! You would play upon me, you would seem to know my stops, you would pluck out the heart of my mystery, you would sound me from my lowest note to the top of my compass; and there is much music, excellent voice, in this little organ, yet cannot you make it speak. 'Sblood, do you think I am easier to be played on than a pipe? Call me what instrument you will, though you can fret* me, yet you cannot play upon me.

Note: 'Fret' - double meaning of causing him anxiety or irritation, and the finger frets on a musical instrument such as a guitar.

RE-ENTER POLONIUS.

HAMLET (CONT'D) (*to Polonius*) God bless you, sir!	**HAMLET** God bless you, sir!
POLONIUS My lord, the queen wishes to speak with you, right away.	**POLONIUS** My lord, the queen would speak with you, and presently.
HAMLET Do you see that cloud over there that's almost the shape of a camel?	**HAMLET** Do you see yonder cloud that's almost in shape of a camel?
POLONIUS (*humouring him*) By heavens, it is indeed like a camel.	**POLONIUS** By th' mass and 'tis, like a camel indeed.
HAMLET I think it's like a weasel.	**HAMLET** Methinks it is like a weasel.
POLONIUS Its back is like a weasel's.	**POLONIUS** It is backed like a weasel.
HAMLET Or like a whale.	**HAMLET** Or like a whale.
POLONIUS Very like a whale.	**POLONIUS** Very like a whale.
HAMLET I will visit my mother shortly. (*aside*) They fool with me, to my very limit. (*to Polonius*) I'll be there right away.	**HAMLET** Then I will come to my mother by and by. [*Aside.*] They fool me to the top of my bent. [*To Polonius.*] I will come by and by.

141

POLONIUS

I will tell her.

POLONIUS

I will say so.

EXIT POLONIUS.

HAMLET

(*to the departing Polonius*) 'Right away' is easy to say.

(*to R & G*) Leave me, my friends.

HAMLET

` By and by' is easily said. Leave me, friends.

EXEUNT ALL BUT HAMLET, WHO NOW RECITES HIS 5TH SOLILOQUY.

HAMLET (CONT'D)

It's now the witching hour of night, when graves gape open, and hell itself breathes disease into the world. Now I could drink hot blood, and do such evil things that the day would tremble at the sight of them. Shush!

– Now I'll go to my mother. Oh, my heart, don't lose your good nature, never let the spirit of that mother killer, Nero, enter this steadfast bosom. Let me be ruthless, not evil. I'll speak daggers to her, but not use them. My words and thoughts will be hypocrites.

However my words against her are meant,

Making them happen, my soul would prevent!

HAMLET

'Tis now the very witching time of night,

When churchyards yawn, and hell itself breathes out

Contagion to this world. Now could I drink hot blood,

And do such bitter business as the day

Would quake to look on. Soft! - now to my mother.

O heart, lose not thy nature; let not ever

The soul of Nero* enter this firm bosom.

Let me be cruel, not unnatural:

I will speak daggers to her, but use none.

My tongue and soul in this be hypocrites:

How in my words soever she be shent,

To give them seals never my soul consent!

Note: Nero was a Roman Emperor famed for killing his own mother, among many other atrocities.

ACT III SCENE III

A ROOM IN THE CASTLE.

THE KING IS TALKING TO ROSENCRANTZ AND GUILDENSTERN.

KING CLAUDIUS

I don't trust him, nor is it safe to allow his madness to have free range. So prepare yourselves, I'll ready your documents immediately to travel to England and he shall accompany you. Someone in my position cannot allow such peril so close by and it grows hourly with his wild moods.

KING

I like him not, nor stands it safe with us
To let his madness range. Therefore prepare you;
I your commission will forthwith dispatch,
And he to England shall along with you.
The terms of our estate may not endure
Hazard so near us as doth hourly grow
Out of his brows.*

Note: Some editions replace 'his brows' with 'his lunacies'.

GUILDENSTERN

We will make preparations. It is a most honourable, devout duty to be concerned for the many souls of Denmark whose welfare depends on your majesty.

GUILDENSTERN

We will ourselves provide.
Most holy and religious fear it is
To keep those many many bodies safe
That live and feed upon your majesty.

ROSENCRANTZ

Each individual will protect himself from harm with all the strength and fortitude of mind he can muster, but how much more of that spirit is needed in the one upon whom the welfare and lives of many depend? When the king dies, he does not die alone, like a whirlpool it draws in those around him. Or it's like a massive wheel fixed to the top of a mountain, to which is attached ten thousand smaller items to each spoke. When it falls, each small attachment, each tiny part, becomes part of the whole calamitous ruin. The king never sighs alone, if he sighs, the nation groans.

ROSENCRANTZ

The single and peculiar life is bound
With all the strength and armour of the mind
To keep itself from noyance; but much more
That spirit upon whose weal depends and rests
The lives of many. The cease of majesty
Dies not alone, but like a gulf doth draw
What's near it with it. Or it is a massy wheel
Fixed on the summit of the highest mount,
To whose huge spokes ten thousand lesser things
Are mortised and adjoined, which, when it falls,
Each small annexment, petty consequence,
Attends the boist'rous ruin. Never alone
Did the king sigh, but with a general groan.

KING CLAUDIUS

Prepare yourselves to leave quickly, we'll shackle this peril which roams too freely.

KING

Arm you, I pray you, to this speedy voyage, For we will fetters put about this fear Which now goes too free-footed.

ROSENCRANTZ

We will hurry.

ROSENCRANTZ

We will haste us.

EXEUNT ROSENCRANTZ AND GUILDENSTERN.

ENTER POLONIUS, URGENTLY.

POLONIUS

Your majesty, he's going to his mother's chamber. I'll secrete myself behind the drapes to hear the conversation. I'm sure she'll pressure him, and, as you said – and wisely said too – it's better that more than a mother hears him, since nature makes her biased. Farewell, your highness. I'll call on you before you go to bed and tell you what I learn.

POLONIUS

My lord, he's going to his mother's closet. Behind the arras I'll convey myself To hear the process. I'll warrant she'll tax him home; And, as you said - and wisely was it said - 'Tis meet that some more audience than a mother, Since nature makes them partial, should o'erhear The speech of vantage. Fare you well, my liege. I'll call upon you ere you go to bed, And tell you what I know.

KING CLAUDIUS

Thank you dearly, my lord.

KING

Thanks, dear my lord.

EXIT POLONIUS.

KING CLAUDIUS (CONT'D)

(*aside*) Oh, my crime is hideous, it stinks to high heaven. It has the curse of Cain on it, a brother's murder!

KING

O, my offence is rank, it smells to heaven. It hath the primal eldest curse* upon't, A brother's murder!

Note "Primal eldest curse" – the curse God put on Cain who murdered his own brother. In The Bible, Cain and Abel are the first two sons of the first two humans on earth, Adam and Eve. Cain was a farmer, his younger brother, Abel, a shepherd. The two brothers each made a sacrifice of his own produce to God. God favoured Abel's over Cain's. Cain in jealousy murdered Abel, which angered God. God punished Cain to a life of wandering.

KING CLAUDIUS (CONT'D)

I cannot bring myself to pray, my desire is keen, but my strong will is overpowered by an even stronger guilt, and like a man with two courses of action before me, I hesitate, not knowing which to take first, and so neglect both. What if this accursed hand were covered with my brother's blood? Isn't there rain in the sweet heavens to wash it as white as snow? What point is mercy if not to counteract sin? And what use is prayer if not for this double force to either prevent us falling from grace, or pardon us when we are down there? So I'll pray to the heavens and my sin will be behind me. Oh, but what kind of prayer would fit my crime? (*pretending to pray*) "Forgive me, lord, for my foul murder?"

That's not right, I'm still in possession of the proceeds of the murder I committed – my crown, my fulfilled ambition, and my queen. Can one be pardoned and still retain the proceeds of the crime? In the corrupt ways of this world, a wealthy criminal's hand may push aside justice, and often it is the criminal gains themselves which bribe the law. But it's not the same in heaven. There's no hiding things up there. Our actions are on display in their full glory, and we are compelled to face our faults head-on and give evidence. What then? What else can I do? See what repentance can do? What can't it do? Yet what good can it do when one can't repent?

Oh, what a wretched position! Oh, my heart, as black as death! Oh, my snared soul, the more it struggles to be free, the more it entraps itself! Help, angels of mercy! Rescue me! Bow, stubborn knees, and may my heart, be as hard as steel, but as soft as a new born babe. Make everything well.

KING

Pray can I not,
Though inclination be as sharp as will,
My stronger guilt defeats my strong intent,
And like a man to double business bound
I stand in pause where I shall first begin,
And both neglect. What if this cursed hand
Were thicker than itself with brother's blood,
Is there not rain enough in the sweet heavens
To wash it white as snow? Whereto serves mercy
But to confront the visage of offence?
And what's in prayer but this twofold force,
To be forestalled ere we come to fall,
Or pardoned being down? Then I'll look up;
My fault is past. But O, what form of prayer
Can serve my turn? `Forgive me my foul murder'?

That cannot be, since I am still possessed
Of those effects for which I did the murder -
My crown, mine own ambition, and my queen.
May one be pardoned and retain th' offence?
In the corrupted currents of this world
Offence's gilded hand may shove by justice,
And oft 'tis seen the wicked prize itself
Buys out the law. But 'tis not so above:
There is no shuffling, there the action lies
In his true nature, and we ourselves compelled
Even to the teeth and forehead of our faults
To give in evidence. What then? What rests?
Try what repentance can. What can it not?
Yet what can it when one can not repent?

O wretched state! O bosom black as death!
O limed soul* that struggling to be free
Art more engaged! Help, angels! Make assay!
Bow, stubborn knees; and heart, with strings of steel,
Be soft as sinews of the new-born babe.
All may be well.

> *Note 'Limed soul' – trapped soul. From birdlime, a sticky substance spread on twigs placed in bird's nests to trap small birds. The more the bird struggles the more it covers itself in the sticky substance.*

KING CLAUDIUS KNEELS.

ENTER HAMLET, BEHIND, UNSEEN. HE RECITES HIS 6TH SOLILOQUY.

HAMLET	HAMLET
(*aside*) Now I could do it easily, now he is praying. And now I'll do it, and send his soul to heaven.	Now might I do it pat, now a' is a-praying. And now I'll do't, and so a' goes to heaven;

DRAWING HIS SWORD.

HAMLET (CONT'D)	HAMLET
And then I have my revenge…	And so am I revenged. That would be scanned:
(*he hesitates*) This needs careful consideration… A villain kills my father, and for that, I, his only son, send this same villain to heaven.	A villain kills my father, and for that I, his sole son, do this same villain send To heaven.
Oh, but this is a helping hand, not revenge. He killed my father, still full of sin, with all his crimes in full bloom, in his lusty prime, and who knows how the balance of his sin stood? Only heaven. Our state of affairs and thoughts lie heavy only with God. Am I avenged if I take him while he is purging his soul of sins? When he is fit and ready to pass on? No.	O, this is hire and salary, not revenge. A' took my father grossly, full of bread,* With all his crimes broad blown, as flush as May; And how his audit stands who knows save heaven? But in our circumstance and course of thought 'Tis heavy with him; and am I then revenged To take him in the purging of his soul, When he is fit and seasoned for his passage? No.

HAMLET SHEATHES HIS SWORD.

> *Note: 'Full of bread' is taken from the bible, Ezekiel, 6.49. where the sins of Sodom were described as pride, fullness of bread, and abundance of idleness. Hamlet is referring to the Catholic religious practise of purging your sins before God through confession. His father was not given the opportunity to do so when he was murdered. But Claudius is now purging his sins before God. This would not be proper revenge as his sins would be cleansed and he would go to heaven.*
>
> *It seems Hamlet is looking for excuses not to do the deed.*

HAMLET (CONT'D)

Away sword, till you find a more sinful occasion. When he is asleep drunk, or in a rage, or in the incestuous pleasures of his bed, or while gambling, swearing, or some other act that has no trace of godliness in it. Then I'd trip him so that his feet may kick at heaven's door but his soul is as damned and black as hell, where it is headed for.

My mother she awaits, for me she stays.
This praying just prolongs your sinful days.

HAMLET

Up, sword, and know thou a more horrid hent:
When he is drunk asleep, or in his rage,
Or in th' incestuous pleasure of his bed,
At gaming, swearing, or about some act
That has no relish of salvation in't,
Then trip him that his heels may kick at heaven,
And that his soul may be as damned and black
As hell, whereto it goes. My mother stays.
This physic but prolongs thy sickly days.

HAMLET QUIETLY TURNS AND LEAVES.

THE KING STANDS.

KING CLAUDIUS

My words rise up, my thoughts remain below.
Words not meant, will never to Heaven go.

KING

[Rising.] My words fly up, my thoughts remain below.
Words without thoughts never to heaven go.

ACT III SCENE IV

THE QUEEN'S CLOSET.

THE QUEEN IS SITTING WAITING IN HER APARTMENT.

POLONIUS ENTERS IN HASTE.

POLONIUS

He'll be here right away. Make sure you give it to him straight. Tell him his pranks have been too outrageous to put up with, and that only your kind intervention has kept the heat of retribution from him. I'll hide myself here. I beg you, be direct with him.

. POLONIUS

A' will come straight. Look you lay home to him,
Tell him his pranks have been too broad to bear with,
And that your grace hath screened and stood between
Much heat and him. I'll silence me e'en here.*
Pray you, be round with him.

> *Note: "I'll 'silence' me e'en here" – the 'silence' makes little sense here, unless he means, "I'll speak no more" or "I'll quietly" hide in here. Many scholars believe the word should have been 'sconce' – a shortened version of 'ensconce' - commonly used in Elizabethan English, and many editors now chose to use sconce.
>
> To further strengthen this argument, in The Merry Wives of Windsor, Falstaff says, "She shall not see me; I shall ensconce myself behind the arras".

HAMLET

(off) Mother, mother, mother!

HAMLET

[Within.] Mother, mother, mother!

QUEEN GERTRUDE

(to Polonius) I will, don't worry. Hide, I hear him coming.

QUEEN

I'll warrant you; fear me not. Withdraw, I hear him coming.

POLONIUS HIDES BEHIND THE ARRAS (DRAPES).

ENTER HAMLET.

HAMLET

(entering) Now, mother, what's the matter?

HAMLET

Now, mother, what's the matter?

QUEEN GERTRUDE

Hamlet, you have greatly offended your father.

QUEEN

Hamlet, thou hast thy father much offended.

HAMLET
Mother, *you* have greatly offended *my* father.

HAMLET
Mother, you have my father* much offended.

Note: The Queen means Claudius, Hamlet mean his late father. Note the use of 'thou' and 'you'. Thou was then a term used for those close to you, You was more formal.

QUEEN GERTRUDE
Come now, your answer is foolish.

QUEEN
Come, come, you answer with an idle tongue.

HAMLET
Go now, your question is wicked.

HAMLET
Go, go, you question with a wicked tongue.

QUEEN GERTRUDE
What is the meaning of this behaviour, Hamlet!

QUEEN
Why, how now, Hamlet!

HAMLET
What's the matter now?

HAMLET
What's the matter now?

QUEEN GERTRUDE
Have you forgotten who I am?

QUEEN
Have you forgot me?

HAMLET
No, by all that's holy, not at all. You are the queen, your husband's brother's wife, and, though I wish it were not so, you are my mother.

HAMLET
No, by the rood,* not so.
You are the queen, your husband's brother's wife,
And, would it were not so, you are my mother.

Note: 'Rood' – the cross Jesus Christ was crucified on.

QUEEN GERTRUDE
(*angered*) In that case, I'll send for those who can teach you to talk to me in a proper manner.

QUEEN
Nay, then, I'll set those to you that can speak.

SHE GETS UP TO LEAVE, HAMLET BLOCKS HER WAY.

HAMLET
Come, come, sit yourself down. You're staying here. You're not going anywhere till I set up a mirror so you can see your innermost self.

HAMLET
Come, come, and sit you down. You shall not budge;
You go not till I set you up a glass
Where you may see the inmost part of you.

HE FORCES HER TO SIT.

149

QUEEN GERTRUDE	QUEEN
What will you do? Murder me?	What wilt thou do? Thou wilt not murder me?
(*calling out*) Help, Help me!	Help, help, ho!
POLONIUS	POLONIUS
(*behind the drapes*) Anyone! Help, help help!	[*Behind the arras.*] What, ho! Help, help, help!

HAMLET DRAWS HIS SWORD.

HAMLET	HAMLET
What's this? A rat? A dead rat, you can bet on it, dead!	[*Drawing.*] How now, a rat? Dead for a ducat,* dead!

HAMLET THRUSTS HIS SWORD THROUGH THE ARRAS
AS HE SAYS THE WORD 'DEAD'.

> Note: "For a ducat" was a saying which meant "you can put your money on it" – meaning you can bet on it being a certainty. A Ducat was a gold coin used to trade between nations. Although each country had its own design the ducat was valid due to its value in precious metal. Ducats are still traded today, mostly as investments, similar to gold sovereigns or Krugerrands. Shakespeare used the word a lot in his works to the point where the word became slang for money.

POLONIUS	POLONIUS
(*behind the drapes*) Oh, he's killed me!	[*Behind the arras*] O, I am slain!

POLONIUS FALLS AND DIES.

QUEEN GERTRUDE	QUEEN
Oh my, what have you done?	O me, what hast thou done?
HAMLET	HAMLET
Well, I don't know. Is it the king?	Nay, I know not. Is it the king?
QUEEN GERTRUDE	QUEEN
Oh, what a rash and bloody deed this is!	O what a rash and bloody deed is this!
HAMLET	HAMLET
A bloody deed, my good mother, almost as bad as killing a king and marrying his brother.	A bloody deed; almost as bad, good mother, As kill a king and marry with his brother.
QUEEN GERTRUDE	QUEEN
(*shocked*) As killing a king?	As kill a king?
HAMLET	HAMLET
Aye, lady, those were my words.	Ay, lady, 'twas my word.

HAMLET LIFTS UP THE ARRAS AND DISCOVERS POLONIUS, DEAD.

HAMLET (CONT'D)

(*to the dead Polonius*) Farewell, you wretched, rash, intruding fool. I mistook you for your master. Accept your fate, you've found that snooping is a dangerous game.

(*to Queen*) Stop wringing your hands.

HAMLET

Thou wretched, rash, intruding fool, farewell.
I took thee for thy better. Take thy fortune;
Thou find'st to be too busy is some danger.
[*To Queen*] Leave wringing of your hands.

THE QUEEN ATTEMPTS TO SAY SOMETHING, HAMLET STOPS HER.

HAMLET (CONT'D)

Quiet! Sit yourself down and let me wring your heart, for that's what I'll do if it's not impenetrable, and if habitual wickedness has not so hardened it that it's now armoured and fortified against reasoning.

HAMLET

Peace! Sit you down;
And let me wring your heart, for so I shall
If it be made of penetrable stuff;
If damned custom have not brazed it so
That it be proof and bulwark against sense.

QUEEN GERTRUDE

What have I done that you dare speak against me in so rude a voice?

QUEEN

What have I done that thou dar'st wag thy tongue
In noise so rude against me?

HAMLET

An act that blurs the goodness and shame of innocence, makes a mockery of virtue, takes the colour from the cheeks of innocent love and puts a sore in its place, and makes marriage vows as false as a gambler's oath. Oh, such a deed, the like of which plucks the very soul from the holy contract, and jumbles up the words of the sacred vow. The heaven's glower with anger over this world and everything in it with a sad face, as if it were doomsday, it is so sick at the thought of what you've done.

HAMLET

Such an act
That blurs the grace and blush of modesty,
Calls virtue hypocrite, takes off the rose
From the fair forehead of an innocent love
And sets a blister there, makes marriage vows
As false as dicers' oaths. O, such a deed
As from the body of contraction plucks
The very soul, and sweet religion makes
A rhapsody of words. Heaven's face doth glow
O'er this solidity and compound mass
With tristful visage, as against the doom,
Is thought-sick at the act.

QUEEN GERTRUDE

Me? What have I done that makes the heavens roar and thunder in protest so?

QUEEN

Ay me, what act,
That roars so loud and thunders in the index?*

*Note: Index, meaning prelude to something, after the index at front of book.

HAMLET WRENCHES OUT A MINIATURE PORTRAIT IN A LOCKET ON A CHAIN
AROUND HIS MOTHER'S NECK OF THE NEW KING.

HAMLET	HAMLET
Look here at this picture.	Look here upon this picture,*

HAMLET THEN SHOWS HIS MOTHER A MINIATURE PORTRAIT OF HIS LATE
FATHER, IN A LOCKET ON A CHAIN AROUND HIS OWN NECK, SIDE BY SIDE
WITH HER OWN PORTRAIT.

*Note: In some productions Hamlet points to two large paintings hanging on the
wall, in others he shows photographs. The choice will be up to the director and the
budget of the production. There is argument about whether Shakespeare meant
Hamlet to show two pictures or merely describe the two characters, effectively
painting a picture of them in words. As miniatures of the king were common at the
time, (they are referred to earlier in Act 2, Scene 2), it would be strange if two mock
miniatures were not used on stage, they were the photographs, or selfies, of the
day. Shakespeare often used 'counterfeit' to describe a portrait or painting.

HAMLET (CONT'D)

And now this one. The likeness of two brothers. See how honourable this one looks – hair radiant like the sun god Hyperion, the presence of Jove, the mightiest god of all, the threatening and commanding gaze of the war-god Mars, the stance of the eloquent messenger Mercury, newly alighted on a hill touching heaven. A combination and a product in which it seems every god has made his mark to give the world a man to look up to. This was your husband.

(*he holds up his mother's locket*) And look now at what follows. Here is your *husband,* like an infected grain contaminating his healthy brother. Can you not see? Could you leave this bountiful mountain to feed and gorge on this barren moor? Ha, are you blind? You can't call it love, for at your age the youthful blood is tamed, it's sensible, and awaits the day of judgement. But what judgement would step from this (*indicating his father*) to this? (*indicating his uncle*).

HAMLET

and on this,

The counterfeit presentment of two brothers.
See what a grace was seated on this brow -
Hyperion's curls, the front of Jove himself,
An eye like Mars, to threaten and command,
A station like the herald Mercury
New-lighted on a heaven-kissing hill;
A combination and a form indeed
Where every god did seem to set his seal
To give the world assurance of a man.
This was your husband.

Look you now what follows:
Here is your husband, like a mildewed ear
Blasting his wholesome brother. Have you eyes?
Could you on this fair mountain leave to feed,
And batten on this moor? Ha, have you eyes?
You cannot call it love, for at your age
The heyday in the blood is tame, it's humble,
And waits upon the judgement;* and what
 judgement
Would step from this to this?

Note: "Waits upon the judgement" – Judgement day, the day you die and are judged by the balance of your sins and good deeds whether you go to heaven or to hell (the good place or the bad place) Hamlet then puns on how his mother's judgement in marrying her husband's brother will be judged by God.

HAMLET (CONT'D)	HAMLET
You've still got your senses, or you wouldn't be able to get about, but your common sense is paralysed, for madness would not make such a mistake. Never was the sense of pleasure so overcome by madness that it didn't reserve some ability to choose between such a notable difference.	Sense sure you have, Else could you not have motion; but sure that sense Is apoplexed, for madness would not err, Nor sense to ecstasy was ne'er so thralled But it reserved some quantity of choice To serve in such a difference.

Note: He means the difference between the two brothers.

HAMLET (CONT'D)	HAMLET
What devil was it that cheated you at blind man's bluff? Seeing without feeling, feeling without seeing, hearing without feeling or seeing, or by smell alone? Only a sickly part of any one sense could be so hoodwinked, not all of them. Where is your shameful blush? Oh, depraved hell, if you can corrupt an old matron's bones, then morality in hot blooded youth will melt in its own fire like candlewax. Declare it no shame then when young compulsive lust takes charge, since it burns so hotly in frosty old age, and common sense still panders to desire.	What devil was't That thus hath cozened you at hoodman-blind?* Eyes without feeling, feeling without sight, Ears without hands or eyes, smelling sans all,* Or but a sickly part of one true sense Could not so mope. O shame, where is thy blush? Rebellious hell, If thou canst mutine in a matron's bones, To flaming youth let virtue be as wax And melt in her own fire; proclaim no shame When the compulsive ardour gives the charge, Since frost itself as actively doth burn, And reason panders will.*

Note: Hamlet says that if the elderly can so easily be a slave to lust, what chance do the young have to resist it?

'Hoodman-blind', now known as 'Blind Man's Bluff' is a children's game where one child is blindfold (eyes covered) and has to find other children by hearing and touch alone.

'Sans' is French for 'without'. 'Sans all' means without any other sense.

QUEEN GERTRUDE	QUEEN
Oh, Hamlet, say no more. You've turned my eyes to look into my very soul, and there I see blemishes so black and ingrained they cannot be cleansed away.	O Hamlet, speak no more. Thou turn'st mine eyes into my very soul, And there I see such black and grained spots As will not leave their tint.

HAMLET

Indeed, but to live in the rank sweat of a greasy bed, wallowing in corruption, flirting and making love in a filthy pigsty...

HAMLET

Nay, but to live
In the rank sweat of an enseamed bed,
Stewed in corruption, honeying and making love
Over the nasty sty -

QUEEN GERTRUDE

(*interrupting*) Oh, say no more! These words are like daggers stabbing my ears. No more, my sweet Hamlet.

QUEEN

O, speak to me no more!
These words like daggers enter in my ears.
No more, sweet Hamlet.

HAMLET

A murderer and a villain, a wretch that isn't worth one twentieth of one tenth of your former lord and master, the laughing stock of a king, a thief of the empire and the reign, who stole the crown from a shelf and put it in his pocket...

HAMLET

A murderer and a villain,
A slave that is not twentieth part the tithe
Of your precedent lord, a vice* of kings,
A cutpurse* of the empire and the rule,
That from a shelf the precious diadem stole
And put it in his pocket -

Note: The 'Vice' was a ridiculous character in medieval morality plays who would run around throwing firecrackers and making mischief.

'Cutpurse' – thief. A purse was hung from the belt, thieves would cut it off.

QUEEN GERTRUDE

(*interrupting*) No more!

QUEEN

No more!

HAMLET

A king in worn out clothes...

HAMLET

A king of shreds and patches* -

Note: 'Shreds and patches' – Hamlet puns on the reverse of a beggar in fine clothes, and a jester whose clothing was made from coloured patches.

ENTER GHOST, UNSEEN BY HAMLET OR QUEEN AS YET.

HAMLET (CONT'D)

(*calling to the heavens*) Save me and hover over me with your wings, you heavenly angels!

HAMLET

Save me and hover o'er me with your wings,
You heavenly guards!

HAMLET SEES THE GHOST, THE QUEEN CANNOT SEE IT.

HAMLET (CONT'D)

(*to Ghost*) What is your gracious figure's wish?

HAMLET

[*To Ghost.*] What would your gracious figure?

154

QUEEN GERTRUDE
Alas, he's mad!

HAMLET
(to Ghost) Have you come to rebuke your lazy son, whose emotions allow time to slip by, neglecting the important action of your urgent command. Oh, tell me!

GHOST
Do not forget. This visit is to sharpen your almost blunted purpose. But look at the bewilderment of your mother. Oh, step between her and her inner torment. Imagination is stronger in weaker bodies. Speak to her, Hamlet.

HAMLET
Are you alright, mother?

QUEEN GERTRUDE
Alas, are *you* alright? You direct your gaze at nothing, and hold conversations with thin air. Your eyes stare wildly, and like soldiers awoken by a call to arms, your flattened hair is startled and stands on end like living extensions. Oh, gentle son, quench the heat and flame of your distemper by sprinkling some self-control on it. What are you staring at?

QUEEN
Alas, he's mad!

HAMLET
[To Ghost.] Do you not come your tardy son to chide,
That, lapsed in time and passion, lets go by
Th' important acting of your dread command?
O, say!

GHOST
Do not forget. This visitation
Is but to whet thy almost blunted purpose.
But look, amazement on thy mother sits.
O, step between her and her fighting soul.
Conceit in weakest bodies strongest works.
Speak to her, Hamlet.

HAMLET
How is it with you, lady?

QUEEN
Alas, how is't with you,
That you do bend your eye on vacancy,
And with th' incorporal air do hold discourse?
Forth at your eyes your spirits wildly peep,
And, as the sleeping soldiers in th' alarm,
Your bedded hair, like life in excrements*,
Start up and stand an end. O gentle son,
Upon the heat and flame of thy distemper
Sprinkle cool patience. Whereon do you look?

*Note: 'Excrement' - from Latin 'ex-crescere', meaning to grow out of, is anything which grows out of the body, such as fingernails or hair. Because hair is lifeless its standing on end suggests the presence of something ominous and unnatural. The famous 18th century actor David Garrick wore a trick wig which enabled him to make his hair stand on end.

HAMLET
(pointing) At him, at him. Look, though pale see how he shines. A combination of his majestic form and strength of cause alone could make even boulders rise up.

HAMLET
On him, on him. Look you how pale he glares.*
His form and cause conjoined, preaching to stones,
Would make them capable.

*Note: 'Glare' - The common meaning back then was as in 'the glare of the sun'. Shining bright. Glare, meaning angry, was a new meaning starting circa 16th C.

155

HAMLET (CONT'D)

(to Ghost) Don't look at me, or you'll convert my stern resolve into one of pity, then I'll be acting with the wrong motive – tears instead of blood.

HAMLET

[To Ghost.] Do not look upon me,
Lest with this piteous action you convert
My stern effects; then what I have to do
Will want true colour - tears perchance for blood.

QUEEN GERTRUDE

Who are you speaking to?

QUEEN

To whom do you speak this?

HAMLET

Can you see nothing there?

HAMLET

Do you see nothing there?

QUEEN GERTRUDE

Nothing at all, though I can see everything there.

QUEEN

Nothing at all; yet all that is I see.

HAMLET

You didn't hear anything either?

HAMLET

Nor did you nothing hear?

QUEEN GERTRUDE

No, nothing but us.

QUEEN

No, nothing but ourselves.

HAMLET

Why, look there. Look how it steals away. My father, dressed as when he lived. Look, there, right now he leaves through the door.

HAMLET

Why, look you there. Look how it steals away.
My father, in his habit as he lived.
Look, where he goes even now out at the portal.

EXIT GHOST THROUGH DOOR, NEVER TO BE SEEN AGAIN.

QUEEN GERTRUDE

This is a figment of your imagination. Madness is very clever at inventing such illusions.

QUEEN

This is the very coinage of your brain.
This bodiless creation ecstasy
Is very cunning in.

HAMLET

Madness! My pulse keeps time and rhythm as steadily as yours. It is not from madness I have spoken. Test me, I will repeat anything on the matter, madness would shy away from doing that. Mother, for the love of God, stop applying soothing balm to your soul, and admit that it is your sin not my madness at fault. It will only cover the ulcerous place with a thin skin, whilst under the surface a foul infection burrows away unseen.

HAMLET

Ecstasy!
My pulse as yours doth temperately keep time,
And makes as healthful music. It is not madness
That I have uttered. Bring me to the test,
And I the matter will re-word, which madness
Would gambol from. Mother, for love of grace,
Lay not that flattering unction to your soul
That not your trespass but my madness speaks.
It will but skin and film the ulcerous place
Whiles rank corruption, mining all within,
Infects unseen.

HAMLET DROPS TO HIS KNEES BEFORE HER, GRASPING HER HAND.

HAMLET (CONT'D)

Confess your sins to heaven, repent your past, prevent the punishment to come, don't spread compost on the weeds to make them fester. Forgive me, for having the good virtue to tell you what's wrong, for in the grossness of these self-indulgent times, even virtue must beg the pardon of vice, and even bow and beg for permission to offer assistance.

QUEEN GERTRUDE

(*pulling Hamlet to his feet*) Oh Hamlet, you have torn my heart in two.

HAMLET

Oh, throw away the worst part of it and live a purer life with the other half. Good night - but don't go to my uncle's bed. Feign decency even if you have none. That monster, custom, which eats away our common sense and feeds upon the habits of the devil, can also hide our intentions if dressed in the clothes of angels to look good and fair. Stay away tonight, and that will make the next absence easier, and the next easier still. Repetition can change the course of one's nature, and either house the devil or throw him out with wonderful potency. Once more, good night, and when you are ready to receive a blessing yourself, I'll beg a blessing from you.

(*pointing to Polonius*) As for this man I do regret my actions, but heaven has seen fit to punish me with this action, and used me to punish him, making me both their slave and their master. I will dispose of him, and face any questions over the death I caused in him. So again, good night. I have to be cruel to be kind. This is a bad beginning and worse is to come. One more word, good lady…

HAMLET

Confess yourself to heaven,
Repent what's past, avoid what is to come,
And do not spread the compost on the weeds
To make them ranker. Forgive me this my virtue,
For in the fatness of these pursy times
Virtue itself of vice must pardon beg,
Yea, curb and woo for leave to do him good.

QUEEN

O Hamlet, thou hast cleft my heart in twain.

HAMLET

O, throw away the worser part of it,
And live the purer with the other half.
Good night: but go not to my uncle's bed.
Assume a virtue if you have it not.
That monster, custom, who all sense doth eat,
Of habits devil, is angel yet in this,
That to the use of actions fair and good
He likewise gives a frock or livery
That aptly is put on. Refrain tonight,
And that shall lend a kind of easiness
To the next abstinence, the next more easy;
For use almost can change the stamp of nature,
And either house the devil, or throw him out
With wondrous potency. Once more, good night.
And when you are desirous to be blest,
I'll blessing beg of you.
[*Pointing to Polonius.*] For this same lord
I do repent; but heaven hath pleased it so
To punish me with this, and this with me,
That I must be their scourge and minister.
I will bestow him, and will answer well
The death I gave him. So, again, good night.
I must be cruel only to be kind.
This bad begins, and worse remains behind.
One word more, good lady.

QUEEN GERTRUDE	QUEEN
But what shall I do?	What shall I do?
HAMLET	HAMLET
None of the following things, whatever happens: do not let the bloated king tempt you again to his bed, or pinch your cheek amorously, or call you his mouse, and don't let him, for a pair of loathsome kisses or by stroking your neck with his damned fingers, make you reveal you know that I am not essentially mad, but merely pretending.	Not this, by no means, that I bid you do: Let the bloat king tempt you again to bed, Pinch wanton on your cheek, call you his mouse, And let him, for a pair of reechy kisses Or paddling in your neck with his damned fingers, Make you to ravel all this matter out, That I essentially am not in madness, But mad in craft. 'Twere good you let him know;
(*sarcastic*) It's right that it's your duty to let him know, for what serene, sober, wise queen would hide such important matters from even a toad, a bat or a cat? Who would do such a thing? No, contrary to sense and decency, do not open the door of the cage and let the birds fly, lest like the monkey who leapt from the cage copying the birds you fall and break your neck.	For who that's but a queen, fair, sober, wise, Would from a paddock, from a bat, a gib,* Such dear concernings hide? Who would do so? No, in despite of sense and secrecy, Unpeg the basket on the house's top, Let the birds fly, and, like the famous ape,* To try conclusions, in the basket creep And break your own neck down.

> *Note: Toad (paddock), bat and cat (gib) are all associated with witches.*
>
> *The ape and the basket. This is from a long forgotten fable, which seems to have been about a monkey who took the lid off a basket, probably a trap at some height, such as up a tree or on a roof, freeing the birds trapped inside, crawled in himself, and assuming he could fly as the birds had done, leapt out and broke his neck.*

QUEEN GERTRUDE	QUEEN
Rest assured, if words are made of breath, and breath gives life, I haven't the life in me to breathe what you have said to me.	Be thou assured, if words be made of breath And breath of life, I have no life to breathe What thou hast said to me.
HAMLET	HAMLET
I must go to England. You know that?	I must to England; you know that?*
QUEEN GERTRUDE	QUEEN
Alas, I had forgotten. It has been so decided.	Alack, I had forgot. 'Tis so concluded on.

> *Note: It is unclear just how Hamlet knew this, unless he overheard the conversation between the king and R & G.*

HAMLET

(*See note below*) The documents have been raised, and my two school friends, whom I trust as much as fanged snakes, bear a message to the English king. They're to sweep me away and lead me into some kind of a trap. Let it proceed, for it's the occupational hazard of the soldier to be blown up by his own bomb. It will be easy to tunnel one yard below their mines and blow them to the moon. Oh, it will be most sweet when the first plot meets the second.

HAMLET

There's letters sealed, and my two schoolfellows,
Whom I will trust as I will adders fanged,
They bear the mandate; they must sweep my way
And marshal me to knavery. Let it work,
For 'tis the sport to have the engineer
Hoist with his own petard;* and't shall go hard
But I will delve one yard below their mines
And blow them at the moon. O, 'tis most sweet
When in one line two crafts directly meet.

> *Note: Hamlet's speech above about the letters does not appear in later versions of the original printings, possibly removed by Shakespeare himself as this speech not only reveals what is to come but is a problem in that Hamlet did not know the plot against him at this point.*
>
> *'Hoist with his own petard' means to die by his own bomb. Ironic justice.*

HAMLET (CONT'D)

(*about Polonius*) This man will see to it I'm packed off quickly. I'll drag the body into the next room. Mother, good night indeed. This counsellor
Who now is still, most quiet and most grave,
Was once in life a foolish prattling knave.

HAMLET

This man shall set me packing.
I'll lug the guts* into the neighbour room.
Mother, good night indeed. This counsellor
Is now most still, most secret, and most grave,
Who was in life a foolish prating knave.

HAMLET GRABS THE DEAD BODY OF POLONIUS.

HAMLET (CONT'D)

(*to body*) Come sir, my business with you draws to an end. Good night, mother.

HAMLET

Come, sir, to draw toward an end with you.
Good night, mother.

EXIT HAMLET DRAGGING THE DEAD BODY OF POLONIUS.

> *Note: 'Lug the guts' means to drag or carry the body, 'guts' being a term used often to describe a person unkindly, e.g. I hate his guts, greedy guts etc. 'Draw toward' is a pun on dragging the body. You draw (or pull) water or something towards you etc.*

ACT IV

THE LADY DOTH PROTEST TOO MUCH

ACT IV

ACT IV SCENE I

THE QUEEN'S CLOSET.

THE QUEEN IS PRESENT, LOOKING UPSET.

ENTER THE KING, WITH ROSENCRANTZ AND GUILDENSTERN.

KING CLAUDIUS

(*to Queen*) These sighs, these shuddering breaths, there must be a reason for them, you must explain yourself, it's right I should know. Where is your son?

KING

There's matter in these sighs, these profound heaves;
You must translate, 'tis fit we* understand them.
Where is your son?

> *Note: Again, the king is speaking as the 'royal we'. He refers to himself as the whole nation. It is excluded from the translation as it is confusing to those whose first language is not English, and to those not familiar with royal speak.*

QUEEN GERTRUDE

(*to R and G*) Leave us for a little while.

QUEEN

Bestow this place on us a little while.

EXEUNT ROSENCRANTZ AND GUILDENSTERN.

QUEEN GERTRUDE

Oh, my husband, the things I've seen tonight!

QUEEN

Ah, mine own lord, what have I seen tonight!

KING CLAUDIUS

What things, Gertrude? How is Hamlet's mind?

KING

What, Gertrude? How does Hamlet?

QUEEN GERTRUDE

As mad as the sea and the wind when they fight to prove which is the mightier. In his uncontrolled madness, hearing something behind the drapes, he whipped out his sword, crying 'A rat, a rat!', and with this crazy notion in his head he killed the concealed good old man.

QUEEN

Mad as the sea and wind when both contend
Which is the mightier. In his lawless fit,
Behind the arras hearing something stir,
Whips out his rapier, cries `A rat, a rat!'
And in this brainish apprehension kills
The unseen good old man.

KING CLAUDIUS

Oh, deplorable act! It would have been my fate had I been there. His liberty is a threat to us all, to you yourself, to me, to everyone. Alas, how shall I explain this bloody deed? The blame will be laid on me for not keeping this mad young man in check, restrained and out of circulation. But I loved him so much I didn't know what was best to do, so, like a man with a foul disease, to prevent it becoming public knowledge I let it fester and feed on the body which carries it. Where is he now?

KING

O heavy deed!
It had been so with us had we been there.
His liberty is full of threats to all,
To you yourself, to us, to every one.
Alas, how shall this bloody deed be answered?
It will be laid to us, whose providence
Should have kept short,* restrained, and out of
  haunt,
This mad young man. But so much was our love,
We would not understand what was most fit,
But, like the owner of a foul disease,
To keep it from divulging, let it feed
Even on the pith of life.* Where is he gone?

*Note: 'Short' here means 'short rein' – keeping someone on a short rein is to keep them close and under control. It is derived from horse control.

'Pith of life' means 'bone marrow of life' – the core of life.

The King is really thinking only of his own position and safety.

QUEEN GERTRUDE

He's removing the body he killed, over which he weeps for what he has done - his madness, like a vein of gold in an iron mine, shows itself as pure at least.

QUEEN

To draw apart the body he hath killed,
O'er whom - his very madness, like some ore
Among a mineral* of metals base,*
Shows itself pure - a' weeps for what is done.

*Note: She's not being truthful. Hamlet was not so upset.

The ore is probably gold in a mine (mineral) of base metals. Gold was once thought to be the only pure metal. Famously alchemists tried to create gold from other base metals, the quest for the fabled philosopher's stone. Though unsuccessful it led to the founding of chemistry as a science.

KING CLAUDIUS

Oh Gertrude, come with me! The sun shall no sooner touch the mountain tops than we'll have him shipped out, and with all our majesty and skill we'll both publicly admit and excuse this vile deed.
(calls) Ho there! Guildenstern!

KING

O Gertrude, come away!
The sun no sooner shall the mountains touch
But we will ship him hence; and this vile deed
We must, with all our majesty and skill,
Both countenance and excuse. Ho, Guildenstern!

RE-ENTER ROSENCRANTZ AND GUILDENSTERN.

163

KING CLAUDIUS (CONT'D)	KING
Friends, both of you, go get some help. Hamlet in his madness has slain Polonius. He's dragged the body from his mother's chamber. Go find him, treat him calmly, and take the body to the chapel. I beg you, hurry.	Friends both, go join you with some further aid. Hamlet in madness hath Polonius slain, And from his mother's closet hath he dragged him. Go seek him out, speak fair, and bring the body Into the chapel. I pray you, haste in this.

EXEUNT ROSENCRANTZ AND GUILDENSTERN HASTILY.

KING CLAUDIUS (CONT'D)	KING
Come, Gertrude, we'll call on our wisest friends and let them know what we plan to do and what untimely deed has been done. So, hopefully, the poisonous slander, whose whisper travels round the world as fast and level as the shot from a cannon to its target, will miss my name and be *Lost in the harmless air. Oh, come away.* *My soul is full of discord and dismay.**	Come, Gertrude, we'll call up our wisest friends And let them know both what we mean to do And what's untimely done. So, haply, slander, Whose whisper o'er the world's diameter, As level as the cannon to his blank, Transports his poisoned shot, may miss our name *And hit the woundless air. O, come away.* *My soul is full of discord and dismay.*

EXEUNT.

Note: the last speech of King Claudius has lines and words ommited in some editions. Some versions omit from "untimely done." and jump to, "O, come away". The words, "so, haply, slander", are thought to have been added at a later date. The alternate shorter speech is below.

KING
(*alternate last speech - see note above*)
Come, Gertrude, we'll call up our wisest friends
And let them know both what we mean to do
And what's untimely done. O, come away.
My soul is full of discord and dismay.

ACT IV SCENE II

ANOTHER ROOM IN THE CASTLE.

HAMLET HAS JUST FINISHED HIDING THE BODY OF POLONIUS.

HAMLET
(*aside, about the body*) Safely stowed away.

HAMLET
Safely stowed.

ROSENCRANTZ & GUILDENSTERN
(*off, calling*) Hamlet! Prince Hamlet!

ROSENCRANTZ & GUILDENSTERN
[*Within.*] Hamlet! Lord Hamlet!

HAMLET
(*aside*) What's the noise? Who's calling me?

HAMLET
What noise? Who calls on Hamlet?

ENTER ROSENCRANTZ AND GUILDENSTERN.

HAMLET (CONT'D)
(*aside, sarcastic*) Oh, here they come...

HAMLET
O, here they come.

ROSENCRANTZ
My lord, what have you done with the dead body?

ROSENCRANTZ
What have you done, my lord, with the dead body?

HAMLET
It's mixed with the dust from whence it came.

HAMLET
Compounded it with dust,* whereto 'tis kin.

*Note: From the Christian burial service, where the body is placed in the earth with the words, "Ashes to ashes, dust to dust".

ROSENCRANTZ
Tell us where so we can get it and carry it to the chapel.

ROSENCRANTZ
Tell us where 'tis, that we may take it thence And bear it to the chapel.

HAMLET
Don't believe it.

HAMLET
Do not believe it.

ROSENCRANTZ
Believe what?

ROSENCRANTZ
Believe what?

HAMLET

That I can keep your secrets and not my own. Besides, to be interrogated by a sponge - what reply should the son of a king make?

ROSENCRANTZ

You think I am a sponge, my lord?

HAMLET

Yes sir, that soaks up the King's favours, his rewards, his orders. But such officers do the king the best service in the end. Like an ape he keeps them in the corner of his mouth, he sucks them dry, then swallows. When he needs to know what you've learned, he only needs to squeeze you, and sponge, you will be dry again.

ROSENCRANTZ

I don't understand you, my lord.

HAMLET

I am glad of that. Satire sleeps in a fools ear.

ROSENCRANTZ

My lord, you must tell us where the body is, and accompany us to the king.

HAMLET

The body is with the king, (*Hamlet*) but the king (*Claudius*) is not with the body. The king is a thing... (*he pauses*)

GUILDENSTERN

A thing, my lord?

HAMLET

...Of nothing. Take me to him. We'll play hide and seek.

HAMLET

That I can keep your counsel and not mine own. Besides, to be demanded of a sponge - what replication should be made by the son of a king?

ROSENCRANTZ

Take you me for a sponge, my lord?

HAMLET

Ay, sir, that soaks up the king's countenance, his rewards, his authorities. But such officers do the king best service in the end. He keeps them, like an ape, in the corner of his jaw, first mouthed to be last swallowed. When he needs what you have gleaned, it is but squeezing you, and, sponge, you shall be dry again.

ROSENCRANTZ

I understand you not, my lord.

HAMLET

I am glad of it. A knavish speech sleeps in a foolish ear.

ROSENCRANTZ

My lord, you must tell us where the body is, and go with us to the king.

HAMLET

The body is with the king, but the king is not with the body. The king is a thing -

GUILDENSTERN

A thing, my lord?

HAMLET

Of nothing. Bring me to him. Hide fox,* and all after.

---

*Note: 'Hide Fox...' was a children's game, now known as hide and seek – children hide while others look for them. Hamlet is pretending he is mad and this is all a silly game and they have to go look for the body.

ACT IV SCENE III

ANOTHER ROOM IN THE CASTLE.

THE KING IS SPEAKING WITH TWO OR THREE LORDS.

KING CLAUDIUS

I have sent some to seek him, and to find the body. It's dangerous to have this man on the loose! But we must not apply the full strength of the law on him, he's loved by the mindless masses who judge only by appearances, and as such, the offender's suffering is considered and not the actual offence committed. To keep everything smooth and calm, this sudden sending away must be seen as if it were deliberated on previously. Acute diseases require acute measures to cure them, nothing else will suffice.

KING

I have sent to seek him, and to find the body.
How dangerous is it that this man goes loose!
Yet must not we put the strong law on him:
He's loved of the distracted multitude,
Who like not in their judgement, but their eyes;
And where 'tis so, th' offender's scourge is weighed,
But never the offence. To bear all smooth and even,
This sudden sending him away must seem
Deliberate pause. Diseases desperate grown
By desperate appliance are relieved,
Or not at all.

KING CLAUDIUS (CONT'D)

Well? What has happened?

KING

How now! What hath befall'n?

ROSENCRANTZ

We can't get out of him where the dead body is hidden, your majesty .

ROSENCRANTZ

Where the dead body is bestowed, my lord,
We cannot get from him.

KING CLAUDIUS

But where is he?

KING

But where is he?

ROSENCRANTZ

Outside, your majesty, cautious as to your welcome.

ROSENCRANTZ

Without, my lord, guarded to know your pleasure.

KING CLAUDIUS

Bring him before me.

KING

Bring him before us.

ROSENCRANTZ

(*Calling*) Guildenstern! Bring in the prince.

ROSENCRANTZ

Ho, Guildenstern! Bring in the lord.

ENTER GUILDENSTERN WITH HAMLET.

KING CLAUDIUS Now, Hamlet, where is Polonius?	KING Now, Hamlet, where's Polonius?
HAMLET At supper.	HAMLET At supper.
KING CLAUDIUS At supper! Where?	KING At supper!* Where?

*Note: Supper is an evening snack or small meal.

HAMLET Not where he eats, but where he is eaten. A certain gathering of discerning worms are with him even now. The worm is the true connoisseur of diet. We fatten our animals to fatten us, and we fatten ourselves for the maggots. Your fat king and your lean beggar are just two ways of serving the same dish, – that's how it ends.	HAMLET Not where he eats, but where he is eaten. A certain convocation of politic worms are e'en at him. Your worm is your only emperor for diet. We fat all creatures else to fat us, and we fat ourselves for maggots; your fat king and your lean beggar is but variable service - two dishes, but to one table: that's the end.
KING CLAUDIUS Alas, alas!	KING Alas, alas!
HAMLET A man may fish with a worm that has dined on a king, and then eat the fish that has fed on that worm.	HAMLET A man may fish with the worm that hath eat of a king, and eat of the fish that hath fed of that worm.
KING CLAUDIUS What do you mean by this?	KING What dost thou mean by this?
HAMLET Nothing more than to show you how a king may make a state journey through the guts of a beggar.	HAMLET Nothing but to show you how a king may go a progress* through the guts of a beggar.

*Note: 'Progress' A royal progress was a state ceremony where the king would travel among his subjects in great pomp and ceremony. Elaborate celebrations were laid on throughout the journey.

KING CLAUDIUS (angry) Where is Polonius!	KING Where is Polonius?

HAMLET

In heaven. Send for him there. If your messenger doesn't find him there, seek for him in the other place yourself. But if you don't find him within a month, you'll smell him as you go upstairs into the lobby

HAMLET

In heaven; send thither to see. If your messenger find him not there, seek him i'th' other place* yourself. But if indeed you find him not within this month, you shall nose him as you go up the stairs into the lobby.

*Note: "The other place" is hell, suggesting Claudius is going to hell.

KING CLAUDIUS

(*to Attendants*) Go look for him there.

KING

[*To some Lords.*] Go seek him there.

HAMLET

He'll be waiting for you.

HAMLET

A' will stay till you come.

EXEUNT LORDS.

KING CLAUDIUS

Hamlet, for your own safety - which we hold dear, as dearly as we grieve for the act you have done – we must send you away with great speed. Therefore make preparations. The ship is ready, and the wind is favourable, your companions await, and everything is set for England.

KING

Hamlet, this deed, for thine especial safety -
Which we do tender, as we dearly grieve
For that which thou hast done - must send thee hence
With fiery quickness. Therefore prepare thyself.
The bark is ready, and the wind at help,
Th' associates tend, and everything is bent
For England.

HAMLET

For England?

HAMLET

For England?

KING CLAUDIUS

Yes, Hamlet.

KING

Ay, Hamlet.

HAMLET

Good.

HAMLET

Good.

KING CLAUDIUS

For us as well, if you knew my intentions.

KING

So is it, if thou knew'st our purposes.

HAMLET

I see an angel that sees them. But for now, to England. Farewell, dear mother.

HAMLET

I see a cherub that sees them. But come, for England. Farewell, dear mother.

KING CLAUDIUS

It is your loving father's doing, Hamlet.

KING

Thy loving father, Hamlet.

HAMLET	HAMLET
No, my mother. Father and mother is man and wife, man and wife is one flesh, therefore it is my mother. (*To R & G, dramatically*) Forward, to England.	My mother. Father and mother is man and wife, man and wife is one flesh, and so - my mother. Come, for England.

EXIT HAMLET.

KING CLAUDIUS	KING
(*to R and G*) Follow him closely, get him aboard quickly. Don't delay, I'll have him away tonight.	[*To Rosencrantz and Guildenstern.*] Follow him at foot; tempt him with speed aboard. Delay it not; I'll have him hence tonight.

ROSENCRANTZ AND GUILDENSTERN HESITATE, AWAITING ANY MORE ORDERS.

KING CLAUDIUS (CONT'D)	KING
Away! The documentation is all sealed and complete for the other purpose of your mission. Now, make haste.	Away! - for everything is sealed and done That else leans on th' affair. Pray you, make haste.

EXEUNT ROSENCRANTZ AND GUILDENSTERN HURRIEDLY.

KING CLAUDIUS (CONT'D)	KING
(*aside*) And, King of England, if you hold any value in my friendship, and my great power over you, may it give you the good sense - since your wounds are still red raw from the last Danish invasion, and your freedom only dependant on your due payments to me – to not ignore my sovereign request, which is described in full in my letters to that effect, namely, the immediate death of Hamlet. Do it, King of England, for like a fever in my blood he rages. *You hold my cure, and till I know it's done, Whate'er my fortune, my joy's not begun.*	And, England, if my love thou hold'st at aught - As my great power thereof may give thee sense, Since yet thy cicatrice* looks raw and red After the Danish sword, and thy free awe Pays homage to us - thou mayst not coldly set Our sovereign process, which imports at full, By letters congruing to that effect, The present death of Hamlet. Do it, England; For like the hectic in my blood he rages, *And thou must cure me. Till I know 'tis done, Howe'er my haps, my joys were ne'er begun.*

*Note: "cicatrice" – the scar of a healed wound.

ACT IV SCENE IV

A PLAIN IN DENMARK.

ENTER THE KING OF NORWAY'S NEPHEW, FORTINBRAS,
WITH A CAPTAIN, AND SOLDIERS MARCHING.

THEY COME TO A HALT.

FORTINBRAS
Captain, go to the Danish king bearing my greetings. Tell him that as agreed, Fortinbras requests the safe passage of his troops across his kingdom. You know the appointed rendezvous. And let him know that if his majesty so wishes, I shall humbly put my request in person.

CAPTAIN
I will do it, my lord.

FORTINBRAS
(*to his army*) Proceed at a measured pace.

FORTINBRAS
Go, captain, from me greet the Danish king.
Tell him that by his licence Fortinbras
Craves the conveyance of a promised march
Over his kingdom. You know the rendezvous.
If that his majesty would aught with us,
We shall express our duty in his eye;
And let him know so.

CAPTAIN
I will do't, my lord.

FORTINBRAS
Go softly on.

EXEUNT FORTINBRAS AND ARMY.

HAMLET, ROSENCRANTZ, GUILDENSTERN, AND ATTENDANTS, HEADING FOR THE SHIP, MEET THE CAPTAIN. THEY SEE THE ARMY IN THE DISTANCE.

HAMLET
Good sir, whose army is this?

CAPTAIN
It's from Norway, sir.

HAMLET
For what purpose, sir, may I ask?

CAPTAIN
A campaign against a region of Poland.

HAMLET
Who is in command, sir?

CAPTAIN
The nephew of the old King of Norway, Fortinbras.

HAMLET
Good sir, whose powers are these?

CAPTAIN
They are of Norway, sir.

HAMLET
How purposed, sir, I pray you?

CAPTAIN
Against some part of Poland.

HAMLET
Who commands them, sir?

CAPTAIN
The nephew to old Norway, Fortinbras.

HAMLET
Is the campaign against the whole of Poland or some border dispute?

CAPTAIN
To be honest, and in plain terms, our aims are to gain a small patch of ground that has no benefit to us except in name. I wouldn't pay five ducats - five - to rent it. Nor would it be worth anything to Norway or to Poland if it were sold outright.

HAMLET
Surely then, the Poles would never defend it.

CAPTAIN
Yes, there is a garrison stationed there.

HAMLET
Two thousand souls and twenty thousand ducats are not worth arguing over this worthless land. This is the abscess of excessive wealth and peace, which bursts inside and shows no outward cause as to why the man died. I humbly thank you, sir.

CAPTAIN
God be with you, sir.

HAMLET
Goes it against the main of Poland, sir,
Or for some frontier?

CAPTAIN
Truly to speak, and with no addition,
We go to gain a little patch of ground
That hath in it no profit but the name.
To pay five ducats, five, I would not farm it;
Nor will it yield to Norway or the Pole
A ranker rate should it be sold in fee.

HAMLET
Why, then the Polack never will defend it.

CAPTAIN
Yes, it is already garrisoned.

HAMLET
Two thousand souls and twenty thousand ducats
Will not debate the question of this straw.
This is th' impostume of much wealth and peace,
That inward breaks, and shows no cause without
Why the man dies. I humbly thank you, sir.

CAPTAIN
God-buy-you, sir.

EXIT CAPTAIN.

ROSENCRANTZ
Shall we be going, my lord?

HAMLET
I'll be right with you. You go ahead.

ROSENCRANTZ
Will't please you go, my lord?

HAMLET
I'll be with you straight; go a little before.

EXEUNT ALL BUT HAMLET, RECITING HIS 7TH AND FINAL SOLILOQUY.

HAMLET

(*aside*) Everything I see around me only reminds me how weak and lacklustre my revenge has been! What is a man, if his main interest and use of his time is just sleeping and eating? No better than a beast. Surely, he who created us with such great ability to make decisions based on past and future events, did not give us that capability and godlike reasoning to let it fester unused in us. I don't know why, other than from a beast-like forgetfulness, or some cowardly fear from over-thinking the consequences – logic which consists of one part wisdom and three parts cowardice – I live to say "This thing's yet to be done", when I still have the reason, the will, the strength, and the means to do it.

HAMLET

How all occasions do inform against me,
And spur my dull revenge! What is a man
If his chief good and market of his time
Be but to sleep and feed? A beast, no more.
Sure, he that made us with such large discourse,
Looking before and after, gave us not
That capability and godlike reason
To fust in us unused. Now, whether it be
Bestial oblivion, or some craven scruple
Of thinking too precisely on th' event -
A thought which, quartered, hath but one part
  wisdom
And ever three parts coward - I do not know
Why yet I live to say `This thing's to do',
Sith I have cause, and will, and strength, and
  means,
To do't.

> Note: A strange statement, he is being shipped to England so the means of doing the deed has slipped away from him.

HAMLET (CONT'D)

Examples too numerous to count incite me – witness this army of such size and power, led by an inexperienced young prince, whose courage and swollen ambition laughs in scorn at the unknown to come, risking lives to fate and dangers untold all for a worthless shell. To be great, one should take action only with great reason, not to find great reason in a useless patch of land to prove one's honour.

HAMLET

Examples gross as earth exhort me;
Witness this army of such mass and charge,
Led by a delicate and tender prince,
Whose spirit with divine ambition puffed
Makes mouths at the invisible event,
Exposing what is mortal and unsure
To all that fortune, death, and danger dare,
Even for an eggshell. Rightly to be great
Is not to stir without great argument,
But greatly to find quarrel in a straw
When honour's at the stake.

> Note: Hamlet is sarcastically suggesting that Fortinbras is trying to prove himself, (after the death of his father to Hamlet's father), by attacking a bit of useless land, the irony being that Hamlet can't even prove himself by revenging his own father's death.

HAMLET (CONT'D)

Where do I stand then? I've a murdered father, a dishonoured mother, incitements to my reasoning and passion, yet they lie dormant, while, to my shame, I see the imminent death of twenty thousand men, who for a moment of glory go to their graves like they would to their beds, fighting for a plot of land not big enough to hold the number of men fighting for it, nor big enough to bury the fallen.

Oh father, my thoughts from this moment forth,

Shall be murderous, or they have no worth!

HAMLET

How stand I then,
That have a father killed, a mother stained,
Excitements of my reason and my blood,
And let all sleep, while, to my shame, I see
The imminent death of twenty thousand* men
That, for a fantasy and trick of fame,
Go to their graves like beds, fight for a plot
Whereon the numbers cannot try the cause,
Which is not tomb enough and continent
To hide the slain? O, from this time forth,
My thoughts be bloody, or be nothing worth!

Note: Hamlet here says twenty thousand men, whereas earlier he had said two thousand men and twenty thousand ducats.

ACT IV SCENE V

ELSINORE. A ROOM IN THE CASTLE.

QUEEN GERTRUDE IS SPEAKING WITH HORATIO
AND AN UNNAMED GENTLEMAN.

QUEEN GERTRUDE
I will not speak with her.

GENTLEMAN
She is insistent, she's quite troubled. In her state she needs some compassion.

QUEEN GERTRUDE
What does she want?

GENTLEMAN
She talks constantly about her father, says the world is unfair, and coughs and beats her chest, and takes spiteful offence in the smallest thing saying wild things that make little sense. She talks nonsense, yet her rambling use of words attracts attention, people listen and then mix up the words to fit their own opinions, which, as she delivers them with winks and nods and gestures, one would think there might be some inferred meaning, though nothing for certain it suggests it is shocking in nature.

HORATIO
It would be wise to speak with her, she may spread dangerous rumours among those with trouble in mind.

QUEEN GERTRUDE
Let her come in then.

QUEEN
I will not speak with her.

GENTLEMAN
She is importunate,
Indeed distract. Her mood will needs be pitied.

QUEEN
What would she have?

GENTLEMAN
She speaks much of her father, says she hears
There's tricks i'th' world, and hems and beats her heart,
Spurns enviously at straws, speaks things in doubt
That carry but half sense. Her speech is nothing,
Yet the unshaped use of it doth move
The hearers to collection; they aim at it,
And botch the words up fit to their own thoughts,
Which, as her winks and nods and gestures yield them,
Indeed would make one think there might be thought,
Though nothing sure, yet much unhappily.

HORATIO
'Twere good she were spoken with, for she may strew
Dangerous conjectures in ill-breeding minds.

QUEEN
Let her come in.

THE GENTLEMAN AND HORATIO LEAVE TO FETCH OPHELIA.

QUEEN GERTRUDE	QUEEN
(aside) To my troubled soul, as with sinners is,	*[Aside.] To my sick soul, as sin's true nature is,*
Each little thing seems signs of great amiss.	*Each toy seems prologue to some great amiss.*
So full of groundless suspicion is guilt,	*So full of artless jealousy is guilt,*
Truth shows itself in fearing to be spilt	*It spills itself in fearing to be spilt.*

HORATIO LEADS OPHELIA IN. SHE CARRIES A LUTE.

HER MIND IS OBVIOUSLY ELSEWHERE, SHE IS NOT HERSELF.

OPHELIA	OPHELIA
Where is the beautiful Queen of Denmark?	Where is the beauteous majesty of Denmark?

QUEEN GERTRUDE	QUEEN
How are you, Ophelia?	How now, Ophelia?

OPHELIA	OPHELIA
(sings) How should I know your true love	*[Sings.] How should I your true love know*
From any other one?	*From another one?*
By his pilgrim's hat and staff,	*By his cockle hat and staff,**
And his sandals worn.	*And his sandal shoon.**

*Note: From a popular ballad of the time. The cockle hat and staff and sandals were worn by pilgrims who made the pilgrimage to the shrine of Saint James in the Cathedral of Santiago de Compostela, in Galicia, north western Spain.

QUEEN GERTRUDE	QUEEN
My sweet lady, what is the meaning of this singing?	Alas, sweet lady, what imports this song?

OPHELIA	OPHELIA
You don't know? Well, I ask you, listen.	Say you? Nay, pray you, mark.
(sings) He is dead and gone, lady,	*[Sings.] He is dead and gone, lady,*
He is dead and gone:	*He is dead and gone:*
At his head is grass-green earth,	*At his head a grass-green turf,**
At his heels is stone.	*At his heels a stone.**
Oh ho!	*O ho!**

*Note: The 'O ho!" could have been a finale to the verse or her sighing.

Green turf and a stone describe a pauper's grave. Not befitting her father, especially as the headstone is placed at his feet.

QUEEN GERTRUDE	QUEEN
Oh, but Ophelia…	Nay, but Ophelia -

OPHELIA	OPHELIA
I beg you, listen.	Pray you, mark.
(sings) His shroud as white as mountain snow-	*[Sings.] White his shroud as the mountain snow -*

176

ENTER KING CLAUDIUS.

QUEEN GERTRUDE (*to King*) Alas, my lord, look.	QUEEN Alas, look here, my lord.
OPHELIA (*continues singing*) *All covered with sweet flowers,* *Which in tears to the grave did <u>not</u> go* *With true-love showers.*	OPHELIA [*Sings.*] *Larded all with sweet flowers,* *Which bewept to the grave did not* go* *With true-love showers.**

*Note: The word 'not' above was added by Ophelia to make her point that her father was buried in a hurry with no tearful mourners. 'True-love showers' are the tears of loved ones.

KING CLAUDIUS How are you, pretty lady?	KING How do you, pretty lady?
OPHELIA Well, may God bless you! They say the owl was a baker's daughter. Lord, we know what we are, but not what we might become. God be at your table!	OPHELIA Well, God-dild you! They say the owl* was a baker's daughter. Lord, we know what we are, but know not what we may be. God be at your table!

*Note: The 'owl' is a reference to an old folktale of Jesus entering a baker's shop in disguise and asking for bread. The baker feeling sorry for him put a large piece of dough in the oven to bake for him. The baker's daughter told her father off. For her unkindness she was turned into an owl, and flew away never to be seen again.

KING CLAUDIUS She is moping for her father.	KING Conceit upon her father.
OPHELIA Now, let's not discuss this, but when they ask you what it means, say this: (*sings*) *Tomorrow is Saint Valentine's day,* *Early in the morning time,* *A maid I'll be at your window,* *To be your Valentine.* *Then up he rose, and donned his clothes,* *Opened his bedroom door,* *Let in the maid, who as a maid,* *Would never leave no more.*	OPHELIA Pray, let's have no words of this, but when they ask you what it means, say you this: [*Sings.*] *Tomorrow is Saint Valentine's day,* *All in the morning betime,* *And I a maid at your window,* *To be your Valentine.* *Then up he rose, and donned his clothes,* *And dupped the chamber-door;* *Let in the maid, that out a maid* *Never departed more.**

*Note: In folklore, on Valentine's day, the first woman seen by a man in the morning would be his true Valentine. In the verse above the 'maid' is taken into his house and when she leaves is no longer a virgin.

KING CLAUDIUS
(*aghast at the bawdiness*) Innocent Ophelia!

KING
Pretty Ophelia!

OPHELIA
Indeed, and without an oath, I'll bring it to an end.
(*sings*) *By Jesus and Saint Charity,*
Alas, and oh for shame!
Young men will do it, if they come to it,
By Cock, they are to blame.
Quoth she "Before you slept with me,
You promised we'd be wed."
And he answers,
"I would have done, under the sun,
If you'd not come to my bed."

OPHELIA
Indeed la; without an oath, I'll make an end on't:
[Sings.]   By Gis and by Saint Charity,
Alack, and fie for shame!
Young men will do't, if they come to't,
*By Cock, * they are to blame.*
Quoth she ` Before you tumbled me,
You promised me to wed.'
He answers,
` So would I ha' done, by yonder sun,
An thou hadst not come to my bed.'

> *Note: "Cock" was slang for 'God'. Here she uses the term as an innuendo for men being led by their genitals.*
>
> *Ophelia references what her brother Laertes had said to her earlier about Hamlet when he told her to hold onto her precious virginity, if she gave it up to Hamlet before they were wed he would lose interest in her, as he didn't truly love her.*

KING CLAUDIUS
(*to Queen*) How long has she been like this?

KING
How long hath she been thus?

OPHELIA
I hope it all turns out well. We must be patient. But I cannot help but weep to think they have laid him in the cold ground. My brother shall hear of this. And so I thank you for your good advice.
(*theatrically*) Come, my coach! Good night, ladies, good night. Sweet ladies, good night, good night.

OPHELIA
I hope all will be well. We must be patient; but I cannot choose but weep to think they would lay him i'th' cold ground. My brother shall know of it. And so I thank you for your good counsel. Come, my coach! Good night, ladies, good night; sweet ladies, good night, good night.

OPHELIA MAKES A DRAMATIC EXIT.

KING CLAUDIUS
Follow her closely, keep a good watch on her, I beg you.

KING
Follow her close; give her good watch, I pray you.

HORATIO LEAVES HURRIEDLY.

KING CLAUDIUS

Oh, this is the poisonous effect of deep sorrow. It's cause was in her father's death, and now look what's happened! Oh Gertrude, Gertrude, when sorrow comes, it never comes alone, but in swarms. First her father is slain, next, your son is gone, he being the most violent author of his own justifiable banishment. The people are suspicious, whispering wild and rebellious rumours about the death of good Polonius. I was naïve to bury him in such secret haste. Poor Ophelia, beside herself and losing her wits, and without them we are mere shadows of our former selves, or just wild beasts. Lastly, and as much as all these put together, her brother has secretly returned from France with unknown intentions and surrounded by busy-bodies infecting his ear with malicious talk about his father's death he feeds on these rumours,. And because they know nothing on the matter, they think nothing of accusing me in their whisperings. Oh my dear Gertrude, this is like a scatter-bomb, causing multiple deaths in me.

KING

O, this is the poison of deep grief. It springs
All from her father's death, and now behold!
O Gertrude, Gertrude,
When sorrows come, they come not single spies,
But in battalions. First, her father slain;
Next, your son gone, and he most violent author
Of his own just remove; the people muddied,
Thick and unwholesome in their thoughts and
  whispers
For good Polonius' death; and we have done but
  greenly
In hugger-mugger* to inter him; poor Ophelia
Divided from herself and her fair judgement,
Without the which we are pictures, or mere
  beasts;
Last, and as much containing as all these,
Her brother is in secret come from France,
Feeds on this wonder, keeps himself in clouds,
And wants not buzzers to infect his ear
With pestilent speeches of his father's death;
Wherein necessity, of matter beggared,
Will nothing stick our person to arraign
In ear and ear. O my dear Gertrude, this,
Like to a murd'ring-piece, in many places
Gives me superfluous death.

Note: Hugger-mugger – secretive.

A COMMOTION IS HEARD OUTSIDE.

QUEEN GERTRUDE

Oh no, what's that noise?

QUEEN

Alack, what noise is this?

KING CLAUDIUS

(*calls*) Attendants! Where are my personal guards? Tell them to guard the door.

KING

Attend! Where is my Switzers?* Let them guard the door.

Note: 'Switzers' – Swiss guards were employed in palaces of Europe because they were from a neutral country and so less influenced by local politics and therefore less likely to turn against the king.

A MESSENGER ENTERS HURRIEDLY.

179

KING CLAUDIUS
What's going on?

KING
What is the matter?

MESSENGER
Save yourself, my lord! The ocean, towering over its shores, overwhelms the beaches with less speed than young Laertes at the head of a rebellious mob overwhelms your guards. The rabble call him their ruler, and, as if the world were just born, its history forgotten, with no traditions - the building blocks of every civilisation - they cry, "We choose Laertes! Laertes shall be King!" Caps, hands, and mouths cheer the cry to the skies. "Laertes, shall be king. Long live King Laertes!"

MESSENGER
Save yourself, my lord!
The ocean, overpeering of his list,
Eats not the flats with more impetuous haste
Than young Laertes in a riotous head
O'erbears your officers. The rabble call him lord,
And, as the world were now but to begin,
Antiquity forgot, custom not known,
The ratifiers and props of every word,
They cry `Choose we! Laertes shall be king!'
Caps, hands, and tongues applaud it to the clouds,
`Laertes shall be king, Laertes king!'

THE MESSENGER EXITS. THE KING LOCKS AND BARS THE DOOR BEHIND HIM.

QUEEN GERTRUDE
How eagerly the cry to follow a false trail.

QUEEN
How cheerfully on the false trail* they cry!

*Note: False trail was a term used when hunting dogs picked up and followed the wrong scent. Hence calling them dogs in the next line.

NOISE AND SHOUTS ARE HEARD OUTSIDE GETTING CLOSE.

QUEEN GERTRUDE (CONT'D)
Oh, this is treason! You treacherous Danish dogs!

QUEEN
O, this is counter, you false Danish dogs!*

THE RABBLE ATTACK THE LOCKED DOORS.

KING CLAUDIUS
They've broken down the doors!

KING
The doors are broke.

ENTER LAERTES, ARMED, WITH A DANISH MOB FOLLOWING HIM.

LAERTES
Where is the king?

LAERTES
Where is the king?

LAERTES SEES THAT THE KING AND QUEEN ARE ALONE.

180

LAERTES

Men, stand outside all of you.

LAERTES

Sirs, stand you all without.

DANISH MOB

No, let us come in.

DANES

No, let's come in.

LAERTES

I implore you, wait for me outside.

LAERTES

I pray you, give me leave.

DANISH MOB

We will, we will.

DANES

We will, we will.

LAERTES

I thank you. Guard the door.

LAERTES

I thank you. Keep the door.

THE DANISH MOB WAIT OUSIDE.

LAERTES RAISES HIS SWORD THREATENINGLY AT THE KING.

LAERTES (CONT'D)

Oh, you vile king, what have you done with my father!

LAERTES

O thou vile king,

Give me my father.

QUEEN GERTRUDE STEPS BETWEEN THEM.

QUEEN GERTRUDE

(*restraining Laertes*) Calm down, good Laertes.

QUEEN

[*Holding Laertes.*] Calmly, good Laertes.

LAERTES

If there's a single drop of calm blood in my body, it proves I'm a bastard, makes my father a cuckold, and places the title 'whore' on the chaste, unblemished brow of my true mother.

LAERTES

That drop of blood that's calm proclaims me
  bastard,
Cries cuckold to my father, brands the harlot
Even here, between the chaste unsmirched brow
Of my true mother.

KING CLAUDIUS

What has caused you to raise such a large rebellion, Laertes?

(*to Queen*) Let him go, Gertrude, have no fear for my safety, a king has divine protection, treason has no hope of rising against me.

KING

What is the cause, Laertes,
That thy rebellion looks so giant-like?
Let him go, Gertrude; do not fear our person.
There's such divinity doth hedge a king,*
That treason can but peep to what it would,
Acts little of his will.

Note: It was believed that the King was appointed by God, and therefore protected by him, making him a divine being. Anyone who took action against the king was damning their soul to hell for eternity (as Laertes says a little later will happen to him if he kills the king). Strange for Claudius to be so confident when he had done the same to the late king.

KING CLAUDIUS (CONT'D)
(*to Laertes*) Tell me, Laertes, why you are so incensed.
(*to Queen*) Let him go, Gertrude.
(*to Laertes*) Speak up, man.

LAERTES
Where is my father?

KING CLAUDIUS
Dead.

QUEEN GERTRUDE
(*indicating the King*) But not killed by him.

KING CLAUDIUS
Let him have his say.

LAERTES
How did he die? – I'll not be toyed with. To hell with allegiance! I'll side with Satan himself! Conscience and decency can go to the deepest pit! I'm not afraid of damnation. I stand by my words, I don't care about this world or the next, let what comes, come. I will have complete revenge for my father.

KING CLAUDIUS
Who would stop you?

LAERTES
No one else in the world but me. And as for my means, I'll use them sparingly, what little I have will go a long way.

KING CLAUDIUS
Good Laertes, in your quest to know the facts about your dear father's death, is it your plan in revenge to sweep away everyone indiscriminately? Friend or foe? Winner and loser regardless?

KING
Tell me, Laertes,
Why thou art thus incensed? Let him go,
  Gertrude.
Speak, man.

LAERTES
Where is my father?

KING
Dead.

QUEEN
But not by him.

KING
Let him demand his fill.

LAERTES
How came he dead? - I'll not be juggled with.
To hell, allegiance! Vows, to the blackest devil!
Conscience and grace, to the profoundest pit!
I dare damnation. To this point I stand,
That both the worlds I give to negligence,
Let come what comes; only I'll be revenged
Most thoroughly for my father.

KING
Who shall stay you?

LAERTES
My will, not all the world's.
And for my means, I'll husband them so well
They shall go far with little.

KING
Good Laertes,
If you desire to know the certainty
Of your dear father's death, is't writ in your
  revenge
That, sweepstake*, you will draw both friend and
  foe,
Winner and loser?

Note: Sweepstake is a gambling term. In a sweepstake, each horse in a race is bet on by a different person. The pot – total money bet by everyone - is won by the backer of the winning horse.

182

LAERTES
Only his enemies.

KING CLAUDIUS
You know who they are then?

LAERTES
To his good friends, I'll open my arms this wide, and like the kind, life giving pelican, feed them with my blood.

LAERTES
None but his enemies.

KING
Will you know them then?

LAERTES
To his good friends thus wide I'll ope my arms, And, like the kind life-rend'ring pelican, Repast them with my blood.*

Note: It used to be thought that the pelican spread its wings and its young would peck at its breast and feed from blood straight from the heart.

KING CLAUDIUS
Why, now you are talking like a faithful son and a true gentleman. The fact I am guiltless of your father's death, and most deeply grieve for it, shall be made as plainly clear to you as daylight is to your eye.

KING
Why, now you speak Like a good child and a true gentleman. That I am guiltless of your father's death, And am most sensibly in grief for it, It shall as level to your judgement pierce As day does to your eye.

OUTSIDE OPHELIA CAN BE HEARD SINGING.

VOICES OF THE MEN OUTSIDE CAN ALSO BE HEARD.

DANISH MOB
(*outside*) Let her in.

DANES
[*Within.*] Let her come in.

THE DOOR OPENS.

LAERTES TURNS TO THE DOOR.

LAERTES
What's going on! Why the noise?

LAERTES
How now! What noise is that?

RE-ENTER OPHELIA CARRYING A MIXTURE OF FLOWERS, SHE IS DANCING AS IF INSANE.

THE MOB OUTSIDE CLOSE THE DOOR BEHIND HER AND SOME SEMBLANCE OF QUIET RETURNS TO THE ROOM.

LAERTES IS NEWLY UPSET AGAIN AT THE SIGHT OF HIS SISTER IN THIS CONDITION.

LAERTES (CONT'D)

Oh, fire dry up my brains! Tears seven times saltier burn out the sense and innocence of my eye! By the heavens, your madness will be outweighed by the scale of my revenge! Oh, rose of May, dear maiden, kind sister, sweet Ophelia!

Oh, heavens above, is it possible a young maiden's sanity should be as easily destroyed as an old man's life? Nature thrives in love, and where it thrives, it sends precious proof of itself following the loss of a loved one.

LAERTES

O, heat dry up my brains! Tears seven times salt
Burn out the sense and virtue of mine eye!
By heaven, thy madness shall be paid with weight
Till our scale turn the beam. O rose of May,*
Dear maid, kind sister, sweet Ophelia!
O heavens, is't possible a young maid's wits
Should be as mortal as an old man's life?
Nature is fine in love, and where 'tis fine
It sends some precious instance of itself
After the thing it loves.

> *Note: He calls her 'rose of May'. A Rose represents beauty and May represents springtime of life, youthfulness. In a similar vein, 'buds of May' refers to young flowers opening to the Spring sunshine, whereas the rose has matured.
>
> Laertes is saying that because of her great love for her departed father, nature has taken her sanity as a sign of her true love, it will accompany the departed loved one.

OPHELIA

(sings) They bore him bare-face on the bier,
Hey non nonny, nonny, hey nonny,
And in his grave rained many a tear –
(she stops singing) Farewell, my dove.

OPHELIA

[Sings.] They bore him barefaced on the bier;*
Hey non nonny, nonny, hey nonny;*
And in his grave rained many a tear -
Fare you well, my dove.

> *Note: 'Bier' - a frame upon which a body is carried to the grave. Barefaced meant the body wasn't covered in a shroud. Similar to 'open coffin' today.
>
> 'Hey nonny' – a nonsense expression, commonly inserted in Elizabethan period folk songs. It provides a jolly break or a chorus everyone can join in.

LAERTES

If you had your sanity and pleaded for revenge, it could not have been more moving than this display.

LAERTES

Hadst thou thy wits and didst persuade revenge,
It could not move thus.

OPHELIA

(to King) You must sing, 'A-down, a-down',
(to Queen) and you 'Call him a-down-a'.
(to all) Oh, how the refrain suits it! The song's about a cheating manager who stole his master's daughter.

OPHELIA

You must sing `A-down a-down', and you `Call him a-down-a'. O how the wheel becomes it! It is the false steward that stole his master's daughter.

LAERTES

This nonsense has more impact on me than meaningful words.

LAERTES

This nothing's more than matter.

OPHELIA DANCES AROUND HANDING OUT SYMBOLIC FLOWERS.

OPHELIA

(*handing flowers to Laertes*) Here's some rosemary, they're for remembrance. I beg you, love, remember. And here are pansies, they are for thoughts.

LAERTES

(*taking flowers*) A meaning in her madness – thoughts and remembrance, aptly fitting.

OPHELIA

(*handing flowers to King*) Here's fennel for you, and columbines.

(*handing flowers to Queen*) Here's rue for you, and some for me, On Sundays we call it the herb of grace. Oh, you must wear your rue for a different reason. And here's a daisy. I would give you violets, but they all withered when my father died. They say he met a good end.

(*sings*) For bonny sweet Robin is all my joy.

OPHELIA

There's rosemary, that's for remembrance. Pray you, love, remember. And there is pansies, that's for thoughts.

LAERTES

A document in madness - thoughts and remembrance fitted.

OPHELIA

There's fennel* for you, and columbines.* There's rue for you; and here's some for me. We may call it herb of grace a Sundays. O, you must wear your rue* with a difference. There's a daisy.* I would give you some violets, but they withered all when my father died. They say a' made a good end.

[Sings.]   *For bonny sweet Robin is all my joy.*

> *Note: Columbines and fennel are for unfaithfulness, ego and foolishness. She cannot say what she means directly to the King so she gives symbolic meaning with the flowers. She hands rue to the Queen and herself. This symbolises sorrow and repentance. Sorrow for Ophelia, repentance and regret for the Queen. Finally she hands a daisy to the Queen, symbolising false appearances, the violets she didn't hand out are symbols of faithfulness.*
>
> *In the original manuscripts no mention was made of handing out flowers, so we have to surmise who she is giving them to and for what reason. In some publications the King and the Queen are reversed. King first is the more common interpretation. There are also variations of the flower's meanings, regardless of this, Ophelia is making a dramatic show of her feelings.*

LAERTES

Sorrowful thoughts, passionate suffering, she can make even hell itself sound charming and lovely.

LAERTES

Thought and affliction, passion, hell itself, She turns to favour and to prettiness.

OPHELIA

(sings) And will he not come again?
And will he not come again?
No, no, he is dead.
Go to your deathbed,
He will never come again.
His beard was white as snow,
His flaxen hair all aglow
He is gone, he is gone,
We can but wail and moan.
God have mercy on his soul!
- And on all Christian souls, I pray that God be with you.

OPHELIA

[Sings.] And will a' not come again?
And will a' not come again?
No, no, he is dead,
Go to thy death-bed,
He never will come again.
His beard was as white as snow,
All flaxen* was his poll.
He is gone, he is gone,
And we cast away moan.
God ha' mercy on his soul!
And of all Christian souls, I pray God. God-buy-you.

*Note: Flaxon is a pale yellow colour, almost blond, common in Scandinavia.

EXIT OPHELIA DRAMATICALLY.

LAERTES LOOKS UP TO THE HEAVENS ABOVE.

LAERTES
Oh God, do you see this!

LAERTES
Do you see this, O God?

KING CLAUDIUS
Laertes, I must share in your grief, or you do me wrong. We'll meet privately later, choose your wisest friends and they shall hear our argument and judge between you and I. If directly or indirectly they find me responsible, I will forfeit my kingdom, my crown, my life and all that I call mine to you in settlement. If they do not, lend me your patience and we shall join forces to appease your soul and give it justice.

KING
Laertes, I must commune with your grief,
Or you deny me right. Go but apart,
Make choice of whom your wisest friends you will,
And they shall hear and judge 'twixt you and me.
If by direct or by collateral hand
They find us touched, we will our kingdom give,
Our crown, our life, and all that we call ours,
To you in satisfaction; but if not,
Be you content to lend your patience to us,
And we shall jointly labour with your soul
To give it due content.

LAERTES
Let it be so. The means of his death, his clandestine funeral – no memorial, sword or headstone over his bones. No noble service, no formal ceremony – it cries out to be explained so loudly from heaven to earth, that I must call it into question.

LAERTES
Let this be so.
His means of death, his obscure funeral -
No trophy, sword, nor hatchment o'er his bones,
No noble rite, nor formal ostentation -
Cry to be heard, as 'twere from heaven to earth,
That I must call't in question.

KING CLAUDIUS

And so you shall, and where the guilt lies, let the great axe fall. I beg you, come with me.

KING

So you shall;
And where th' offence is, let the great axe fall.
I pray you go with me.

EXEUNT.

ACT IV SCENE VI

ANOTHER ROOM IN THE CASTLE.

HORATIO IS PRESNT TALKING WITH ONE OF THE CASTLE SERVANTS.

HORATIO Who are these men that wish to speak with me?	HORATIO What are they that would speak with me?
SERVANT Seafaring men, sir. They say they have letters for you.	SERVANT Seafaring men, sir. They say they have letters for you.
HORATIO Let them come in.	HORATIO Let them come in.

THE SERVANT LEAVES.

HORATIO I don't know what part of the world sends me greetings, unless it is from Prince Hamlet.	HORATIO I do not know from what part of the world I should be greeted, if not from Lord Hamlet.

THE SERVANT RETURNS ACCOMPANIED BY A COUPLE
OF ROUGH LOOKING SAILORS.

1ST SAILOR God bless you, sir.	1ST SAILOR God bless you, sir.
HORATIO May he bless you too.	HORATIO Let him bless thee too.
1ST SAILOR That he shall sir, if it pleases him.	1ST SAILOR A' shall, sir, an't please him.

THE SAILOR TAKES OUT A LETTER.

1ST SAILOR (CONT'D) Here's a letter for you, sir. It comes from the Danish ambassador who was heading for England. If your name is Horatio, as I am led to believe it is.	1ST SAILOR There's a letter for you, sir. It came from th' ambassador that was bound for England.* If your name be Horatio, as I am I let to know it is.

Note: The sailor (or probably pirate) says the letter comes from the ambassador traveling to England. This we know was Hamlet, so it would seem that Hamlet did not reveal his true identity, possibly because that would have made him too valuable for the pirates to release.

HORATIO TAKES THE LETTER, OPENS IT, AND READS ALOUD.

HORATIO

(*reads*) "*Horatio, when you have read this, give these fellows access to the king – they have letters for him too. Before we were two days at sea, a heavily armed pirate ship gave us chase. Finding ourselves too slow to escape, we were compelled to fight, and as they came alongside I boarded their ship. At that moment they broke away from our ship and I became their only prisoner. With the cunning of thieves they have shown me mercy – they knew exactly what they were doing - for in return I am to do a good turn for them. Let the king have the letters I have sent, and join me with as much speed as you would flee death. I have words to speak in your ear that will make you speechless, even though mere words could only make light of such heavy matter. These good fellows will bring you to where I am. Rosencrantz and Guildenstern are still on their way to England. About them I have much to tell you. Farewell.*
Yours faithfully, HAMLET."

HORATIO

[*Reads.*] "*Horatio, when thou shalt have overlooked this, give these fellows some means to the king: they have letters for him. Ere we were two days old at sea, a pirate of very warlike appointment gave us chase. Finding ourselves too slow of sail, we put on a compelled valour, and in the grapple I boarded them. On the instant, they got clear of our ship, so I alone became their prisoner. They have dealt with me like thieves of mercy - but they knew what they did: I am to do a good turn for them. Let the king have the letters I have sent, and repair thou to me with as much speed as thou wouldst fly death. I have words to speak in thine ear will make thee dumb, yet are they much too light for the bore of the matter. These good fellows will bring thee where I am. Rosencrantz and Guildenstern hold their course for England; of them I have much to tell thee. Farewell. He that thou knowest thine, HAMLET.*"

HORATIO LOOKS UP FROM THE LETTER AND ADDRESSES THE SAILORS.

HORATIO (CONT'D)

(*to sailors*) Come, I will grant you access to deliver your letters. And do it quickly so you can take me to the man you brought them from.

HORATIO

Come, I will give you way for these your letters;
And do't the speedier that you may direct me
To him from whom you brought them.

EXUENT.

ACT IV SCENE VII

ANOTHER ROOM IN THE CASTLE.

KING CLAUDIUS IS IN EARNEST DISCUSSION WITH LAERTES.

KING CLAUDIUS

Now you've listened with a knowing ear, your conscience has to acquit me of guilt, and you must take me to your heart as a friend, since hearing that the man who killed your noble father, sought my life too.

LAERTES

So it appears. But tell me why you took no action against these acts, such heinous capital offences, it would have been wise for your own safety and everyone else's, in response to such great provocation.

KING CLAUDIUS

Oh, for two important reasons, which to you may perhaps seem very feeble, though to me are strong. The queen is his mother and worships the sight of him, and as for myself – by my strength or weakness of character, one of the two - she is so much part of my life and soul that, like a star fixed in its orbit around her, I could not go against her. The other reason, why I don't take it to a public trial, is the great love the general public have for him. They affectionately gloss over all his faults, and like the lime water spring coats wood and turns it to stone, they convert his weaknesses to strengths, so that my arrows, too light for so strong a wind, would have flown back to my bow, and not where I had aimed them.

KING

Now must your conscience my acquittance seal,
And you must put me in your heart for friend,
Sith you have heard, and with a knowing ear,
That he which hath your noble father slain
Pursued my life.

LAERTES

It well appears. But tell me
Why you proceeded not against these feats,
So criminal and so capital in nature,
As by your safety, wisdom, all things else,
You mainly were stirred up.

KING

O, for two special reasons,
Which may to you, perhaps, seem much
  unsinewed,
But yet to me they're strong. The queen his
  mother
Lives almost by his looks; and for myself -
My virtue or my plague, be it either which -
She's so conjunctive to my life and soul
That, as the star moves not but in his sphere,
I could not but by her. The other motive,
Why to a public count I might not go,
Is the great love the general gender bear him;
Who, dipping all his faults in their affection,
Would, like the spring that turneth wood to
  stone,
Convert his gyves to graces, so that my arrows,
Too slightly timbered for so loud a wind,
Would have reverted to my bow again,
But not where I have aimed them.

LAERTES

And so I've lost a noble father, and have a sister driven into mad desperation, who was once regarded - if I may recall her praises from the past - as ranking amongst the highest of the age for her perfections. But I'll have my revenge!

KING CLAUDIUS

Don't lose sleep over that never happening. You must not think I am made of such lacklustre stuff that I can let danger taunt me in the face and think it a game. You'll hear more about it shortly. I loved your father as I love myself, and that, I hope, will help you to think... (*he is interrupted*)

LAERTES

And so have I a noble father lost;
A sister driven into desp'rate terms,
Whose worth, if praises may go back again,
Stood challenger on mount of all the age
For her perfections. But my revenge will come.

KING

Break not your sleeps for that. You must not
  think
That we are made of stuff so flat and dull*
That we can let our beard be shook with danger,*
And think it pastime. You shortly shall hear
  more.
I loved your father, and we love ourself;
And that, I hope, will teach you to imagine -

ENTER A MESSENGER, WITH LETTERS.

Note: To pluck a hair from a man's beard was considered a dire insult and a threat. The defeat of the Spanish Armada was said to have 'singed the king of Spain's beard', taking the insult to the next level.

Flat and dull – flat refers to liquid that has lost its fizz or gone off.

KING CLAUDIUS

What news do you bring?

MESSENGER

Letters, my lord, from Hamlet. These are for your majesty, this one's for the queen.

KING

How now, what news?

MESSENGER

Letters, my lord, from Hamlet.
These to your majesty; this to the queen.*

Note: What was in the letter to the Queen? It's never mentioned again. Nor is Claudio (in the Messenger's next statement) mentioned again. Did Shakespeare have plans? Were they edited out? We will probably never know.

KING CLAUDIUS

From Hamlet? Who brought them?

MESSENGER

Sailors, your majesty, so they say, I didn't see them. They were given to me by Claudio. He received them from the man who brought them.

KING

From Hamlet? Who brought them?

MESSENGER

Sailors, my lord, they say; I saw them not.
They were given me by Claudio. He received
  them
Of him that brought them.

191

KING CLAUDIUS
Laertes, you shall hear them.
(*to Messenger*) Leave us.

KING
Laertes, you shall hear them.
Leave us.

EXIT MESSENGER.

THE KING OPENS THE LETTER AND READS IT ALOUD.

KING CLAUDIUS
(*reads*) *"High and gracious majesty, this is to let you know I am returned naked to your kingdom, stripped of all my belongings. Tomorrow I beg leave to see your kingly face, when I shall, with your permission, recount the ordeal of my sudden and even more remarkable return.*
HAMLET."
- What does this mean? Are the others coming back? Or is it deception of some kind with no truth in it?

KING
[*Reads.*] *"High and mighty, you shall know I am set naked on your kingdom. Tomorrow shall I beg leave to see your kingly eyes, when I shall, first asking you pardon, thereunto recount the occasion of my sudden and more strange return.*
HAMLET."
What should this mean? Are all the rest come back?
Or is it some abuse, and no such thing?

LAERTES
Do you recognise the handwriting?

LAERTES
Know you the hand?

KING CLAUDIUS
It's Hamlet's way of writing. *'Naked'*! And in a postscript here he says *'alone'*. Can you explain it to me?

KING
'Tis Hamlet's character. `Naked'!
And in a postscript here he says `alone'.
Can you devise me?

LAERTES
I am at a loss, my lord. But let him meet you. It warms my sick heart to think I shall live and tell him to his face, "Now you shall die."

LAERTES
I am lost in it, my lord. But let him come;
It warms the very sickness in my heart
That I shall live and tell him to his teeth,
`Thus diest thou.'

KING CLAUDIUS INDICATES THE LETTER.

KING CLAUDIUS
If this is correct, Laertes – and if it isn't why else would he send it? – will you follow my orders?

KING
If it be so, Laertes -
As how should it be so, how otherwise? -
Will you be ruled by me?

LAERTES
Yes, your majesty. As long as you do not order me to make peace.

LAERTES
Ay, my lord;
So you will not o'errule me to a peace.

KING CLAUDIUS

Peace only within yourself! If he has now returned, abandoning his voyage and with no intention of remaking it, I will lead him into a trap I am planning that cannot fail to bring about his downfall, and upon his death no whisper of blame could be breathed, even his mother will be convinced it was an accident.

LAERTES

Your majesty, then I will follow your orders, especially if you could arrange that I might be the instrument to carry it out.

KING CLAUDIUS

That works well. You have been spoken of often since you left, and in front of Hamlet, for a skill at which you excel. Your other skills added together did not raise such envy in him as that one alone, though in my mind not the most important of skills.

LAERTES

What skill was that, your majesty?

KING CLAUDIUS

A mere feather in the cap of youth, but useful too. For youth suits the light and careless clothes it wears just as fur lined cloaks and sturdier attire suits the wealth and wisdom of older years. Two months ago, a gentleman from Normandy was here – I've seen and fought against the French myself, and know how exceptional they are on horseback - but this dashing gentleman was a wizard at it. Firmly planted in the saddle, and such wondrous control of his horse he might have been part of it, as if half beast himself. He exceeded what I thought possible by so much that any tricks and feats I could imagine fell short of anything he did.

KING

To thine own peace. If he be now returned,
As checking at his voyage, and that he means
No more to undertake it, I will work him
To an exploit now ripe in my device,
Under the which he shall not choose but fall;
And for his death no wind of blame shall
  breathe,
But even his mother shall uncharge the practice
And call it accident.

LAERTES

My lord, I will be ruled;
The rather if you could devise it so
That I might be the organ.

KING

It falls right.
You have been talked of since your travel much,
And that in Hamlet's hearing, for a quality
Wherein they say you shine. Your sum of parts
Did not together pluck such envy from him
As did that one, and that in my regard,
Of the unworthiest siege.

LAERTES

What part is that, my lord?

KING

A very riband in the cap of youth,
Yet needful too; for youth no less becomes
The light and careless livery that it wears
Than settled age his sables and his weeds,
Importing health and graveness. Two months
  since
Here was a gentleman of Normandy -
I've seen myself, and served against, the French,
And they can well on horseback; but this gallant
Had witchcraft in't. He grew unto his seat,
And to such wondrous doing brought his horse
As had he been incorpsed, and demi-natured
With the brave beast. So far he topped my
  thought
That I, in forgery of shapes and tricks,
Come short of what he did.

LAERTES
A Norman was he?

KING CLAUDIUS
A Norman.

LAERTES
I'll bet my life it was Lamond.

KING CLAUDIUS
The very same.

LAERTES
I know him well. He is the pinnacle and gem in the nation's crown.

KING CLAUDIUS
He spoke of you, and gave such a glowing report of your skill and mastery in swordsmanship, and with the rapier especially, that he declared that it would be a rare sight indeed if there was another who could match you. He swore the fencers of his nation had neither the movement, stance or keen eye to oppose you. Sir, this report he gave made Hamlet so enraged with envy that he could do nothing but wish and beg for your immediate return to fence with you. Now, from this...

LAERTES
A Norman was't?

KING
A Norman.

LAERTES
Upon my life, Lamord.

KING
The very same.

LAERTES
I know him well. He is the brooch indeed,
And gem, of all the nation.

KING
He made confession of you,
And gave you such a masterly report
For art and exercise in your defence,
And for your rapier most especial,
That he cried out 'twould be a sight indeed
If one could match you. The scrimers of their
 nation
He swore had neither motion, guard, nor eye,
If you opposed them. Sir, this report of his
Did Hamlet so envenom with his envy
That he could nothing do but wish and beg
Your sudden coming o'er, to play with you.
Now, out of this -

THE KING PAUSES AND IF A THOUGHT HAD STRUCK HIM.

LAERTES
What from this, your majesty?

KING CLAUDIUS
Laertes, were you fond of your father? Or are you like the sorrowful painting, a face with no feelings?

LAERTES
Why do you ask this?

LAERTES
What out of this, my lord?

KING
Laertes, was your father dear to you?
Or are you like the painting of a sorrow,
A face without a heart?

LAERTES
Why ask you this?

KING CLAUDIUS

It's not that I think you did not love your father, but I know love has a beginning in time, and as I see it, with periods where love is tested, time weakens the spark and the fire of love. There lives inside the flame of love itself, a kind of wick or snuff that slowly kills it, and nothing stays perfect forever - growing like a parasite, it dies in its own excess. What we can do, we should do when we can, for this 'can' changes and finds excuses and delays as much as any words, hands or accidents can cause. And then the 'should' is like a waster's sigh, it gives pain in its relief. But, to the point of the argument – So, Hamlet returns, what would you undertake to show you are your father's son in actions rather than words?

LAERTES

I'd cut his throat in the church!

KING CLAUDIUS

Indeed, nowhere should be sanctuary against murder. Revenge should have no restraints. But, good Laertes, do this; keep to your room, when Hamlet returns he should not know you have arrived. I'll arrange for people to praise your excellence and set a double gloss on the fame the Frenchman gave you, and bring you, finally, together with a wager on your heads. He, trusting me and suspecting nothing, will not study the rapiers, so that with ease, or a little underhandedness, you may chose a sword with no protective tip, and in a deadly thrust, avenge your father.

KING

Not that I think you did not love your father,
But that I know love is begun by time,
And that I see, in passages of proof,
Time qualifies the spark and fire of it.
There lives within the very flame of love
A kind of wick or snuff that will abate it;
And nothing is at a like goodness still,
For goodness, growing to a plurisie,
Dies in his own too much. That we would do,
We should do when we would; for this `would'
    changes,
And hath abatements and delays as many
As there are tongues, are hands, are accidents,
And then this `should' is like a spendthrift's sigh
That hurts by easing. But, to the quick of th'
    ulcer:
Hamlet comes back; what would you undertake
To show yourself your father's son
More than in words?

LAERTES

To cut his throat i'th' church.

KING

No place indeed should murder sanctuarize;*
Revenge should have no bounds. But, good
    Laertes,
Will you do this? - keep close within your
    chamber.
Hamlet returned shall know you are come home.
We'll put on those shall praise your excellence,
And set a double varnish on the fame
The Frenchman gave you; bring you, in fine,
    together
And wager on your heads. He, being remiss,
Most generous and free from all contriving,
Will not peruse the foils; so that with ease,
Or with a little shuffling, you may choose
A sword unbated, and, in a pass of practice,
Requite him for your father.

---

*Note: 'Sanctuary'. There was a time when a man on the run from the law or his enemies could claim 'sanctuary' in a church. There he would be protected, his pursuers could not harm him; to cut his throat in church was unthinkable.

LAERTES

I will do it, and to make doubly sure I'll poison the tip of my sword. I bought a potion from a charlatan, so deadly that by dipping a knife in it and drawing blood, no rare antidote, even if collected from all the medicinal herbs and plants under the moon, can save a man from death who has so much as been scratched by it. I'll dip the point in this potion, so that even if I slightly graze him it will be death.

LAERTES

I will do't;
And for that purpose I'll anoint my sword.
I bought an unction of a mountebank,*
So mortal that, but dip a knife in it,
Where it draws blood no cataplasm* so rare,
Collected from all simples that have virtue
Under the moon,* can save the thing from death
That is but scratched withal. I'll touch my point
With this contagion, that, if I gall him slightly,
It may be death.

*Note: 'Cataplasm' – a poultice, a kind of bandage soaked in herbs and medicines tightly wound around a wound.

A Mountebank was a traveling quack doctor who mounts his dubious wares on a bench.

'Under the moon' – double meaning of anywhere on earth and the belief that herbs gathered at night (especially under a full moon) have an increased potency.

KING CLAUDIUS

Let's plan this out. Decide a convenient time and means to suit our purpose. If this fails and our intentions reveal themselves due to bad execution of our plans, it's better not attempted, therefore this project should have a back-up plan that we could use if this one should blow itself apart in operation. Wait... let me see. We'll make a solemn wager on your skills – I have it! When you are duelling and get hot and thirsty - so make your bouts all the more exertive to ensure this – he'll call for a drink. I'll have prepared for him a cup for the purpose. If he takes a sip – if by chance he escapes your poisoned thrust, our purpose will still be fulfilled. But wait, what's that noise?

KING

Let's further think of this;
Weigh what convenience both of time and means
May fit us to our shape. If this should fail,
And that our drift look through our bad
  performance,
'Twere better not assayed; therefore this project
Should have a back or second that might hold
If this did blast in proof.* Soft, let me see.
We'll make a solemn wager on your cunnings: -
I ha't!
When in your motion you are hot and dry -
As make your bouts more violent to that end -
And that he calls for drink, I'll have prepared him
A chalice for the nonce,* whereon but sipping,
If he by chance escape your venomed stuck,
Our purpose may hold there. But stay, what
  noise?

*Note: 'Blast in proof' – a test for a cannon was to load it with a larger charge of explosive to prove quality of manufacture. If faulty it would blow apart.

'Chalice for the nonce' – cup for the one occasion. nonce = for the once.

ENTER QUEEN GERTRUDE WAILING.

QUEEN GERTRUDE

One sorrow treads upon the heels of another, so quickly one after the other. Your sister's drowned, Laertes.

LAERTES

Drowned! On no, where?

QUEEN GERTRUDE

There is a willow that grows over the brook, its silvery leaves reflecting in the glassy stream. Using the willow branches she was making garlands of buttercups, nettles, daisies and purple orchids which the unrefined shepherds call by a ruder name but our demure maidens call 'dead men's fingers'. There, clambering to hang her coronet shaped garland of flowers on the overhanging branches, one malicious bough broke. Down fell both her flowery trophies and herself into the weeping brook. Her clothes spread out wide, and like a mermaid they held her afloat, during which time she chanted snatches of old ballads, like someone not understanding the danger of their predicament, or like a creature native and at home to the water. It was not very long before her garments, heavy with the water they had drunk, pulled the poor wretch from her tuneful song to muddy death.

QUEEN

One woe doth tread upon another's heel,
So fast they follow. Your sister's drowned, Laertes

LAERTES

Drowned! O, where?

QUEEN

There is a willow* grows ascaunt the brook,
That shows his hoar leaves in the glassy stream.
Therewith fantastic garlands did she make
Of crow-flowers, nettles, daisies, and long
   purples,*
That liberal shepherds give a grosser name,
But our cold maids do dead men's fingers call
   them.*
There on the pendant boughs her crownet weeds
Clamb'ring to hang, an envious sliver broke,
When down her weedy trophies and herself
Fell in the weeping brook. Her clothes spread
   wide,
And mermaid-like a while they bore her up;
Which time she chanted snatches of old lauds,
As one incapable of her own distress,
Or like a creature native and indued
Unto that element. But long it could not be
Till that her garments, heavy with their drink,
Pulled the poor wretch from her melodious lay
To muddy death.

Note: Quite how the Queen knows such meticulous detail of the drowning is not known.

*Again, many editions differ on the significance of the flowers used by Ophelia. The willow is a symbol of forsaken love, a forsaken lover would make a garland of willow when their beloved had left them. The crow-flowers, nettles, daisies, and long purples are all wild flowers considered weeds by gardeners. The "grosser name" of the "long purples" (orchids) is sexual in nature as the plant has a long stem with two bulbs, resembling male genitalia. The word 'orchid' is the basis for many medical terms relating to male testicles.

Crow-flowers (known today as buttercups) were sent to remind someone of their ungrateful or unfaithful behaviour, they also represent the virginal state of a woman. The nettle's sting represents pain and suffering, daisies symbolise false feelings, the orchid love and fertility.

LAERTES
Alas, then she is drowned.

QUEEN GERTRUDE
Drowned, drowned.

LAERTES
You already have too much water, poor Ophelia, therefore I will hold back my tears.
(*he struggles to control himself*)
But it is our response, customary in nature. Let shame say whatever it likes.
(*he weeps openly*)
When these tears are finished the womanly emotion will be out of my system. Adieu, my lord. I have a fiery speech that wishes to blaze it's way out, but these foolish tears douse it.

LAERTES
Alas, then she is drowned.

QUEEN
Drowned, drowned.

LAERTES
Too much of water hast thou, poor Ophelia,
And therefore I forbid my tears. - But yet
It is our trick; nature her custom holds,
Let shame say what it will.
[*Weeps.*] When these are gone,
The woman will be out. Adieu, my lord.
I have a speech o' fire that fain would blaze,
But that this folly douts it.

LAERTES LEAVES THE ROOM SOBBING.

KING CLAUDIUS
Let's follow him, Gertrude. How hard I had to work to calm his rage! Now I fear this will start it over again. Therefore we'd better follow him.

KING
Let's follow, Gertrude.
How much I had to do to calm his rage!
Now fear I this will give it start again;
Therefore let's follow.

EXEUNT.

198

ACT V

A TRAGIC END TO A TRAGIC TALE

ACT V

ACT V SCENE I

A CHURCHYARD.

TWO COMIC GRAVEDIGGERS ARE AT WORK WITH SPADES AND PICKAXES.

Note: This scene offers some light relief from the tension and emotion that has been building. Shakespeare was a master at inserting a comic interlude to relieve the tension before throwing us back into the turmoil even deeper than before. It also gave the actors a respite and a chance for the comedians among the repertoire to have some fun.

They speak in prose as this is comedic (as opposed to blank verse).

1ST COMIC GRAVEDIGGER
Is she to be buried with a Christian ceremony even though she took her own life?

2ND COMIC GRAVEDIGGER
I tell you she is. So get on and make her grave. The coroner has already sat on her - her case that is - and deemed it a Christian burial.

1ST COMIC GRAVEDIGGER
How can that be right? Unless she drowned herself in self-defence.

2ND COMIC GRAVEDIGGER
Well, that's the judgement.

1ST COMIC GRAVEDIGGER
It must be 'self-offence', it can't be anything else. For here lies my point – if I drown myself knowingly, it is a deliberate act, and an act has three parts - that is; to act the part, to do the part and to perform the part. 'Argo', she drowned herself knowingly.

1ST CLOWN
Is she to be buried in Christian burial that wilfully seeks her own salvation?

2ND CLOWN
I tell thee she is; therefore make her grave straight. The crowner hath sat on her, and finds it Christian burial.

1ST CLOWN
How can that be, unless she drowned herself in her own defence?

2ND CLOWN
Why, 'tis found so.

1ST CLOWN
It must be se offendendo,* it cannot be else. For here lies the point: if I drown myself wittingly, it argues an act, and an act hath three branches - it is to act, to do, and to perform. Argal, she drowned herself wittingly.

200

> *Note: 'se defendendo' is self-defence in Latin, he jokingly makes up a Latin name for self-offence, 'se offendendo'. Something which doesn't exist.*
>
> *'Argal' is a mispronounced 'Ergo' (Latin for 'therefore') – he is someone trying to sound learned but getting the words wrong.*

2ND COMIC GRAVEDIGGER	2ND CLOWN
No, but listen, good Mister Digger…	Nay, but hear you, Goodman Delver.

THE 1ST GRAVEDIGGER IGNORES THE INTERRUPTION.

1ST COMIC GRAVEDIGGER	1ST CLOWN
Let me finish. Here lies the water, OK?	Give me leave. Here lies the water; good.

HE LAYS HIS SPADE ON THE GROUND AS AN IMAGINARY BODY OF WATER.

1ST COMIC (CONT'D)	1ST CLOWN
Here stands the man, OK?	Here stands the man; good.

HE STANDS HIS PICKAXE ON THE GROUND APART FROM THE SPADE.

1ST COMIC (CONT'D)	1ST CLOWN
If the man…	If the man

HE PICKS UP THE PICKAXE.

1ST COMIC (CONT'D)	1ST CLOWN
goes to this water…	go to this water

HE PUTS THE PICKAXE AGAINST THE SPADE.

1ST COMIC (CONT'D)	1ST CLOWN
and drowns himself, it is, whether he likes it or not, the end of him - take note of that.	and drown himself, it is, will he nill he,* he goes - mark you that;

> **Note: 'will he nill he' – whether one likes it or not. From this we get the expression, 'willy-nilly'.*

HE MOVES THE PICKAXE AWAY FROM THE SPADE AGAIN.

1ST COMIC (CONT'D)	1ST CLOWN
But, if the water comes to him…	but if the water come to him…

HE PICKS UP THE SPADE AND PUTS IT AGAINST THE PICKAXE.

1ST COMIC (CONT'D)

And drowns him, he doesn't drown himself. 'Argo', he that is not guilty of his own death so doesn't shorten his own life.

1ST CLOWN

and drown him, he drowns not himself. Argal, he that is not guilty of his own death shortens not his own life.

2ND COMIC GRAVEDIGGER

But is that the law?

2ND CLOWN

But is this law?

1ST COMIC GRAVEDIGGER

Yes, indeed it is. The Inquest Coroner's law.

1ST CLOWN

Ay, marry, is't; crowner's quest law.

2ND COMIC GRAVEDIGGER

Well, if you want the truth the way I see it, if this hadn't been a posh woman, she would not have been given a Christian burial.

2ND CLOWN

Will you ha' the truth an't? If this had not been a gentlewoman, she should have been buried out o' Christian burial.

1ST COMIC GRAVEDIGGER

Why, that's the truth, and more's the pity that posh folk should be allowed in this world to drown or hang themselves more than their fellow Christians. Come, my spade.

1ST CLOWN

Why, there thou sayst, and the more pity that great folk should have count'nance in this world to drown or hang themselves more than their even Christian. Come, my spade.

HE STOOPS TO PICK UP HIS SPADE AND CLIMBS INTO THE HOLE.

1ST COMIC (CONT'D)

The only real gentlemen in ancient times were gardeners, ditch diggers and gravediggers, upholding Adam's profession.

1ST CLOWN

There is no ancient gentlemen but gardeners, ditchers, and gravemakers: they hold up Adam's profession.

HE STARTS DIGGING DOWN.

2ND COMIC GRAVEDIGGER

Was he a gentleman?

2ND CLOWN

Was he a gentleman?

1ST COMIC GRAVEDIGGER

Aye, the first to have arms.

1ST CLOWN

A' was the first that ever bore arms.

2ND COMIC GRAVEDIGGER

He didn't bear arms.

2ND CLOWN

Why, he had none.*

*Note: He means heraldic 'coat of arms' of a gentleman, whereas the 1st Comic means he was the first man, so the first with arms who could dig.

Modern Version	Original Text
1ST COMIC GRAVEDIGGER What? Are you a heathen? Do you not read the Scriptures? The Bible says, 'Adam digged'. How could he dig without arms? I'll put another question to you. If you twist the answer, you prove you are…	**1ST CLOWN** What, art a heathen? How dost thou understand the Scripture? The Scripture says Adam digged. Could he dig without arms? I'll put another question to thee. If thou answerest me not to the purpose, confess thyself *-

Note: 'Confess thyself and be hanged' is an old saying he doesn't finish. It means confess your sins before God before you are executed - deathbed confessions being a recurring theme in Hamlet. It is also suggested that the missing end could have been the word 'ass' - prove yourself an ass.

2ND COMIC GRAVEDIGGER (*interrupting*) Get on with it!	**2ND CLOWN** Go to.
1ST COMIC GRAVEDIGGER Who is it that builds stronger things than either a stonemason, a ship builder or a carpenter?	**1ST CLOWN** What is he that builds stronger than either the mason, the shipwright, or the carpenter?

THE 2ND GRAVEDIGGER PONDERS A MOMENT BEFORE REPLYING.

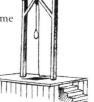

2ND COMIC GRAVEDIGGER A gallows maker. Because the frame outlives a thousand tenants.	**2ND CLOWN** The gallows-maker; for that frame outlives a thousand tenants.*

Note: Gallows - a wooden structure from which criminals were hanged.

1ST COMIC GRAVEDIGGER I like your wit, I do indeed. The gallows is a good answer. But how is gallows good? It's good to those who do bad. But, you do not speak good to say the gallows are built stronger than a church. 'Argo', the gallows might do *'you'* some good. Try again, come on.	**1ST CLOWN** I like thy wit well, in good faith; the gallows does well. But how does it well? It does well to those that do ill. Now, thou dost ill to say the gallows is built stronger than the church; argal, the gallows may do well to thee. To't again, come.
2ND COMIC GRAVEDIGGER (*thinking out loud*) Who builds stronger than a stone mason, a ship builder or a carpenter?	**2ND CLOWN** Who builds stronger than a mason, a shipwright, or a carpenter?
1ST COMIC GRAVEDIGGER Aye, answer me that, and put an end to it.	**1ST CLOWN** Ay, tell me that, and unyoke.*

Note: A yoke was the wooden bar attached to working oxen to pull things. Unyoking an ox meant the end of the day's work for the ox.

2ND COMIC GRAVEDIGGER	2ND CLOWN
Oh, now I can answer.	Marry, now I can tell.

1ST COMIC GRAVEDIGGER	1ST CLOWN
Go on...	To't.

THE 2ND GRAVEDIGGER PAUSES AS IF IN DEEP MEANINGFUL THOUGHT.

2ND COMIC GRAVEDIGGER	2ND CLOWN
Damn, I don't know.	Mass, I cannot tell.

HAMLET AND HORATIO APPROACH FROM A DISTANCE UNSEEN.

1ST COMIC GRAVEDIGGER	1ST CLOWN
Don't beat your brains about it, a slow ass will not quicken his pace by beating it, and when you are next asked this question, say "A grave maker". The houses he makes last till doomsday. Now, get you off to Yaughan's tavern and fetch me a flagon of ale.	Cudgel thy brains no more about it, for your dull ass will not mend his pace with beating, and when you are asked this question next, say `a gravemaker'. The houses that he makes lasts till doomsday. Go, get thee to Yaughan; fetch me a stoup of liquor.*

*Note: 'Stoup' was two quarts (four pints/2.26 litres).

2ND GRAVEDIGGER LEAVES, 1ST GRAVEDIGGER STARTS
DIGGING AND SINGING WHILE HE WORKS.

HAMLET AND HORATIO APPROACH AS HE SINGS.

1ST COMIC (CONT'D)	1ST CLOWN
(sings as he digs)	*[Digging and singing.]*
In youth, when I did love, did love,	*In youth, when I did love, did love,*
I thought it was very sweet	*Methought it was very sweet*
To shorten -Oh!- the time for -Ah!- my behove,	*To contract – O* the time for - a my behove,*
-Oh!- I thought there -Ah!- was nothing -Ah!- meet.	*O methought there - a was nothing - a meet.*

Note: The Oh! and Ah! sounds are grunts as he is digging. He is singing a ballad popular at the time but with the wrong wording, "The Aged Lover Renounceth Death", by Thomas Vaux, second Baron of Vaux, (from Tottel's Miscellany, which was the first printed anthology of English poetry, 1557). The audience would have recognised the wording as comically mangled. Originally it meant; what was appropriate when he was a youth, at his age now is no longer appropriate. The original wording was; "I loathe that I did love, / In youth that I thought sweet, / As time requires for my behove, / Methinks they are not meet."

HAMLET
Has this fellow no feelings for his work that he sings while grave digging?

HORATIO
Habit has instilled in him a sense of ease in his work.

HAMLET
That's probably so; a man not accustomed to such work would have a more sensitive nature.

HAMLET
Has this fellow no feeling of his business that a' sings at grave-making.

HORATIO
Custom hath made it in him a property of easiness.

HAMLET
'Tis e'en so: the hand of little employment hath the daintier sense.*

*Note: From a now commonly used saying meaning a hand not accustomed to hard work would be more sensitive. However it is unclear whether the phrase became popular because of Hamlet, or if the phrase existed in some form before Hamlet was written (as many phrases attributed to Shakespeare did, though he would often paraphrase them, making his own version).

1ST COMIC GRAVEDIGGER
(sings) But age with his stealing steps
Has clawed me into his clutch,
And has shipped me back into the land,
As if I had never been such.

1ST CLOWN
[Sings.] But age with his stealing steps
Hath clawed me in his clutch,
And hath shipped me intil the land,
As if I had never been such.*

*Note: This time he has mixed two verses together from the ballad. It basically means old age has taken life from him and returned him to the earth from which he was created.

HE UNEARTHS A SKULL AND THROWS IT UP OUT OF THE GRAVE.

HAMLET
That skull had a tongue in it, and could sing once. How the rogue hurls it to the ground, as if it were the jawbone of Cain, who committed the first murder.

HAMLET
That skull had a tongue in it, and could sing once. How the knave jowls it to th' ground, as if it were Cain's* jawbone, that did the first murder.

*Note: Cain – from the biblical story of Cain murdering his brother Abel and being punished by God to spend a life of wandering.

HAMLET PICKS UP THE SKULL FROM WHERE IT HAD ROLLED TO.

HAMLET (CONT'D)
This could be the head of a politician which this ass now rules over. (*he gestures at the digger*)
(*about the skull*) Someone who would have tried to over-rule God, could it not?

HAMLET
This might be the pate of a politician* which this ass now o'er offices;* one that would circumvent God, might it not?

Note: 'Politician' also means a person who acts in a manipulative or devious way. Different editions use either "over-reaches" or "o'er offices", both mean the same.

HORATIO
It could be, my lord.

HORATIO
It might, my lord.

HAMLET
Or of a courtier, who would say, 'Good morning, sweet lord? How are you, my good lord?'
This might be Lord Such-and-such who praised Lord Such-an-another's horse when he wanted to borrow it, could it not have?

HAMLET
Or of a courtier, which could say ` Good morrow, sweet lord? How dost thou, good lord?' This might be my Lord Such-a-one that praised my Lord Such-a-one's horse when a' went to beg it, might it not?

HORATIO
Yes, my lord.

HORATIO
Ay, my lord.

HAMLET
Why, yes it could. And now Lady Worm has him - jawless and knocked about the bonce with a gravedigger's spade. An ironic spin of fortune, if we think about it. Were these bones bred only to play bowls with? Mine ache to think of it.

HAMLET
Why, e'en so; and now my Lady Worm's, chapless, and knocked about the mazard with a sexton's spade. Here's fine revolution,* an we had the trick to see't. Did these bones cost no more the breeding but to play at loggets* with 'em? Mine ache to think on't.

Note: 'Loggets' is a game which involves throwing sticks at a stake.

'Revolution' - The wheel of fortune had spun to take his life, and now his head is spinning after being thrown like a bowling ball.

1ST COMIC GRAVEDIGGER
(*sings*) A pickaxe and a spade, a spade,
And also a shrouding-sheet,
Oh!, a pit of clay for to be made
For such a guest to meet.

1ST CLOWN
[*Sings.*]   A pickaxe and a spade, a spade,
For and a shrouding-sheet,
O, a pit of clay for to be made
For such a guest is meet.

HE THROWS UP ANOTHER SKULL.

HAMLET
There's another.

HAMLET
There's another.

HAMLET (CONT'D)
Could that be the skull of a lawyer? Where's his evasive arguments now, his petty quibbles, his lawsuits, his legal practices, and his loopholes in the law? Why does he allow this rude rogue to knock him about the bonce with a dirty shovel, and not threaten him with legal action for assault?

HAMLET
Why may not that be the skull of a lawyer? Where be his quiddities* now, his quillets,* his cases, his tenures, and his tricks? Why does he suffer this rude knave now to knock him about the sconce with a dirty shovel, and will not tell him of his action of battery?

Note: 'Quiddity' is a clever pun, it has two meanings, both applicable, one is the method used by lawyers to evade a difficult question by bringing up some other disconnected or irrelevant point, the other meaning is the essential being of something, the life spirit. 'Quillets' are frivolous distinctions.

HAMLET
Hmm! This fellow in his time might have been a great buyer of land, with his covenants, title deeds, mortgages, fines, dual guarantors, possession orders. Is this the final fine, the repossession of his freehold? With his fine cranium filled with his final dirt? Will his dual guarantors no longer guarantee his land any more than the length and breadth of paper the contracts were written on? The transfer of property deeds for his land would barely fit in this... (*points to the skull*) his deed box, and the deed owner can own no more? Huh?

HAMLET
Hum! This fellow might be in's time a great buyer of land, with his statutes, his recognizances, his fines,* his double vouchers, his recoveries. Is this the fine of his fines and the recovery of his recoveries, to have his fine pate full of fine dirt? Will his vouchers vouch him no more of his purchases, and double ones too, than the length and breadth of a pair of indentures?* The very conveyances of his lands will scarcely lie in this box; and must th' inheritor himself have no more, ha?

Note: 'Fines' are legal documents. It also means 'good', 'finish/end', small, and financial penalty. Shakespeare punned heavily on the word here.

An 'indenture' was a legal document with two identical wordings, which was then torn in half to create two copies which could be later matched. Hamlet says the document would be the same size as the land he owns now, that inside his skull, as he has been thrown out of his previous land and cannot buy more.

HORATIO
Not a jot more, my lord.

HORATIO
Not a jot* more, my lord.

*Note: Jot means both small amount and something written, another pun.

HAMLET
Isn't parchment made of sheepskin?

HAMLET
Is not parchment made of sheepskins?*

*Note: Legal contracts were written on parchment which was made from stretched and dried animal skins.

HORATIO
Yes, my lord, and calfskin too.

HORATIO
Ay, my lord, and of calf-skins too.

HAMLET
Those who seek assurance from words on a parchment are sheep and calves themselves. I will speak with this fellow.

HAMLET
They are sheep and calves which seek out assurance in that. I will speak to this fellow.

Note: Shakespeare included a lot of legal references in his works, using terms normally only used by those in the legal profession. We know the subject interested him, whether the knowledge was learned or he had acquaintances in the profession to aid him is not known. But Shakespeare owned property and had shares in the Blackfriar's Theatre and the Globe Theatre right up till his death, so he had experience in the legal side of both land and business.

Interestingly, Shakespeare lived with wigmaker Christopher Mountjoy and his wife in a house on the corner of Silver and Monkwell Street where from 1598 Mountjoy had taken Stephen Bellot on for six years as an apprentice. When the apprenticeship ended Stephen rejected the advances of the Mountjoy's daughter, Mary. Mrs Mountjoy asked Shakespeare to intervene on their daughter's behalf, in which he was successful.

in 1605 Shakespeare testified in court to the facts leading to the marriage after Mountjoy had fallen out with his now son-in-law and refused to pay a dowry and declared he would never give Mary and Stephen a groat. Shakespeare related the facts leading up to the marriage but could not remember the size of the proposed dowry. The court handed the matter over to the church to decide upon, no records of the final outcome are known.

The court records suggest that, despite being wealthy and having the patronage of the king, Shakespeare was willing to support a lowly tradesman in need and stand against the man whose house he himself lived in.

This would have been around the time Shakespeare was writing Hamlet so the legal world was have been fresh in his mind.

HAMLET (CONT'D)
(to gravedigger) You there, whose grave is this?

HAMLET
Whose grave's this, sirrah?

1ST COMIC GRAVEDIGGER

Mine, sir.

(sings) Oh! A pit of clay to be made
For such a guest to meet.

HAMLET

I think it is indeed yours, for you are lying in it.

1ST COMIC GRAVEDIGGER

You lie out of it, sir, and therefore it is not yours. For my part, I don't *lie* in it, but it is mine.

HAMLET

You do *lie* in it, because you are in it and you say it's yours. It's for the dead, not for the living, therefore, you lie.

1ST COMIC GRAVEDIGGER

It's a short living lie, sir, so it runs from me back to you again.

1ST CLOWN

Mine, sir.

[Sings.] O, a pit of clay for to be made
For such a guest is meet.

HAMLET

I think it be thine indeed, for thou liest in't.

1ST CLOWN

You lie out on't, sir, and therefore 'tis not yours. For my part, I do not lie in't, yet it is mine.

HAMLET

Thou dost lie in't, to be in't and say it is thine. 'Tis for the dead, not for the quick; therefore thou liest.

1ST CLOWN

'Tis a quick* lie, sir; 'twill away again from me to you.

Note: 'Quick' – a pun on the two meanings of living and fast.

HAMLET

What man are you digging it for?

1ST COMIC GRAVEDIGGER

For no man, sir.

HAMLET

What woman, then?

1ST COMIC GRAVEDIGGER

For no woman either.

HAMLET

Who is to be buried in it, then?

1ST COMIC GRAVEDIGGER

Someone that '*was*' a woman, sir, but now, God rest her soul, she's dead.

HAMLET

What man dost thou dig it for?

1ST CLOWN

For no man, sir.

HAMLET

What woman, then?

1ST CLOWN

For none neither.

HAMLET

Who is to be buried in't?

1ST CLOWN

One that was a woman, sir; but, rest her soul, she's dead.

HAMLET

(*to Horatio*) How pedantic the rogue is! We must speak correctly, or ambiguity will be our undoing. By the heavens, Horatio, I've noticed that common behaviour has become so pretentious of late that the peasant kicks at the heels of the aristocrat so closely he chafes his chilblains. (*to Gravedigger*) How long have you been a gravedigger?

HAMLET

How absolute the knave is! We must speak by the card,* or equivocation* will undo us. By the Lord, Horatio, these three years I have taken note of it, the age is grown so picked that the toe of the peasant comes so near the heel of the courtier he galls his kibe. How long hast thou been a gravemaker?

*Note: 'Equivocation' – a favourite term of Shakespeare since the Guy Fawkes plot, first referenced in Macbeth. It means using ambiguous wording to mislead or conceal the truth and avoid incriminating oneself.

'By the card', or more commonly today, 'by the book', meaning following the rule book or instructions to the letter.

1ST COMIC GRAVEDIGGER

Of all the days in the year I started it was the day our late King Hamlet defeated Fortinbras.

1ST CLOWN

Of all the days i'th' year I came to't that day that our last
King Hamlet o'ercame Fortinbras.

HAMLET

How long ago is that?

HAMLET

How long is that since?

1ST COMIC GRAVEDIGGER

Don't you know? Every fool can tell you that. It was the very day that young Hamlet was born – him that is mad and sent away to England.

1ST CLOWN

Cannot you tell that? Every fool can tell that. It was that very day that young Hamlet was born - he that is mad and sent into England.

HAMLET

Oh yes, indeed, and why was he sent to England?

HAMLET

Ay, marry, why was he sent into England?

1ST COMIC GRAVEDIGGER

Why? Because he was mad. He will recover his sanity there, or, if he doesn't, it doesn't matter there.

1ST CLOWN

Why, because he was mad. A' shall recover his wits there; or, if a' do not, 'tis no great matter there.

HAMLET

Why's that?

HAMLET

Why?

1ST COMIC GRAVEDIGGER

It won't be noticed in him. There the men are as mad as he is.

1ST CLOWN

'Twill not be seen in him there. There the men are as mad as he.

HAMLET

How did he become mad?

HAMLET

How came he mad?

1ST COMIC GRAVEDIGGER
Very strangely, they say.

HAMLET
What do you mean, 'strangely'?

1ST COMIC GRAVEDIGGER
Frankly, by him losing his wits.

HAMLET
On what grounds?

1ST COMIC GRAVEDIGGER
Why, here in Denmark, I've been working here, man and boy, this last thirty years.

1ST CLOWN
Very strangely, they say.

HAMLET
How `strangely'?

1ST CLOWN
Faith, e'en with losing his wits.

HAMLET
Upon what ground?

1ST CLOWN
Why, here in Denmark. I have been sexton* here, man and boy, thirty years.*

*Note: The Gravedigger has taken the literal meaning of 'ground' as beneath our feet, not as in the 'reason' for the madness.

A 'sexton' was a church worker doing manual work such as bell ringing and grave digging.

This statement puts Hamlet's age as thirty.

HAMLET
How long will a man lie in the earth before he rots?

1ST COMIC GRAVEDIGGER
Truly, if he not be rotten before he dies – as we have many pox-ridden corpses that will barely hold together before being laid to rest – he will last you some eight or nine years. A tanner will last you nine years.

HAMLET
How long will a man lie i'th' earth ere he rot?

1ST CLOWN
Faith, if a' be not rotten before a' die - as we have many pocky* corpses nowadays that will scarce hold the laying in - a' will last you some eight year or nine year. A tanner* will last you nine year.

*Note: 'Pocky' – syphilis ridden. Otherwise known as the great pox.

A 'tanner' converts animal skins into leather by soaking them in tannic acid.

HAMLET
Why does he last longer than others?

1ST COMIC GRAVEDIGGER
Why, sir, his hide is so tanned by his trade that he will keep out water a great while. And as everyone knows, water is a furious decayer of your whoreson dead body.

HAMLET
Why he more than another?

1ST CLOWN
Why, sir, his hide is so tanned with his trade that a' will keep out water a great while; and your water is a sore decayer of your whoreson* dead body.

*Note: 'Whoreson' is an expletive, much like 'son of a bitch'.

HE KICKS AND PICKS UP A SKULL FROM THE GRAVE HE IS DIGGING.

1ST COMIC GRAVEDIGGER

Here's a skull that has lain in the earth three and twenty years.

HAMLET

Whose was it?

1ST COMIC GRAVEDIGGER

A whoreson mad fellow's it was. Whose do you think it was?

HAMLET

I don't know.

1ST COMIC GRAVEDIGGER

A plague on him, he was a mad rogue! He poured a flagon of Rhine wine on my head once. This same skull, sir, was Yorick's skull, the king's jester.

HAMLET

This?

1ST COMIC GRAVEDIGGER

This very one.

HAMLET

Let me see.

1ST CLOWN

Here's a skull now hath lain you i'th' earth three-and-twenty years.

HAMLET

Whose was it?

1ST CLOWN

A whoreson mad fellow's it was. Whose do you think it was?

HAMLET

Nay, I know not.

1ST CLOWN

A pestilence on him for a mad rogue! A' poured a flagon of Rhenish on my head once. This same skull, sir, was Yorick's skull, the king's jester.

HAMLET

This?

1ST CLOWN

E'en that.

HAMLET

Let me see.

HAMLET TAKES THE SKULL FROM HIM AND STUDIES IT.

HAMLET

Alas, poor Yorick. I knew him, Horatio – a fellow of endless mirth, and the most inventive imagination. He has carried me on his back a thousand times, and now, how repulsed I am to think of it! I feel sick in my throat. Here hung those lips that I have kissed countless times.

HAMLET

Alas, poor Yorick. I knew him, Horatio; a fellow of infinite jest, of most excellent fancy. He hath bore me on his back a thousand times; and now, how abhorred in my imagination it is! My gorge rises at it. Here hung those lips that I have kissed I know not how oft.

HAMLET NOW SPEAKS TO THE SKULL ITSELF.

Modern	Original
HAMLET (CONT'D) (*to skull*) Where are your jeers now, your capers, your songs, the quick quips that would set the table roaring? Not got one now to mock your toothy grin? Quite the fallen chin. Now go to my lady's chamber and tell her even if she paints her make-up on an inch thick, she'll still end up looking like this. Make her laugh at that. (*to Horatio*) Here, Horatio, tell me something.	**HAMLET** Where be your gibes now, your gambols, your songs, your flashes of merriment that were wont to set the table on a roar? Not one now to mock your own grinning? - quite chap-fallen. Now get you to my lady's chamber and tell her, let her paint an inch thick, to this favour she must come. Make her laugh at that. Prithee, Horatio, tell me one thing.
HORATIO What's that, my lord?	**HORATIO** What's that, my lord?
HAMLET Do you think Alexander the Great looked this way in the ground?	**HAMLET** Dost thou think Alexander looked o' this fashion i'th' earth?
HORATIO Exactly the same.	**HORATIO** E'en so.
HAMLET And smelled the same? Pah!	**HAMLET** And smelt so? Pah!

HAMLET PUTS DOWN THE SKULL.

Modern	Original
HORATIO Exactly the same, my lord.	**HORATIO** E'en so, my lord.
HAMLET What lowly use we may be recycled for, Horatio! Could we not conceivably trace the noble dust of Alexander to find it used to plug a barrel?	**HAMLET** To what base uses we may return, Horatio! Why may not imagination trace the noble dust of Alexander till a' find it stopping a bung-hole?
HORATIO It would be too bizarre to think it possible.	**HORATIO** 'Twere to consider too curiously to consider so.
HAMLET No, truly, not a bit. Follow it through, logically, and step by step. Alexander died. Alexander was buried. Alexander turned to dust, the dust to earth, from earth we make clay, and when that clay is used, why not for a beer-barrel bung?	**HAMLET** No, faith, not a jot; but to follow him thither with modesty enough, and likelihood to lead it, as thus: Alexander died, Alexander was buried, Alexander returneth to dust, the dust is earth, of earth we make loam, and why of that loam, whereto he was converted, might they not stop a beer-barrel?

HAMLET (CONT'D)
(reciting a rhyme)
Imperial Caesar, dead and turned to clay,
Might stop a hole to keep the wind away.
Oh, that earth which kept the world in awe
Should patch a wall to keep out winter's roar!

HAMLET
Imperious Caesar, dead and turned to clay,
Might stop a hole to keep the wind away.
O, that that earth which kept the world in awe
Should patch a wall t' expel the winter's flaw!

ENTER BEARERS WITH A BODY IN A SHROUD FOLLOWED BY A PRIEST, THE KING, THE QUEEN, LAERTES, AND WITH LORDS ATTENDING.

Note: It was common practice to bury a body in a shroud, or lay a body in a shroud in a mausoleum (as in Romeo and Juliet) rather than use a coffin.

HAMLET (CONT'D)
But wait, wait a minute! Here comes the king, the queen, the courtiers... Who are they following? And with such lack of ceremony? This suggests the corpse they follow did with desperate hand take its own life. Someone of importance. Let us conceal ourselves and observe.

HAMLET
But soft, but soft awhile! Here comes the king, The queen, the courtiers. Who is that they follow?
And with such maimed rites? This doth betoken The corpse they follow did with desp'rate hand Fordo it own life. 'Twas of some estate.
Couch we awhile, and mark.

HAMLET AND HORATIO STAND ASIDE OUT OF SIGHT.

LAERTES
(to priest) What about funeral rites?

LAERTES
What ceremony else?

HAMLET
(hushed to Horatio) That is Laertes, a very noble youth. Listen.

HAMLET
That is Laertes, a very noble youth. Mark.

LAERTES
What about funeral rites?

LAERTES
What ceremony else?

PRIEST
Her funeral rites have gone as far as we are permitted to give. Her death was open to question. If not for orders from high authority over-ruling normal procedure, she would be buried in unsanctified ground till the doomsday trumpets sounded, with rubble thrown on her instead of sympathetic prayers. Yet we have allowed her virginal garland, her maiden bouquets, the last rites and bell ringing of a burial in hallowed ground.

PRIEST
Her obsequies have been as far enlarged As we have warranty. Her death was doubtful, And but that great command o'ersways the order She should in ground unsanctified* have lodged Till the last trumpet; for charitable prayers, Shards, flints, and pebbles should be thrown on her.
Yet here she is allowed her virgin crants, Her maiden strewments, and the bringing home Of bell and burial.

214

> Note: Taking one's own life was seen as an act against God. Only he had the right to choose if we live or if we die. In such cases bodies were buried without ceremony in 'unsanctified' ground - ground not blessed by the church. Because of royal intervention some ceremonial rites have been allowed.

LAERTES	LAERTES
Can nothing more be done?	Must there no more be done?
PRIEST	PRIEST
Nothing more can be done. We would violate the Holy Service of the Dead if we were to sing a solemn hymn and lay her to rest like souls who died at peace with God.	No more be done. We should profane the service of the dead To sing sage requiem and such rest to her As to peace-parted souls.

THE CHURCH BELL RINGS AND THEY LOWER HER BODY INTO THE GRAVE.

LAERTES	LAERTES
Lay her in the earth, and may violets spring forth from her fair and pure body. (*angry*) I tell you, ungracious priest, my sister shall be an angel performing the deeds of the lord, when you lie howling in hell.	Lay her i'th' earth, And from her fair and unpolluted flesh May violets spring. I tell thee, churlish priest, A minist'ring angel shall my sister be When thou liest howling.
HAMLET	HAMLET
(*aside*) What! The beautiful, pure Ophelia!	[*Aside.*] What, the fair Ophelia!*

> *Note: There had been no mention of her by name, Hamlet only realised it was Ophelia they were burying when Laertes said, 'my sister'.

QUEEN GERTRUDE SCATTERS FLOWERS ON THE GRAVE.

QUEEN GERTRUDE	QUEEN
(*scattering flowers*) Sweets to the sweet. Farewell. I had hoped you would have been my Hamlet's wife. I had planned to adorn your bridal bed with flowers, sweet maiden, not scatter them on your grave.	[*Scattering flowers.*] Sweets to the sweet; farewell. I hoped thou shouldst have been my Hamlet's wife. I thought thy bride-bed to have decked, sweet maid, And not have strewed thy grave.

LAERTES

Oh, may triple sadness fall ten times triple on that cursed head whose wicked act deprived you of your most talented senses!
(*to gravedigger*) Hold back the earth a while, I want to hold her once more in my arms.

LAERTES

O, treble woe
Fall ten times treble on that cursed head
Whose wicked deed thy most ingenious sense
Deprived thee of! Hold off the earth a while,
Till I have caught her once more in mine arms.

LAERTES LEAPS INTO THE GRAVE AND LIES DOWN HOLDING OPHELIA.

LAERTES (CONT'D)

Now pile your dust upon the living and the dead, till you've made a mountain on this spot taller than Mount Pelion, or the cloud tipped blue head of Mount Olympus.

LAERTES

Now pile your dust upon the quick and dead,
Till of this flat a mountain you have made
T' o'ertop old Pelion, or the skyish head
Of blue Olympus.

HAMLET HEADS PURPOSEFULLY FOR THE GRAVE.

HAMLET

(*advancing*) Who is it that grieves so over-dramatically? Whose words of sorrow cause the wandering stars to stop in disbelief like wounded listeners? This is I, Hamlet, Prince of Denmark!

HAMLET

[*Advancing.*] What is he whose grief
Bears such an emphasis, whose phrase of sorrow
Conjures the wand'ring stars, and makes them stand
Like wonder-wounded hearers? This is I,
Hamlet the Dane.

HAMLET LEAPS INTO THE GRAVE.

LAERTES

(*threateningly*) May the devil take your soul!

LAERTES

The devil take thy soul!

LAERTES GRAPPLES WITH HAMLET AND GRABS HIM BY THE THROAT.

HAMLET

Not a good prayer! I demand you take your fingers from my throat, I may not be hot-tempered and rash, but I have a dangerous streak in me which it would be wise to fear. Unhand me.

HAMLET

Thou pray'st not well.
I prithee take thy fingers from my throat,
For though I am not splenative and rash,
Yet have I in me something dangerous,
Which let thy wiseness fear. Hold off thy hand.

KING CLAUDIUS

Pull them apart.

KING

Pluck them asunder.

QUEEN GERTRUDE
Hamlet, Hamlet!

QUEEN
Hamlet, Hamlet!

LORDS
Gentlemen!

LORDS
Gentlemen!

HORATIO
My good lord, calm yourself.

HORATIO
Good my lord, be quiet.

THE LORDS PART THEM, AND THEY COME OUT OF THE GRAVE. THE TWO
MEN, THOUGH RESTRAINED, STILL LUNGE FOR EACH OTHER.

HAMLET
No, I'll fight him on this point until my eyelids blink no longer.

HAMLET
Why, I will fight with him upon this theme
Until my eyelids will no longer wag.

QUEEN GERTRUDE
Oh, my son, for what reason?

QUEEN
O my son, what theme?

HAMLET
I loved Ophelia.
(to Laertes) Forty thousand brothers with their combined love could not equal my love. What will you do for her?

HAMLET
I loved Ophelia. Forty thousand brothers
Could not, with all their quantity of love,
Make up my sum. What wilt thou do for her?

KING CLAUDIUS
Oh, he is mad, Laertes.

KING
O, he is mad, Laertes

LAERTES LAUNCHES A FRESH ATTACK ON HAMLET.

QUEEN GERTRUDE
For the love of God, leave him be.

QUEEN
For love of God, forbear him.

HAMLET
(to Laertes) Streuth, show me what you'd do. Will you cry, will you fight, will you starve, will you cut yourself? Will you drink acid, eat a crocodile? I'd do it. Do you come here to whine? To out-grieve me by leaping into her grave? To be buried alive with her? Well, so will I. And if you prattle about mountains, let them throw millions of acres of earth on us, till the ground above us singes its head against the burning sun, making Mount Ossa look like a wart! No, if you want to talk big-talk, I can rant as well as you.

HAMLET
'Swounds, show me what thou'lt do.
Woo't weep, woo't fight, woo't fast, woo't tear
  thyself,
Woo't drink up eisel, eat a crocodile?
I'll do't. Dost thou come here to whine?
To outface me with leaping in her grave?
Be buried quick with her, and so will I.
And if thou prate of mountains, let them throw
Millions of acres on us, till our ground,
Singeing his pate against the burning zone,
Make Ossa like a wart! Nay, an thou'lt mouth,
I'll rant as well as thou.

217

QUEEN GERTRUDE

This is sheer madness. The fit will be upon him for a while. Afterwards he'll be as calm as a female dove whose golden chicks have hatched, sitting in dejected silence.

HAMLET

Listen, sir. Why are you behaving like this towards me? I've always loved you. But it doesn't matter, even the might of Hercules could not stop a cat mewing, or a dog having its day.

QUEEN

This is mere madness,
And thus a while the fit will work on him;
Anon, as patient as the female dove
When that her golden couplets are disclosed,
His silence will sit drooping.

HAMLET

Hear you, sir.
What is the reason that you use me thus?
I loved you ever; but it is no matter.
Let Hercules himself do what he may,
The cat will mew, and dog will have his day.*

Note: An obscure way of Hamlet saying no matter how powerful the forces against him, nature will take its own course. Playing on the old adage, "Every dog will have his day", meaning that every dog, no matter how good or bad, will eventually find something good in life.

HAMLET STORMS OFF.

KING CLAUDIUS

I beg you, good Horatio, go see to him.

KING

I pray thee, good Horatio, wait upon him.

EXIT HORATIO, FOLLOWING HAMLET.

KING CLAUDIUS (CONT'D)

(*to Laertes*) Strengthen your patience with the talk we had last night. We'll start the matter right away.

(*to Gertrude*) Good Gertrude, ensure your son is watched. This grave will have a lasting memorial built for it.

(*to Laertes*) *We'll wait an hour for him to quieten down.*

Till then, be patient until we can plan.

KING

Strengthen your patience in our last night's speech.
We'll put the matter to the present push.
Good Gertrude, set some watch over your son.
This grave shall have a living monument.
An hour of quiet shortly shall we see;
Till then, in patience our proceeding be.

EXEUNT

ACT V SCENE II

A HALL IN THE CASTLE.

HAMLET AND HORATIO ARE IN DEEP DISCUSSION TOGETHER.

HAMLET INDICATES THE LETTER HORATIO HOLDS IN HIS HAND. IT IS THE
LETTER HAMLET HAD SENT HIM AFTER HE HAD BEEN SENT AWAY. THEY APPEAR
TO HAVE BEEN IN DEEP DISCUSSION ABOUT ITS CONTENTS.

Note: This is the last scene, and it's another long scene.

HAMLET
(*indicating the letter Horatio holds*)
So much for this, sir. Now you shall learn the rest. You remember all the details?

HORATIO
I remember, my lord!

HAMLET
Sir, in my heart there was a kind of turmoil that prevented me sleeping. I lay there feeling worse than a mutineer in shackles. Rashly – and heavens be praised for rashness, sometimes our instincts serve us well when our scheming plans fail, and that should teach us there is a divinity that shapes our destinies, no matter what we plan.

HAMLET
So much for this, sir; now shall you see the other.
You do remember all the circumstance?

HORATIO
Remember it, my lord!

HAMLET
Sir, in my heart there was a kind of fighting
That would not let me sleep. Methought I lay
Worse than the mutines in the bilboes.* Rashly -
And praised be rashness for it: let us know
Our indiscretion sometimes serves us well
When our deep plots do pall, and that should
   teach us
There's a divinity that shapes our ends,
Rough-hew them how we will.

*Note: Bilboes were iron shackles used to restrain mutinous crew members. Possibly named after the Spanish town of Bilboa. Examples of them can be seen in the Tower Of London, salvaged from the defeated fleet of the Spanish Armada.

HORATIO
That is most certain.

HORATIO
That is most certain.

HAMLET

I rose from my cabin, my sailing coat wrapped around me, in the dark I groped my way to find them, which I did, and stole their documents, and then withdrew back to my own cabin again. My fears overcoming my manners, I made so bold as to unseal their official papers, where I found, Horatio – such royal treachery! – precise orders, embellished with various reasons, concerning the king of Denmark's welfare, and England's king too, with oh! so many myths and horrors about me, that on first reading, without hesitating even to sharpen the axe, my head would have been cut off!

HORATIO

Is it possible?

HAMLET

Up from my cabin,
My sea-gown scarfed about me, in the dark
Groped I to find out them; had my desire,
Fingered their packet, and in fine withdrew
To mine own room again; making so bold,
My fears forgetting manners, to unseal
Their grand commission; where I found, Horatio -
O royal knavery! - an exact command,
Larded with many several sorts of reasons,
Importing Denmark's health, and England's too,
With ho! such bugs and goblins in my life,
That, on the supervise, no leisure bated,
No, not to stay the grinding of the axe,
My head should be struck off.

HORATIO

Is't possible?

HAMLET HANDS HORATIO THE OFFICIAL PAPERS.

HAMLET

Here's the orders, read it when you get a chance, but would you like to hear what I did?

HORATIO

Please, I beg you.

HAMLET

Being surrounded by a net of villains – before I could think up a prologue my mind had already begun on the plot – I sat down and worked out new orders, and wrote them down in the official style. I used to believe, as our statesmen do, it is a style befitting lowly ranks, so I had worked hard to unlearn it, but now, sir, it did me a trusty service. Would you like to know what I wrote?

HAMLET

Here's the commission, read it at more leisure.
But wilt thou hear now how I did proceed?

HORATIO

I beseech you.

HAMLET

Being thus benetted round with villainies -
Ere I could make a prologue to my brains,
They had begun the play - I sat me down,
Devised a new commission, wrote it fair.
I once did hold it, as our statists do,
A baseness to write fair, and laboured much
How to forget that learning;* but, sir, now
It did me yeoman's* service. Wilt thou know
The effect of what I wrote?

Note: Yeomen were considered most trustworthy.

Men in power had very bad signatures, leaving all their writing to their clerks and assistants who wrote beautifully. It was a sign of wealth and status if you could barely write.

HORATIO
Yes, my good lord.

HAMLET
An urgent demand from the Danish king, *as* the English king is his faithful dependant, *as* the love between them, like the evergreen palm, should flourish, *as* peace should be maintained and be a token to their mutual friendship, and many other such like *"as's"* of great statesmanship, and that upon reading and learning the letter's contents, without further debate one way or another, he should put the bearers of the document to immediate death, not even allowing time for absolution.

HORATIO
Ay, good my lord.

HAMLET
An earnest conjuration from the king,
As England was his faithful tributary,
As love between them like the palm* should
 flourish,
As peace should still her wheaten garland* wear
And stand a comma 'tween their amities,
And many suchlike as'es of great charge,
That, on the view and knowing of these contents,
Without debatement further more or less,
He should the bearers* put to sudden death,
Not shriving-time* allowed.

> Note: 'Shriving' - Again Hamlet mentions dying without cleansing (absolving) of the sins.
>
> The palm is a symbol of everlasting, being it is evergreen, the wheaten garland is a symbol of peace and plenty.
>
> The letter bearers to be put to death were Rosencrantz and Guildenstern.

HORATIO
How did you seal it?

HORATIO
How was this sealed?*

> *Note: Official documents were 'sealed' with an official seal to prove they were genuine and had been unopened. The seal was made by pouring hot wax on the folded document where the outside flap closed, and then pressing an official 'seal' into the hot wax, leaving an exact impression of the embossed design of the metal seal – often worn as a signet ring by nobility. To open the document one would have to break the wax seal or cut the parchment.

HAMLET
Why, even in that heaven intervened. I had my father's signet ring in my purse, which that other Danish king's seal was copied from. I folded the one I'd written the same as the other, signed it, gave the impression of my seal, and safely replaced the counterfeit undetected. Now, the next day was our sea battle, and what happened subsequently you already know.

HAMLET
Why, even in that was heaven ordinant.
I had my father's signet in my purse,
Which was the model of that Danish seal;
Folded the writ up in the form of th' other,
Subscribed it, gave't th' impression, placed it safely,
The changeling never known. Now, the next day
Was our sea-fight; and what to this was sequent
Thou know'st already.

HORATIO

So Guildenstern and Rosencrantz go to their death.

HAMLET

Why, sir, they enjoyed their employment so much they are not on my conscience. Their downfall was caused by their own attempts to win favour. It's dangerous for lesser beings to come between the cut and thrust of the swords of mightier opponents.

HORATIO

My, what a king this is!

HAMLET

Do you not think it now rests upon me – he has killed my father and made a whore of my mother, come between my hopes for the throne, cast his hook and line to take my very life, and with such deception – wouldn't it be poetic justice to end him with my own hand? And wouldn't it be a damnation to allow this cancer in our nature to grow in its evil?

HORATIO

So Guildenstern and Rosencrantz go to't.

HAMLET

Why, man, they did make love to this employment;
They are not near my conscience. Their defeat
Does by their own insinuation grow.
'Tis dangerous when the baser nature comes
Between the pass and fell-incensed points
Of mighty opposites.

HORATIO

Why, what a king is this!

HAMLET

Does it not, think thee, stand me now upon -
He that hath killed my king and whored my
  mother,
Popped in between th' election and my hopes,
Thrown out his angle* for my proper life,
And with such coz'nage - is't not perfect conscience
To quit him with this arm? And is't not to be
  damned
To let this canker of our nature come
In further evil?

Note: 'Thrown out his angle' – Fishing reference, catching a fish, angling.

HORATIO

He must find out shortly from the king of England the nature of the business there.

HAMLET

It will be soon, I have a short time, and it takes no longer than counting to 'one' to end a man's life. But, good Horatio, I am very sorry that I lost my temper with Laertes. I now see the mirror image of my anger reflected in his. I'll endeavour to win his favour. It was the exaggeration of his grief that drove me into a towering rage.

HORATIO

Wait, someone's coming.

HORATIO

It must be shortly known to him from England
What is the issue of the business there.

HAMLET

It will be short. The interim is mine,
And a man's life's no more than to say `one'.
But I am very sorry, good Horatio,
That to Laertes I forgot myself;
For by the image of my cause I see
The portraiture of his. I'll court his favours.
But, sure, the bravery of his grief did put me
Into a tow'ring passion.

HORATIO

Peace, who comes here?

OSRIC APPROACHES, A YOUTHFUL MEMBER OF THE ROYAL COURT,
FLAMBOYANT IN DRESS AND SPEECH.

HE EXAGGERATES HIS BOWING AND SCRAPING AS HE GREETS HAMLET.

OSRIC
Your highness is super welcome back in Denmark.

HAMLET
(*dryly*) I humbly thank you, sir.
(*aside to Horatio*) Do you know this social butterfly?

HORATIO
No, my good lord.

HAMLET
(*aside to Horatio*) It is in your favour, it would be a sin to be acquainted with him. He has large, fertile estates. If a beast is lord of many beasts, his feeding trough can stand in the king's kitchen. He's a jackdaw, but, as I said, plentiful in the possession of acres of dirt.

OSRIC
Your lordship is right welcome back to Denmark.

HAMLET
I humbly thank you, sir.
[*Aside to Horatio.*] Dost know this water-fly?

HORATIO
No, my good lord.

HAMLET
[*Aside to Horatio.*] Thy state is the more gracious, for 'tis a vice to know him. He hath much land, and fertile. Let a beast be lord of beasts, and his crib shall stand at the king's mess. 'Tis a chough,* but, as I say, spacious in the possession of dirt.

Note: 'Chough' is a jackdaw, a member of the crow family that can mimic human sounds and words without knowing their meaning. Pronounced 'chuf'.

Hamlet suggests that the king is only friendly with Osric because of his land and the animal produce from it, but he is really just like his cattle.

OSRIC BOWS AND SWEEPS THE FLOOR WITH THE
FEATHERS IN HIS OVERLY LARGE HAT.

OSRIC
(*overly pretentious*) Sweet lord, if your lordship is at leisure to spare the time, I would impart a message from his majesty.

OSRIC
Sweet lord, if your lordship were at leisure I should impart a thing to you from his majesty.

HAMLET MIMICS THE PRETENTIOUS MANNER OF OSRIC IN HIS SPEECH.

HAMLET
(*mimicking*) I will receive it, sir, with all diligence of spirit.
(*condescending*) Put your hat to its right use – it's for the head.

HAMLET
I will receive it, sir, with all diligence of spirit. Put your bonnet to his right use; 'tis for the head.

OSRIC
I thank your lordship, but it is very hot.

HAMLET
No, believe me, it's very cold, the wind is from the north.

OSRIC
It is moderately cold, my lord, indeed.

HAMLET
But, then again I think it is too hot and humid for my temperament.

OSRIC
Exceedingly so, my lord, it is very humid, as it were... I don't know how to say it... But anyway, my lord, his majesty commanded me to let you know he has laid a large wager on your head. So, the situation is...

OSRIC
I thank your lordship, it is very hot.

HAMLET
No, believe me, 'tis very cold, the wind is northerly.

OSRIC
It is indifferent cold, my lord, indeed.

HAMLET
But yet methinks it is very sultry and hot for my complexion.

OSRIC
Exceedingly, my lord; it is very sultry, as 'twere - I cannot tell how. But, my lord, his majesty bade me signify to you that he has laid a great wager on your head. Sir, this is the matter -

HE PAUSES AND FANS HIMSELF WITH HIS HAT, ANNOYING HAMLET.

HAMLET
I won't remind you again.

HAMLET
I beseech you, remember.

HAMLET INDICATES TO OSRIC TO PUT HIS HAT ON.

OSRIC
No, my good lord, I assure you, it is for my comfort. - Sir, Laertes has returned to court, an absolute gentleman, believe me, full of most excellent qualities, of very refined manners, and pleasing appearance. Indeed, to speak of his merits, he is the very pinnacle of good breeding, you will find in him the refinement a gentleman only learns from his grand tour.

OSRIC
Nay, good my lord, for mine ease, in good faith. Sir, here is newly come to court Laertes; believe me, an absolute gentleman, full of most excellent differences, of very soft society, and great showing. Indeed, to speak feelingly of him, he is the card or calendar of gentry, for you shall find in him the continent* of what part a gentleman would see.

*Note: 'Continent' - The Grand Tour was a cultural journey through continental Europe undertaken by the privileged few and the upper classes to absorb the art, knowledge and cultures of Europe. Shakespeare was not of the privileged few, or the highly educated, being self-taught mainly. He certainly knew of European culture, but this may have been from studies and those around him who had completed the tour and shared their experiences. The double meaning is that you see in Laertes the complete continent, not just individual parts of it.

HAMLET

(*pretentiously*) Sir, your description of him suffers no lacking, though I know, to itemise his qualities would strain even the most mathematical of minds, and even they follow in the wake of the quickness of his. But in furtherance of acclaim, I take him to be a soul of great note, endowed with qualities so scant and rare, he - to truly surmise him – is matched only by his own semblance in the mirror, and anyone trying to imitate him, would be merely his shadow, nothing more.

OSRIC

Your lordship speaks most impeccably of him.

HAMLET

The relevancy, sir? Why do we wrap the gentleman in our insufficient utterances?

OSRIC

Sir?

HORATIO

(*to Osric*) Is it not possible to understand when another tongue speaks your language? You can do it, sir, really.

HAMLET

What is the significance of nominating this gentleman?

OSRIC

Of Laertes?

HORATIO

(*about Osric sarcastically*) His purse is empty already, all the golden words are spent.

HAMLET

Of him, sir.

OSRIC

I know you are not ignorant...

HAMLET

Sir, his definement suffers no perdition in you, though, I know, to divide him inventorially would dozy th' arithmetic of memory, and yet but yaw neither in respect of his quick sail. But in the verity of extolment I take him to be a soul of great article, and his infusion of such dearth and rareness as, to make true diction of him, his semblable is his mirror, and who else would trace him, his umbrage, nothing more.

OSRIC

Your lordship speaks most infallibly of him.

HAMLET

The concernancy, sir? Why do we wrap the gentleman in our more rawer breath?

OSRIC

Sir?

HORATIO

Is't not possible to understand in another tongue? You will to't, sir, really.

HAMLET

What imports the nomination of this gentleman?

OSRIC

Of Laertes?

HORATIO

His purse is empty already; all's golden words are spent.

HAMLET

Of him, sir.

OSRIC

I know you are not ignorant -

HAMLET
(*interrupting*) I'd like to think you did, sir, but truly, even if you did it would not be to my credit. Well, sir?

HAMLET
I would you did, sir; yet, in faith, if you did it would not much approve me. Well, sir?

OSRIC
(*continuing*) You are not ignorant of what excellence Laertes has...

OSRIC
You are not ignorant of what excellence Laertes is -

HAMLET
I dare not admit that, unless I was claiming to be his equal in excellence, for to know a man well one must first know oneself.

HAMLET
I dare not confess that, lest I should compare with him in excellence; but to know a man well were to know himself.

FINALLY OSRIC GETS HIS POINT ACROSS.

OSRIC
I mean, sir, for his weaponry. By the reputation laid on him by others, in his field he has no match.

OSRIC
I mean, sir, for his weapon. But in the imputation laid on him by them, in his meed he's unfellowed.

HAMLET
What's his weapon?

HAMLET
What's his weapon?

OSRIC
Rapier and dagger.

OSRIC
Rapier and dagger.

HAMLET
That's two weapons - but still...

HAMLET
That's two of his weapons - but well.

OSRIC
The king, sir, has wagered with him six Barbary horses, against which he has 'imponed', as I understand it, six French rapiers and daggers, with their scabbards, belts, and so on, indeed, three of the carriages are very fancy, well matched to their hilts, most delicate contraptions, and of very elegant design.

OSRIC
The king, sir, hath wagered with him six Barbary horses, against the which he has imponed,* as I take it, six French rapiers and poniards, with their assigns as girdle, hanger, and so: three of the carriages, in faith, are very dear to fancy, very responsive to the hilts, most delicate carriages, and of very liberal conceit.

*Note: 'Imponed' was used to emphasise the pretentious talk of Osric. He means 'staked' as his bet. It derives from the latin, 'imponere' – to place upon. Hamlet will pull him up on the use of the word a little later.

HAMLET
What do you mean by carriages?

HORATIO
I knew you'd be requiring footnotes before it was over.

OSRIC
The carriages, sir, are the belts and straps.

HAMLET
The phrase would be more relative to the subject if we were carrying cannons at our sides. I will call it straps till then. But go on: six Barbary horses against six French swords, their accessories, and three elegantly designed 'carriages'. That's the French bet against the Danish king. Why is this 'imponed', as you call it?

OSRIC
The king, sir, has laid the wager, sir, that in a dozen rounds between yourself and Laertes, he shall not exceed three more hits than you. Laertes has wagered on nine hits in twelve rounds, and it could be arranged immediately if your highness would agree to answer.

HAMLET
What if I answer no?

HAMLET
What call you the carriages?

HORATIO
I knew you must be edified by the margent ere you had done.

OSRIC
The carriages, sir, are the hangers.

HAMLET
The phrase would be more germane to the matter if we could carry a cannon by our sides. I would it might be hangers till then. But on: six Barbary horses against six French swords, their assigns, and three liberal-conceited carriages; that's the French bet against the Danish. Why is this `imponed', as you call it?

OSRIC
The king, sir, hath laid, sir, that in a dozen passes between yourself and him, he shall not exceed you three hits. He hath laid on twelve for nine, and it would come to immediate trial if your lordship would vouchsafe the answer.*

HAMLET
How if I answer* no?

> *Note: Osric means 'answer the challenge', Hamlet twists it to mean answer the question. 'Answer the challenge' is a duelling term where one man has challenged another to a duel. The correct reply would be "I accept" or "I decline". 'No' would not be a valid answer.

OSRIC
I mean, my lord, the opposition to yourself by trial.

OSRIC
I mean, my lord, the opposition of your person in trial.

HAMLET

Sir, I will take a walk here in the hall. If his majesty will allow it, it is the time of day I take my exercise. Fetch the foils. If the gentleman is willing, and the king's wager still stands, I will win for him if I can. If not, I will gain nothing but my shame, and the odd hit.

HAMLET

Sir, I will walk here in the hall. If it please his majesty, it is the breathing time of day with me. Let the foils* be brought, the gentleman willing, and the king hold his purpose, I will win for him an I can. If not, I will gain nothing but my shame, and the odd hits.

> *Note: A 'foil' is a light, blunt edged fencing sword with a protective button on the tip for safety.*
>
> *Note the repeated use of the word 'will' in the sentence.*

OSRIC

Shall I deliver your message as such?

OSRIC

Shall I deliver you e'en so?

HAMLET

To this effect, sir, answer with whatever flourish your character sees fit.

HAMLET

To this effect, sir, after what flourish your nature will.

OSRIC BOWS DEEP AND GRACIOUSLY.

OSRIC

I commend my duty to your lordship.

OSRIC

I commend my duty to your lordship.

HAMLET

And to yours.

HAMLET

Yours, yours.

OSRIC EXITS FLAMBOYANTLY.

HAMLET (CONT'D)

(*to Horatio*) He does well to commend himself, no one else would.

HAMLET

He does well to commend* it himself; there are no tongues else for's turn.

> *Note: 'Commend' has many meanings. Osric means he entrusts his duty to Hamlet, Hamlet takes the alternative meaning of 'praises'.*

HORATIO

This foolish bird runs away with its shell on its head.

HORATIO

This lapwing* runs away with the shell on his head.

> *Note: The 'lapwing' was considered a foolish bird in such a hurry that when hatched it would run away with its own shell on its head. As the hat had feathers and may have been shell shaped, as was a fashion of the day, this would make sense.*

HAMLET

He would curtsy to his mother's nipple before he sucked it. Like he – and many others of the same ilk which this sad age deems fashionable – they've learnt to sing the tune and talk the talk of the times, with a collection of frothy words which carry them through conversations on the most popular and musty old opinions, but blow on them to test them and their bubbles burst.

HAMLET

He did comply with his dug before a' sucked it. Thus has he - and many more of the same bevy that I know the drossy age dotes on - only got the tune of the time and outward habit of encounter, a kind of yeasty collection which carries them through and through the most fanned and winnowed opinions; and do but blow them to their trial, the bubbles are out.

ENTER A LORD.

LORD

My lord, his majesty commended his message to you by way of young Osric, who brought back the reply that you await him in the hall. He wishes to know if you await there to duel with Laertes now, or if you require a while longer?

LORD

My lord, his majesty commended him to you by young Osric, who brings back to him that you attend him in the hall. He sends to know if your pleasure hold to play* with Laertes, or that you will take longer time?

Note: 'Play' was a technical term in fencing for a contest, you 'played' for a prize. In a similar way to playing a game of football, for example.

HAMLET

My intentions have not changed, they are at the king's service. If he is fit and ready, then so am I, now or whenever, providing I am as ready as I am now.

HAMLET

I am constant to my purposes; they follow the king's pleasure. If his fitness speaks, mine is ready; now or whensoever, provided I be so able as now.

LORD

The king and queen and everyone else are on their way.

LORD

The king and queen and all are coming down.

HAMLET

Good timing.

HAMLET

In happy time.

LORD

The queen desires that you show some gentle courtesy to Laertes before you commence the duel.

LORD

The queen desires you to use some gentle entertainment to Laertes before you fall to play.

HAMLET

She gives me good advice.

HAMLET

She well instructs me.

EXIT LORD.

HORATIO

You will lose this wager, my lord.

HAMLET

I do not think so. Since he went to France, I have been in continual practise. The odds are in my favour. But you have no idea how uneasy I feel inside. But that is of no consequence now.

HORATIO

But, my good lord...

HAMLET

It is foolish, it is the kind of misgiving that would perhaps trouble a woman.

HORATIO

You will lose this wager, my lord.

HAMLET

I do not think so. Since he went into France, I have been in continual practice; I shall win at the odds. But thou wouldst not think how ill all's here about my heart; but it is no matter.

HORATIO

Nay, good my lord -

HAMLET

It is but foolery; but it is such a kind of gain-giving as would perhaps trouble a woman.*

*Note: Women back then were considered the weaker sex and the expressions reflected this, but also traditionally recognised as the more intuitive of the sexes.

HORATIO

If your mind tells you something is not right, obey it. I will postpone their arrival and say you are not ready.

HAMLET

Not a bit. We'll not heed premonitions. There is a special predetermination, as in the 'fall of a sparrow' speech by Jesus. If it's to be now, then it will not come later. If it is to be later, it will not be now. But it will come. Being in readiness for it is what's important. Since no man knows what future he leaves behind, it is no loss to leave early. Let it be.

HORATIO

If your mind dislike anything, obey it. I will forestall their repair hither, and say you are not fit.

HAMLET

Not a whit; we defy augury. There is special providence in the fall of a sparrow.* If it be now, 'tis not to come; if it be not to come, it will be now; if it be not now, yet it will come. The readiness is all. Since no man has aught of what he leaves, what is't to leave betimes? Let be.

*Note: The 'fall of a sparrow' is from a bible passage (Mathew 10) where Jesus tells his disciples that two small sparrows are of little value, costing nothing to buy, but when one fell (died) it would meet the Father (God). The timing was predetermined and everything, no matter how small, was of value to God.

ENTER KING CLAUDIUS, QUEEN GERTRUDE, LAERTES,
LORDS, OSRIC, AND ATTENDANTS WITH TRUMPETS,
DRUMS, CUSHIONS, FOILS AND GAUNTLETS, AND A TABLE
WITH FLAGONS OF WINE ON IT.

KING CLAUDIUS

Come, Hamlet, come and take Laertes' hand which I now offer.

KING

Come, Hamlet, come, and take this hand from me.

THE KING PUTS LAERTES'S HAND INTO HAMLET'S.

HAMLET

(*to Laertes*) Grant me your forgiveness, sir. I have done you wrong. Please forgive me as the gentleman you are. This present company knows, and you must surely have heard, how I am punished with a mental disorder. Whatever I have done that might have upset your nature, honour or roughly stirred up your disapproval, I hereby declare was caused by my madness. Was it Hamlet who wronged Laertes? It was never Hamlet. If the real Hamlet is absent, and when he is not himself he does wrong to Laertes, then Hamlet does not do it. Hamlet denies it. Who does it, then? His madness? If so, Hamlet is the one who is wronged. His madness is poor Hamlet's enemy. Sir, before this audience, let my declaration that I intended no evil, free me in your mind, so far as your generosity will allow, as if I had shot my arrow over the house and unintentionally injured my brother.

HAMLET

Give me your pardon, sir. I have done you wrong;
But pardon't as you are a gentleman.
This presence knows,
And you must needs have heard, how I am
 punished
With sore distraction. What I have done
That might your nature, honour, and exception
Roughly awake, I here proclaim was madness.
Was't Hamlet wronged Laertes? Never Hamlet.
If Hamlet from himself be ta'en away,
And when he's not himself does wrong Laertes,
Then Hamlet does it not, Hamlet denies it.
Who does it, then? His madness? If't be so,
Hamlet is of the faction that is wronged;
His madness is poor Hamlet's enemy.
Sir, in this audience,
Let my disclaiming from a purposed evil
Free me so far in your most generous thoughts
That I have shot mine arrow o'er the house
And hurt my brother.*

*Note: 'Shot my arrow over the house and hurt my brother', an adage told to young boys warning them about the danger of firing blindly without thinking.

LAERTES

I am satisfied in my feelings, which had motive enough in this case to stir me strongly to seek revenge. But in terms of honour I am unmoved, and will not consider reconciliation until some elder masters in the field of honour have voiced their opinion as to whether I can keep the honour of my name unblemished. But until that time I accept your offer of love as honest, and will not decline it.

LAERTES

I am satisfied in nature,
Whose motive in this case should stir me most
To my revenge. But in my terms of honour
I stand aloof, and will no reconcilement
Till by some elder masters of known honour
I have a voice and precedent of peace
To keep my name ungored. But till that time
I do receive your offered love like love,
And will not wrong it.

HAMLET

I welcome your acceptance with open arms, and will earnestly partake in this friendly wager between brothers.
(to attendants) Give us the foils. Come on.

HAMLET

I embrace it freely,
And will this brother's wager frankly play.
Give us the foils. Come on.

LAERTES

Come, one for me.

LAERTES

Come, one for me.

HAMLET

I'll be your 'foil', Laertes. My lacking will make your skill shine fiery bright, like a star in the darkest night.

HAMLET

I'll be your foil,* Laertes. In mine ignorance
Your skill shall, like a star i'th' darkest night,
Stick fiery off indeed.

*Note: 'Foil' here is used for a number of puns. First it is the sword they fight with, second he is being a foil to Laertes, preventing him winning, third it is something that contrasts two things showing up one to be better, forth, it is a setback, fifth, a reflecting metal placed under a gem or behind a lantern to reflect the light making it even brighter, like silver baking foil used in cooking.

LAERTES

You mock me, sir.

LAERTES

You mock me, sir.

HAMLET

No, by this hand I solemnly swear.

HAMLET

No, by this hand.

KING CLAUDIUS

Give them the foils, young Osric. Hamlet, my son, you know the wager?

KING

Give them the foils, young Osric. Cousin* Hamlet, You know the wager?

"Note: 'Cousin' was used for any family member. It meant they were kin. Now it is only used for relatives who are children of a parent's sister or brother.

HAMLET

Very well, my lord. Your grace has laid odds on the weaker side.

HAMLET

Very well, my lord;
Your grace has laid the odds o'th' weaker side.

KING CLAUDIUS

I am not worried, I have seen you both.
But since then he's improved, so we have
the handicapped odds.

KING

I do not fear it; I have seen you both.
But since he's bettered, we have therefore odds.*

Note: According to Osric, Hamlet has been given a three hit head start.

OSRIC PASSES FOILS, THEY CHECK THE WEIGHT AND
BALANCE. LAERTES NOTICES HIS IS NOT THE POISONED FOIL.

LAERTES

This is too heavy. Let me try another.

LAERTES

This is too heavy; let me see another.

HAMLET SWISHES HIS FOIL ABOUT IN THE AIR.

HAMLET

This suits me well. These foils are all of
equal length?

HAMLET

This likes me well. These foils have all a length?

OSRIC

Yes, my good lord.

OSRIC

Ay, my good lord.

THEY PREPARE TO DUEL.

KING CLAUDIUS

Put the flagons of wine on this table. If
Hamlet wins the first or second hit, or
draws level with the third hit, let all the
battlements fire off their cannons. The
king shall drink to Hamlet's further luck,
and into the cup will throw a pearl more
valuable than the one worn in the crown
of four successive kings of Denmark. Give
me the cups, and let the kettle drums
signal the trumpets to sound, the
trumpets signal the cannons to fire, the
cannons signal the heavens, the heavens
signal the world that "The king drinks to
Hamlet". Come, begin.

KING

Set me the stoups of wine upon that table.
If Hamlet give the first or second hit,
Or quit in answer of the third exchange,
Let all the battlements their ordnance fire;
The king shall drink to Hamlet's better breath,
And in the cup an union shall he throw,
Richer than that which four successive kings
In Denmark's crown have worn. Give me the cups,
And let the kettle to the trumpet speak,
The trumpet to the cannoneer without,
The cannons to the heavens, the heaven to earth,
`Now the king drinks to Hamlet'. Come, begin;

A GOBLET IS PASSED TO THE KING. TRUMPETS SOUND.

KING CLAUDIUS (CONT'D)
And you judges, keep a keen eye.

KING
And you, the judges, bear a wary eye.

HAMLET
Come on, sir.

HAMLET
Come on, sir.

LAERTES
Come, my lord.

LAERTES
Come, my lord.

THEY PRESENT FOILS AND START THE DUEL.

HAMLET GAINS THE FIRST HIT.

HAMLET
One!

HAMLET
One.

LAERTES
No.

LAERTES
No.

HAMLET
(*to judges*) A ruling?

HAMLET
Judgement.

OSRIC
A hit, a very definite hit.

OSRIC
A hit, a very palpable hit.

LAERTES
Very well. Again.

LAERTES
Well, again.

LAERTES RAISES HIS FOIL TO START ROUND TWO.

KING CLAUDIUS
Wait. Give me a drink.

KING
Stay, give me drink.

THE KING'S GOBLET IS FILLED WITH WINE.

THE KING PUTS POISON IN THE GOBLET AND RAISES IT ALOFT.
HE DROPS A PEARL INTO IT.

KING CLAUDIUS (CONT'D)
Hamlet, this pearl is yours.
Here's to your health.

KING
Hamlet, this pearl is thine;
Here's to thy health.

DRUM AND TRUMPETS SOUND, AND CANNONS ARE FIRED AS
ORDERED EARLIER BY THE KING.

KING CLAUDIUS (CONT'D)
Give Hamlet the cup.

KING
Give him the cup.

HAMLET
I'll fight this bout first, put it aside for a
while.
(*to Laertes*) Come.

HAMLET
I'll play this bout first; set it by a while.
Come.

THEY ADDRESS EACH OTHER AND COMMENCE DUELLING.

HAMLET
Another hit! What do you think?

HAMLET
Another hit; what say you?

LAERTES
A touch, a touch, I have to confess.

LAERTES
A touch, a touch, I do confess.

KING CLAUDIUS
Our son shall win!

KING
Our son shall win.

QUEEN GERTRUDE
He's sweating and short of breath.
(*to Hamlet*) Here, Hamlet, take my napkin,
mop your brow. The queen drinks to your
good fortune, Hamlet.

QUEEN
He's fat and scant of breath.
Here, Hamlet, take my napkin, rub thy brows.
The queen carouses to thy fortune, Hamlet.

HAMLET
Thank you, madam.

HAMLET
Good madam.

THE QUEEN RAISES THE POISONED GOBLET IN TOAST AND PUTS IT TO HER LIPS.

KING CLAUDIUS
Gertrude, do not drink it.

KING
Gertrude, do not drink.

QUEEN GERTRUDE
I shall, my lord. Begging your pardon.

QUEEN
I will, my lord; I pray you pardon me.

THE QUEEN TAKES A DRINK OF THE POISONED WINE.

KING CLAUDIUS
(*aside*) It is the poisoned cup. It is too late.

KING
[*Aside.*] It is the poisoned cup; it is too late.

HAMLET
I dare not drink yet, madam. Later.

HAMLET
I dare not drink yet, madam; by and by.

QUEEN GERTRUDE
Come, let me wipe your face.

QUEEN
Come, let me wipe thy face.

LAERTES
(*to King*) My lord, I'll hit him this time.

LAERTES
My lord, I'll hit him now.

KING CLAUDIUS
(*to Laertes*) I think not.

KING
I do not think't.

LAERTES
(*aside, looking at his poisoned rapier*)
There again, it almost goes against my
conscience.

LAERTES
[*Aside.*] And yet it is almost against my conscience.

HAMLET
Come on, for the third, Laertes. You are
wasting time. I beg you, come at me with
your best shot, I am sure you are treating
me with kid gloves.

HAMLET
Come for the third, Laertes; you do but dally.
I pray you, pass with your best violence;
I am sure you make a wanton of me.

LAERTES
You think so? Come on then.

LAERTES
Say you so? Come on.

THEY RESUME DUELLING AND PLAY THE THIRD BOUT WITH NEITHER SCORING
A HIT. OSRIC STEPS IN AND SEPARATES THEM, JUDGING IT A DRAW.

OSRIC
It's even, no one scored a hit.

OSRIC
Nothing neither way.

LAERTES SNEAKS IN A HIT CATCHING HAMLET UNAWARES AND CUTTING HIM.

LAERTES
Have that!

LAERTES
Have at you now!

THEY RENEW THEIR SCUFFLING, IN EARNEST SO FIERCELY THEY DROP RAPIERS
AND PICK UP THE WRONG ONES.

THEY RESUME FIGHTING AND THIS TIME HAMLET WOUNDS LAERTES WITH THE
POISONED RAPIER. THE KING SEES THIS.

KING CLAUDIUS
Part them. They are incensed!

KING
Part them; they are incensed.

HAMLET
No, come on, again!

HAMLET
Nay, come again.

THE QUEEN FALLS DOWN FROM THE EFFECTS OF THE POISON.

OSRIC
See to the queen there.
(*to the duellists*) Stop!

OSRIC
Look to the queen there, ho!

HORATIO
They are both bleeding.
(*to Hamlet*) How bad is it, Hamlet?

HORATIO
They bleed on both sides. [*To Hamlet.*] How is it,
my lord?

OSRIC
How is your wound, Laertes?

OSRIC
How is't, Laertes?

LAERTES
Why, like a woodcock caught in my own trap, Osric, I am rightly killed by my own treachery.

LAERTES
Why, as a woodcock* to mine own springe, Osric; I am justly killed with mine own treachery.

Note: The woodcock is a notoriously stupid bird.

HAMLET
What's happened to the queen?

HAMLET
How does the queen?

KING CLAUDIUS
She fainted at the sight of the blood.

KING
She swoons to see them bleed.

QUEEN GERTRUDE
No, no, the drink, the drink! Oh, my dear Hamlet. The drink, the drink! I am poisoned.

QUEEN
No, no, the drink, the drink! O my dear Hamlet; The drink, the drink! I am poisoned.

THE QUEEN DIES.

HAMLET
Oh, treachery! Stop! Lock the doors! Find the source of this treachery!

HAMLET
O villainy! Ho! Let the door be locked. Treachery, seek it out!

OSRIC FLEES OUT THE DOOR.

LAERTES COLLAPSES.

LAERTES
It's the end, Hamlet. You are doomed. No medicine in the world can do you any good. There is not half an hour of life left for you. You are holding the treacherous instrument, its guard is off and it's poisoned. The foul deed has turned itself back on me. Look, here I lie, never to rise again. Your mother's poisoned. I am no more. (*struggles to speak*) The king... the king's to blame.

LAERTES
It is here, Hamlet. Hamlet, thou art slain. No med'cine in the world can do thee good; In thee there is not half an hour of life. The treacherous instrument is in thy hand, Unbated and envenomed. The foul practice Hath turned itself on me; lo, here I lie, Never to rise again. Thy mother's poisoned. I can no more. The king, the king's to blame.

HAMLET
The point poisoned too! Then, venom, do your worst!

HAMLET
The point envenomed too! Then, venom, to thy work.

237

HAMLET TURNS TO FACE THE KING.

HE LUNGES AT THE KING WITH THE POISONED RAPIER,
PENETRATING HIS CHEST.

ALL
Treason! Treason!

ALL
Treason! Treason!

KING CLAUDIUS
Oh, defend me, friends, I'm only wounded.

KING
O yet defend me, friends; I am but hurt.

HAMLET
Here, you incestuous, murderous, damned Dane! Finish this poisoned drink. - Is your pearl here? Follow my mother!

HAMLET
Here, thou incestuous, murd'rous, damned Dane, Drink off this potion. - Is thy union* here? Follow my mother.

HAMLET FORCES THE DRINK DOWN THE THROAT OF THE KING.

KING CLAUDIUS DIES.

Note: The 'union' - a common name for a pearl then, but also a pun for the union between husband and wife. They are both poisoned.

'Union' derived from the fact no two pearls were alike, making them unique, or 'unio' in Latin, corrupted to 'union'.

LAERTES
(*weakly*) He got his just desserts. It is a poison mixed by himself. Exchange forgiveness with me, noble Hamlet. Be pardoned for mine and my father's death, and I for yours.

LAERTES
He is justly served;
It is a poison tempered by himself.
Exchange forgiveness with me, noble Hamlet.
Mine and my father's death come not upon thee,
Nor thine on me.

LAERTES DIES. HAMLET ADDRESS THOSE ASSEMBLED ONE AT A TIME.

HAMLET
(*to Laertes*) May Heaven acquit you of it! I follow you.
(*to Horatio*) I am dead, Horatio.
(*to mother*) Wretched queen, farewell!
(*to all*) You who look pale and tremble at this misfortune, but stay silent onlookers to this act, if I had the time – as the cruel agent of death is strict in his duties – Oh, I could tell you – but leave it at that.
Horatio, I am dead, you live on, relate my case to those who do not know the truth.

HAMLET
Heaven make thee free of it! I follow thee.
I am dead, Horatio. Wretched queen, adieu!
You that look pale, and tremble at this chance,
That are but mutes or audience to this act,
Had I but time - as this fell sergeant Death
Is strict in his arrest - O, I could tell you -
But let it be. Horatio, I am dead;
Thou livest; report me and my cause aright
To the unsatisfied.

HORATIO

Don't bank on it. I have more of the old Roman warrior in me than any Dane.

HORATIO

Never believe it.
I am more an antique Roman* than a Dane.

> *Note: Romans typically chose suicide before dishonour.*
>
> *Notice how the poison killed Laertes quite quickly, yet for some reason Hamlet seems to last a significant amount of time longer.*

HORATIO PICKS UP THE POISONED CUP.

HORATIO

There's some drink left.

HAMLET

Give me the cup, if you are a real man!

HORATIO

Here's yet some liquor left.

HAMLET

As thou'rt a man,
Give me the cup.

HAMLET TRIES TO GRAB THE CUP. THEY STRUGGLE.

HAMLET (CONT'D)

Let go, by heavens I'll have it.

HAMLET

Let go; by heaven I'll ha't.

HAMLET MANAGES TO WREST THE CUP FROM HORATIO.

HAMLET (CONT'D)

Oh God, Horatio, what a damaged reputation I'd leave behind if things were left standing with the truth unknown! If you ever held me dear to your heart, put off the joys of heaven for a while, and instead suffer the pains of this harsh world so you live to tell my story.

HAMLET

O God, Horatio, what a wounded name,
Things standing thus unknown, shall live behind me!
If thou didst ever hold me in thy heart,
Absent thee from felicity a while,
And in this harsh world draw thy breath in pain,
To tell my story.

MARCHING FROM AFAR AND A CANNON SHOT CLOSE BY IS HEARD.

HAMLET (CONT'D)

What warlike noise is this?

HAMLET

What warlike noise is this?

OSRIC RUSHES BACK IN.

OSRIC

Young Fortinbras, returning from his conquest in Poland, fires a warlike volley in honour of ambassadors newly arrived from England.

HAMLET

(*struggling to speak*) Oh, I'm dying, Horatio. The potent poison overpowers my spirit. I will not live to hear the news from England, but I do predict that Fortinbras will be elected king of Denmark. He has my dying support. So tell him, with the events, more or less, which have transpired. The rest is silence...

OSRIC

Young Fortinbras, with conquest come from Poland,
T' the ambassadors of England gives
This warlike volley.

HAMLET

O, I die, Horatio.
The potent poison quite o'ercrows my spirit.
I cannot live to hear the news from England,
But I do prophesy th' election lights
On Fortinbras. He has my dying voice;
So tell him, with th' occurrents, more and less,
Which have solicited. The rest is silence.*

Note: 'Rest is silence' - double meaning, the rest of what he has to say and the rest he will have in the grave, like the saying "rest in peace".

HAMLET SLUMPS AND DIES.

HORATIO

Now a noble heart cracks apart. Good night, sweet prince, may flights of angels serenade you to your rest.

HORATIO

Now cracks a noble heart. Good night, sweet prince,
And flights of angels sing thee to thy rest.

SOUNDS OF MARCHING TO DRUMS WITHIN THE CASTLE.

HORATIO (CONT'D)

What is that approaching sound of drums?

HORATIO

Why does the drum come hither?

ENTER FORTINBRAS, AND THE ENGLISH AMBASSADORS, WITH DRUM, COLOURS, AND ATTENDANTS.

FORTINBRAS

What is this spectacle?

HORATIO

What would you like it to be? If one of sorrow or disbelief, look no further.

FORTINBRAS

Where is this sight?

HORATIO

What is it you would see?
If aught of woe or wonder, cease your search.

FORTINBRAS STUDIES THE SCENE FOR A MOMENT.

FORTINBRAS

This heap of corpses suggest a massacre. Oh, proud death, what feast is planned in your eternal quarters that you take so many noble bodies in one swoop, striking so bloodily.

FORTINBRAS

This quarry cries on havoc. O proud death, What feast is toward in thine eternal cell That thou so many princes at a shot So bloodily hast struck?

1ST AMBASSADOR

The sight is wretched, and our news from England comes too late. The ears are deaf that should be hearing us tell that his orders were fulfilled. Rosencrantz and Guildenstern are dead. From where should we receive our thanks?

1ST AMBASSADOR

The sight is dismal; And our affairs from England come too late. The ears are senseless that should give us hearing To tell him his commandment is fulfilled, That Rosencrantz and Guildenstern are dead. Where should we have our thanks?

HORATIO INDICATES THE KING'S BODY.

HORATIO

Not from his mouth, even if it had the ability of life to thank you. He never gave the order for their death. But since you've walked in on such a bloody time...

HORATIO

Not from his mouth, Had it th' ability of life to thank you; He never gave commandment for their death. But since, so jump upon this bloody question,

---

HORATIO INDICATES FORTINBRAS.

HORATIO (CONT'D)

You from the Polish conflict...

HORATIO

You from the Polack wars,

HORATIO INDICATES THE ENGLISH AMBASSADORS.

HORATIO (CONT'D)

And you from the King of England, I order that these bodies be placed high on a platform for all to view, and then let me speak to the ignorant world how it came to this. You shall hear of carnal, bloody, inhuman acts, of divine intervention, of accidental killings, of deaths planned with deception and false motives, resulting in plots misfiring and then backfiring on the instigator's heads. All this I can truly relate.

HORATIO

and you from England, Are here arrived, give order that these bodies High on a stage be placed to the view; And let me speak to th' yet unknowing world How these things came about. So shall you hear Of carnal, bloody, and unnatural acts, Of accidental judgements, casual slaughters, Of deaths put on by cunning and forced cause, And, in this upshot, purposes mistook Fall'n on th' inventors' heads. All this can I Truly deliver.

FORTINBRAS

Let us hear it in all haste. And assemble the nobility. As for me, with some sorrow I seize my opportunity. I have some rights within recent memory to this kingdom, which, as the time is appropriate, I now claim.

FORTINBRAS

Let us haste to hear it,
And call the noblest to the audience.
For me, with sorrow I embrace my fortune;
I have some rights of memory in this kingdom,
Which now to claim my vantage doth invite me.

HORATIO

I shall also have reason to speak of that, and from the mouth of one whose voice will draw support from others. But let this ceremony take place immediately, even while men's minds are still heated, before any more mishaps or mistakes can happen.

HORATIO

Of that I shall have also cause to speak,
And from his mouth whose voice will draw on
  more.*
But let this same be presently performed,
Even while men's minds are wild, lest more
  mischance
On plots and errors happen.

Note: Horatio means the voice of Hamlet naming Fortinbras as his successor.

FORTINBRAS

Let four captains bear Hamlet like a soldier to the platform, for had he lived to be crowned he was likely to have proved a good king. To mark his passing, soldier's trumpets will play, and military salutes will sound loudly for him.

(*to his men*) Carry the bodies.

FORTINBRAS

Let four captains
Bear Hamlet like a soldier to the stage,
For he was likely, had he been put on,
To have proved most royal; and for his passage,
The soldiers' music and the rites of war
Speak loudly for him.
Take up the bodies...

HIGH RANKING SOLDIERS LIFT THE BODIES AND CARRY THEM ON THEIR
SHOULDERS TO A PLATFORM AT THE END OF THE HALL FOR ALL TO SEE.

MILITARY TRUMPETS PLAY SOMBRE MUSIC AND DRUMS SOUND.

FORTINBRAS (CONT'D)

A sight such as this is more befitting to a battlefield, it is inappropriate here. Go, order the military salute.

FORTINBRAS

Such a sight as this
Becomes the field, but here shows much amiss.
Go, bid the soldiers shoot.

EXEUNT, MARCHING, BEARING OFF THE DEAD BODIES;
AFTER WHICH A PEAL OF ORDNANCE IS SHOT OFF.

Made in the USA
Las Vegas, NV
26 September 2023

78185152R00133